the
Sow's Ear
Café

a novel

Holly Quan

 FriesenPress

Suite 300 - 990 Fort St
Victoria, BC, V8V 3K2
Canada

www.friesenpress.com

Copyright © 2018 by Holly Quan
First Edition — 2018

Front cover photo: Gervais Goodman
Author photo: Ken Wong

ISBN
978-1-5255-1575-0 (Hardcover)
978-1-5255-1576-7 (Paperback)
978-1-5255-1577-4 (eBook)

1. FICTION

Distributed to the trade by The Ingram Book Company

The only view is forward when your
back's against the wall.

—James Keelaghan, "Hold Your Ground"

To the many **friends** in Millarville, Turner Valley, and Black Diamond who welcomed us into small-town life. *"Look where we live!"* We say that every day, and it's not just the scenery.

And

To **Dr. Rob Mitchell** who made many things possible. Birds! Leaves! Stars! I had no idea.

the Sow's Ear Café

PROLOGUE

She plows against the wind and muscles through the accumulating drifts, head down like a big old thug of a draft horse determined to push the wind aside. Determined to not think about the love of her life, the anchor of her soul, the husk of the man she left behind in the bar. Instead she thinks about Ray and Lucie working hard to make The Sow's Ear a dependable source of income for all of them. She thinks about how much whisky and beer Tom will need to forget how old and broken he is, about how much it will all cost, and where the money might come from.

She lurches on through the storm, eyes down, feet moving. The wind becomes inconsequential to her, the cold brushed aside — it's to be endured. Endured like mad cow disease, endured like the auction of her home, her possessions. Endured like this early storm that's even now bending tree limbs to the snapping point. She keeps going because what else is there to do but keep on keeping on?

A tiny vessel lurching hard against a frozen sea, she comes to the four-way stop and does not pause because there is not a moving vehicle in sight, She keeps pushing, kneeing aside the drifts. Turns up the hillside road, pushing pushing. She becomes encrusted, barely discernible from the storm itself.

THE CHILL IN YOUR EMBRACE

Look at them, gathered around their table. They are lacquered dolls. Scarabs. Brilliant — brittle. Men and women both. Luminous skin. Gleaming hair. Likewise their clothing, even their conversation, is polished to a high sheen. They are gorgeous. Smooth. Buffed. At the top of their game, whatever game that might be.

How can we not envy them, snugged together as they are around a too-small table in a loud, costly restaurant, not caring about the crush or the music volume or the ridiculous prices? Some of them have just come from seeing a movie together, and the rest have been at this table for hours: eating, drinking, telling lies, and spreading gossip until the moviegoers arrived.

In the shadows beyond the table's glow, their server pulls a cork with a deliberately loud pop. Everyone grins, glasses offered, held languidly in long fingers. The server fills their waiting glasses quickly, splashing dots of dark liquid onto the table. Nobody cares. They only want their share. They tip their heads back, drinking. They laugh with perfect smiles. Lipstick and long fingernails in rich, thick shades of vermillion and ochre and fuchsia bounce the candlelight.

A circle of friends, talking, laughing, leaning toward one another to share a joke: "Jeez, did you catch the wiggle on that waiter? Can you *get* any more *gay*?"

"To friends!"

"To *straight* friends!" says Brad. Their hero, their macho golden boy. Laugh laugh laugh. Clink clink clink.

A girl with milky skin frowns and sits back from the circle.

Nobody notices her concern.

Look around the table. It's very early spring, but the evening is unseasonably warm and humid, so everyone's dressed ahead of the season — they think it's summer. The men wear slim pants moulded to their butts, trim at the waist, just right. Their jackets, perhaps slightly too heavy for this warm night, are open to trap any passing wisp of cool air. Their skinny floral ties are loose and crooked. They look wanton and drunk. They are.

Because it's an unusually warm night, the women wear skimpy dresses hastily retrieved from last summer's wardrobe to accommodate this unexpectedly spring-like night. Bare shoulders, cleavage exposure just right — fun and fashionable, not lewd — firm, slim arms, graceful necks. Throats tender, soft, inviting caresses. Skirts showing lots of leg, but really it's about staying cool and comfortable. No, really. Silkily they cross and re-cross their legs. Cool, smooth. Their feet are delicately arched, supported by shoes with crisscrossing straps and tiny stiletto heels.

Every garment is black.

Despite their dark clothes, the friends are luminous. They radiate elegance and ease. Their laughter is loud.

Outside, sirens bray past the restaurant on their way to some fresh disaster, some crushed skull, bashed vein, demolished vehicle, demolished marriage. The friends around this table hear none of it. The city's crash and crisis — and, just now, the first few huge raindrops and even a roll of thunder — are beyond them, beyond the restaurant's brick walls, beyond the fresh oysters and venison chops, chocolate mousse and raspberry coulis. Beyond the wine.

"What did you mean by that — *straight* friends? You can't say stupid things like that…"

"Stupid!" he cries to the circle. "My *sweetheart* has just called me stupid!" His eyes rove the table, looking for support.

Oh, Baby, don't start. I'm sorry. I didn't mean it. You're just drunk. You've had a tough week and you're taking it out on the waiter. I get it. I just wish you wouldn't treat people that way.

Glaring straight into his girlfriend's pale eyes, daring her to take the waiter's side, Brad stands and mimics the server. Dangling a limp wrist, he wiggles his ass to the increasing laughter of the circle.

The server returns to refresh their drinks but hangs back, watching this theatre from the shadows; he doesn't quite come forward to the noisy crowd. Finally he steps into the light and every eye at the table is raised to him — the wronged, the ridiculed. With shark grins, they wait for his rage to pour over them, to provoke them in the name of entertainment.

But he says, "No, no, you've got it all *wrong*. Honestly, there's not a straight guy in town who can wiggle like little old me." The server prances around the table, wine bottle raised like a banner, a caricature of himself. He leans over, stretches long fingers to caress Brad's cheek.

Grins freeze.

"Brad, sit down." His milk-skinned girlfriend glares at the ringleader and then reconfigures her face to address the server, her eyebrows raised, trembling. She's all Bette Davis. "I'm so sorry... "

"Never mind, Cupcake. He's not my type. And..." the server leans across the full width of the table to top up her glass. "It looks to me like he's not *your* type, either. Ha!" He spins like Nureyev and is instantly swallowed by the darkness beyond the table's pool of light.

Brad sits down. "Faggot." Delivered with his trademark giggle and sneer.

The circle closes around Brad, insulating but not quite forgiving or condoning his behaviour, not quite on his side. "Yeah, whatever," someone says.

The conversation moves on.

"Bottoms up, people, it's a school night. I've got an eight o'clock meeting."

"That's nothing. I've got a running date at five-thirty. *Five-thirty*! What was I thinking?"

"Is it even daylight then?"

"Barely. Running in the dark, in the rain. At five-thirty…"

"That's dedication."

Their car is as shiny as their friends. Pale-skinned Lucie, lips pressed into a narrow, clamped slit of dried-blood red, heels tapping her embarrassment on the parkade's concrete floor, gets to the car first. She stands, stiff and icy, waiting for Brad to punch the button, unlock the car doors.

He does not. He walks to his own side, uses the key to unlock his door, and gets in. The slam echoes from every concrete surface. For a moment she thinks he will start the car, drive away in a showy screech of tires, and leave her standing there with her righteous fury, her embarrassment, her need.

He starts the car before finally unlocking her door from the inside. She gets in, seething. Boiling. Defeated. Says through clenched teeth, "I should drive. You're drunk."

"The hell I am."

To prove his sobriety, he revs the car and steers expertly around the pillars of the almost-empty parkade, tires complaining with each tight turn. He breathes noisily as he cranks the steering wheel right, left, right, left. She lets herself go limp, lets gravity fling her back and forth, restrained only by her seatbelt. Point made, he drives up two levels to the exit, pays without a word, and pulls out into the pouring, streaming rain to swish along with Tuesday night traffic. Streetlights, stoplights, store lights, all reflect in the sheen of rain on pavement. She turns away from him, jaw tense, shoulders tight, willing herself to look aside, not ahead where danger lies. He's too drunk to drive, drunk on fury if not on beer.

He jerks to a stop and despite herself she glances ahead to see a red light and the whirl of crossing traffic. She sees trucks, insect-like buses with their antennae attached to overhead wires, and a slow-moving old man carrying a sodden cloth shopping bag.

Walk faster buddy. Please walk faster.

The man limps to the sidewalk, safe and sound. As she looks away again, she catches the reflection of green light on the rain-slicked street. Brad charges forward. Bangs the driver-side front wheel onto the median on the intersection's far side. Her gaze whips forward as the tire jolts back down to the street and the car reels sideways.

"*Whatthefuckareyoudoing?*"

"Shut up!" He corrects the car's trajectory.

She realizes she's shaking, her teeth clenched, her hands fisted. She forces herself to take a slow, long, silent breath, to consciously relax her shoulders, her jaw. Her head is pounding, and it's not from too much wine. She slowly releases her tension, one knotted muscle at a time. It's a long drive home. Her mind replays tonight's little drama.

I know why you do this. You've done it so many times, and I know just what you're going to say so there's no point in me even calling you on it. Besides, I've already pushed you too far tonight. I know that being a stockbroker is a hard job, and you're trying to live up to your clients' expectations. You're under so much pressure. You deserve to unwind with a few beers. I know, I know... I know what you need...

Lucie herself is exhausted and only marginally less drunk than Brad. She regrets her outburst, wants to calm him, restore what passes for peace between them these days. She knows exactly how to do that. She reaches over, touches his thigh, traces a finger suggestively up and down. Starts massaging, gently, working up his leg.

"Should you be doing that while I'm driving?" He glances toward her, grinning.

Twenty minutes of incident-free travel later, he turns into the drive of their condo tower, which is surrounded by carefully clipped bushes and trees. Rhododendron flowers are now ghostly by streetlight, although by day they are lovely, pale blue. Glossy black leaves sparkle with rain. The lawn is a soaked carpet. The garage door rolls open, revealing sulphurous light within. Brad pulls sedately into the correct stall and shuts off the engine. They each disembark, close doors civilly, no slamming. As they walk toward the elevator, she takes his hand, he rewards her with that sidelong 'I can't wait to have you' look she can't resist. They wordlessly await the elevator, elevate, walk to their door, and enter.

Lucie flings her raincoat off, then her light, lacy top. She rubs against him like a hungry cat. Trying hard to be sweet, to forget her anger and embarrassment. He responds with rough kisses, reaching around her back to unclip her bra. But she murmurs into his neck, "So my sweet golden boy, what *was* that about?" She can't stop herself. "I mean, really — was he worth the trouble?"

"Shut up, Lucie," he mutters, burying his face between her breasts.

Ah, whatever. Another crisis drowns in sex. At least I know how to distract you.

"Luce," says Glenda, the perennially perky receptionist, as Lucie slumps into the office lobby. "Late night? You look terrible."

"Yeah, thanks for that. Went to that new chichi restaurant in West Van. And then I couldn't sleep for some reason."

Ha, you know damn well why you were wide awake. Fighting with yourself, trying to think of some adult way to fix this relationship. To fix Brad. To make us work, to click like we used to.

Lucie closes her office door to concentrate on the presentation she's supposed to deliver, but she's bleary and distracted. Her cell phone buzzes.

"Hey, Gwen."

"Hey, Lucie. Sorry we missed dinner last night."

"You didn't miss much." Lucie sighs. "OK, actually you missed a *circus*. Brad was showing off again, making fun of our uber-gay waiter. So I yelled at him. Stupid me. But we worked it out later."

"Oh, in the usual fashion?"

"Well, yeah. He may be childish in public, but once I get him home, he grows up, in more ways than one." Lucie giggles in spite of herself. "What did you and Patrick get up to?"

"Nothing. We walked the dog and called it a night."

"Lazy bums. What's up for the weekend?"

"Drinks at BiBi's on Saturday. You in?"

"Probably. Though I'll have to work. I'm way behind on this presentation."

"So stop going out on Tuesdays."

"Yeah, yeah. You're not my mother. See ya Saturday."

Lucie wanders to the office kitchen, makes an extra-strong coffee. She can hear murmured conversations elsewhere in the office but encounters no one. She drifts back to her desk, closes the door, and tries again. The coffee is scalding and too bitter to drink.

Her job is no less stressful than Brad's, especially at the moment — she's part of a team trying to win a new client. Lucie works for a human resources firm. Her specialty is helping small busi-nesses design compensation and benefits packages. It's a difficult task to balance what a company can afford against paying enough to attract and keep talented employees. Normally she's good at it, creative and resourceful. She invents ideas the clients love, and she's well paid for her brilliance.

Her desk phone buzzes. She punches the speaker button.

"Hey, Mark."

"Lucie," her manager snaps. "I need to see some progress. Today."

"I'm not feeling great this morning, but I'll at least get you an outline, OK? And I'll finish at home over the weekend so we can finalize next week."

"That's not exactly what I had in mind."

Well it's what you're getting, boss man.

"Yeah, I'm on it. Still lots of time." She punches the button, cutting him off before he can harangue her further.

She knows Brad will be annoyed when she brings work home — he demands her full attention on weekends. With bribery in mind, at noon she scoots out to buy him a couple of expensive shirts and herself some racy lingerie. She returns to the office, spends an unproductive afternoon, and leaves early, claiming to have a crashing headache. Once at home, she puts on the new lace garments that serve to accentuate her creamy skin, her mass of black hair, and startlingly pale eyes. She wraps herself in a satin cover-up, displays Brad's new shirts on the coffee table and stretches on the sofa, awaiting his arrival. She can barely stay awake. But her plot works its intended magic. He loves her gifts, all of them. They romp and play on the sofa, and then she darts upstairs to their cozy, dark bedroom where they remain for hours, forgoing dinner. Another late night, another bleak day will be her reward. But she's warmed him to the idea that she'll have to work the entire weekend, except of course for Saturday night at a local café they frequent because it's raucous, jammed, and famous for good wine. That alone will placate him.

But Saturday dawns and Brad complains loud and long when she sits at the dining table, coffee at hand, laptop open, notes strewn about. He whines that he's not getting any breakfast — she's ignoring him and should have finished her assignment during the week. After what seems like hours of tedious argument, he stomps out, bound for the gym, leaving her utterly unable to focus. She considers going for a walk or phoning a girlfriend. Instead she paces around the table, opens the kitchen windows, does a load of laundry. It's mid-afternoon when she finally sits again, rouses her sleeping computer, and at last applies herself. Three hours later, drained and knowing this is not her best work, she runs a hot bath and nearly falls asleep amid a cloud of lavender-scented bubbles.

She dresses. Waits. The kitchen clock ticks ticks ticks. She considers ordering pizza. Finally her cell phone buzzes.

"Where the fuck are you, *Cupcake*?" Brad yells over loud music and conversation. Clearly he's already at BiBi's. Clearly he's been there for hours.

"On my way," she chirps, trying to keep the razor edge from

her voice.

BiBi's is a long, narrow room, much of which is taken up by the bar and open kitchen. It's hot, it's ridiculously noisy with electronic music punched to what must surely be dangerously high decibels. As usual it's standing room only. Lucie elbows her way through the crush, looking for familiar faces. It takes a good five minutes to push to the back where her friends are clustered. Brad is shouting a drink order, bending to scream directly into the face of a diminutive Asian girl who nods and turns toward the bar.

"Cupcake!" He passes her a huge globe-shaped glass half-full of thick red wine. Gratefully she takes it, flashes her famous grin, kisses him long and full, and then takes a deep swig of the rich, juicy liquid. She looks around, then muscles her way to Gwen, who is seated in a corner. They shout into each others' ears to make themselves heard, so Lucie doesn't notice when the server returns. But she's fully aware of Brad's displeasure as he refuses to take the glasses from the tray. Even above the din, Lucie hears him curse, "Stupid slut," as the server retreats.

Lucie can't believe her ears. Such an awful word. She stops in mid-sentence, mouth open, shocked and dismayed. Gwen places a hand on Lucie's arm. "Let it go, Luce. The damage is done. You can't undo it, and you sure as hell can't apologize for him this time."

"I can't believe it. I've got to get out of here. *Now.*"

Deeply committed to his tantrum, Brad fails to see Gwen and Lucie leaving. But he's furious by the time he arrives home well past midnight.

"Oh there you are, *Cupcake*! What do you think you're doing, deserting me like that? All day I've had to entertain myself, then you leave me standing there alone..."

"You were hardly alone. I had to leave. Brad, you can't use language like that. You used a dirty word on that poor girl. And stop calling me 'Cupcake'."

He coughs out a short, mean laugh and grabs her, pulls her toward him, but she yelps and twists away. He staggers but regains his balance. Stares at her in disbelief as he slowly opens the fridge, pulls out a beer. Unzips his pants. The sound tears through her, shredding her nerves.

Oh, no. Not this time. I'm done with this dance. She backs away from him.

"What, you don't want it? That's not like you, *Cupcake*. And I'll call you whatever I want. Besides, since when are you such a defender of civility?"

"Oh, get off it. You were a jerk. Looking for attention like a spoiled brat."

"Don't be calling names, Lucie. You're not good at it."

"I'm serious, Brad. One more time and I swear *you are gone.* Gone, like yesterday's news. Do you read me?"

Lucie, what are you doing? Don't set him off. Just calm down, calm him down. You don't want a fight.

A long pull on the bottle, a smug belch. "You don't say. And just exactly how would you do that, little miss don't-fuck-with-me?"

Rage makes her bold. "Could I just remind you who leases this lovely piece of real estate?"

Another exuberant swig. "Could I just point out that if not for *both of u*s paying for it, you could not afford this lovely real estate. And if I won't leave, and you walk out, I'm still here, and I get the condo. Checkmate."

She rolls her eyes, her head, her shoulders toward the ceiling. "Oh, stop. Just stop. You think you're so damn smart, like you can do whatever you want, and I can do exactly nothing about it. What if I kick your ass out?"

"What if I leave?"

"What if you do?" she yells. Her voice is high and squeaky, she's hysterical. Anger is taking her to places she knows she'll regret.

He finishes the beer in one long gulp. "You should be so lucky." Drops the bottle on the tile floor, where of course it smashes on the hard tile. Bits of dark amber glass and beer scatter and splash. "This place is a pigsty, Lucie. Why don't you ever clean up?"

"Son of a bitch!"

Don't cry, don't cry, don't give him the win.

"Don't be calling my mother names, either." He stalks upstairs.

She remains, seething by the kitchen sink, wondering why she lets him get away with such ridiculous behaviour. Eventually, she gets out the mop and broom and sweeps up the broken glass.

"I said things I shouldn't have, but he made me so mad, I lost it. I *never* lose it, Jude, I'm always the tough girl. Ohmygod what is wrong with me? Then he took off upstairs to bed, expecting the little woman to clean up."

"And did the little woman comply?"

Lucie shakes her head sadly. "Of course."

"Lucie! You could have left the whole mess right there." Judith spoons soup from her brimming bowl. "You're not his maid."

"Come on, this is Brad we're talking about. He would have walked on glass for weeks, ground it into the floor, before admitting he was wrong."

"Lucie, my sweet friend, why aren't you getting this? He is abusing you." Judith leans forward over the table and lowers her voice confidentially. "You're right, he behaves like an ass, and I know you thought you could get him to grow up, act his age. You said that to me a dozen times when you started seeing him, 'He's got so much potential, Jude.' But he has not changed, not lived up to whatever you saw in him. In fact, I think he's worse because he knows how much it bugs you. It's a game with him now."

Lucie sighs. "Did I really say he had *potential*? Fergodssake."

"Never mind. Listen. What he's doing to you is emotional abuse, mental cruelty. But still you defend him, you forgive him. You give him sex instead of standing up to him. How long are you going to let him jerk you around? Listen to me. You. Don't. Need. Him." These last words delivered with smart raps of Judith's spoon on the table. Ting ting ting.

"Yes, I get it. He is such a child. He has no self-control. Maybe I'm lucky he didn't throw the bottle at me."

"Good behaviour or bad, he gets what he wants from you."

Lucie smirks and blushes. "Yeah, but that's mutual."

Judith rolls her eyes. "Can you *hear* yourself? Christ, Lucie! He is poison. Get rid of him. Lots of other fish..."

Lucie stares down at her plate. Why did she order such a huge meal? She hasn't touched a bite. "It's just ... I'm such a sucker for a great body and cute smile. All this trouble is just as much my fault as his. You know I can't get enough of him. He makes me feel so amazing, so sexy. I mean, look at me, I'm a freak. Who would want me?"

"Oh fergodssake. Men look at you like they'd leave their wives in five minutes flat, and that's got nothing to do with Brad. You don't need to be grateful to him, for anything."

In fact, Lucie is not freakish, but her appearance is arresting. Apart from rather wide hips and generous breasts, she is petite and slender, muscular, graceful, energetic. She moves with cocky confidence and bravado. She's often mistaken for someone much younger than she is.

But it's her unusual face that is so compelling. Lucie is a porcelain doll. Her complexion is milky, her skin so thin it's stretched taut over her forehead and cheekbones, shot through with the fine lines of underlying veins. Her cheeks seldom show any blush or natural colour, instead she is pallid to the point of transparency. Her eyes are light, the clear, soft blue of faded denim, circled by long but sparse dark lashes — frequently augmented with mascara — and capped by carefully sculpted, arching brows. Full, moist lips frame a wide mouth. Her heavy, long mop of curly hair — true black with the iridescent blue and green highlights of a raven's feathers — tumbles over her shoulders and ripples halfway down her back.

Despite her ghostly appearance, her smile is radiant. When she

employs that famous smile, her eyes illuminate with fun and possi-
bility, her shoulders lift and tilt. She knows exactly how to use that
smile, how to get what she wants. All her life it's been her armour,
her key to open new doors. She's the original coquette.

Her pallor notwithstanding, Lucie is irresistibly sexy. Every pore,
every muscle, every movement and glance transmits a certain
lasciviousness, a lushness, a readiness. Lucie presents as someone
who loves sex and can't wait for her next encounter. It drives her
girlfriends mad and attracts men like wasps to honey. It is impossible not to notice her, not to look twice. People do. Men especially.
She's used to it, in fact, she enjoys it. On the street, she glances
back over her shoulder, catches someone's eye, winks and grins,
turns to fling her black mane — 'I know you want me but you can't
have me' — and walks on.

Today, Lucie gives up the pretence of eating her meal and puts
her fork down. "I just don't know, Jude. I'm so tired these days.
He's sucked the air out of my life. I feel like I'm thirty-nine going
on ninety-three. Plus Mark is pissed with me because I'm not doing
a stellar job on the presentation, which is coming up. Sorry, Buddy,
I know you're trying to help, but I've got to get back to work. I've
been the worst lunch date ever."

"Hey, I'm your friend. I've known you for a decade, remember?"
Judith reaches to tap Lucie's hand. "Seriously. Get rid of Brad. He's
damaging you. Tell him to get the hell out."

"Phhhh!" Lucie lays some bills on the table. "Maybe you're right.
But it's sad, I'm not ready to let him go. Giving up on him now
seems like such a defeat. You know, 'Lucie tries again...and fails
yet again...'"

"Oh fergodssake," says Judith, finishing the wine in her glass —
a glass that rang with a clear sweet note when the two friends
toasted each other earlier.

Lucie pushes her plate away. "I really have to go."

"Just promise me you'll think about dumping Brad. Seriously,
Luce. He is not the last guy in the world and he is Not. Worth. Sex."

Again the spoon, ting ting ting.

"Yeah, I'll think about it. I've *been* thinking about it. I've got to do something."

"Yes, you do. Listen, Gwen and Elaine are coming to my place Friday night for drinks and a movie. You should come, too. We'll talk more."

"OK, gotta go. Thanks, Hon." Lucie bends to give her friend a quick hug, then flees the restaurant.

Four friends sprawl on the floor and the worn leather couch in Judith's living room, drinking wine and half-heartedly watching a movie but far more interested in analyzing Lucie's latest situation.

Judith again tries to impress upon Lucie that her relationship with Brad is toxic, bordering on dangerous. "If he smashed a bottle on the floor, how long until he takes a swing at you?" she reasons.

Gwen nods but seems less convinced than Judith about what Lucie should do. "What about counselling?" she asks.

Lucie, quite tipsy, snorts as she laughs. "C'mon, can you see that? He's barely inclined to tell me whether he'll be home for dinner. Hell would freeze solid before he'd share details of his life with a counsellor."

Elaine, curled into an oversized rocking chair, sips thoughtfully but seems preoccupied and doesn't contribute her opinion. Her expression is troubled, her forehead furrowed. Judith glances her way but doesn't ask what Elaine thinks. Instead Lucie stands unsteadily to fill the empty glass Elaine holds up.

"Argh, this is just going in circles," Lucie complains. "I can see this relationship has some serious cracks, but honestly I'm not afraid he'll hurt me physically. I'm more afraid he'll leave. And he's right. Without two incomes my condo is unaffordable."

"So you're going to stick it out with him to keep the condo?" Gwen asks. "Pardon me, but I can't say that seems like a good idea."

"At the moment, it's the only idea I've got."

Elaine, who normally jumps into such discussions with both feet, seems almost bored. Lucie suspects her friend is impatient and distant because this is yet another in a long string of Lucie's personal crises. It's a recurring pattern, and Lucie wouldn't blame her friends for their boredom and frustration. Lucie's progressive falling out with Brad is just more of the same; she's been here before. Among her friends, Lucie has a reputation for seeking advice when yet another relationship crumbles, asking over and over for help but never seeming to learn from her mistakes.

The only thing Elaine contributes to the conversation is, "I'm sure it will all work out. Meanwhile, I think we all need some retail therapy. Who's up for Holt Renfrew tomorrow? I personally could use a new purse for spring. Something funky, with flowers. Kate Spade, you know?"

Gwen and Elaine eventually call it a night and take taxis home, but Lucie's not finished despite the advancing hour. Judith, ever supportive and patient, continues to listen and talk talk talk. Eventually, she drags out a blanket and pillow and makes Lucie — now incapable of locomotion — to lie down on the couch. "You are my bestest buddy ever," Lucie mumbles as Judith tenderly wraps a blanket around her and settles her head on the pillow. Within five minutes Lucie is sound asleep. Judith regards her friend for a few minutes, then shakes her head and goes to her own soft bed.

The next day, hung over and despondent, Lucie declines Elaine's invitation for a shopping spree. Instead she sleeps fitfully on Judith's couch, finally rousing to drink sweet tea and choke down honey-smeared toast before heading home late in the day. When she arrives, Brad is nowhere to be seen but the kitchen countertop is decorated with no fewer than four empty pizza boxes, and the sink is stacked with soiled plates and glasses. Clearly Brad and the boys entertained themselves last night, watching hockey or who-knows-what. Lucie, who likes her home clean and orderly, grits her teeth, clears the mess, and turns on the dishwasher. Her head is still pounding. She takes a hot shower and crawls into bed.

She spends Sunday similarly occupied, tidying the condo, doing laundry. She wants to get outdoors but the clouds are emptying themselves from drizzle to downpour. Instead she reads and dozes. Once again she's brought work home, but she's unable to summon enough energy to review her ideas for Wednesday's proposal. She'll just have to work late tomorrow.

No Brad, no call, no text — nothing. In spite of herself, Lucie wanders from room to room, lonesome and sad.

The radio wakes her at seven a.m., the announcer forecasting another sodden day. If Brad has come and gone overnight, she was unaware of his presence — but nothing in the kitchen or den appears to have been moved, and there's no sign of him having used the bathroom. She suspects he's punishing her by staying away with one of his friends, waiting for her to panic and start phoning around, searching for him.

Which is precisely what I'll do if he's still gone tonight. Oh, Lucie, get a grip on yourself. Make a damn decision. Do you want him or don't you?

After work it's still pouring, cold, deeply overcast. The rain has been incessant since that odd warm evening when they were all out for dinner. Today the earth is soaked, gutters flow like rivers. Vancouver is in a foul mood. What happened to spring?

Like me and Brad, Lucie muses as she slops her way home, her purse and briefcase swinging heavily from her shoulder, umbrella unfurled but not terribly effective. *Are we a couple or not? We started out so strong, so full of life. I thought I loved him. I thought he loved me. But here we are, raining on each other. Pouring. What happened?*

She stops at a corner clotted with pedestrians waiting to cross. A sleek car pulls around the corner, splashing several people who yell, swear, and step back into others waiting behind, who in turn push and curse.

Oh, what would I give to be someplace where people look out for each other!

The stoplight changes. She surges forward with the crowd.

And where would that be? I don't want to go anywhere. I love Vancouver, really. I just don't like the greed and speed, but you'd get that anywhere. Cities are cities. But Vancouver has a heart. And great shopping, restaurants, bars, fun stuff to do, and fun people to do it with. My friends are here, my life is here. This is home. I could never go back to Toronto. So if I want to stay here — and I do — then I have to make some changes. Starting with: lose Brad. I'll figure out the condo situation. OK. He's gotta go. He's gotta go.

Her pace takes on a determined tempo. Ting ting ting.

He's gotta go. Gotta go. I can do this. Gotta go. Gotta go. Gotta go.

She arrives at the condo building, uses all her exhausted weight to push open the thick smoked-glass doors, wondering, not for the first time, why they have to be so heavy. In the lobby, she shakes and folds her umbrella, careless that she spatters water over the floor and the bamboo plants in glossy black pots that remind her of Brad's glossy car. She pushes the elevator button. The brushed steel doors glide open. She pushes her floor number. The elevator bumps to a halt and emits her into a corridor lined with soft mustard-yellow tiles. She wonders, not for the first time, why the designer chose such a hideous colour.

Form over function. She thinks this every day.

Lucie turns right and pushes through less weighty glass doors into an open-air courtyard. The courtyard aspires to be a garden, except it's surrounded by seven storeys of looming walls and balconies on all four sides, creating a narrow funnel of light and a glimpse of sky. Despite the gloom, a modest fountain splashes into a reflecting pool tiled in greens, blues, and whites. It takes up most of the courtyard's area, with a bit left over for walkways and planters full of cheerful pansies and marigolds. In summer, when the sun is high enough to shine directly into this canyon to light up the pool, reflections bounce into her apartment and spots of light fly about her living room in an endlessly changing dapple. But it's too early in the year for that. Right now, she's met only with the restful sound of splashing water and the soft pish of rain falling on the pool.

She unlocks her door and steps inside.

Home. That word used to mean peace and rest. Now, I never know.

To her surprise, Brad is there. He is sprawled on the sofa, one arm crooked to support his head. A half-finished beer stands within reach on the coffee table. No fewer than four empties also decorate the table's surface, along with empty chip bags. He is at ease. Lord of his realm. "Hi, *Cupcake*. Had a good day?"

"What are you doing here?" She drops her bags, shucks off her wet shoes, and props her umbrella by the door.

"I live here, remember?"

She replies in a dull, exhausted monotone. "No, I mean what are you doing here *now*? You're never home at this hour, but here you are, and you've been here for hours, judging from the empties."

"You're right." He pushes himself upright with considerable effort. "I have been here all day. What a great day, Lucie, I tell ya! Drinkin' beer and watchin' TV — this is the life." He grins broadly. His cheeks are flushed, his nose red from drinking.

She pictures him in a clown suit with big fuzzy buttons running down his vest. Floppy feet. Demented grin. Red bulb nose. "So. What's up?"

"What's up?" he asks the universe, lifting his eyes to the ceiling, raising his arms with his voice like a preacher's. "What, indeed, is *up*?"

She does not move. She wants to stride around the table and smack his drunken face. But she stands by the door, damp and shivering, and says evenly, "Brad, what's going on?"

He lowers his arms and his hands come to rest in his lap. He swings his gaze down to her. He is so strong, so present. Despite his inebriation, his youthful, square-jawed face is full of energy. His thick, red-blond hair is spiky and electric, his broad shoulders lift and fall with every breath, his chest heaves with power. He is a lion, a president, a boy with a slingshot in his pocket.

His gaze transfixes her. "I'll tell ya what's up, Cupcake. I am leeee-ving you." He sings out the words. Folds both arms behind his head and leans back like someone who's just won the lottery.

Silence ensues. Minutes pass, a century maybe, she's not sure. She feels glued to the wall, a battered moth pinned but not quite dead.

At last, a decision. Gotta go. Gotta go...

Finally she says, "So. Leave already."

He stands. "That's it? No protest, no argument? Don't you want to know *why*?"

"I couldn't fucking care less. You've poisoned my life enough. So go. Good riddance."

To her surprise he darts forward, remarkably agile for someone who's been drinking for hours. He plants one foot then the other onto the foursquare solid oak coffee table, takes two steps, leans forward to wing his right arm up, then down, and strikes the side of her head with his open hand. It's not a skull-cracking blow, but she is so tired and the hit so unlikely and unexpected, that he knocks her over. She collapses down the wall and comes to rest on her side, gazing forlornly at the floor upon which her cheek rests.

I really need to vacuum. This rug is a mess. I should rent a rug cleaner.

He bends at the knees, reaches down from his height on the coffee table, grabs the front of her coat and yanks her from lying on her side to sitting more or less upright. Her legs splay awkwardly before her. She feels like a rag doll.

"Did you hear me? *I am leaving you, Lucie.* I am going to live with Elaine. Elaine. Your buddy Elaine. Don't you want to know why?"

Again she shakes her head. She is so tired. So very tired.

What is this about? What do you want?

"I'll tell you anyway." He booms from his great height atop the table. "Elaine never works weekends. No crowd of friends she's out with all the time. Her daddy is rich, and she has a house, not a condo but a *house*, are you listening to me? And she doesn't piss me off all the time by telling me how to live my life, how I should *behave*. Plus Elaine is the best little fuck I've had for years. So think about this, Lucie. While you were out spending too much time with your nosy girlfriends, Elaine and I were right here, fucking, getting it on, being at one with the universe, know what I mean? Do you really want to know what is *up*? Let me show you." He reaches down, oh so slowly.

Lucie wants to close her eyes but her gaze is fixed on his right hand as he kneads his crotch. In some kind of bemused and distant horror, she watches a bulge form. She's repelled but fascinated, like seeing an especially horrible sea slug. She can't tear her eyes away.

"Oh don't worry, *Cupcake*. I'm not going to fuck you one last time. That would not be much fun for me. I would rather do it with someone who *wants* it."

What do you mean? Didn't we have fun together? Didn't I show you a great time, always?

He thrusts his swollen crotch toward her. "Like you don't know what you're missing. Just think about it. Me and Elaine. Me." He grabs himself again. Squeezes. "And," another squeeze, "E. Laine." Each syllable delivered with a thrust. Ting ting ting.

She closes her eyes and slowly collapses to the floor. She is a heap of clothing and fear and disappointment and grief. He jumps from the table and strides up the stairs. She hears the bathroom door slam.

In the silence, Lucie pushes herself up to sit, then she stands and finally removes her wet raincoat. Mechanically she hangs it up, stows her shoes, umbrella, purse, and briefcase, putting each article in its place. She drifts into the kitchen and turns on the light over the stove. Fills the kettle, sets it onto the burner. Gets out a cup, teapot, teabag, and stands in the dim light until the kettle whistles. Pours searing water into the pot. Overhead she hears nothing. No footfalls, no doors slamming, no sound of someone packing.

The tea steeps. She pours a cupful, drinks a slow careful sip of hot liquid. Still no sound overhead. She is paralyzed with fatigue. She stands at the kitchen counter and sips hot tea, refills, and drinks until the pot is empty.

What does he want? Is he waiting for me to come upstairs and beg him to stay? Or maybe he's passed out. Oh, I can't do this.

She wanders into the den, a cozy, windowless room lined with bookshelves. Turns on the television but does not watch, Instead she pulls a blanket over her head and curls up on the sofa where she and Brad used to nestle into each other, watching movies. She rolls onto the floor and adjusts the blanket around her, a cocoon. The television murmurs.

Whatever else Brad might have had in mind for a dramatic closing scene does not happen. When Lucie wakes up she is clenched on the floor, stiff and aching. She lies still for a long time, listening. She hears nothing. She sits up, pushing away the blanket, her hips and shoulders complaining from hours on the hard surface. She stands, wanders up the stairs into the bedroom.

Nobody home. He is gone. He has taken his ties, shirts, jackets. His shiny, gorgeous shoes. The bathroom is equally vacant. He's taken his razor, cologne...special shampoo. It does not occur to her that this transfer of goods to Elaine's house has been going on for some time. She hasn't noticed the gradual thinning of his belongings.

Lucie trails back to the kitchen, not sure whether she is relieved or enraged that Brad is gone. But anger needs energy, and she is drained. She microwaves a bowl of popcorn and turns back to her happy friend, the television.

At some point she lifts herself from the floor, abandons the yapping television, and gropes her way upstairs to the bedroom. It's dark in the apartment except for the dancing reflections from the poolside lights in the courtyard. She finds their bed — hers and Brad's. To her surprise, the bed is soft and embracing. The mattress floats her, the duvet hugs her. How could this be? It's been the carnival spot for her loving with Brad. But now he's gone. Now it's her refuge. Hers alone.

What day is this, what time? She has no idea. The room is dark, but she faintly registers rain drumming the window. Her eyes are gummy. She's not hungry.

There's a sound. Rhythmic, insistent, an annoying buzz, yet far away like a distant siren or barking dog. It's making her mad, but she can't do anything about it. It stops.

It starts again. She struggles to roll over, so swaddled by blankets and pillows that she can barely move. Thin daylight warms the silky curtains but rain beats on the window. Must be some great storm for rain to be hitting her window here, so far down the narrow courtyard shaft.

What is that noise?

It has stopped, but she's now conscious enough to think it might have been the phone. She has never allowed a phone in the bedroom. There's only one rarely used landline in the condo. It's downstairs in the kitchen, and it's ringing, again.

You're persistent, whoever you are.

Lucie sits up into a tangle of sheets and duvet, long hair flopping over her face. There's a flight of stairs between her and the phone, and a ton of fabric pinning her legs to the mattress. Even if she wanted to pick up the call she wouldn't make it in time. Instead she sighs and thrusts aside the bed linens, rises, stretches, and rakes her fingers through her sticky jungle of hair.

Again the phone.

"Oh leave a damn message."

Eventually Lucie makes her way to the kitchen. Every few minutes, the phone rings, stops, rings again. Finally she is poised over the instrument, waiting for the next series to begin. When it does she lifts the receiver and says, in the most annoyed voice she can muster, "_Yes?_"

There's a long pause. Lucie starts to replace the handset when a panicky voice says, "_Lucie?_ Lucie, are you there? Don't hang up, it's me, Glenda."

"Hi."

"Hi. It's me, Glenda. From work. You remember work, right?"

Lucie sighs. "Hi."

There's an awkward pause.

"Hi," Lucie says again. It's all she can think of.

"Lucie we've been worried about you. Especially Mark. They had to do that presentation without you. He's really pissed. Lucie, if you want the truth he's more pissed than worried, I'd say."

"OK, thanks."

Glenda seems stunned. "I didn't call to... I mean.... What do you mean, 'thanks'? Lucie, are you OK? Are you on some kind of bender? Do you need help? Because Mark really wants to see you. He told me to phone you and keep phoning, but your cell must be dead so I've been calling your home phone..."

"OK. Mission accomplished. Thanks. I'm... um, I'm having a bad time right now. Personal. Like a crisis. Tell him I'm sorry, I'm sure they did the presentation fine without me."

"They didn't, actually."

"Um. Well. OK, I'll let you go."

"No, you won't. Mark asked me to tell you to get your butt into the office. Today."

Lucie laughs as she disconnects.

She makes coffee. She is hungry but can't find the energy to operate the toaster. The fridge smells sour. She turns off the television, which has been talking away to itself in the den for hours. Days maybe.

The phone rings.

I bet that would be Mister Mark, calling to personally tell me how concerned he is.

"Hello."

"Lucie?"

"Who else?"

Even over the phone, her manager's voice is squeaky with rage.

"You know, Lucie, if you're having some personal difficulty that's OK, we all have problems and things come up that we have to sort out. But you have been absent, totally absent, missing in action, since Monday. It is now Thursday morning, are you aware of that?"

"Um, no. Thursday? Really?"

She hears the hiss of his breath inhaled between clenched teeth.

"Plus you missed the presentation. We were counting on you, Lucie. You know the material better than anyone. But you let us down. The client called this morning to say they're awarding the contract elsewhere."

His voice is like a dentist's drill piercing her brain. She shifts the receiver to the other ear, takes a swig of coffee.

"Anything to say?" He speaks the exact phrase her mother used in the old days. Her mother, endlessly lecturing and criticizing, only pausing her diatribe to make sure Lucie was listening.

"Sorry." Lucie delivers it with a shrug Mark cannot see.

"And will you be gracing us with your presence any time soon?"

"Yes, actually. Yes, you instructed Glenda that I should present myself today. Which I will do. And I will have an explanation. Really."

"What time?"

"Huh? Right now? It's, um..." she glances at the stove's clock, "nine-thirty."

"I mean *what time will you be here*?"

"God, Mark, don't yell at me, OK? Look, I'm sorry. I'm really sorry. I just... Look, never mind. I'll be there before noon, OK?"

"Fine."

Coffee in hand, she climbs upstairs to be greeted by a damply unpleasant smell in her bedroom — the fug of heavily used sheets, farts, feet, and sweat, the same air breathed in and exhaled over and over for too long. She yanks open a window, strips the bed, starts the washing machine, and takes a shower. Tries to focus on finding suitable clothing for her meeting with Mark.

In the mirror, she regards her reflection. There's no evidence of Lucie the street-wise, sassy girl looking back from her mirror.

She looks broken, sad, uncertain. Ghastly. Her skin is so white her face and hands have a blue cast. Everything about her seems see-through, exposed and temporary.

She applies mascara and a dark lipstick she retrieves from a basket on the dresser, then practices her famous smile. The makeup only highlights her pallor. There's a faint but unmistakable purplish bruise on her cheek where Brad made contact, and blue-black circles stain the puffy skin under her eyes. Again she rummages through the basket, but there's no concealer or foundation to be found. "Oh well. Guess lipstick is as good as it gets," she declares to her reflection.

Lucie could capitalize on her odd features and unruly hair to make some kind of bold fashion statement, but she dresses conservatively and has no tattoos, no piercings or body hardware except two holes in each earlobe. She utterly rejects wearing power suits, unlike most of her female colleagues. Her wardrobe tends toward neutral shades, even in summer. Impatiently, she flips through her closet and chooses the most cheerful tunic she can stand to wear today — royal blue with a pattern of tiny black hearts. She pulls it over a long-sleeved sweater of light and dark grey stripes. She rolls up black tights and finds silver hoops for her ears.

She dons boots and coat, grabs umbrella and purse. Decides to leave her briefcase, which is loaded with the failed presentation, at home.

OK, he's gone. And for once in your life, you are the dumpee not the dumper. Forget it. The point is, he's gone. You are free of him. Open the windows, get some fresh air into your life. Turn the page. Get going. Confront your angry boss.

Feeling more or less lucid, Lucie sets out to her downtown office. As she leaves the condo building, a ferocious wind whips her coat around her knees and shreds the clouds to reveal scraps of fiercely blue sky so clear and hard it looks scrubbed. She takes heart. The sun might even show later.

Head up, she walks quickly. Her arrival at the office generates an odd look from Glenda, who is on the phone but nods a greeting, eyebrows raised, eyes wide with some kind of alarm.

Mark's door is open. Lucie enters and starts to unbutton her coat.

"Don't get comfortable. Close the door," he barks.

She complies.

He picks up a large envelope and hands it to her. "I'll get right to the point, Lucie. I'm sorry to do this, but I need someone I can depend on. I can't have people disappearing from the face of the earth just when I need them most. You didn't even have the courtesy to call. I might have been able to forgive your *behaviour...*" his voice becomes tighter with each word, "...but you didn't even bother to let us know where you were. I nearly called the *police*, Lucie. We called your home every day, called your cell until the battery died. Didn't you get the messages? Where the hell have you been?"

Shut up, Mark. You sound like my mother.

She barely hears him. She has withdrawn a sheaf of pages from the envelope and started reading. The printed words hit like hurled rocks: 'Termination. For cause. Inappropriate behaviour.' And the last line, telling her she will be paid up to and including last Monday.

She looks up to see his bulging eyes and his lips pressed into a thin, straight line. He so resembles a monster cartoon character she almost laughs out loud. She thinks he is probably waiting for her to speak, to explain. To apologize. Maybe to beg. Instead, she gives him her most impertinent, flirtatious grin.

Just call me Marilyn. Manson, Monroe, take your pick.

"I'll clear out my office. Gimme twenty minutes."

March fades, it's now well into April. Lucie has been unemployed for more than a month. She's been trolling online job sites, submitting her resumé. She's phoned business colleagues, personnel agencies. But so far nobody has said, "Try this company," or "Here's a contact, I know these guys are looking for people, I've told them how great you are, they'd be crazy to pass you up."

Reluctant to go out and have to face streets teeming with the happily employed, at first Lucie passes the time by spending hours on LinkedIn and Facebook. But gradually she stops posting and only browses through friends' pages, reading the cheerful, hollow details of their lives: their chirps about weekend parties or vacation plans or what they're having for dinner. Sweet nothings. Finally she quits altogether, impatient and angry.

She's gone underground, burrowed like a hunted fox. She doesn't go out, she doesn't call her friends. She has told no one about her breakup with Brad, though she's certain Brad himself has informed their circle about his glorious new circumstance. In fact, she's certain her so-called friends have known about Brad's infidelity, his liaison with Elaine, for some long time — and they've all been having a good laugh at her expense.

Likewise, she's told no one about losing her job. She has simply stopped calling people in her circle, stopped going out for cocktails or movies. Definitely no dinners or shopping trips. She has no income, therefore she's become invisible.

When she's not angry, she's embarrassed, and oh so disappointed in the people she trusted. She's afraid of their ridicule. She would sooner be alone than have to be her usual sassy self, knowing they all see straight through her. She almost physically feels the swirl of gossip around her like a riptide. She has no idea how to defend herself; she's utterly unprepared for this exposure.

She's chewed her fingernails to rags. She can't sleep. The dark shadows under her eyes solidify and take up residence in a previously untroubled face. Some mornings when she gazes forlornly into the bathroom mirror, it looks like someone has hit her square in the face, although Brad's bruise has long since faded. She is a prizefighter, knocked down. Knocked out.

Occasionally she summons enough courage to leave her flat and pass empty time with increasingly long walks. She keeps her cell phone close, its ringer volume at maximum, afraid she'll miss a call from someone who's bowled over by her resumé and ready to offer her a job. But the phone remains silent.

Today as she slowly paces along the Seawall, she unexpectedly encounters Patrick and Gwen out walking their dog. They were shifty-eyed when they spotted her, but it was too late for them to turn away. So here the three of them stand, engaged in halting conversation. Do Gwen and Patrick know about Brad and Lucie and Elaine? Whose side are they on? Lucie is trying to show them her usual lippy, sardonic self, but in fact she's so very happy to see familiar faces and have a chance to offer her point of view. She's known these two for a long time — she attended their wedding. She hopes they'll support her, recognize her desperation and need, and transmit her message back to the group of friends. But their evasiveness puzzles her.

How much do I tell you? I know you guys well, or so I believe — but do I tell you the truth about my anxiety... that I'm on the edge of some disaster? How do I know what story you'll spread around? I don't know, I don't know who to trust any more.

"So what was I going to do?" she ventures, midway through their conversation. "Tell my boss that my boyfriend walked out on me? And that maybe I deserved a few days to get myself back in order?"

"Well, your manager did have a point about not calling," says Patrick, snapping the leash as his dog strays to investigate an interesting bush.

"Never mind, it's behind you now," says Gwen, trying not to get tangled in the leash. "On to better things."

"Right. I'll get another job. I've sent out tons of resumés," Lucie says.

"I don't suppose your company gave you a reference letter?" All three laugh, but Lucie says, "Seriously, they should. I've spent years with them, gave them good work, brought in some great clients. Then I make one mistake and whammo, I'm out the door with no help, barely even a final paycheque."

"You'll find something. There's lots of work around."

"Oh, yeah," Lucie says lightly. "No worries."

But in fact, worries abound. Bills are coming in. Her credit cards. The condo lease payments. And no job in sight — not so much as an interview. Her confidence is ebbing, replaced by impatience and just the tiniest nagging what if, what if. What if — *what*? The truth is, she's on a creaky, unstable limb with no Plan B. Her bank account is draining rapidly despite her efforts to be frugal.

Back on the Seawall, Gwen asks, "So will we see you at Bill's party on Saturday?"

"Maybe, I'm not sure," says Lucie, who knows nothing about this party. She hasn't been invited.

"Let us know if you change your mind, we'll give you a lift," Patrick offers as they part company.

"Yeah, will do. Thanks, see ya."

That's how it is now. Parties she's not invited to, movie nights and concerts nobody tells her about. No one has come over to spend time with her or suggested going for coffee, a walk, a gallery visit. Judith, for instance: radio silence. Lucie's most trusted friend. All that advice over lunch, Judith emphatically rapping her spoon on the table. Solidarity, support, *ha*. It's all vanished like smoke. Friends shun Lucie as though she has a contagious skin rash.

"You do have a reputation for being, ahh, headstrong," a placement counsellor told her when Lucie first started looking for work.

"I do? That's news to me."

The woman gave Lucie a no-nonsense look across her cluttered desk. "This might be a big city but, as I'm sure you know, your kind of work is specialized and only a handful of companies are hiring right now. I've made calls, but people seem to know who you are. And they're not biting."

"But I've done great work," Lucie responded, exasperated, trying not to sound desperate and scared. "My company promoted me, I brought in good clients. I must have *some* talent. Come on, there can't be that many closed doors."

"You'd be surprised."

"I guess I am."

The lack of employment frightens her even more than her friends' abandonment. Jobs have always come easily for Lucie. For that matter, throughout her decade in Vancouver, everything has come easily: work, money, men, her circle of friends. She's never had to think about any of it or try too hard. Her favourite motto — 'If stuff happens easily, it's meant to be' — has more or less defined her hand-to-mouth life. She falls in love, she finds a new job, she sees a great new band. She falls out of love, moves on to a new job, finds new bands to follow. New friends. Waves in, waves out. And when her latest relationship went sideways, as they all did, Lucie could always count on her well-worn cloak of cynicism and dismissal. A familiar piece of clothing, this. She's put it on for every prince who turned out to be a toad, every gal pal who secretly mocked her pale face and dark, bloody-looking lips.

But this, now. Not the same, not at all. Like swimming in murky water, she can't see the bottom and she doesn't know which way is up. After each increasingly rare conversation with a friend who offers no real help, Lucie reacts with a mental *Fuck you* and deletes yet another contact from her iPhone.

Speaking of which, she needs to pay the cell phone bill.

Today as she says good-bye to Patrick and Gwen, with some reluctance she crosses them off her list too. Patrick and Gwen have survived several of Lucie's shifts to new friends, new passions, and pastimes. They have considerable longevity in her life; she'd thought they were good buddies. But have they called? Oh, no. Did they avoid eye contact today? Oh, yes.

She walks slowly now, no destination in mind, no deadline. Nothing to do, nobody waiting on her. So strange to not stride along, head up, turning to glance at the men who inevitably stare at her, and flash her provocative smile. She has no confidence. She is empty.

And another thing: Lucie has no car. She enjoys driving and isn't

unnerved by big-city traffic. But now, there's no Brad and his glossy
car. She's also relinquished her drive-share account. The lack of a
vehicle is creating trouble she never anticipated. Getting groceries
has become a chore involving bags, backpacks, and bus rides. And
what if she lands a job in Burnaby or Surrey or someplace off the
map like that? Hours commuting? Move to the suburbs?

Get over it, Lucie. Brad was never a long-term life partner pros-
pect. Actually he was just a pretty-boy chauffeur. Nothing more.
Not a love affair. Lust, at best. Face facts, Lucie. A good car, a good
fuck, period. And mostly it was about the car.

She sits on a beach log, crosses her legs, and joggles one foot rapidly.

Argh! No, it was more than a car; of course it was more. He made
me laugh, we had fun. He's gorgeous. But in the end — he hit me.
Like my mom hit me, sometimes. I swore I'd never let that happen
again. Maybe that hit has unnerved me more than anything.

She glances around, taking in her surroundings. The afternoon
is empty. The tide is out. Little kids are playing in the mucky sand,
a few couples are walking hand in hand, they talk and laugh. Gulls
hang in mid-air, aloof. The sunshine is warm but the cool wind
makes her wish she'd worn a scarf. She's afraid to go home to face
the stack of bills, afraid to wander the streets in case she meets
someone she knows. Afraid to spend money on anything — not a
coffee, not a dishtowel, nothing.

Her fingers worry the buttons on her coat as her thoughts delve
yet again into the cause of this dilemma. She can't stop herself
from picking it apart. She can't let it go.

My golden boy. What happened? You got tired of me because I
tried to make you see how your life could be better, how you could...
improve. And you couldn't stand it. You were fed up with me. Like
you said. Before you hit me.

She swipes cold tears from her cheeks.

Face it, Lucie. You picked him up because it was easy, then you
nagged the hell out of him until he found sweet Elaine, who would
never think of criticizing him. It's your fault, it's always your fault

when this happens. They're never good enough. Like you were never good enough. Your sweet mother made sure you got that message. Over and over.

She fumbles in her pocket for a tissue. Shaking her head like a wet dog, clearing her mind from this constant loop of worry, Lucie stands, turns, and comes face to face with Elaine.

"Lucie."

"Oh hel-*lo*," Lucie says. Delivered with a brilliant smile that feels false even to herself.

They stare, hands dangling. Uncertainty hangs in the air like the seagulls. Then Elaine extends a gloved hand and touches Lucie's arm. "You were too much for him, you know," she says in a conspiratorial tone.

Lucie tilts her head forward as if to bring Elaine into better focus. "Sorry? Meaning...?"

Elaine withdraws her hand. "You were always telling him off. He never felt like he measured up."

"That's news to me," Lucie lies, facing Elaine with her usual tough-girl persona.

"He never knew how to please you, what you wanted. More than he could give, I guess."

"More news." Lucie, to her own surprise, stands tall and folds her arms across the chest just as her mother used to do. Belligerent.

"I'm trying to explain."

"Save it," Lucie snaps, stepping around Elaine. Head high. The wind whips hair into her eyes. Stings. Tears.

"He says you were never home," Elaine yells at Lucie's retreating back. "You have too many friends, you're into movies and parties. You're shallow and you're afraid to be alone. Well you're alone now, aren't you?"

Damn right.

—➤ɱɤ—

April May June. Three months. *Three months!* Still no job. No calls, except the almost-polite one from a collection agency and the frightening one from the condo management company. Plus the weather is abysmal; it's the coldest, wettest spring anyone can recall, in a city accustomed to cold, wet weather.

Lucie is walking aimlessly, killing time yet again, finding diversion through window shopping. Avoiding her reflection, her own pale, pleading eyes. Stopping outside of bakeries and bookshops, looking through her mirror image in the windows, never going inside. The price of croissants appalls her. The price of everything appalls her. Only a few months ago she would heedlessly buy whatever she wanted, but today purchasing even a cookie or newspaper, a bottle of water, a pair of socks, a lottery ticket, any discretionary item, any tiny bit of pleasure or distraction is absolutely not on. She can't believe she's previously been so loose with her money, never thinking ahead, never saving a dime.

Today is another damp, drizzling day, so it surprises her to see clothing hung outside of a boutique across the street, until she realizes the clothes are protected from the rain by a high awning. The bodyless outfits swing and flutter enticingly. One ensemble in particular captures her attention: a fawn-brown A-line skirt peeking from beneath a long cream sweater. She crosses the street for a closer look and finds the skirt is fine wool tweed and the sweater is fluffy soft cashmere.

What a life she could create, wearing those clothes! Dark stockings and flat-soled slippers, a slender silk scarf of teal or salmon looped around her neck and shoulders. She would move soundlessly through an old house that's peaceful but for the ticking clocks and the purring cat. She would sip Earl Grey tea from vintage bone china and read, curled in a window seat, listening to classical music, and bathed in clear, white winter light from a tall window. Quiet, serene, soft. Worry-free.

Someone touches her shoulder and she yelps.

"Sorry!" says the equally startled store clerk. "Want to try those on?"

"How much is the skirt?" Lucie asks, recovering. Heart slamming.

"Um, about $400. I can check."

"That's OK." She keeps walking.

Which comes first, a new life or a new look? Is it that easy — buy different clothes and suddenly you act differently, you create a new personality? Maybe all I need is wardrobe.

Her cell phone chimes. She fumbles eagerly in her pocket, grabs the phone, a huge, relieved grin lighting her face.

At last, at long fucking last!

But it's not a job offer. It's Judith.

"Lucie?"

"Jude? MygodIthoughtyouweredead." Lucie says, the familiar phrase they use to signal too much time between calls or contact. She tries to keep disappointment and hungry relief from her voice.

Normal, Lucie. Just be normal. So it's not a job, but it is Jude.

Judith's voice, so comforting. "I'm sorry, Luce. I've been away for a few weeks. My mom had surgery so I scooted to the island for a while."

"She OK?"

"She had a hip replacement. The surgery was pretty good, but I had to help her, took longer than we thought. Anyway, yes, she's fine. Which is not what I hear about you."

Lucie is now leaning against a bus shelter. She can't see for the tears smearing her vision. "Jude, can we have coffee or something? And... can you buy?"

"Where are you?"

In twenty minutes they are leaning over steaming mugs in a noisy café.

"When did life get this complicated? One minute I had a job and friends and a social life and a guy. Now I'm an outcast. What a word, 'outcast.' Castaway, like garbage. Jude, I feel like *garbage*, like I've just been cluttering up other peoples' lives all these years, and now they're only too happy for an excuse to dump me."

"Come on. Lucie, you know that's not true. The girls have been asking about you, nobody's heard from you for weeks. Is your life really that hard? I mean, look at you — smart, funny, gorgeous, ambitious."

"Unemployed."

Judith sits back as if to gain perspective, to place Lucie in a bigger frame of view. Her gaze strays to the poster hanging behind Lucie's right shoulder: the Eiffel Tower at night. Judith pauses, bites her lower lip, squirms and fidgets, folding and re-folding her hands around her mug. She doesn't drop her gaze from the poster, doesn't make eye contact with Lucie.

"*What?*" Lucie says. "Jeez, Sweet Pea, whatever you've got to say, just say it. You know you're my best buddy. I need straight talk from you."

Judith draws a deep breath and lets it go, slowly, forcing her shoulders to relax. "OK, this is about as straight as I've ever been with you."

"You have my full and rapt attention."

Judith shakes her head. "Ugh, this is hard. I'm trying to think of a gentle way to..."

"Oh fergodssake."

Judith's gaze snaps to Lucie's pale face. "OK then, straight up, no nice. Think about this: you are how old now, thirty-eight?"

"Just turned thirty-nine, but who's counting?"

"That's my point. You are staring down the big four-oh, but you behave like a teenager. Lucie, you are so... ah, I'm just going to say it. You're not taking responsibility for your decisions. You're not... making any *progress*, Luce. You've got to get a grip on your life and start being an adult. You flit from guy to guy, one circle of friends to the next, passion to passion — one minute you're into vintage French movies, the next you're into Lebanese cooking, and then you're raising poodles. You mould your life to fit your current boyfriend, then for whatever reason, he's no longer in the picture, and you change shape again.

"Lucifer, my friend, you need to grow up. Believe in yourself, trust your own judgment about who you are and what you want from life. You're such a dilettante. You dabble, but you don't stick with anything, or anyone. I never know who you are, except you're ever the tough girl, always with a wisecrack, pushing people away, 'I'm fine, I don't need you, thank you very much and buzz off.' But what do you believe in, really? I don't think you believe in yourself, for one thing. You're as Peter Pan as the men you complain about. You need a dream, a new plan. Something big."

"I'd be happy to make my condo payment. That would certainly be big. The payment, I mean."

Judith thumps the table in frustration. "You're not listening! You're all about sarcasm and self-defence. Which proves my point. You never seem to understand that you have choices. You are not a victim, Lucie, although you behave that way, as if things just happen to you, events wash over you like the wind or the waves, and you're powerless. Well, you're not."

Where is her bravado? Lucie starts to cry, not dramatic sobs but a slow leak of sadness and apprehension.

Judith fishes in her pocket for a tissue, hands a tattered rag to Lucie. "Sorry, this is all I've got."

Lucie gratefully accepts the gift and dabs her eyes, wipes at her nose. Rolls and clutches the tissue like it's a life preserver.

Judith continues, "OK, physical abuse is never deserved, of course that's not your fault. But Lucie, you've painted yourself into a corner and wallowing is not going to solve anything."

"*Wallowing*?" Lucie is incredulous, incensed. This tirade is nowhere near the support she wanted from Judith. "Are you kidding me? Is this some kind of tough-love treatment? Because if that's the best you can do, I am not interested. I'm not looking for sympathy, but I need ideas. What am I gonna do?"

"Lucie, listen to me! There is no magic here, except the magic you could create yourself by maybe stepping up to take an active role in your own life. I don't have pixie dust to sprinkle on your head and make it all better. But *you* do. Change your life, Sweet

Pea. Because you can. You're thinking small. You're only focused on finding a job. OK, that's important, but you need a bigger horizon, you need a whole-life change. Think *big*, girlfriend. You could actually do something different. Don't you see the freedom you have? Take your life in your hands. Make your own damn pixie dust."

"By thinking big do you mean declaring bankruptcy?"

"Maybe. What have you got to lose?"

Now Lucie sits back, gripping her mug, seething. She contemplates tossing coffee across the table.

"What do I have to lose? Let me count the ways." She slams her cup down, splashing liquid over the rim and onto her fingers. She does not stop to dry her hand but raises one dripping finger after another as she speaks. "One: job — oh no, make that *career*. Two: condo and all the stuff inside it. Three: friends in general and male companionship in particular."

Judith raises a sceptical brow but says nothing.

"*Fine*. Where was I? Oh yeah, financial security. Credit rating. What have I got to lose? My *life*. My entire fucking screwed-up life."

"That's the spirit! Look, you even have colour in your cheeks for once."

"You make me crazy. I need serious help, and you're telling me how suddenly fetching I look." But Lucie has stopped weeping and even offers Judith a wan smile.

"I'm not convinced you need your old life back, Luce. Turn a page, girlfriend. Please, please, do something for yourself for a change."

Lucie knocks back the remainder of her now-tepid coffee. "I need a job, I need a way out of this mess, and you're telling me I should grow up, which I entirely deny and refute. I may be a teenager in an adult's ever-aging body, but that life model has served me well for many years. What's wrong with the way I live?"

They lock eyes. Neither states the obvious.

"Well Lucifer, you've been on a certain, ah... trajectory ever since I've known you. It's been like watching fireworks. Bang bang, light and fun. But eventually the show's over and everyone goes home." Judith reaches to squeeze Lucie's hand, which is still wet from spilled coffee. "Listen, do you want another coffee, sandwich, anything? I should go."

"No, thanks. Where's the bathroom?" As Lucie leaves the table, Judith stands, pulls on her jacket, a bemused look on her softly lined, maternally pleasant face. She sits down again and grins enormously when Lucie returns.

"Now what?"

"Lucifer, I can't do much, but I can give you a car."

"More crazy-making. I can't afford it. Seriously."

"You need a car because you're going to take a trip."

"Oh, please."

"Think about it, would you just *think* about it? You need a break. Go away, breathe some different air. A change of scene will help you look at things differently. Give your life a serious review. I'm not kidding. You can come up with a plan. Maybe you could go back to school in the fall. Maybe move to a whole different place. Get out of the rut you're in, which is a rut you don't even see. Whatever. My point is — get outa town."

"Maybe take up hang gliding?" Delivered with a sidelong glance — this is an old joke between them. Lucie waits for Judith to laugh, which, after a beleaguered sigh, Judith does. Lucie continues, "Jude, look. Thanks, but come on, where would I go? I have no money, sister. You had to buy coffee today fergodssake. Road trip? That is a sweet fantasy but it's utterly, totally not on. Not. On." Lucie is tempted to snatch up her plastic coffee spoon and rap it on the table for emphasis. Ting ting.

Judith persists. "Whistler?"

"What did I just say? Don't they charge admission just to look around?"

"Ever been to Banff?"

"*Where*? Are you actually insane?"

"How about this: I can give you a car and two thousand dollars to take a trip. Go wherever you want: Abbotsford, White Rock.

Mexico. Montreal. Whatever. The catch is, you must come home with a plan, a solid, realistic plan for moving your life forward, and I'm not talking about just finding a new job. Or hang gliding."

Lucie says nothing.

"OK, and there's another catch," Judith says. "In the interest of full disclosure, it's not exactly a Maserati."

Lucie shakes her head, slowly. Not smiling, but not arguing. Not a refusal.

"So you'll think about it?"

"Yeah, in my spare time."

"Ha ha. Ever the tough girl. You make me crazy. Have I said that already?"

On the sidewalk, Lucie opens her arms wide and embraces Judith with a fierce, long hug. "You are my best bud, you know that, right? Who else would listen to me whine like this? And who else would tell me straight out what's screwed up about my life, then come up with some crazy-ass scheme to help me reform?"

"I love you dearly, and I'll always be here. I'm the bookmark in your life so you can always find your place. My advice is: go away, have some adventures, come back with a new attitude and a plan. OK?" Judith stands back, grasps Lucie's shoulders and shakes gently. "Lucie are you listening? OK?"

Lucie squeezes her eyes tight shut to keep the telltale tears from speaking. "Yeah, OK already."

Lucie arrives home. Among the bills crammed into her mailbox, there's an odd envelope with her name hand-written on it. Once in her apartment, she slits it open and slides out a simple one-sheet letter that bears the condo management company's logo. She only needs to read the first line, its bold, all-capitals type sends a chill through her, buckles her knees: 'NOTICE OF EVICTION.'

Well, Lucie, even if you didn't believe this day was coming, it's here.

—)⫯⫰⫯⟨—

To Lucie's surprise, Gwen calls. Her voice is cheerful and most welcome to Lucie's anxious ears.

"Hi Lucie. Want to meet us for sushi? Haven't seen you since we ran into you on the Seawall. We'll buy — I think you're still looking for work, yes?"

So here they are, three abreast along a polished granite bar, sipping tiny cups of sake. Lucie is still uncertain about these two. She is nearly afraid of them. But they've bubbled back to the surface of her life and invited her out for dinner, so over raw fish and miso soup she's rewarding them with an honest accounting of her current situation, trusting them to guard what she tells them.

It's all about presentation. Appearance. Ugh, my life as sushi.

Patrick drains his tiny sake cup and holds it up for replenishment. Gwen pours. He takes a sip, sets his cup on the counter with a soft click, and says, "Lucie, I feel like we owe you an apology. We haven't called, and it's mostly because we don't know what to say. We're Elaine's friends too, we like her a lot."

Gwen quickly adds, "But I talked to Jude and thought, 'OK this is bullshit. Lucie needs friends now and we're just being stupid and lazy about it.' So, we're sorry."

Lucie only raises her cup to them. "Thanks, guys. No need to apologize. I'm happy to know I still have some support."

"So what are you going to do, Lucie? Maybe you need a change." They exchange glances but Lucie doesn't notice.

"I love Vancouver but right now I can't live the life I want here. It costs too much. Until I find another job. Then things will pick up."

"Really? Same old same old? No change?"

Lucie frowns. "The road trip idea?"

Again the conspiring looks. "Yes in fact. We think Jude has a great idea. Get out of town, Lucie. Do some thinking. You never know what might turn up."

Right. Maybe I'll move to Alberta and meet a cowboy.

"So, Lucie, you have no savings, right?" Gwen asks innocently.

Lucie feels a weight on her shoulders, pressure in her chest.

"Nope, I spent every last cent on having a great time. And now I guess I'm about to lose the condo."

A pause, a beat, as they absorb this information.

"OK," Gwen says after a deep breath, "then there's really nothing holding you here. If you go with Jude's plan, we'd kick in some money."

Lucie takes a long draw on her sake.

"I have no job. Apparently I have no home. Guess I'm taking a trip." She gives her friends a forthright but resigned look. "What I really need right now is a place to store my furniture."

"We can cover that — help you move, put stuff in storage for a while."

Lucie holds up her cup for more sake and says, "That would be a big help. Thank you, thanks so much. I'll pay you back when I can."

"Listen, don't even think about it. Friends help each other. No strings, Lucie. Some people have left you hanging for sure, but we're happy to help you, and we'll miss you. Just come back, OK?"

WHAT A ROAD I'VE TRAVELLED

"It's my brother's car," Judith explains. "He went to do his master's degree in Ontario, and now he's got a job there. He won't be coming back. So he asked me to sell it. But really, it's not worth much. It would cost more to advertise than I would get."

Lucie walks around the silver Civic, giving it a cursory inspection. Two-door hatchback. Manual transmission. A bit of rust.

Judith says, "It's mechanically sound, I drive it occasionally myself. Nothing wrong with it. But it has a lot of miles or kilometres or whatever. It's old. No on-board navigation, no iPod plug-in. But it does have a radio."

"If it's going to be my chariot to a new life, it needs a name," Lucie muses. "Something heroic."

"Ha! OK, um, Hercules? Perseus? Agememnon?"

"Agememnon. That'll do."

"It's good on gas," Judith offers as they walk from the garage to her modest house. Summer has finally arrived, and the day is hot. Roses along the fence perfume the air and hop with bees. Recently mown grass lends a sharp, fresh vegetal scent to the mix. The two friends sit under a large patio umbrella, pouring lemonade into tall glasses.

Judith says, "All right girlfriend, you've got a bit of money in the bank, you've got a car. Now let's figure out where you should go."

"Not much choice, is there?" Lucie says. "Nothing west of here except islands and a whole lot of ocean. And I can't afford to go north to Whistler or south to the States. So it's eastward-ho, I guess — through the mountains, see what's on the other side. I've never been there."

"Want a few travel tips?"

"Yeah, of course."

"Take your time, for one thing. This is a journey, not a marathon. Get off the main roads, stop long enough to look around. Enjoy yourself. Relax, if you remember how to do that."

"Right, coach."

"You'll be going through some national parks, and they charge admission unless you're passing straight through. Pay it. If they spot your car parked anywhere in a national park and you don't have a pass, they'll ding you with a big fine. Which will come in the mail to me, since the car is registered in my name. I'm just saying— I don't want parking tickets courtesy of you. Ditto speeding."

"OK, I get it."

"It's nearly summer now, vacation time, so the roads will be thick with everything from huge trailers to guys on Harleys. That's fine, they'll get where they're going, but don't let them push you. Just be calm, take your time — the scenery's stunning. Stop a lot, look around. And remember to call ahead for reservations, the campgrounds will be really full."

"Campgrounds? Hold it right there. I'm allergic to sleeping on the ground with worms and spiders. Besides, I don't own a tent or sleeping bag or whatever else you need. And what do you do about food? Roast weenies over an open fire?"

Judith fixes Lucie with an exasperated look. "Hmm. Fine, no camping. Accommodation will cost you more if you stay in hostels or motels or even B&Bs. But are you going to hike at least? Get out of your car, see stuff?"

"Maybe..."

"I'm guessing you need boots and a backpack?"

Lucie nods reluctantly.

"OK. Let's go shopping. I'll buy."

Great. Holt Renfrew to Mountain Equipment Co-op. Such is my life.

Although the sun is climbing above the tall trees that line both sides of the highway, it's still cool — the trees' indigo shadows extend across both eastbound lanes, which are already humming with long-weekend traffic. Lucie, piloting Judith's Honda, has joined the traffic stream and is patiently following behind an enormous trailer. Impatient drivers whip by in the left lane, but she's content to flow along with whatever the traffic dictates. Her car radio plays softly. She's focused on driving, keeping her distance from the trailer ahead, obeying the speed limit. Taking her time, as Judith instructed.

Rear seats in the rugged Agememnon have been folded flat to accommodate gear and luggage. Judith insisted on lending Lucie a sleeping bag and also bought her some basic hiking gear — a small backpack, new boots, several pairs of socks, a first-aid kit, water bottle, a water-repellent jacket. Sunscreen. High-energy snacks. Lucie doubtfully added these items to her luggage: two suitcases, one for clothes, the smaller one for shoes, accessories, makeup. A few novels.

One thing Lucie has forgotten: the roadmap. It was lying right there on the dresser in Judith's spare room where Lucie has been living since moving her furniture and belongings out of the condo. But in her eagerness to get away from Judith's well-meaning but constant advice — and before her nerve failed — early this morning Lucie hugged her friend and fled, literally leaping the three steps from Judith's porch to the back lawn and dashing to the waiting car, apparently eager to begin her road trip. Although she could use the map function on her iPhone to guide her, Lucie is trying to be frugal, including curtailing cell phone use.

Nor does Lucie have a hotel reservation — despite Judith's warning — but she's not going far. Today's destination is Hope, a town only a couple of hours' drive east from Vancouver.

Who would stay there on a long weekend? They'll all be going farther into the mountains where they can fish and hike and sit around campfires or do whatever people do.

Hope. Seems like a good place to spend her first night away from home.

Hopeful in Hope. Ha ha.

Maybe she'll locate a friendly bed-and-breakfast place where the owners will be so surprised to have a guest they'll invite her in for lunch and a tour of their back garden. Then she'll stroll the town's quaint streets, browsing through craft shops and bookstores. At dusk she'll join the B&B owners over a glass of...

Lucie suddenly realizes the traffic ahead of her has slowed. She hits the brake hard and nearly stalls the car, remembering to shift down just in time.

Manual transmission. Who does that any more?

And that's how it goes for the next three hours. Traffic runs freely, then clots. She passes farms, the fecund odour of silage and manure and cropland filling the car through the open window. It's hot now. Agememnon has no air conditioning, so she's got the fan on high and her windows rolled down, occasionally resting her elbow on the doorframe.

Oh the mountains. The Coast Range draws ever nearer, larger, darker. Once a faint line on the horizon and nearly lost in the day's humid haze, the mountains are now becoming real, solid and terrifying. She wonders how steep the mountain highways are, how roadways can possibly penetrate this fortress of rock. She realizes her heart is pounding, and her breathing is shallow and rapid. Lucie forces herself to take deep breaths and flexes her fingers. She's gripping the steering wheel like it's a lifeline.

The road begins to climb away from the farms and flatland, turning and twisting between looming cliffs and peaks. Over her right shoulder a waterfall sprays down shadowed cliffs, while on her left the brown Fraser River roils thickly westward, headed to the ocean. Signs inform her that the next exits will take her to Hope. Relieved to be nearing the end of this ordeal, she takes the first exit.

She finds herself on a main thoroughfare clogged with traffic. She passes fast-food outlets and notices a visitor information centre. She pulls in.

"Hi," says the cheerful clerk behind a desk strewn with maps and brochures. "Welcome to Hope. How can I help you?"

"I need a place to stay."

"Tonight?"

"Yes. Just the one night."

"Ooh, I don't know. You might be out of luck. No reservation, I take it? Town's pretty full up for the weekend. How much do you want to spend?"

The clerk makes several phone calls on Lucie's behalf and comes up empty each time. "I'm so sorry, there's really nothing I can do. You can try farther up the highway, there's a bunch of little towns north of here — Yale might have something. Or you could go all the way up to Kamloops, depending on whether you're headed north or east, of course."

"I don't think I want to drive any more today. Is there really nothing at all? I'd take a bed and breakfast."

"I tried a couple of B&Bs, but they're full. I don't blame you about the driving, it's crazy on long weekends. The only thing I can suggest is that you could go to each hotel after dinnertime, see if they've had any cancellations. Here's a street map. The hotels are marked. Most are along this main street." The clerk indicates the busy roadway just outside.

Lucie sighs, exasperated with her own lack of planning. "OK, thanks, I'll try that. And I'd like a provincial highway map too, please."

Armed with maps, brochures, and guidebooks, Lucie goes back to her oven of a car. She pulls out into traffic, and then immediately turns onto a side street and drives aimlessly until she finds a tree-lined avenue where she parks in the shade. Only then does she realize how hungry she is. She locks the car and starts wandering, the distant roar of traffic leading her back to the main road, where she settles for a burger and cold lemonade. She lingers in the restaurant's air-conditioned interior until she's chilled, then walks back to find her car.

Where is her car? Isn't this the street where she parked? But the silver Civic is nowhere to be seen.

Don't tell me. There's a time limit on parking and some crank had my car towed.

But then she notices a gaudily painted house she doesn't recall. Panic subsiding, Lucie walks around the block to a parallel street and spots Agememnon, faithfully waiting in the shade. She gets in and tries to interest herself in reading about local attractions, but heat and exhaustion make her drowsy.

She wakes with a start. Her neck and back are aching, but the air is deliciously cooler now. She starts the engine and, guided by her street map, visits several motels. No vacancy, no vacancy, sorry, try next door. It's now dusk, although not yet seven o'clock. Lucie is puzzled by the gloom until she realizes that this town, surrounded by high peaks, loses daylight earlier than Vancouver. Streetlights are already popping on.

Ah, poor Lucie. Say farewell to long, slow sunsets over the beach.

Discouraged, she pulls a sweater and jeans from her luggage and finds another fast-food restaurant where she changes in the restroom, then orders soup and a bagel for dinner. Leaving, she finds the night air is choked with diesel fumes and the continuing grind of holiday traffic. Consulting her map once more, she discovers a narrow road and drives east from the town to a peaceful, tree-filled park near a large lake. She pulls into a roadside rest area behind several campers and trailers, hoping her tiny car will be inconspicuous amid these travelling fortresses. Lucie retrieves her new sleeping bag, fluffs it around her in the passenger seat, and settles in with the radio playing country music.

Welcome to the Hotel Agememnon. Isn't there a song about that?

Sunlight through the windshield wakes her. The car's side windows are slightly open, and the air is damp and fresh with pine. *Or is it spruce? What's the difference, anyway?*

Lucie trudges to the campground's shower building. The concrete floors are chilly and wet, but there's a fresh scent and the toilets seem clean. She bolts the shower stall door and gingerly tests water temperature before stepping into the pelting stream that needles her skin. She shampoos, soaps, and rinses before remembering that she lacks a towel. Cursing and shivering, she uses her shirt to dry herself and stomps back to the car, flinging drops of water from her mane of hair into the bright, ever-warming morning.

She consults her map and decides on an ultimate trip destination: Banff.

She returns to Hope's visitor information centre. "Next stop, Princeton," she says to the same perky clerk she spoke to yesterday. "Can you get me a reservation there?"

This time, success: The Tall Timber Motel awaits.

Farewell, sweet Hope. I bid you fond adieu.

Today's trip on Highway 3 is fizzing with traffic but less frantic than yesterday's hell-bent swarm on Highway 1. She passes the remnants of a massive rockslide that covered the road in the 1960s. She continues into lush Manning Provincial Park where she stops for a short stroll, sending cell phone images to Judith. Continuing east, the road becomes steeper and more winding, traffic crawling behind an armada of heavy transport trucks.

Lucie crosses over a mountain divide and sees the scenery change dramatically, from dense, green, rain-fed forest on the west side of the divide to open range and sparse bluffs of tall, reptilian trees with scaly red bark and very long needles. The velvety short grass cloaking the hillsides is yellow-brown, and the heat is direct and relentless. Although she's concentrating on the road and traffic, she's also conscious that she's moving through a landscape she's never seen before. It's harsh and haunting and strangely gorgeous.

The road churns and turns, rises and descends. On and on. Slow, so slow.

After several hours she reaches the town of Princeton. She is sweat-soaked and spent from her harrowing drive, so she's grateful to learn her room is ready, equally grateful to take a long hot shower — this time with a towel close at hand — and to lie down, albeit on a bed that's too soft and bouncy. She sleeps deeply for hours, then wakes to make her way to a small roadside restaurant.

Another day, another burger.

She returns to her room. Having slept the afternoon away, she's now wide awake. She restlessly watches television, and says out loud, "I bet Ma is doing this exact same thing right now. I should phone her and see what she's watching. Maybe we can compare notes. Watch a reality show together."

Not enough social contact. It's been two days and I'm talking to myself.

But now she's thought about her mother, the past becomes lodged in Lucie's head. She seldom dwells on her childhood in Ontario: her chronically dissatisfied mother, the physical and emotional abuse. What's the point of revisiting all that pain? The past is done, the distant past, anyway. But tonight it grabs her and won't be ignored.

An only child, Lucie used to joke that her mother never had the chance for a second baby because her father left the family home—a dingy apartment in suburban Toronto—when Lucie was barely three months old. Of course, Lucie remembers not one thing about him. He exists only in her surname, and apparently, in her curly dark hair and pale complexion. By contrast, her mother is fleshy and florid-faced, her once light brown hair long since faded to grey.

Ah, her mother. Without so much as a high-school diploma, alone in Toronto where she knew nobody and with tiny Lucie to care for, somewhat improbably her mother found work as a baker. That job obliged her to leave the apartment at three in the morning, returning by mid-afternoon to sourly do the cleaning, shopping, and cooking, and then go early to bed. During the week, Lucie and her mother rarely crossed paths. Instead, Lucie was raised by a merry-go-round of neighbours and babysitters, which suited her because it meant escape, however briefly, from her mother's constant criticism and occasional — all right, more than occasional — pinches and slaps and smacks with whatever weapon was at hand. No matter what Lucie did — what she wore, whom she befriended, how good her grades — her mother nagged and barked and scolded. And hit. Which served to make Lucie wary, judgmental, demanding, and utterly self-reliant. And needy. As an adult, others' opinions matter to her, more than they should. She's easily wounded by cruel or unfounded remarks or unfair judgments, though she doesn't hesitate to inflict such judgment herself.

Yet Lucie also learned she could protect herself by being charming, flirtatious, and funny. Smile, make people laugh, and they're less likely to yell or to hit, and more likely to smile in return, hug and offer friendship of some kind. Love, or what passes for it.

Suddenly Lucie sits up, her spine rigid, her eyes unfocused. The memory of a distant conversation intrudes with startling clarity.

It's Judith's voice. "You know Sweet Pea, at some point we have to stop blaming our parents for screwing us up. We have to take responsibility for who we are." Judith had made this observation several years back, when she and Lucie were dissecting the collapse of Lucie's latest romance.

"Maybe. But I think as adults we're all trying to overcome our childhoods, we can't help it," Lucie had countered, swirling fragrant red wine in her glass. "I'm convinced I'm constantly trying to compensate for my mother's lack of affection by always needing a man in my life, however unsatisfactory he turns out to be. But it's Ma's fault that I'm such a nag."

"You might have a point there — about compensating for our childhoods — but I still say you need to own up and fix it yourself. That's what grown-ups do, Lucifer. I get that your mom damaged you, and you have every right to be wary of people. You've never learned how to trust, yourself or anyone else." Affronted, Lucie had scowled at this remark but said nothing. Judith continued, "Trust is not in your background. But you get what you give, Luce."

Ignoring Judith's advice, Lucie had continued, "But it always seems so obvious to me that everyone has some trait or habit that needs fixing. As Ma used to say, 'If you'd just do what I tell you, your life would be a lot better.' I'm cursed with that so-called wisdom. It won't let go, like an earworm. Maybe if I sing *O Canada* in reverse I'll get rid of it." She'd laughed extravagantly at her own joke.

"Jeez, you've never tried fixing me."

"But Jude, you're perfect."

"Liar. The thing is, Luce, you're really good at figuring people out, but you never wait for them to ask you for advice or guidance, you always beat them to it. It's like, 'Ta-da! Do this and *shazaam*, instant personal improvement.' And people don't necessarily want to hear that, unless they ask," Judith's words were harsh and truthful, but she'd grinned hugely as she presented Lucie with this insight.

"I know you're right. I jump to conclusions and I can't stop myself from pointing out peoples' shortcomings. I'm just trying to help. I never mean to be hurtful." Pensively, Lucie sipped her wine. "OK, I'm judgmental for sure. But the other thing my mother did to me — and I think I'm pretty grateful for it — is I've grown a pretty thick skin. And now I'm living inside that shell. I don't know how to break free, and maybe I don't want to. It's been my armour for years and it works. I'm all tough and sarcastic. It's a necessary protective device. Pass the wine."

"Sometimes you're tough, yes. But I know how disappointed and damaged you are every time a relationship runs aground."

"Arrr, captain! More grog, there, matey... Anyhow, my latest dude is dust, good riddance to him. And stop telling me I'm not allowed to blame my mother. She's the root of all evil."

Here in this stifling Princeton motel room, Lucie's memory of that distant conversation stops playing as suddenly as it began. She sighs, stretches her arms, and looks around the room. Princeton's streetlights illuminate the windows. She rolls off the lumpy bed, parts the curtains, and looks up to catch the rising quarter-moon, tiny and white, inconsequential above the town.

You and me tonight, girlfriend. We'll keep each other company.

In her lost Vancouver life, if Lucie was at loose ends and fretting about her past and present lovers, she would pick up the phone. Someone was always available for a movie, a drink. A laugh. But tonight she's in a small highway town, far from anything familiar. She drifts back to the bed and cycles once again through TV channels. Considers taking a bath, until she sees the bathtub is tiny and shallow, offering no kind of comfort or relaxation, and there's an ant struggling for escape near the drain. Back to the television. Back to musing about her mother, her past life, her path to this motel in Princeton of all places.

The past seizes her again.

Lucie doesn't recall many happy moments with her mother though there were special times that were, if not exactly joyful, at least temporary releases from her mother's simmering rage and blame: weekly baking. On most Saturday nights and all day Sundays, her mother baked at home with Lucie at her side. Her mother sold the results of her weekend baking to friends and neighbours for a bit of extra income. Mother and daughter worked together over flour, sugar, baking powder, eggs, flavourings, and fillings. Lucie's mother seemed soothed and transformed then, from an angry woman railing against the misfortunes of her life to someone at least in control of her abilities and a few spare hours to put her knowledge to use. Lucie had no idea what her mother was like at the bakery — calm, organized, purposeful? She only saw her mother in their own cramped kitchen and how the mixing, kneading, preparation, and the resulting loaves, cookies, cakes, and pastries gave her mother such pleasure, so much satisfaction she actually smiled. For Lucie, those times were about absorbing her mother's skills and knowledge — the difference between folding and mixing, the ratio of liquid to dry, how to be careful with salt, how cold butter and cold hands made flaky pie crust. How to separate eggs. How to knead, pulling and pushing the dough; how to tell when the dough was right simply by its spring and stretch beneath her hands. Baking was a rhythm that substituted for talk or touch between them. Baking became their conversation.

Mostly they baked bread: several different doughs started Saturday night and left to rise, filling the apartment with the bubbly tang of working yeast. Rye, whole wheat, sourdough, pumpernickel. Potato bread. But there were also cakes — sponge, spice, chocolate of course, angel food and devil's food. They made cookies too, and soft fluffy croissants when they could afford the quantity of butter required. Sometimes pizza dough or pretzels. At Christmas and Easter, special breads and cookies, always for sale, never for home. Her mother's specialty — though opportunities were few — wedding cake, made to order and gorgeously decorated with fondant and candy flowers, beads and braids and scrolls, every bride's dream. But it's the bread Lucie remembers most of all. A sourdough starter always percolated on the kitchen counter, called into action each weekend to make a loaf for Lucie's school lunch sandwiches , the only thing her mother made for home consumption.

Beyond baking together, Lucie recalls not one happy moment, no fun-filled Christmas or birthday or vacation. She can barely conjure an image of her mother's smile, remembering instead a face darkened with scowls and a voice of strident lectures. She sees her mother standing in the dim apartment, arms crossed over chest, feet planted, waiting for Lucie to offer an explanation, an excuse or apology for whatever sin she had committed — and Lucie's sins were apparently legion, from leaving the apartment without permission, to less than perfect grades, wearing lipstick, staying out late, or not calling home to say where she was. But even when Lucie did call, her mother yelled because the phone woke her and how was she supposed to get enough rest to rise at three in the morning to work at the bakery if Lucie kept calling at all hours of the night?

Damned if I did or didn't. Never mattered. Whatever I did was wrong.

Finally, when she was nearly finished high school, Lucie rebelled against seventeen years of carrying the freight of her mother's disappointment. One day, Lucie yelled back. "I *am* good enough!" she screamed. "You're a terrible mother! You've made sure that I'm now my own worst enemy because all you do is nag at me and find fault no matter what. I'm so done with that, Ma! I don't need you to tell me how bad I am at everything because *it's not true.* From now on, I'm going to concentrate on what's *good* about me. And Ma, there's lots that is good about me. Lots! You just can't see it, or if you do, you never, never say so."

Their fight went on for days until Lucie packed some clothes and left one night to stay in a friend's basement. She never lived under her mother's roof again. After high-school graduation — which she attended in a borrowed dress and pinchy high heels one size too small, not knowing whether or not her mother was in the audience to see Lucie limp across the stage to get her diploma and shake the principal's hand — Lucie was determined to live a life of indulgence and enjoyment. "I'm making up for what I've been missing," she said to a boyfriend at the time.

She found work waiting tables and collecting tips, making just enough income to finance rent and a serious party habit. Lucie was usually just a paycheque away from eviction, but it hardly mattered. Whatever cheap apartment or basement suite she rented was merely a place to store her clothes and nurse her hangovers.

"I was out virtually every night for five years," she confided to Judith soon after they met. "I had more men than I can remember; I was a first-class tramp. I'm amazed that I never caught any disease or got picked up for public drunkenness, vagrancy, whatever it's called. Then I got tired of my life going nowhere, so I sobered up and went back to school."

She had no savings at the time, so applied for and won scholarships to pay her way through university. Then, armed with her newly minted commerce degree, she bought a train ticket and journeyed about as far west from her Ontario roots as Canada's geography allowed. She left Toronto behind to settle in Vancouver, and only speaks to her mother occasionally now: terse conversations that last a few minutes at best.

And my life has been an upward spiral since I moved to Vancouver. Not that you've ever said you're proud of me, or happy for me. Maybe you're not. Maybe you think I ran out on you just like my useless dad did, and you've never forgiven me, either. Well if you were as miserable to him as you were to me, I guess you deserve to be alone. But I've looked after myself and I'm still doing that, right now, right here in beautiful Princeton. You did one good thing for me, Ma. Made me tough.

Lucie glances at the motel's clock radio and is shocked to see it's three in the morning. She turns the television off and gets back into the lumpy bed to remain awake until early light seeps through the curtains.

Lucie follows the Similkameen River eastward, upstream, then turns north into the Okanagan Valley. Again the scenery changes, from a wild western landscape to orderly vineyards, orchards, gardens, small towns, and fruit stands. She stops at a couple of wineries, sips free samples, and buys a bottle or two. She's reserved another motel in advance and spends two nights in the town of Penticton.

It's a beach town, but nothing like the coastal beaches she's used to in Vancouver. No tides for one thing, though the breeze kicks up waves on the big lake that are reminiscent of ocean waves. As she strolls the strand, she notices the splashing water, gulls floating motionless in the air, people in kayaks and on paddleboards. And the kids.

Children are everywhere on the rough beach. Occasionally she has to stop walking or has to dodge around running, screaming, laughing kids. They dart and cavort, and above all they laugh laugh laugh. They are accompanied by, or chased by, dogs or parents or older siblings. Their delight lends music to the wind and lapping waves, a joyful hullaballoo of families and fun that makes her think along an entirely different track.

Does she want kids? Does this scene of domestic fun and contentment generate envy or longing in her? Or does she cringe at the very idea of diapers and strollers and days at the beach, the mall, daycare? Lucie considers herself anti-maternal, again blaming her haphazard, somewhat violent and largely solitary upbringing. Who would want to perpetuate that? But casually observing these families, she's not so sure. Given the right circumstances, the right man, perhaps this could be her future. Then again, maybe she should just get another job and start splashing again in the current of her perfectly fun, if shallow, social life in Vancouver.

Or get a dog instead of having a kid or a man. You can dress dogs up, take them for walks. Then again, even a dog will bite you if provoked. Can't trust men, can't trust kids, can't trust dogs.

After two sunny, lazy, aimless and dreamless days, it's time to leave. The route takes her north, skirting Okanagan Lake to Kelowna, where she buys cheese, sausage, olives, and bread for a picnic. The sky is clear, the warmth and sunlight are honey-sweet. This entire valley is a paradise of fresh food, local produce, and wine. The enormous lake itself is deep blue and beckons her to swim. She could stay here. Find a job picking fruit maybe, or serving wine in a vineyard tasting room, speaking with authority about Pinot Gris and Chardonnay.

Nothing doing. This place is pretty, but I have places to go. A life to change. I'm busy, don't ya know. Goin' to Banff, wherever that is.

As Lucie drives north, the road climbs away from Kelowna toward Vernon, her next stop. From a musty roadside motel, she decides to treat herself to a phone call with Judith.

But Judith does not answer. Lucie tries to leave an upbeat message — "Hi, I'm in Vernon. Bet you don't know where that is," — but she's sure her voice sounds forlorn and uncertain. She's made only scant progress on figuring out a plan for her life. Instead, she's mostly thought about the past and the patterns that have shaped her. Banff, and whatever lies beyond it, seems a million miles away.

A plan, a challenge, a change? Ha, as if. Really what I want is another job, a movie night, and some good wine with my gal pals. What's so hard about that? What's so wrong?

The next morning, Lucie resolves to drive as far as she can in a single day. "Enough of this puddle-jumping. Get on with it," she says aloud as she stuffs her bags. She unfolds the entire roadmap on the motel bed to determine a forward route. She sees it's perhaps ninety minutes to the town of Sicamous. "How the hell do you pronounce that?" she wonders aloud. "Sick-a-mouse? Seek-a-mooz? Maybe Shika-moose, moose, moose-moose?" She makes herself giggle.

Once there, however it's pronounced, she'll turn onto the Trans-Canada Highway, which she figures will be a major freeway on which she can fly eastward, pushing to Banff. Then a few days' rest in the mountains before plotting her return home to Vancouver, new life mission in hand.

Having a route in mind makes her feel better. After paying an appalling price for mere coffee and toast in the motel's coffee shop, she sets off through rolling farmland: low round hills on both sides of the road. Next she follows a twisting lakeside highway that makes her grin with the fun of steering and shifting. She is relaxed and having a fine time when she stops for gas in Sicamous.

Then she joins the Trans-Canada Highway eastbound. Ahead are round and lushly forested mountains that look friendly and welcoming. But as she drives eastward, the mild, low mountains shoulder in to crowd the highway. Cliffs and steep slopes bully forward, pushing ever closer to the road until Lucie is surrounded by extreme landscape: sheer rock faces on her right hand and a deep, dark lake on the other. She and tiny Agememnon are hemmed in by slow holiday trailers ahead and aggressive transport truckers behind. There's no alternative but to keep driving on. She grips the wheel, terrified.

And now the weather is turning. Menacing clouds bunch and crash against the mountain wall ahead like waves hitting a breakwater. Blotting out sunlight, the gathering storm drains colour from the landscape, turning the towering rock faces from rich green forest to forbidding purple and black.

She settles behind a transport truck lumbering eastward. Far from being the multi-lane, high-speed motorway she'd expected, this stretch of the so-called national highway consists of one lane in each direction and only the narrowest of shoulders. No passing lanes. The road curves and climbs. Soon Lucie's mouse-sized car is sandwiched between two enormous trucks. As the road bends this way and that, she catches occasional glimpses of an unbroken line of vehicles ahead of her, more behind. Fat raindrops splash on her windshield. "This is insane," she mutters as her wiper blades swish. Now the rain is pouring, slicking the road surface, and sheeting over her windshield. Helpless to leave the line of traffic, she surrenders to the situation and tries to stay calm.

There's no radio signal.

Breathe. Relax.

Luckily, the deluge has slowed the pace of the long snake of vehicles. Nobody seems to be impatient, though the truck behind her is much too close for comfort, the huge front grill entirely filling her rear-view mirror.

Yeah, Lucie. How tough are you now?

There are no towns, no rest stops, only occasional points of interest that come up too fast for Lucie to make a decision about pulling off. And anyway, how would she get back into traffic if she should stop? She might be stuck for hours. Days. The rest of her life.

Highway signs slowly count down the distance remaining between Lucie and the next settlement, Revelstoke. After an eternity of rain and agitation, the road spills into a wide valley, and there is the town. Almost panting with anxiety and relief, Lucie swings off the highway and cruises the town's streets, up and down, searching for a likely place to stay. "Plan B," she tells Agememnon.

She calls Judith again. This time, success.

"I *do* know where Vernon is," Judith says as a greeting. "Is that where you are now?"

"Nope, Revelstoke. I wanted to get to Banff today, but jeez Jude, I couldn't do it. The rain, ohmygod it started raining like crazy and the road is only one lane... *one lane each way,* and the trucks and huge trailers, do you know some of those trailers could sleep a whole *town*? So I was stressed, and I just couldn't keep going. I had to stop here."

"Whoa, Lucie, come up for air. Slow down. Just. Slow. Down. Breathe. I'm not kidding, come on, we'll do it together. Inhale. Exhale."

"OK, stop, no yoga needed. I'm all right — and I know I'm whining. This trip is just more intense than I expected, that's all. A bigger adventure than I was ready for."

"And that's not a bad thing, though I doubt you believe me right now. So why not take a few days where you are? Relax, look around."

"Because I want to get on with it. I want to get somewhere, feel like I'm making progress."

"You are missing the point. Besides, you *are* somewhere."

Lucie pauses to consider this remark. "OK, you're right again. I *am* missing the point. Guess I'm accustomed to instant success. This slow-down-to-smell-the-roses bit is killing me."

Judith laughs and changes the subject. "How's the weather?

Clearing up? OK, so tomorrow you should take a drive up to Mount Revelstoke National Park, and remember what I said about getting a park pass. It's spectacular up there, wildflowers like you've never seen, great views, and it's not hard walking. Go there, Luce. Give yourself a break, see something different. Do you even *know* how to take a vacation?"

"Vacation. Is that what this is?"

A pause.

Lucie sighs. "Sorry, Jude. Sorry. I know you're trying to help. Don't think I'm not grateful. I do appreciate it, really. So, flowers. OK, I'm in. How do I get there?"

"You're at a bed and breakfast, yes? Ask the owners, they can give you directions. How's your money holding out?"

"Fine," Lucie lies.

"Good. Hang out in Revelstoke for as long as it feels right before you go again. It's a cool town, maybe a place you should consider for your future. I'm serious."

A pause.

Judith picks up the conversation. "OK, you're not saying anything so... When you head east again, you've got one more tough piece of driving through Rogers Pass, but after that the road gets much better. But really, don't push. Your next biggish town is Golden. It's nice and funky, another good prospect if you'd just open your mind, Lucie. Or you could carry on to Lake Louise, though it's probably booked to the gills right now. OK? Lucifer, sorry, I've been lecturing again. Are you OK?"

"Yep. I'll send you a selfie from the top of Mount Revelstoke so I can prove I'm taking your advice."

"Atta girl."

"Jude?"

"Luce?"

"Thank you. Always."

—⫛—

Lucie is speaking aloud. "'Meadows in the Sky Parkway.' Yikes, who came up with *that*? Sounds like an advertising slogan." She navigates a narrow road, switch-backing up the flank of Mount Revelstoke. Contrary to her promise to Judith that she would stay a while in the town, Lucie asked her hosts for directions to the mountaintop, then packed her bags and checked out. Judith may have advised a slow pace, but Lucie is focused on forward motion — getting where she's going and back again.

But Judith did make this side trip seem worthwhile. So here is Lucie, ears popping as she gains altitude along a crazy pinwheel road.

The day is brilliant, and the road is already hectic with traffic. Arriving at the parking area, Lucie puts on her new hiking socks and boots, loads her new backpack with water, snacks, and fresh socks — and Band-Aids — shoulders the pack, and sets off.

Although there are plenty of adults and kids scampering about, she feels instantly peaceful as she trudges up the wide trail. It climbs gently, winding through an open meadow. A light breeze flutters the amazing assortment of wildflowers — blue, orange, white, and many shades of yellow. Judith was right; this is a true spectacle. Lucie slows her steps and breathes deeply. The air is tangy with evergreen sap and warm grass. Each blossom is bright and freshly washed by yesterday's rain. Lucie's progress is slow because every few steps she stops to take in the view, gazing from the distant peaks to the tiny flowers at her feet.

The trail is less than a kilometre long, but it takes her nearly three hours to make the round trip. She arrives back at her car, heels off her boots, and swings her backpack to the ground. Opens the car door to admit fresh air. She slides barefoot into the driver's seat and inserts the key, turns it...

To her alarm, the car won't start.

She tries several times before the engine catches and revs. "Come on, buddy. What was that about?"

OK, now you're talking to your car.

Relieved, Lucie exits the parking lot and snakes her way back down the mountain to re-join the eastbound highway. It's only when she's nearing the bottom of the mountain that remembers she neglected to take the selfie she promised Judith.

Never mind, I was there. I can speak with authority about the experience. And it was fine, just exactly fine. As advertised.

She turns east toward Rogers Pass, a driving route that proves less difficult than Judith warned. The biggest surprise turns out to be snow sheds. Built to protect the roadway from winter avalanches, the snow sheds are dimly lit tubes, tunnels of roaring traffic. While most of the sheds' interiors are reasonably bright, one particularly long one is dark and cavernous, with trucks and buses speeding in both directions. Upon entering this shed, Lucie has a moment of panic. She actually shrieks, but keeps driving and pops out of the far end unscathed.

The scenery is a jaw-dropping spectacle of glaciated peaks, deep lush valleys, and rich dark forests, but Lucie doesn't look closely. She is relentless, and keeps driving, driving, goal in mind. Descending from Rogers Pass, she enters another broad valley where the roadway continues an exhausting twist and turn, twist and turn. Eventually she arrives at the town of Golden. She's deeper into the mountains than ever — and farther from Vancouver and its cafés, theatres, shops, beaches, her acquaintances, social spin — all that's been familiar. Lucie is utterly alone amid the roar of cross-country traffic.

She pulls off the highway and drives along Golden's streets where the shops and restaurants are closed; the façades are dark, turning her away. It's late. She hasn't kept track of time. She drives back to a strip of motels and fast-food restaurants along the highway, all with lights ablaze.

Tonight it's a stuffy room in another roadside motel. The windows don't open. Instead she turns on the air conditioner, but it rattles like an old tractor, and she quickly turns it off again. Now she can hear the constant grind of trucks gearing down on the highway right outside. The lightness and peace she felt this morning on her walk through the mountain meadow have evaporated. She cranks open the tiny bathroom window that offers not a whisper of fresh air, then flicks listlessly through television channels in search of diversion. Finding none, she resorts to her map.

"Lake Louise. It's a side trip, but it's on the way. Why not? Let's go see world-famous Lake Louise tomorrow, Lucie. What do you say? Sure Lucie! Sounds like a plan. Atta girl."

The next morning — overcast and chilly but not yet raining — finds her on the road early, bleary after a sticky night disturbed by traffic noise. She is tired and in no way ready for what the route presents. Climbing steeply from Golden in the valley bottom, she's suddenly on the most serpentine piece of road she's encountered yet. It's astonishing, crazy, who would allow such a piece of insane road — ostensibly the nation's main east-west highway? The route crawls up, carved into an appallingly sheer slope on her left side with an equally appalling gorge below on her right. When at last, after just twenty minutes that seems much longer, the road emerges from the canyon and straightens, Lucie opens the driver-side window to recover her nerve with gulps of bracingly frigid air.

If you can drive that piece of shit, you can drive anything. National highway? Sheesh.

Nearing the tiny village of Field, she notices another visitor information centre and stops to pick up brochures and an Alberta roadmap. Shakily she gets back into Agememnon and once again has trouble getting the engine to catch. But it does, and she's off with one more push remaining to get over the Great Divide, the spine of the continent: Lake Louise is waiting on the other side, with Banff its distant cousin beyond.

More spectacle, more unimaginably jagged mountains. Snow. Glaciers. The Kicking Horse River, thick with silt, an incredible, milky-opal blue. A broad valley bottom strewn with river gravel and braided channels. But she's concentrating her strength and energy on driving. Highway signs and flags welcome her to Alberta as she crosses the divide.

Keep going, keep going. When you're going through hell, keep going. Lake Louise. Then Banff. Then home.

Lake Louise. She turns off the highway to join yet another line of trailers and campers on yet another winding road that climbs and climbs, until finally she reaches a jammed parking lot where she circles several times before finding a spot to leave her car. When she gets out to stand and stretch, her legs feel wobbly, but the air is crisp and refreshing. She shrugs into a sweater and jacket as tiny needles of rain spit from the sky. She joins a throng headed for the lakeshore.

Ah, Lake Louise, prime among the many iconic Canadian Rockies locations according to her travel literature. Today the lake is steely grey, the bordering mountain slopes are dark, but the great glacier beyond is huge and impressive as the wind chases clouds about and sunlight occasionally glints through, illuminating the ice to a dazzling brightness.

"You should see it on a nice day," says a cheerful-looking young man in scuffed hiking boots, shorts, and a woolly lumberjack shirt. He's the perfect cliché of an outdoor enthusiast, the kind of person Lucie would normally deride. But today she pivots to crack open her famous smile and catch his eye as he strides past. She loses her balance, staggers, and nearly falls.

He swiftly grabs her elbow, says, "Whoa, hey, are you OK? A bit dizzy? Might be the altitude. Where are you from?"

"Vancouver."

"Yep, definitely altitude. Don't worry, you'll get used to it after a couple of days. Where are you staying? Tomorrow's supposed to be nice. You really should see the lake on a sunny day, the colour is unreal." He has released her arm but stands close, ready to catch her again if needed. He's smiling down at her through a neatly trimmed blond beard and moustache.

"I'm, um, passing through," she says weakly.

"You look like you're passing *out*, if you don't mind me saying. Look, there's a coffee shop in the hotel, would you like a coffee? Or at least some water? Seriously, you look kinda pale."

She manages a tight smile. "I *am* kinda pale. But a coffee would be outstanding, thanks."

"I'm Kevin."

"Lucie."

And so it is with her. A smile and an opening — and here she is again, engaging, flirting, and skating across someone else's life. And who is this man who's picked up on her need, whatever that need might be?

Coffee and a sandwich fortify her, but she feels as though a vise is tightening on her head. With minimal polite protest on her part, she allows Kevin to pay for her meal. She explains a little about her journey: "I'm between jobs so thought I would, you know, look around a bit. Take a break."

She learns he's spending the next week hiking in the area. "Just short hops, day hikes," he explains, seeming embarrassed. "I broke my ankle earlier this year, and I'm getting back into shape. No back-country marathons for me yet."

She has no doubt it's only a matter of time until he'll be doing exactly that. She also learns there's a hostel in the tiny village in the valley below. "Too expensive to stay in the fancy hotels around here at the lakeshore," he says, "but the hostel is perfect."

"I've never stayed in a hostel," she admits. "I'm such a city girl. I think of them as 'hostiles', but I guess I don't know much."

"Hostile, yeah they can be , but this one's better than most. Want to see if they've got a room for you? I walked up here to the lake, so if you can give me a lift back down, we can see whether they've got any vacancies."

As they walk to Lucie's car, the pavement and their heads and shoulders become damp from a light but persistent drizzle. "Could you drive?" she asks. "I'm absolutely beat."

Kevin adjusts the driver's seat to accommodate his long legs and tries the ignition. Agememnon sputters once, twice, then catches. "That's been happening for a few days," Lucie says.

"Could be the altitude, it can affect the fuel mix," he says and adds, "if you're going to be in Alberta for a while you might want to get it adjusted."

The hostel does indeed have a room for her. It's Spartan, but there's a clean bed, which is all she wants. Kevin offers dinner but she declines. "Nope, think I'll take a pill for my headache and get some sleep. Thanks, I totally appreciate your help. Sorry you hooked up with an altitude sufferer."

"Drink lots of water, it helps," he advises. "I'm hiking early tomorrow so I probably won't see you, but if you still feel crappy, tell the hostel staff. They're really helpful. And here," he opens his wallet and hands her a business card. "Look me up when you get to Calgary."

"OK. Thanks for lunch and for rescuing me."

"No problem. Always happy to assist a damsel in distress." He leans forward to swiftly kiss her cheek, and his moustache tickles her skin. He nods, grins, and turns to stride back outside to the rain.

Two painkillers and a full glass of fresh cold water later, Lucie is stretched flat on the firm bed, arms and legs extended like a four-pointed star. Gusts of rain splash the window, which she's opened to admit the fortifying scent of cold forest. Tall pines sway and creak in the sighing wind that sounds to her like distant surf.

"You could hike up to Lake Agnes," says the Australian girl at the hostel's front desk. "It's not too far, and there's a very cute teahouse at the top where you can have lunch." She shows Lucie how to find the trail, which skirts the shore of Lake Louise before climbing a ridge to the hidden tiny lake above.

Under the lemony morning sun, the teal-green colour of Lake

Louise is — as Kevin promised — surreal. Inspired by her happy time amid meadow flowers at Mount Revelstoke, Lucie is ready for more. But this time the path is challenging as it becomes steeper and rougher. She has to stop frequently to catch her breath. She picks her way over rocks and exposed roots, gaining a little altitude with every step.

"A little altitude, a little attitude," she tells herself. Her knees and lungs ache. The sound of falling water gets louder, but she's watching the ground in front of her, carefully placing her feet to avoid obstacles until she turns a corner and looks up to see a gushing waterfall and stairs leading to the top of a sheer rock face. "Stairs. Fergodssake." This final push seems to suck all her remaining strength, but she's rewarded at the top by a jewel-lake held in the cupped hands of the surrounding mountains. And there's the promised teahouse, a petite log cabin where she buys cookies and a pot of tea. Seated at an outdoor table, she drinks in the view along with tea and the muted chatter of other hikers. The tea is strong and hot, the cookies chewy and sweet. She catches herself grinning. This time, she does remember to take some photos to send to Judith.

OK, mighty conquering hero. Get moving. Places to go.

Her walk down takes a fraction of the time she needed for the ascent. Still, by the time she's back beside her car, it's mid-afternoon. Banff is less than an hour away, and with another tank of gas Lucie presses eastward along a stretch of dual-lane divided highway. Effortless driving and — a welcome miracle — radio reception. Within forty minutes, she glides into Banff but sees instantly there will be no chance of scoring a room. The town's main street is bumper-to-bumper, as is pedestrian traffic on the sidewalks. She can't even find a place to drop the car. She pulls into a grocery store parking lot to consult her map and sees it's only a half-hour to Canmore, a town just outside Banff National Park.

"Huh. I spend days aiming for Banff, and I don't even get to walk around. OK. Onward ho."

Approaching Canmore, a town hugging the national park's eastern boundary, she spots another visitor centre. With no reservation and no confidence that she'll be able to find a room, Lucie enters the surprisingly quiet office where three people behind the desk eagerly greet her.

"I don't suppose there's any chance I could find a room here tonight?"

"We can probably scare up something but it could be pricey," says the young man behind the desk. University student. Clearly flummoxed by Lucie's odd but appealing appearance.

"I'm on a pretty tight budget." Delivered with her trademark diamond-bright grin and a helpless shrug.

"Let's see what I can do."

But after a series of phone calls, the clerk shakes his head sadly, maybe wishing he could offer Lucie his own bed. "I'm sorry. Everything's either completely full, or they want a minimum three-night stay. You could keep going another hour to Calgary, but I suspect you'll have trouble there too. The Calgary Stampede is on. You won't find a hotel anywhere near downtown, although there might be something farther out in the burbs."

"I don't think I can drive that far today."

"Then my only suggestion is to head east about fifteen minutes. There's a hotel and casino on the First Nation land. The hotel is reasonably priced because they want you to spend your cash in the casino. Want me to try that?"

"Sure, thank you."

Success. *Six Feathers Resort and Casino here I come.*

On a narrow grassy plain, the casino building stands squarely against the pummelling west wind. The mountains extend their arms to the north and south as if to embrace the building, but eastward Lucie sees the sweep of an open horizon with nary a mountain peak to block the view.

She bought some food before leaving Canmore, and six bottles of beer. Over her in-room picnic, once again Lucie spreads a map and considers where to go next. Calgary is out of the question. Although Kevin might be good for a free couch or even a companionable bed, she's not inclined toward a quick liaison now, despite his cheerfulness. Is he the right guy, a free spirit, a path to a new life? She'll never know.

Don't open a door you don't want to walk through. I've learned that much at least.

She regards the map carefully and sees she can circumvent the city entirely by taking a route through the hamlet of Bragg Creek, then hooking up with Highway 22 south. That road in turn connects to Highway 3, where she could turn westward again, homeward bound.

Is that what she wants?

Will her road trip be a simple, albeit challenging, loop through the mountains and back, maybe three weeks in total? Will she arrive back at Judith's house with her traveller's tales — or more to the point, with a plan for her future? From hotel rooms to gas stations and the odd diversion, this trip's logistics and difficult driving have so occupied Lucie's mind and energy that she's given little thought to anything else, least of all a plan for her future. So far, she has to admit the trip has been more or less pointless, except for a couple of nights musing about her mother's impact on her character, a few nice hikes amid mountain flowers, and some unexpected gentle care from a passing stranger clad in a lumberjack shirt.

A plan for my future? As if.

She flings the map to the floor and opens another beer.

ALL THE THINGS YOU
THOUGHT WERE YOURS

Lucie's car shoots away from the mountains into a landscape that's broad and relatively flat, as though it's been smoothed by the wind. It's such a surprise to see far horizons on all sides that she laughs out loud as the mountains, her constant companions and erstwhile enemies over the past days, quickly recede to a jagged blue line in her rear-view mirror.

Jubilant, she sings out loud with the radio. She is a liberated prisoner. She breathes deeply, turns the radio's volume up, tips her head back and gives a cowboy yell. "Yahoo yahoo! Oh look at me, coming through the mountains. All by my little self. Look what I did! *Woo hoo!*"

She flies along the highway, embedded in a stream of traffic moving well above the posted speed limit. Whatever. She's elated.

When was the last time she felt *elated*?

The exit she wants comes into view. With some reluctance, Lucie turns south onto a narrower, less busy highway. Maybe she should reconsider, continue eastward and find a room in the city, call Kevin, visit the rodeo, and participate in street dancing and other Calgary Stampede fun she's read about in her tourist guidebooks. But no — she's got a route in mind and somehow a citywide cowboy party doesn't appeal to her. She's set instead on a different journey: spend a few days in Alberta slipping along the eastern flank of the mountains, then turn west and go home, draining her savings all the way. With any luck, this newfound energy will stay with her until she reaches Vancouver, then power her search for a new job, another place to live, then, well, who knows? So maybe the trip won't have been a waste of time and gasoline after all.

Singing softly now in her low alto voice, slightly off-key, she reaches a tiny town called Bragg Creek but she doesn't stop. She continues on her circuitous route around the city and finds the southbound turn onto Highway 22. A bright orange and black sign featuring a horse and rider — the sign pocked with holes, clearly somebody has been using it for target practice — welcomes her to The Cowboy Trail.

She is headed south now with the mountains distant over her right shoulder, often hidden altogether by the closer hills. The sun is high, the sky huge, decorated with enormous swirls of wispy cloud. What a difference a far horizon makes. She whizzes past huge fields, thinly dotted with grazing cattle. She passes two riders trotting along a fence, a black and white dog loping at the horses' heels. Both riders are actually wearing cowboy hats and fringed leather chaps. It's like driving through a postcard, an old-time Western movie. Her only irritation is the large pickup truck hauling a horse trailer that has zoomed up behind her out of nowhere and is now hugging her bumper.

Oh, just go around. You've got lots of room, this is the emptiest road I've ever seen. Come on, dude. Pass me and get out of my life.

The driver does so, suddenly pulling out and gunning past in a spray of dust and diesel fumes.

"So long cowboy."

Another hour and it's time to stop for lunch and find a gas station. A highway sign announces a town just ahead: Sweetgrass. She slows.

The town's name is vaguely familiar, but she can't quite make a connection. Perhaps some grisly farmstead murder? Or maybe it's the secluded summer home of a hockey star or pop music diva? She can't remember.

She eases to a stop in front of the only likely looking place on the main street, a restaurant with a name that makes her laugh out loud: The Sow's Ear Café.

The truck and trailer that zoomed around her earlier are parked just up the street. "All that hurry to get here? Must be a damn fine restaurant."

Lucie has some trouble finding the entrance. The building is old-fashioned, with a tall false front and two big windows on either side of a recessed front door. It might once have been a grocery or hardware store, perhaps even a saddlery. But she ascends the front steps to find the front door firmly locked. She is about to give up, thinking the café is closed, but then notices a small sign that reads: 'Please use side entrance.' Yes, but which side?

She backs onto the sidewalk and follows it around to one side of the building, but there's no door. Returning to the front, she notices a small courtyard on the other side, framed by a wrought-iron fence. Several tables and large umbrellas populate the sunny, sheltered space and flowers grow in various large pots. But nobody is seated outdoors, although the afternoon is pleasant and music floats softly from an unseen speaker. Lucie crosses the courtyard and at last locates the entrance — a wide wooden door that stands open, a piece of twine secures the door to a hook on the building's outside wall. The inner screen door is closed to keep bugs at bay, but the door itself is so battered and warped there's a substantial gap between it and the doorframe. Through the screen's mesh, which is dusty but intact, she hears talk and smells coffee.

She enters. The buzz of conversation ebbs for a moment and two or three curious faces briefly turn her way. She's in a large room with hardwood floors that creak musically underfoot as a very young woman, probably high-school age, ferries plates to tables. The tables are of varying vintages and styles. Some are round, others square, some are long enough to accommodate six diners or more, others are tiny, meant for twosomes. The farmhouse-style chairs are similarly mismatched: some with round backs, some upright and square, some painted, others stained or perhaps simply dark from decades of use.

Several large lamps that might once have illuminated an old-time schoolhouse hang from the high ceiling and cast a soft, ivory light, hardly necessary with bright sunlight streaming in through the side windows. The walls are decorated with rusty antique farm implements and hand tools, the use of which Lucie cannot imagine. A chalkboard advertises the daily specials, and there's a short bar along the back wall with several stools parked in front of it. Displayed behind the bar are bottles of whisky and wine — a smallish selection but Lucie notices several labels she recognizes as good quality and not inexpensive.

Rich scents fill her nose as she reads the list of specials on the blackboard to her left. The menu is extraordinary. She'd expected burgers and fries or some such innocuous fare. Instead, the chalkboard offers baked beans with smoked pork hock, homemade ham and split pea soup, lamb shank with lentils, a sample plate featuring mini turkey burgers served three ways. A salad of arugula and romaine with walnuts, cranberries, and pomegranate, crumbled goat cheese, espresso balsamic vinaigrette. What kind of crazy backwater cowboy café is this?

"Sit anywhere you like," says the young server as she hurries by with a precarious armload of dirty dishes. "I'll be right back with coffee."

'Anywhere' proves to be the only unoccupied table, situated in the far corner by one of the front windows. The chairs are awkwardly positioned so that she must either face the window with her back to the room, or face the room and ignore the view of outside, such as it is. She chooses the latter, preferring to watch people instead of the dusty street. The server returns with a sturdy mug, though Lucie has not asked for coffee. "Cream and sugar? Want water too?"

"Just black, thanks. And water would be great."

The girl darts across the room to pick up more empty plates and disappears into the back, returning with a carafe of coffee and two servings of pie and ice cream for a table on the other side of the room. She hurries back and forth, seeming harried, clearly the only person serving the room. Lucie sips her coffee. After nearly ten minutes, the girl finally returns to her table with a pad and pencil but no glass of water.

"Sorry, we're a bit short-staffed today. Can I take your order?"

"Is there a menu?"

The girl looks exasperated. "Just what's on the board."

"I'll try the mac and cheese please."

"Sorry, we're out."

"How about the soup and gourmet grilled cheese sandwich?"

"OK." The girl whirls to dash back to the kitchen.

"And that glass of water please," Lucie calls, louder than she intended. Again, a few faces turn toward her.

She sits back, mug in hand, and surveys the room. There's a table of burly men dressed in overalls and bright orange safety vests, perhaps a road maintenance crew, and another party of four grey-haired women who lean over their table, talking in low tones and laughing occasionally. There's a table of three men, all wearing cowboy hats — she suspects one of them is the driver who roared past her on the highway — and another table seating a family consisting of a young mother and four little kids who are remarkably quiet and well-behaved. Two older couples chat over dessert. A uniformed police officer sits alone. He's one of several single men, most wearing cowboy hats or ball caps, bent over newspapers spread on their tables. Only one man has removed his hat, which hangs on the back of his chair. His forehead has a distinct line — tanned below, pale above.

Her order arrives. The soup is rich and velvety, just enough salt and a hint of lime to bring out the sharply acidic yet sweet tang of perfectly ripe tomatoes. The sandwich oozes with three different cheeses, the bread is golden-crisp. It's by far the best meal Lucie has had on this trip. In fact, it's the best meal she's enjoyed in months.

"More coffee?"

"Sure. And — water? Please?"

"Yeah, sorry. Right away."

But no glass of water appears. Lucie tries not to hurry. The food is so delicious she wants to savour it slowly. Meanwhile, the room empties as the other diners finish, pay, and depart, until Lucie and the group of four intent women are the only ones left. Long swatches of sunlight from the south windows have shifted across the floor. Time to put another tank of fuel into Agememnon and figure out how much farther she wants to drive, and where she'll stay tonight. As she's seen the other diners do, Lucie walks to the bar and waits to pay.

"Never did get that glass of water," she jokes. The girl only gives her a worried look and hands Lucie her change.

Outside, the day is hot. An insistent breeze has sprung up to harry dry leaves and odd bits of paper, kicking dust along the street. Vehicles roll by, mostly farm trucks, some holiday campers and trailers. A pair of raucous motorcycles.

Lucie opens her car door and allows air to circulate a bit before she gets in. She meant to cover the steering wheel with a shirt but forgot, so the wheel is nearly too hot to touch. She gingerly grasps it, inserts the ignition key and turns it.

Nothing. Not a spark, not a cough, no effort of any kind.

"Come on." She tries again. This time there's some clicking noise under the hood — something is trying to happen — but it doesn't sound promising. "Come *on*."

She keeps trying until she smells gasoline. She understands enough about cars to know she's flooded the engine but has no clue what to do about that or about the lack of ignition. Rolling up the windows, she gets out and looks up and down the street for a service station. About a block away is a gas bar and small convenience store. She trudges up the street and enters. "I need some help — my car won't start."

The young Asian man behind the counter shakes his head. "We don't do service here. Just gas."

"Is there a mechanic in town? Anywhere?"

"Sure. That way." He points back in the direction of the café. "About three blocks. Or maybe four."

She plods back up the street feeling utterly alone, her joyful mood evaporated. Finds the auto mechanic: a shop with two bays and a small office. The smell of oil and rubber greets her as she pushes the door open. She can hear noise from the adjoining repair bays, but there's nobody behind the desk. Going to the door leading to the garage area, she calls, "Hello? Hello!"

A tall, loose-boned man appears from behind the truck he's working on. He saunters toward her, a slow smile lighting his soft, deeply lined face. "Hello Missy. Need a hand with something?"

Don't call me Missy, for a start. But she gives him her practiced, pert Lucie-grin and says, "Sure *do*! I'm parked in front of the café and my car won't start."

"All right, let's go take a look." He calls over his shoulder. "Jake! I'm going out for a minute."

The man is in no hurry as they walk up the street. He withdraws a pack of cigarettes from his stained denim overalls and lights one, stopping to cup his massive hands to defend the flame against the insistent breeze. He does not offer a cigarette to Lucie, and he doesn't speak until he's taken two or three good long drags, slowly exhaling. The wind catches the smoke, whirls it away. Finally he says, "Don't recognize you, guess you're passing through?"

"Yes. Doing a road trip. I'm from Vancouver. Never been through the mountains before."

"That so? Quite a trip."

"Yes it is. That's my car there, the silver Honda."

"OK. Won't start, you say? Why don't you just hop in and give 'er a go. And pop the hood for me."

She does as requested, with the same result — there's some kind of sound but no ignition.

"That's good," the man calls. He slams the hood down and comes around to the driver's side window. "Battery's gone. Could be something else too but until we get 'er started I can't really tell."

"OK, so," she gives him another flirty smile, twisting her shoulders and dropping her eyes, the combination of tough girl and clueless girl she relies upon to get her out of a jam. "Sorry, I don't know what to do..." She shrugs and smiles radiantly.

Just call me Marilyn. Monroe that is.

The man seems unimpressed. He simply starts walking back up the street, clearly expecting her to fall in step, which she does. He says, "Well, let's go see if I have a battery in the shop that fits, not sure that I do. We mostly service trucks around here."

They make the return trip to the garage, slowly enough that he has time for a second cigarette. Walking at his elbow, Lucie is directly in the smoke's acrid path, but she doesn't duck around to his upwind side.

"I'm Bob MacDonnell," he says en route, with emphasis on the last syllable, 'Mac-da-NELL,' his tone implying this is a fact she would do well to remember.

"Lucie."

At the service shop, Bob disappears into the back while Lucie takes a seat in the office. She waits for what seems an hour, listening to country music playing on the radio until at last Bob reappears. "Well, Missy. I have good news and bad news."

"OK..."

"The bad news: I don't have a battery for you. The good news: I can spare Jake tomorrow and send him into the city to pick one up. So you'll have to spend the night in our fair town."

He sees the distress on her face. "Now calm down, Missy," he says, his voice deep and fatherly. "We have a couple of nice B&Bs in town, and a good hotel although it's noisy on weekends because of the band in the bar. And you've already found our famous café. Now let me get the tow truck rigged up and we'll pull your little beauty back here. Then I can take you to the hotel. How would that be?"

On the edge of exasperated tears, Lucie nods.

Bob's assessment of the hotel proves to be accurate. It's clean and well kept, but obviously it's the large taproom that generates the establishment's income. In fact, the rooms are so rarely in demand there's no reception area or front desk. Bob instructs her to go into the bar to request a hotel room. "Ask for Amanda," he tells her. He offers to help move her belongings inside but she declines, instead she laboriously drags her bags into the bar herself, a task that requires three separate trips.

It's mid-afternoon and the bar is nearly empty. Still, it takes some time to find the elusive Amanda, who it turns out, is taking her lunch break. Lucie waits, picking and fretting her fingernails until Amanda appears. "We don't get too many people actually wanting a room here," she says, giving Lucie a steady, appraising, but not unfriendly once-over. "Mostly we rent rooms to people who drink too much in the bar here and have no way home. Or sometimes people are in town for weddings or funerals, but I don't recall hearing about either a wedding or a funeral this weekend."

"My car broke down."

"Ah." Amanda searches behind the long curved bar for room keys. "Ah, found the key. Just so you know, people generally don't stay here much because the hotel is actually a bar, mostly. There's nothing wrong with your room, it's clean and safe. But noisy — there's not a room in the place where you don't hear the band. Anyway, come on, I'll show you the way. Want a hand with your luggage? There's no elevator, this might take a bit of back-and-forth. Looks like you're packed for a long trip, where are you headed?"

"I didn't want to leave anything in the car while it's getting fixed," Lucie evades. "Sure, I've love some help, thanks."

"Right," says Amanda, who is rather Scandinavian in appearance — tall, yet sturdy, with graceful hands and muscular arms, high cheekbones, and long, straight, ash-blonde hair. She easily hefts the larger of Lucie's two bags and leads the way through a door marked 'Private' and up a steep staircase. She doesn't pry, although

Lucie has not answered her question about destination. At the end of a dim, stale-smelling hallway, Amanda opens a door using an actual thick brass key, not a plastic key card. She strides straight across the stuffy room to sweep back the heavy curtains and crank open both sides of the window, admitting hot air. "Hmm, not sure that's the best idea. Anyway, it should start to cool off soon, we're on the east side of the hotel here. You'll get street noise but not the late-day heat."

She turns to leave, but pauses and regards Lucie with genuine concern. "Are you OK? You're awfully pale."

"Yes. No. I don't know. Yes, I'm OK. I *am* pale. It's just me."

"You look a little stressed. You get settled and come down to the bar for a nice cool glass of wine. And don't worry about the rest of your stuff, I'll get one of the boys to carry it up for you. Just leave your key in the lock."

Leave my key in the lock. Jeez Louise, I'm in some different universe now.

"The thing is," Lucie tells Amanda, "Bob didn't tell me how much it might cost. And I'm kind of watching my money. A low-budget trip, you know?"

Amanda is working the bar. The afternoon is quiet, and she gives Lucie her full attention, pausing only to fill the occasional order. She seems sincerely interested in Lucie's plight, which is gratifying and makes Lucie unusually talkative and truthful — that, and a second glass of chilled Sauvignon Blanc.

"Can your friend in Vancouver help out?" Amanda asks, tucking errant strands of hair behind her ear. "It's her car after all, right?"

"If it comes to that, yes. But she's already done so much for me. I mean, trusting me with the car, and kicking my butt enough that I'm actually taking this trip. I'd hate to call her and ask for money. Don't get me wrong, I can pay for my room and all. But car repair?

Not in the plan."

"It never is."

Amanda checks her wristwatch, a chunky, mannish affair with a wide metal band. "What are you doing for dinner?"

"I'll probably have a bar burger, maybe take a walk, then early to bed I guess. And wait to hear from Bob tomorrow."

"Why don't you come have dinner with my husband and me? It won't be fancy but it beats bar food."

"Oh, no. Thanks, you've been so nice already."

"Come on. I live on a ranch west of here. It's pretty in the evening, nice sunsets. Good food, if I do say so myself. And I'll get you back here before the band gets started in case you want to dance and party all night," that remark delivered with an actual wink. "OK? I'm off in about twenty minutes."

Half an hour later, they climb into Amanda's enormous, dark-blue pickup truck and drive along the town's summer streets. Kids and dogs play in front yards, and people mow their lawns. The breeze has died down, leaving a fine halo of dust suspended in the air, catching the slanting sunlight. Amanda takes a side road that leads uphill and curves away from town, passing fields scattered with grazing cattle, stands of spruce and poplar, a bobbing pumpjack.

"I've never actually seen one of those before," Lucie says.

"This is one of the oldest oil fields in the country," Amanda replies. "The pioneer oil guys made all their mistakes here and learned, then did a better job elsewhere. You only need those pump things where there's not enough pressure in the reservoir to push oil to the surface. It can be a sign of a badly managed reservoir, or so I understand." Amanda turns onto a gravel road.

"I thought I'd see more horses around here," Lucie comments.

"Oh, they're around. Just about everybody has a horse or two lurking in the back pasture."

"Do you?"

"We have, let's see, thirteen or fourteen on the place right now. We own some, and we use them as saddle horses or for working cows, but my husband also breeds and trains horses. So it's kind of a revolving door — or gate, I guess. Ha, ranch humour. Except for our five keepers, I never know exactly how many we have at any time."

Another turn, and another, until Lucie is completely disoriented. Amanda finally takes a hairpin turn onto a narrow, rutted road, barrels up a sidehill and around a long curve. The view reveals out-buildings and then a large log home, surrounded by trees. "Here we are. Don't mind the dogs, they're loud but harmless."

Lucie disembarks the truck to a chorus of joyful barking welcome. The dogs swarm around but do not jump or nip.

Inside, the house is dim and cool, constructed of fat logs that make it feel like a cozy cabin in the Swiss Alps. Amanda quickly disappears to change into jeans and a light shirt. Returning to the kitchen, she washes hands at the sink and starts preparing dinner. "Thought I might fire up a couple of steaks."

"OK..."

Amanda catches Lucie's hesitation. "Sorry, I didn't even ask. Do you not eat meat?"

"Oh, I do. I'm not a vegetarian by any stretch. But I don't eat a lot of beef, mostly I guess because there's so much good seafood in Vancouver, so that's mostly been my diet. But sure, steak. I'm in beef country, right?" A Lucie grin, met by a wry glance from Amanda that Lucie cannot interpret. She persists. "Give me a job. I can make salad or peel those spuds."

"You're on."

The women work side by side, talking sporadically. The silences feel peaceful and companionable. Lucie relaxes and stretches her back and shoulders as she stands at the sink peeling potatoes.

They hear the back door open and close. "Hello," says a man's voice. Very softly, but making a statement nonetheless.

"Hey. We've got company."

A tall man, thin as a stick, comes into the kitchen. "Keith," he says, holding out a hand to Lucie.

"Lucie."

"Howdy."

Howdy? Lucie nearly laughs out loud.

Amanda says, "Lucie's a stray. Her car broke down in town, and Bob brought her to the hotel for a room."

Keith grins at Amanda. "Really? You actually sold a hotel room?" He disappears into the recesses of the large house, retuning shortly in fresh clothes, his hair wet and clinging to the back of his neck. Opens a beer and offers one to Lucie, but not Amanda.

"Go ahead," Amanda says. "I don't drink."

"You work in a bar but don't drink?"

"Yeah, I know. I just never developed a taste for it, not even wine. Which makes me the favourite for house parties. I'm always the taxi of choice. And that's fine with me. So, Hon," Amanda says, smiling at her husband, "want to get those steaks going?"

The evening passes amicably. The meal is hearty and delicious, the conversation light and pleasant. The steak is fork-tender, with a delectable crunchy crust and tangy blue cheese sauce. It's the best beef Lucie has ever tasted. After dinner, they move to the back veranda to watch the westering sun. Horses graze across the green hillside below the house. Backlit by the long late rays, their manes and tails appear to be on fire. Nearby but hidden from view, a coyote begins to yip and soon the valley rings with a chorus of voices.

"Wolves or coyotes?" Lucie asks. "I've never heard either before, I'm such a city girl. I don't know the difference."

"Coyotes," Keith replies, pronouncing the word in the Spanish way, 'coy-OH-tees.' Lucie, who pronounced it 'KY-oats,' makes a mental note.

Keith says, "Not too many wolves hereabouts, though you hear them sometimes. Way different, less like laughing, instead it's a big long howl. Lonesome sound, makes your hair stand up."

Lucie shivers.

"Want a sweater?" says Amanda.

"No, I should go. Thanks, you've both been so kind. And I'd be happy to help clean up."

"I have a dishwasher for that."

"I'll do the honours," Keith says.

At the door, Amanda gives Lucie a warm and sincere hug. "Listen Lucie, don't worry. Bob's the best mechanic in town. And if you need help, call me. I'm off work tomorrow but here's my cell number. In fact, call me anyway, I want to know that you're OK and on your way." She scribbles on a scrap of paper, which Lucie tucks into her pocket.

Keith is quiet as he pilots them back to the hotel through the orange dusk. "Take care, now," is all he says as Lucie steps down from the gigantic pickup truck. She ducks up the stairwell and walks to the hallway's far end, feeling the vibration of bass and drums from the bar band all along the dark passage. Opening her door, she finds her luggage and assorted gear safe and neatly piled at the foot of the bed.

The band pounds away until two in the morning. When at last it's quiet, Lucie manages a few hours of fitful sleep.

The morning air is cool and scented with grass and shadows, drawing her outside. She walks to the café, but it's still closed. She wonders whether she should wait at Bob's shop, but it's closed too, so she strolls the town's wide and mostly paved streets, marvelling at the elaborate gardens and landscaping in some yards, the half-wrecked cars supported on blocks that occupy others.

Here I am again, wandering around some strange town. From Hope to Sweetgrass. I'm starting to perfect the form.

It's getting late and a coffee would not go amiss. She tries the café again and finds the door is open and there's music playing, but the room is empty. She sits in the same chair as yesterday. She can smell coffee, so somebody must be in the back. She gets up again, aiming for the hallway that probably leads to the kitchen. About halfway along is the coffee station, where one pot is filling and another sits on a warmer. She takes a cup from the shelf above the station, pours, returns to her seat.

Other customers arrive and take seats. A couple stands uncertainly by the door but still nobody appears to greet people and start taking orders. Lucie idly watches the room fill when her cell phone rings. "Hello, yes? This is Lucie," she adds as an afterthought.

"Good morning, Missy. This is Bob MacDonnell. I have good news and bad news."

Lucie takes a breath. "Such as?"

"Jake took a run to the city and got a battery for you, so we got your little beauty fired up. But it could use some work. If you're planning to head back through the mountains, I'd recommend we take care of a few issues."

Lucie knows she should ask what issues Bob is referring to but also knows his answer wouldn't make sense to her anyway. Instead she blurts, "How much will it cost?"

"I'd say with parts and labour we're looking at around $500. I should have all the parts in stock here so we could get 'er done for you by Monday. Tuesday at the latest."

"So there's no chance I'd make it back to Vancouver without this work?"

"I wouldn't say that, exactly. But you don't want to get stuck fifty miles from nowhere in the mountains."

"Yes, I understand." Lucie looks up, distracted by a commotion at the back of the café, perhaps from the kitchen. Raised voices.

"Fuck *you*!" yells a young woman, unseen.

"Right back at ya! You've got some nerve showing up late again when you know we're short this week. I can't depend on you at all." This from a man, also unseen.

"Um, Bob, I'm at the café. I'll come to see you soon as I've had lunch."

"Sure, Missy. Take your time."

The young woman who served Lucie yesterday has stormed into

the dining room, her face red, tears coursing down her cheeks. Pursuing her is a short, robust, athletic-looking man. Short, curly red-blond hair and freckles, clear blue eyes blazing. Wearing a white chef's jacket and apron. Clutching a knife.

"You're fired, you hear me? Outa here, right now. And use the back door," he shouts. But the server tears off her apron, flings it to the floor, and barges to the front door where she stops to scream obscenities at him again, then stomps out, letting the screen slam.

Everyone is riveted. Stunned.

How is it I witness restaurant drama everywhere I go?

The chef, knife in hand, looks around and shrugs. "Sorry, folks," he says. "Just give me a minute and I'll get you all started with coffee, then take your orders. Service will be a little slow today." He stomps away up the hall.

Before she can stop herself, Lucie springs from her chair, strides to the coffee station. She grabs several mugs and the full carafe of hot coffee. She returns to the dining room and goes from table to table, raising the carafe. "Coffee?" she asks, filling mugs. "I'm not sure where the cream and sugar are, but I'll find out." She goes back for more mugs, spots baskets full of sugar packets, and a small fridge where she finds several small pitchers of milk. Back in the dining room, people are waiting at the door. "Sit anywhere," she says. She keeps pouring coffee. Someone asks for tea. "Not sure, I'll find out," she says.

On her third trip to the coffee station, she encounters the chef in the hallway. "Can you make another pot please?" she asks him. "And where would I find tea?"

"What are you doing?" Not challenging or belligerent, just curious.

They are nearly the same height though he is somewhat taller and outweighs her by a wide margin. He has a fighter's powerful shoulders and arms, broad chest, muscular back. His face, now that he's calmed down, is no longer flushed but seems open and friendly, with sky eyes and a constellation of freckles across his cheeks and over the bridge of his nose. A smile tickles his oddly boyish rosebud lips.

"It happens that I need cash, pronto," Lucie says. "And you seem to need a server, pronto. So I appear to be serving coffee."

His full grin reveals small, even teeth. "Done table service before?"

"Not lately, but yes."

"Ray." He holds out his hand.

"Lucie," she says. His grip is firm.

"OK. I'll make more coffee this time, but here are the coffee pouches, here's how you do it," he quickly demonstrates. "Hot water for tea is right there," he indicates a red-handled tap. "Teabags in that cupboard. Pitchers of cold water and milk in the bar fridge under the counter. No menu. Selections are on the board, that's what we serve. No 'can you make me a cheeseburger' — what you see on the board is what we have and be firm about that. There should be an order pad behind the bar, tear off the top copy and clip it to the order board in the kitchen for me. I'll unlock the cash box when I get a minute so you can make change. Thanks." He turns to the kitchen.

She turns to search for an order pad.

"Lucie?"

"Ray?"

"You keep all your tips."

"Best news I've had all day."

The next four hours are quick and chaotic. It's been years since Lucie waited tables, but she finds her stride and clicks into a rhythm of snapping orders onto the kitchen order board, ferrying full plates from kitchen to table and empty plates back again, filling coffee mugs and water glasses, opening beer bottles, and chatting with guests: "You're right, I'm new, just started today." "No I don't know Freddy, do I look like him? I'm not from around here." "Gluten-free pizza crust? I don't know, but I'll ask, hang on." She sees the same Mountie who was in the café yesterday and thinks she recognizes two of the older women who were so intently bent over their table yesterday too. For his part, Ray shows her where to find clean tableware and cutlery; he unlocks the cash box and quickly instructs her on adding tax to the order total, shows her how to use the handheld device for tableside credit and debit. At one point he calls, "No more beef shank," and she erases that item from the chalkboard with her finger.

At last it's mid-afternoon, and the place is empty. She sits on a bar stool, grabs a calculator from under the bar and goes over the day's chits, trying to reconcile cash and credit slips with the orders.

Ray comes out of the kitchen carrying a frosty glass of cold water, his apron smeared. He stands behind the bar and watches her for a moment. "We serve dinner, too."

She looks up. "I'm in."

He laughs and shakes his head, stamps a foot on the floor. "Where have *you* been all my life?"

"Driving a crappy car from Vancouver that won't make it home without fixing some 'issues', according to Bob MacDonnell. Which reminds me, I need to hustle up to his service emporium and find out what those issues are. Can you spare me for half an hour or so?"

"You bet."

They regard each other. Ray takes a long slow sip of water, never breaking eye contact. Slowly licks water from his lips. "Who the hell are you anyway?"

"I'll explain later. I'm on a road trip, and my car broke down here. Bob's my man apparently, but I can't afford whatever he's got in mind for car repair. Lucky for me a job opening came up."

Ray grins warmly and says, "Just so you know, he's fair and he's the best mechanic in town. If he says something needs fixing, it needs fixing. He's also the mayor."

"Thanks. Good to know."

Lucie strides up the street. The afternoon was intense, like being pulled under water and pushed around by heavy surf. Now it's good to feel fresh air, to slow her pace and breathe calmly. But by the time she's walked the few blocks to the service station, she's given in to exhaustion.

As she's come to expect, there is nobody in the front office but she sees through to the service bay, where her car is on a hoist. She pounds the service bell on the desk. Bob does not appear. Instead, a lanky young man in oil-stained overalls materializes from the repair bay. "I'm Jake," he says.

"That's my car," she says, pointing to the suspended Honda.

"Oh, yeah, Bob said you would be around. She needs some work, your little car." Jake's speech rhythm is exactly like Bob's, as though the young man has been taking elocution lessons from his boss.

"What kind of work?"

"Well, I have good news and bad news."

Lucie can barely stop herself from rolling her eyes.

"Bob told me he'd like to explain it to you in person, but he's gone now for the day, and we're closed tomorrow, being Sunday and all, so I guess you can't talk to him 'til Monday."

"And what part of all that would be the good news?"

Jake looks at her quizzically. "Sorry?"

Lucie sighs. "Never mind. Whatever the car needs, just do it. I don't have a lot of money though. So, I don't even know what I'm saying here, but I guess if you think there's a chance to use a cheap part or skip a repair — just please remember that I don't have a lot of money. In fact I've just started working at the café up the street to make some cash so... Oh, I don't even know why I said that. Look, just fix my car, OK? Bob has my cell phone number. Call me when it's ready."

"Okie dokie," Jake responds.

She regards him for a moment and realizes the conversation is over, although the extent of car repair is still undetermined. "Thanks," she says, turns on her heel, and walks back through the late afternoon heat and haze to the restaurant.

She is relieved to see the café is still empty. In the dim hallway leading to the kitchen she calls, "Hey, Ray?"

"Over here."

She finds him by a back sink, peeling shrimp, a stack of vegetables beside him.

"In any ordinary world I'd have other people doing this prep work," he mutters by way of greeting.

"In any ordinary world my friend's car wouldn't break down and leave me stranded," she replies.

He looks up. "You're not stranded. You're in Sweetgrass, a fine little Alberta town, which, may I be so bold as to point out, has already landed you a job. And a good mechanic for whatever ails your car. And, I'm guessing, a place to stay?"

"At the hotel."

He nearly drops the shrimp he's deveining. "You're kidding? That's a bar hotel. Noisy as hell."

"Well, where else? I'm nearly out of money, my car is broken. And what. The. Hell. Else. Should I do?" She pounds her fist into her open palm with each syllable. Smack smack smack.

He gives her a long look. "Sorry," he says, sounding sincere, and raising his hands in surrender. "Guess I speak my mind too much — just ask the girl who quit on me today. Or my sous-chef who didn't turn up either, guess I've pissed her off too. I normally have a staff of five, but right now it's you and me. And believe me, I do not want or intend to annoy you. I don't know how you dropped into my life, but you're all that stands between me and closing for at least a few days. And that would mean throwing out all this fine fresh shrimp and a bunch of other stuff. So — I'm sorry. I don't mean to offend you, and I'm grateful you're here, whoever you are. But seriously, we can find you a better place to stay than the hotel."

"Yeah, that would be good. We'll talk later. Want me to peel spuds?"

For the second day in a row, Lucie is standing before a sink, paring skins from potatoes. She also peels carrots, rinses tomatoes, peels and chops garlic. Then a buzzer sounds. "Customers," says Ray.

She drops the knife, cleans her hands, grabs a fresh apron, and goes out front to greet guests at the door. And so begins the next hectic four hours taking orders, serving, clearing, pouring coffee, beer, wine, dessert, and remembering how to operate the credit card machine.

As if by magic, it's 10 p.m. Lucie and Ray clean and tidy the kitchen and dining room, put away clean mugs and dishes, stow food in the cooler. Their only conversation all night occurred when Lucie brought in a new order or had a question about the menu or where to find whatever a customer wanted — extra salt and pepper, balsamic vinegar. Finally their work is done. "How do I take tips that people gave by credit card?" she asks.

"You total credit card tips and take it out of cash. And if there's not enough cash, you write up a chit for me, and I pay you the next time I get to the bank."

"So even if it's a perfect world and we have two servers and three people working in back, we don't share tips?" Lucie doesn't notice her use of the word 'we.'

"I pay my kitchen staff well, and I believe servers should keep their tips because it's about their service. No pooling." He removes his white jacket and apron and stuffs them into a laundry basket. He's wearing a light-blue tee shirt that hugs his broad chest and shoulders. "Want a drink?" He disappears up the hallway toward the bar and reappears with a bottle of Scotch and two glasses.

"How do you account for after-hours shots?"

He laughs, again shaking his head. "You don't miss anything do you? I don't pour much after hours — two shots, max. Mark it down as a business expense."

"So is this your restaurant?" she asks, accepting a very generous glass of whisky.

"I don't own it, but I run it free rein." They clink glasses. "To rescue," he says and takes a long sip. He tips his head back, sighs. "The guy who owns this café — you'll laugh at this — won it from the previous owner in a poker game."

"Ha, you're kidding! Man, this is the Wild West for sure. Most people try to get out of Dodge. I've stumbled into it."

"Yep, it's crazy here sometimes but no crazier than anyplace else. Where did you say you're from?"

"Did I say?"

He sips his whisky and regards her with such gentle humour in his bright flax-blue eyes that she regrets her suspicious response. He says reasonably, as though speaking to a naughty but not irredeemable child, "Yes. I believe you mentioned driving from Vancouver, though you could actually be from anywhere. Mars, for all I know."

She relents and gives him what she hopes is an open and sincere smile — not her usual tough-girl-Lucie grin — to match his own. For some reason, she feels safe, and she's willing to give him an honest if abbreviated taste of her story. "Here's the scoop on me, Lucie Tanguay," she begins, and provides a synopsis of her current situation. She tells Ray about losing her job in Vancouver and about Judith's help with a car and a plan for renewal through travel and adventure. "So there you have it," she concludes. "My sorry-ass life in a nutshell."

"And you're in Sweetgrass for the time being," he says. "You could have done worse. You've already managed to meet some local luminaries. Bob is a good guy and useful to know way beyond vehicle repair. He knows everyone in town, and then some. And Amanda is a gem. I'm not surprised she took you home for dinner, it's exactly what she would do. Plus I think you're probably now acquainted with a couple of the local Mounties, which is never a bad thing. And me, of course."

"Cheers to that." They clink glasses again, although hers is empty.

"Want more?"

"No, thanks. You're open tomorrow, yes? Lunch and dinner? I need to get some rest. Can you drive me back to the hotel?"

"Yes, yes, and yes."

"Hey, what's with the name? The Sow's Ear?"

He grins, but then his smile fades and he ducks his head — perhaps he's being modest, she can't tell. He says, "When I took over the kitchen, I told the owner — the previous guy, not the poker champ

— I wanted to cook cheap cuts that nobody uses. Brisket, tripe, pork hocks, beef marrow, stuff like that. Two reasons: one, it's what I learned to cook because I grew up poor, and two, you can buy cheap meat and turn it into fantastic food people are willing to pay top dollar for, so your margins are a bit better than most restaurants. Or they were, until everyone in Calgary caught on to pork jowl and beef marrow. Anyway, we were out ahead of the pack long enough that we have a reputation for interesting food. People come here from the city and even beyond. That's the hook: I'm making silk purses out of sow's ears. Although sow's ear itself is currently not on the menu."

"Clever. Where'd you learn to cook?"

He doesn't answer immediately. Then says, "I grew up on a farm, but my dad wasn't much of a farmer, he made some bad decisions and investments — as if a farmer has money to invest in the first place — and he lost the farm. Mom divorced him but she couldn't keep all the kids together — there are seven of us, so we scattered. I went to live with my grandmother, who wasn't exactly rich either. She taught me about making silk purses out of a lot of things. Food. Clothes. Whatever. I guess it's called learning to be resourceful. So I've been cooking since I was twelve. When most prairie boys were into hockey or rodeo, I was getting cookbooks out of the school library. I even tried to take home economics at school instead of mechanics. That raised a few eyebrows. And earned me a few beatings." He stops talking to tip the last drop of whisky from his glass. "Sorry, that was too much information. The short answer is, Gran taught me to cook."

"Your story's a lot like mine."

"Oh?"

"My mom taught me to bake. Maybe I'll tell you about it some time," she says. "Right now, I'm totally beat. Let's close up, I've got to get some sleep."

Back in her room, Lucie muses that she has no idea how much her hourly wage might be, but counts out $130 in tips.

It's dusk. Lucie is on Amanda's back deck, a beer in hand.

After just over a week of Lucie living at the hotel, Amanda took pity and asked her whether she'd like to rent the spare room in the ranch house basement. "It's a bit dark and definitely not fancy, but it beats living above the bar," Amanda said. "Two hundred a month, could you afford that much?" to which Lucie nodded gratefully and joked, "Promise you'll play loud music on weekends so I'll feel at like I'm at home back in the hotel."

Lucie is now installed in a muffled basement bedroom. Double bed with a decent mattress, rather threadbare cotton sheets, many blankets, and a hefty down duvet. The room is full of mismatched furniture, from a chunky wooden dresser to a contemporary Danish bedside table that hosts a clock radio and a vase of dried flowers. In the corner is a rattan chair with a good reading lamp leaning over its shoulder. There's a generous closet. Because it's a basement room, the large window is at shoulder height. One of the two west-facing panes slides open to admit fresh air. The window is concealed by plain white cotton curtains with frills all around. The windowsill is broad enough to accommodate plant pots, sundries, and a pile of books.

This is a clearly meant to be a guest room. To Lucie it feels transient, a place someone would only occupy for a few days. But for now it's home, and she's settled in, hung up clothes, filled dresser drawers, tuned the radio. Maybe at some point she'll find a few more personal items to brighten the room, perhaps a different duvet cover or flower arrangement. Maybe she'll find some other accommodation entirely. For the moment though, she's relieved — astonished, actually — to have been invited to live in such a clean, secure, comfortable place. But Amanda's welcome was genuine, a spontaneous offer not generated by Lucie's *give-me-what-I-want* grin. Lucie never employed that grin; Amanda simply and sincerely offered a place to stay.

It's refreshing. In Lucie's experience, only Judith and Gwen have ever extended such unconditional kindness.

So what is it about these people, this place? Have I stumbled into some pocket of human kindness unknown to the rest of the world?

Without making a conscious decision, Lucie has started settling into Sweetgrass. She's earned enough to pay Bob for car repair, but she's in no hurry to move on. The tide has pushed her far up the beach, and here she stays, driftwood stuck in sand. No regrets. And, for the time being, no need for onward travel.

No plan. But she's found a safe place to stay for now.

On weekdays The Sow's Ear is only open for lunch, so this Monday morning Lucie is not expected at work until 10:30 or so. Amanda's sleeping in after taking the graveyard shift at the bar last night. It's a fine clear morning, getting warm already though it's barely seven. Lucie takes a mug of coffee and wanders out to watch Keith working horses.

He's got a young animal loping around the perimeter of a large, high corral she's learned to call a 'round pen.' The horse, reddish-brown with white socks and a white star on its forehead, wears a halter with a long rope attached. Keith stands in the pen's centre, lightly grasping the rope and flicking the other end behind the horse to keep it moving, but he is speaking softly to the horse, which appears nervous but also curious as it turns its head toward Keith. With commands Lucie doesn't catch — perhaps body position or tone of voice? — Keith gets the horse to stop. He slowly approaches, and places a gentle hand on the horse's neck. The horse flinches but stands. Keith rubs the animal's neck, ears, and chest, then steps away and turns his back. The horse turns around to follow. Keith returns to the centre and gets the animal moving again, now in the opposite direction.

It all looks like magic to Lucie.

Keith is fully focused on the horse and doesn't appear to know Lucie is watching between the pen's railings, so she's startled when he glances over his shoulder and says, "Want to ride?"

"No. Thanks, no." She smiles but her voice is emphatic. *Not a chance, cowboy. Not 'til the devil needs ice skates.*

He glances at her again, yet never seems to lose connection with the tiring horse. Lucie sees a slight but teasing smile cross his face.

"Why not?"

"I've never been on a horse. In fact I've never been this close to one before."

"I know."

"Is it that obvious?"

"Yep."

She's annoyed and mildly insulted, though she knows he's right. She keeps quiet.

Again by some signal Lucie can't discern, he makes the horse stop. The animal is breathing hard, its nostrils flared and red, its neck and chest darkly damp with sweat. Again Keith approaches and rubs his hands over the horse's neck, along its back, down its front legs. Its ears twitch but it stands firm.

"Watch a horse's ears," Keith says, without looking at Lucie. "You can tell what he's paying attention to. Right now, Sunny Boy is paying attention to me. His ears are cocked back, following me. If I move forward, his ears will follow me." And indeed that is what happens.

"I thought when a horse's ears are back it means they're mad. Like with a dog."

"Ears flat back means aggression, or fear. Ears pricked back like this means attention. Exactly what I want."

She's surprised to hear him use a word like 'aggression.' "I had no idea," Lucie says, a bit louder than she'd intended. The horse flicks one ear in her direction, then back again toward Keith, who is now running his hands along its rump and down its back leg. He straightens and moves to the animal's head, grasping the halter and giving it a slight tug. The horse steps forward, and Keith walks alongside. Gradually the animal's head droops a little and its ears seem to flop lazily to the side. "Now he's calm, he's trusting me to watch for danger. I'm now the alpha. I'm in charge."

Lucie is surprised to hear the word 'alpha.' _There's more to you than meets the eye. Or ear._

"That's enough for today Sunny Boy," Keith says, unlatching the gate and leading the horse toward the barn. Lucie follows. The building's wide, dim corridor is flanked by stalls on one side and windows on the other, which overlook the expansive indoor arena. "Come around here, I'll show you how to tie," Keith says to Lucie, who nervously walks around the horse, allowing plenty of room between her and the animal's powerful back legs.

"He won't kick unless provoked."

Provoked. Another strange word from the mouth of a cowboy.

"It's safer to stay close. Watch his ears. Here, this is a quick-release knot." He ties and releases the loop twice, then steps aside. "Your turn."

Lucie passes a loop of rope through a metal ring fixed to a sturdy upright beam, then pulls a second loop through the eye of the first one, just as Keith demonstrated. "Good," he says. "This is a safe knot because the horse is secure, but you can release fast. Pull this end." She does so. The knot easily unfurls. She re-ties the knot as Keith ducks under the horse's neck and disappears, leaving her standing alone next to the animal, without a clue as to what she should do next. Follow Keith? She hears his footsteps echo quietly as he walks away.

Although relaxed — its head drooping, its grapefruit-sized eyes half closed — the horse is daunting. Its head alone is enormous. Lucie has never been so near to such a gigantic, unknown, and unknowable beast. Even most dogs in her previous city life were knee-high or less. Lucie realizes she could rest her chin on the horse's back.

Tentatively Lucie raises her left hand and places it on the horse's neck. The creature doesn't move, but as Lucie looks up — *Ohmygod horses are big!* — she sees its ears are pricked back, paying attention to her, the slim woman at its side. Slowly, Lucie rubs the soft warm hide of its neck, working her hand up and under the coarse, long hair of the horse's mane. She threads the fingers of her other hand through the mane, carefully pulling out knots. The animal smells of sweat and dust, but it's somehow calming and comforting to stand there in the cool barn, touching and combing while the horse breathes softly and swishes its tail.

Lucie is so lost in this simple meditation, she doesn't hear the steps of an approaching horse. Suddenly, Keith comes behind Sunny Boy, leading a small grey horse. A small grey horse with a saddle on its back, reins looped over the saddle horn.

"Hop on," Keith says.

Hop? Are you kidding me? I'll need a ladder to get up there. Besides, didn't I say no? Her fear and doubt must be obvious, because Keith actually reaches out and takes her arm, pulls her gently but with absolute authority around to the horse's left side.

"I'll lead. We'll do a couple circuits in the arena," he says. "To get on, face the horse. Grab the horn with your left hand. Now left foot in the stirrup." He holds the stirrup steady for her. It's high, a difficult stretch. Lucie is wearing tight-fitting city jeans and light slip-on running shoes. She tries once, twice, yet again and can't reach the stirrup, which makes her mad.

Of course I can do this. Come on, city slicker. Show this guy what you're made of.

Hopping on her right foot and pulling herself up by the saddle horn, after three attempts she succeeds in getting her left foot placed in the stirrup. No sooner is her foot anchored than Keith deftly steps behind her and gives an expert boost. Lucie doesn't have time to think or protest.

"Swing your leg over."

She does so, and bumps to a hard landing in the saddle, straddling the horse with left foot in the stirrup, the other foot dangling.

Keith steps around to adjust the length of the right stirrup, guides her foot into position. He does the same adjustment on the left side. Meanwhile Lucie, heart hammering, swallows several times and tries to be brave as she sits astride the horse. It's the strangest sensation, her legs forced apart, her butt slipping on the saddle's smooth, hard surface. She feels very exposed and insecure.

She realizes Keith is looking up at her. "I'll show you how to hold the reins but don't use them, just hang onto the horn. This is Quincy, by the way. She's a good little mare. Real easy ride. Pass the reins between your fingers like this. Now put weight on your feet, push your heels down. Most beginners sit a horse like a sack of spuds. 'Light seat' means your weight is evenly distributed, seat and feet. Here we go."

Distributed. You keep surprising me.

Keith steps forward, and the mare's head pops up. Her ears prick forward and she starts to move. Lucie tries to remember all the things Keith just said. *Weight on feet. Hold the horn. Sack of spuds. Breathe.*

They walk to the far end of the corridor, Lucie looking straight ahead along the amazingly narrow ridge of the horse's neck, and then between the mare's ears. The arena door is open and Keith steps inside, pausing to flick on overhead lights. The arena floor is thickly layered with dirt and sawdust that looks reassuringly deep and soft. Keith walks ahead and Quincy follows along the wall, moving slowly. Lucie feels her hips loosen as she sways slightly side to side in concert with the horse. They make one full circuit, then Keith stops. Quincy likewise comes to a halt.

"This mare neck-reins," he says. "Some horses are trained to direct-rein, where you pull the right line to turn right, left line to turn left. But Quincy responds to a combination of pressure from the rein and from your knees. Turn left by squeezing with your *left* knee and pulling the *right* rein across her neck like this." He demonstrates, and the horse shifts its weight, taking a step to the left. "Let's practice that. I'll lead her, but when I say 'right' or 'left,' you squeeze your knee and lay the opposite rein against her neck. She'll turn. Remember to keep balanced in the saddle. Weight on feet. Heels down."

He steps forward again and Quincy follows. After a few steps, Keith softly says, "Left." With great concentration, Lucie pushes her left knee gently into the mare's side and lifts the reins so the right rein rubs the horse's neck. Nothing happens. Quincy continues to walk forward, following Keith. "Push harder with your knee, there's leather between you and the horse. Make her do what you want. You're the boss. Try again. Left."

This time, the grey mare does turn to the left and begins heading away from Keith toward the middle of the arena.

It's only then Lucie realizes Keith is not using a lead rope. The horse had simply been following him. She's on her own.

"Left again, come around in a big slow circle."

For a split second, Lucie flashes to anger about being duped, but she's far too frightened and preoccupied to pursue that thought. Instead she follows Keith's instructions, pushing Quincy through a manoeuvre that's more a square than a circle. Nonetheless, she comes all the way back to Keith, who has moved to the middle of the arena. "Right," is all he says, and Lucie guides the horse through a rather more circular circle. "Now ride along the wall, down to the end... back toward me... figure eight across the arena on the diagonal to the far wall, ride around the end. Straighten your back, sit up. Watch her ears. Weight on feet. Heels down. Turn right, do a tighter circle this time."

Figure eights. Circles to the right, to the left, tighter each time. Then a leisurely stroll along the wall, and it's over.

"Hop off. Then walk her a bit to cool out." Keith does not come over to assist, but walks away and exits the arena.

Flummoxed, Lucie remains astride the mare, mentally going through the motions needed to dismount. Logically, it should be the reverse of getting on. Gingerly she puts her full weight into the left stirrup, kicks her right foot free and slowly swings her right leg up and over. Her right leg continues its downward arc as she frantically twists. Her right toe comes to rest on the ground, her left foot still suspended in the stirrup. She grasps the stirrup and yanks her foot out, topples backward into the dirt.

The patient mare doesn't move, except to swing her great head around to look at Lucie who is laughing on the ground.

Nothing to see here, girlfriend.

Lucie stands and starts to dust herself off, then considers the dirt on her butt could be a badge of honour, a laugh to share with Keith. She grasps the horse's bridle as she saw Keith do earlier with the young horse. She takes a step forward and Quincy follows. Lucie releases her grip. Woman and horse pace together around the arena once, twice. When she reaches the door again, Keith is waiting.

She looks directly at him. Her cheeks are flushed, her eyes glitter. She sports a wide, amazed grin. She considers hugging him. "That. Was. Awesome."

"Every morning if you like."

"Yes."

Lucie has been utterly occupied with the business of her present life, simply living day-to-day—working at the café, getting settled into her new underground lair in Amanda's house, and taking the odd walk around town to discover her new surroundings. Early morning riding lessons.

Not that Lucie has spared no thought at all for Judith. Every time she gets into the mighty Agememnon — now fully functional and humming smoothly — Lucie reminds herself she owes Judith an update, more than the quick text notes she's sent: 'I'm OK, will send news,' and 'Sorry, things are FINE just busy, will call.' But she knows Judith will want more than a travelogue and weather report, she'll probe for the status of Lucie's life reinvention plan — but

Lucie has no such plan. Vancouver and her previous life lie like a half-read book left face down beyond the jagged western horizon, neglected for the moment but perhaps not forever. Lucie has no idea what she wants for her future, but the present is proving to be more interesting by the day.

So when Lucie finally makes the long-overdue call to her distant friend, Judith's voice on the phone sounds relieved. "Ohmygod-Ithoughtyouweredead. Luce, where are you? What's going on? I've been so worried."

"Relax, Sweet Pea. Pour yourself a drink and settle in. I have a tale for you. I'm in beautiful downtown Sweetgrass, Alberta. No, check that, I'm *close* to Sweetgrass. I'm actually calling you from the deck of a gorgeous big ranch house west of town. I'm watching horses graze. The sky is such an incredible blue. Jude, I had no idea the sky could be so clear, it's like a painting. Like they've invented some kind of special crayon colour here. And the air is sweet and fresh. There's big thunderclouds forming up to the west, we might get a lightning show later. You never get much thunder and lightning in Vancouver, right? But here it's almost a daily occurrence in July."

She doesn't notice her use of the word 'you.'

"And Jude, I've made such good friends here. The couple who own this ranch are so *genuine*. Sweet Pea, I can't think of a better word for them. They have been so kind to me, and they are so real, down-to-earth, I trust them totally. Such a change for me, eh? And I have a *job* here. I'm serving tables in this amazing little restaurant and making a good wage and tips. I'm actually putting money back into my bank account for the first time in months.

"But, hey, more news — Jude, I've been riding horses, can you believe it, *me* on a horse? Just riding around the indoor arena they have here at the ranch, but it's been fun, I've never been on a horse before, but it's amazing. I'm learning so much, and riding is like a full-on vacation from your life because you have to pay attention to the horse... Oh, I have so much to tell you about that. Being on a horse is scary, but Keith is a good teacher — this is his ranch, along with Amanda who works at the hotel bar, you would _love_ them.

"And oh yeah, Agememnon is in better shape than ever. I had some issues with the car, which is why I stopped here in the first place, but it's all fine now. Jude, are you there?"

Judith has not interrupted Lucie's river of talk. Now she says, "Yes. Yes I am right here. You sound terrific, Luce. You sound full of life and fun and energy. That was the point of the exercise, yes? To get your mojo back? Sounds like it's working."

"_Mojo_. Now there's a word I haven't heard in years. You are so right. I just feel, I don't know... lighter. Calmer. Released. I have a job for one thing. That alone has made me feel better about... me."

"And now what?"

Lucie takes a swig of beer before responding. "I might stick around here for a bit."

"Seriously?"

"Yeah, is that OK? I mean about the car? If you want, I could buy it from you. In fact I should, because I'll have to get Alberta license plates pretty soon."

"Yikes, are you thinking about _staying_ there? Where is Long Grass, anyway?"

"Ha, I thought you knew every dot on the map. And it's _Sweetgrass_ not Long Grass. It's about an hour southwest of Calgary, in the foothills. Little town, maybe two thousand people. One high school, two hotels — I was actually living in one of those hotels for a while. I now have a local address, general delivery post office box. Plus we have two gas stations, a library. Several bars, way too many pizza places and liquor stores."

"I get the picture. Small town. Don't worry about the car, it's yours. I guess we need to do some paperwork so it's registered to you. I'll get that going. But Lucie, are you sure about this? About sticking around in ... um, wherever you are? It's a huge step. You've lived in Vancouver more than ten years, and whether you believe me or not, you do have friends here. People have been asking about you. And about your career... I mean, it's fine to take a break and work in a restaurant, live in a small town for a bit, but you can't do that for the rest of your life. Ugh, sorry, do I sound like your mother?"

"Oh, just a little. Or actually a lot. Besides, finding a new course in life was the point of this trip, right? I'm still looking."

"I'm just asking, Sweet Pea. Don't get me wrong, if you think it's the right place for you, I'm behind you one hundred per cent, you know that. It's just... *unexpected*, that's all. So, do you think you'll stay there for the rest of the summer, or what?"

"Can't really say." Lucie takes another gulp of beer. "If I'm going to find myself, or whatever the hell it is I'm doing here, how do I know how long that might take? I have zero reasons to go back to Vancouver right now. You can say hi to all my so-called friends, and you can even tell them I'm waiting tables in a hayseed town in Alberta, which should give them all a laugh. Honestly Jude, I have no clue how long I'll be here. Maybe 'til next week. Maybe next year. I don't know, and at the moment, I don't care. That's all I can say. No life plan. But it's OK here."

"Well good, I guess. I feel like Pandora: I opened a box and look what popped out. Beyond my wildest dreams."

"Don't get *me* wrong, Jude, you know I'm grateful for every last thing you've done for me. But look — you gave me the car and the keys and booted my ass out of town because I was too stuck to know that I was stuck. Maybe I don't know how to really have a life, or take a vacation, as you said. Maybe I'm here in lovely Sweetgrass to figure that out. It's as good a place as any. It's beautiful here. Sweet air, so many birds, frogs singing at night, coyotes too. Who knew?"

"I'm amazed. You're not much of a nature lover."

"Maybe I've never had the chance. Not that I'm going camping any time soon. I still draw the line at sleeping on the ground. And I've got to say, horses are great, but they're dusty and sweaty, you know? After riding lessons it's straight into the shower and my clothes get washed, pronto."

"Good girl. At least you're not compromising your standards. So, you're OK out there with the tumbleweeds and cowboys? Really?"

"Yes I am. Maybe more OK than I've been for a while. I'll send you some pictures so you can get a taste of this place. And Jude?"

"And Lucifer?"

"Thank you. I can't say that enough."

July melts like chocolate into August. The days are uncommonly humid and uncomfortable. Leaves hang limply, clothing sticks to skin, and the neutral grey-blue sky is blurry from the constant moisture haze. Days are slow, hours ooze into one another, the cloying heat is unrelenting. Lucie's customers comment on how unusual it is that the evenings don't cool after sunset. People complain so frequently Lucie becomes impatient with their chatter about sleepless nights and damp sheets, listless kids, fretful dogs, and horses that won't settle down.

It rains nearly every afternoon — another local complaint — but rain doesn't bring relief, only increased humidity and daily instability, lashing wind, thunder, sometimes hail. Even tornado warnings. Obstructive and unusual weather is interfering with the expected way things go around here, and people don't like it. Customers are cranky. Tips diminish. Even Amanda and Keith don't talk much over dinner and retire early, leaving Lucie to read or walk through the rain-wet long grass of the pastures with the ranch dogs and mosquitoes for company.

On the other hand, customers comment on how lush the hay crop is this year and how there's been no fire ban yet. Lucie picks up on all this information, tidbits she can share while topping up glasses of cold water or setting plates on tables. The yin and yang of ranch life.

The café is continually busy. Even with the staff complement back up to five — Ray has hired two assistants in the kitchen, plus a young woman to help Lucie part-time in the front — Lucie is at the restaurant from late morning until closing. She arrives by ten to get things organized, and on days the café is open for dinner, she leaves after midnight, exhausted. The ceiling fans rotate, and the translucent fabric blinds on the south-facing windows are always drawn; still, on some afternoons, the café is stifling. Lucie daydreams about strolling along a Pacific beach in a cooling breeze, but that vision lasts only long enough for her to bang into a wall of personal baggage, which of course she would have to confront and resolve in order to reclaim a life that includes walking on beaches. She puts the image aside and makes another pot of coffee.

During her shifts Lucie doesn't talk much to Ray or the others. Not that she's aloof, it's simply that there's seldom time for chat. There has been no repeat of the after-hours whisky shots with Ray — or anyone else for that matter — which suits Lucie just fine. Undecided about how much longer she'll remain in Sweetgrass, she's reluctant to widen her circle or make an effort toward closer friendships.

It's the same with customers. She's always ready with friendly banter but never anything more. There have been a couple of date offers from local cowboys, even a joking marriage proposal from an especially boisterous table one night, but she's declined all offers for social contact, sincere or not.

She's learned to recognize the café's regulars. The police — there are five altogether — come in for coffee or lunch in various combinations. The older women she encountered on her first visit to the café similarly visit in various combinations of two, three, or all four. There's a lone cowboy who's somewhat heavyset and is never in a hurry. His visits are frequent, two or three times each week, but he only orders coffee, and occasionally a slice of pie. He sits alone at whatever table is available, annoying her if he ties up a large table by himself when she has customers waiting. He simply watches in a detached and distant way, speaking to no one. Once, he was accompanied by a petite, white-haired woman, who also didn't speak, who only nodded and gave a shy smile when Lucie offered a cup of coffee. The woman peered around the room curiously, as though she'd never been in a restaurant before.

One overcast and gloomy Thursday, an oddly quiet day, only Ray and Lucie are working. Ray chalks menu items on the board, Lucie tallies receipts behind the bar, listening absently to country music on the café's stereo as she sips cool water. She's mildly annoyed when the door swings open, and a tall man in a tan-coloured, very grimy cowboy hat and equally dirty jeans shuffles into the restaurant and takes a seat.

"George!" Ray exclaims as if spotting a long-lost cousin. "You been a long time in the bush, buddy. Good to see ya."

George only nods and says, "Coffee. And one of those barbequed sandwiches you make." He pronounces the word in a long drawl, "BAR-bee-kewed," which grates on Lucie though she doesn't know why. Maybe because that item is not on today's menu, and Ray is usually adamant about not preparing anything made to order.

"Coming up," Ray grins as he heads past Lucie to the kitchen. Over his shoulder, he adds, "Meet Lucie, my new hired hand. Luce, why don't you engage George in a debate about the joys of modern living?"

What the hell...? And since when do you call me 'Luce'? With a shrug, Lucie grabs the simmering coffee pot and a mug on her way to the cowboy's table.

"Hey, Honey," he says.

Honey. Not a good start. With arched eyebrows, a raised shoulder, and trademark sneer she replies, "*Hey.*" She omits to add *honey*.

They stare at one another for a beat. Lucie is first to blink. She raises the coffee pot, he nods. As she fills his cup, she tries to keep her tone light and conversational. He is a customer after all, and apparently a friend of Ray's. "Guess I'm supposed to talk to you about modern living. I have no idea what Ray means by that, so go easy on me."

"Pull up a chair."

"I'm working."

He glances around the empty room. "Don't seem all that *occupied* right now." Pronounced OK-yew-pied. From under the brim of his hat, he regards her with an appraising look she's sure he would also use to size up the quality of a horse or a bull or a bale of hay. Then he sits back. "I'll tell you one thing about me, see if it surprises you. My house ain't got no runnin' water nor electricity." He elongates the word, 'EE-lek-TRISS-a-tee.'

"No EE-lek-TRISS-a-tee," she echoes him.

"Nope. Dontcha wanta know why?"

"Maybe." She half expects him to start lecturing, which he does. "Runnin' water an' electricity are the scourge of the modern age," he says evenly, waving his hands for emphasis. "Think about it, girl. If you got a house with runnin' water, why then you got a problem. Say yer toilet gets backed up, or yer sewer runout don't run. You got a problem. Any kinda blockage — say you're datin' a woman with long hair and the drains get fulla hair, and before you know it, you got water water ev-a-ree-where! But a water leak, hell that's nuthin', just an inconvenience. Ee-lec-triss-a-tee—now that stuff'll kill ya."

In the back, Ray bangs the ready bell. "Gotta go," she says quickly.

As she picks up the order she glares at Ray through the pass-through window. "What is this supposed to be about?"

"Tell you later."

But when she takes the order to his table, George only nods. Apparently the lecture is over. He eats his sandwich, drinks a single cup of coffee, pays, and slips out without another word.

Lucie goes into the kitchen with the used plate and mug. "So?"

Ray is chopping vegetables. He doesn't look up. "What did he tell you?"

"All about his girlfriend's long hair clogging his drains."

"Ha! Did he make an impression?"

"Sure did. He called me 'honey' for a start."

Ray chuckles. "I'll admit he lays it on a bit thick, the hillbilly act.

But he's smart as a whip, if whips are, in fact, smart. George lives off the grid. He's got a good fresh water spring on his property, and a woodlot. He's rigged up an outdoor solar-powered shower, he's got a wood-fired hot tub, a composting toilet, and he heats his cabin with wood and solar panels. And I can tell you, his place is about the coziest spot this side of Honolulu in winter. Just in case you think he's some kind of backwoods crazy dude, he's actually smarter and more environmentally informed than most anybody you'll ever meet. Plus he's got at least two engineering degrees and an MBA."

" That's nice. And what was I supposed to learn from that encounter?"

Ray puts the knife down and turns to look at her. "You have got one big chip on your shoulder, don't you?"

She smiles slightly, she's ready to spar with him. "Oh, I see where this is headed. A life lesson for Lucie. Show me how other people can live on next to nothing so I quit feeling sorry for myself about losing my fancy Vancouver condo and job and friends."

"That pretty much sums it up."

"But the thing is, I'm not sorry about all that."

He gives her raised eyebrows and a teasing smile.

"Seriously. Do you think I'm moping around, wishing I could be back in Vancouver? Do you think I'm just slumming here until I get enough cash to take off again? Because that's not true. I'm perfectly happy here."

He fixes her with a direct and rather icy glare that belies the boyishness of his round, freckled face. "People around here are pretty good judges of character, mostly because there's not a lot to do here except analyze the hell out of each other, so they get lots of practice. Small-town life at its finest. Anyway, I'm just trying to help. Thought you might like to meet one of the local characters. Broaden your horizons a bit." He's almost laughing.

"Don't do me any favours."

"OK then I won't invite you to the dance next Saturday."

" Pardon me? Aren't we supposed to be open for dinner on Saturdays?

If you're dancing, who's cooking?"

"Nobody will be here. Everyone who's anyone will be at the dance. We won't be open that day. I just need to remember to put signs up saying there's no service, in case people from the city show up on the fly and wonder what's going on. Which reminds me, can you put a notice on our website?"

"Isn't there some rule about dating staff?"

"It's not a date, it's a dance. And you don't work for me. You work *with* me."

"I'm not clear on the distinction."

As they face each other, Lucie becomes aware that her breathing is fast and shallow, as if she's been running.

"So?" he prompts.

"I hate dancing. By that, I mean I'm a terrible dancer and I know it. So, thanks but no, I don't want to go to a dance."

"You've never been to a square dance, have you? They call out the steps. They tell you what to do. There's nothing to it. Follow along. Easy. Don't drink too much."

"Square dance. God help me, I'm going to a square dance."

"I'll consider that a yes," he says, picking up his knife. "Take the day off, I'll pick you up at five. No need to dress up, jeans are the fashion statement around here."

It's well past nine in the morning, and Lucie is still in bed, having decided sleep was preferable to a riding lesson. Pearly light filters through the curtains of the single high window in her room. She's listening to the radio, stretching her arms and legs, back and shoulders, luxuriating in the deep, soft mattress and the warmth of the light blanket. Her loose agreement with Keith — if she arrives in the arena before eight, she gets a riding lesson — is void for today.

There's a tap tap tap on her door and Amanda's voice. "Lucie? Are you OK?"

"Yes," Lucie calls. "I've got the day off."

"Coffee?"

"Sure. Meet you on the deck." Lucie pulls on a sweatshirt and pads upstairs barefoot. She pushes open the screen door to the west-facing deck, at this hour still cool and shaded. Amanda arrives with coffee and biscotti. "Wow, Amanda — upscale cookies. You treat me too well, you know."

Amanda grins. "Keith hates these things, doesn't see the point of them, says they're too dry and just make sludge when you dip them in your coffee. And he's right, but he's never been to an Italian café. You look like a woman of the world, so I figured you'd appreciate an international treat."

"Ha, woman of the world, as if. I've never been to Italy. But I have dipped a biscotti or two, and yeah they do make sludge in your cup. Yummy though. Thanks."

"I'm surprised. I had you pegged as a world traveller."

"Not so much. I was born and raised in Ontario, then moved to Vancouver to escape my mother. And now I'm on a trans-mountain adventure. Ontario, B.C., Alberta. That's it for my travels — though I did go to New York once. You?"

"I'm from B.C., raised on a ranch near Williams Lake. Know where that is?"

Lucie shakes her head.

"Never mind. It's in the interior, a long way from anywhere. I thought I wanted to live in the city, so after high school I moved to Vancouver for university. Yikes, what a mistake. I hated it. So many people, so much noise. So much rain! But I met a couple of girls who wanted to travel, so we did the classic thing — backpack across Europe. Predictable, eh? But fun, and great to see so many places, hear different languages. When I came back — broke, of course — I'd had enough of seeing the world. Travel opened my eyes to the life I had in Williams Lake, what I loved about it. So I went straight home to the ranch and jumped back into that life with both feet. I met Keith at a dance. We got married and wanted to buy land, but we couldn't find anything around Williams Lake so we came out here and found this place. Took every dime we had, plus his folks and mine put up cash to help us. Which we've paid back, I'm happy to say. And here we are, living the dream."

"Really? You sound a bit cynical. I mean, no return trips to Italy, for a start."

Amanda laughs out loud. "I am dead serious. I *love* this life. *We* love this life, we *are* living our dream. Look where we live. Mountains and fresh air and horses and enough work and good friends. What else could I want? Sure, the occasional trip to Paris or Florence would be nice, but I'm not complaining."

"You never go anywhere?"

"Hawaii or Mexico. Winters are fierce here, you need a dose of sun. I'd like to try Cuba sometime."

Their conversation pauses. As ever with Amanda, the silence is easy. The morning is cheerful, the air is warm. They drink coffee and watch as horses make their way across the pasture below, grazing and flicking their tails.

"How are your riding lessons going?" Amanda asks.

"Fun. Fine. Every morning I learn something new. Keith is so patient. I'm such a city girl, but he never criticizes, he just stays calm and corrects when I'm doing something stupid, which is often, but he does it in a way that I don't *feel* stupid, you know? I'm sure you do know. Mostly we've been working in the arena, but he's taken me on a couple of rides through the field. Oh, that is so great, I had no idea. Riding a horse is like a one-hour vacation because you can't think about anything else; you have to concentrate on exactly what you're doing. It chases all your problems away. When you're in the saddle, you're in the moment."

"I know. I grew up riding horses, and it's still one of my favourite things to do. I think that's why ranch people are generally pretty calm. They live in the moment a lot. No yoga required, *ha*. I guess riding a horse is a kind of meditation." Another companionable pause, until Amanda asks, "So what's up with the day off today?"

Lucie grimaces. "The café is closed, and I'm going to the dance tonight with Ray, very much against my better judgment. But there you have it: the price of a Saturday sleep-in morning is a date with the boss."

"Wow, that's rare. In all the time I've known Ray — not long, he's only been in town maybe three years? — he almost never comes to a local event. I guess he's not very social, though he's friendly at the café and everyone knows him. But this dance is a big deal; it's the annual fundraiser for the volunteer fire department."

"I didn't know that, he didn't say. Just told me the entire town will be there, so I guess that includes me. Are you and Keith going?"

"Yeah, of course. Everyone goes because everyone depends on the volunteer firefighters, so we ante up the money they need. Besides, it's a good time, and you see people you never get to see, because usually everyone is tied to their land all summer haying, tending cows, mending fences, whatever. So for you, it's probably a good window on our world and some of our crazy characters."

"I met George the backwoods wonder recently."

"He'll be there. And he's a terrific dancer. Just sayin'."

"Of course he is, he's apparently brilliant at everything. Plus he has seven degrees and lives in a house without running water. Why do I feel like I'm getting set up?"

"One thing you need to know." Amanda sits up and places her cup on the deck. "Set up or not, you have to arrive at and leave the dance with the same person, period. Or you'll be a major topic of conversation until next Christmas. Besides, you don't need to worry about George, he's been living with the same woman for years."

"Got it," Lucie says, standing and stretching her arms above her head. "Not that there's much chance of me making local history. Besides, I guess I'm pretty wary of men in general right now. So what can you tell me about Ray? I work with him but he's a stranger to me. We never talk at the café because we don't have time."

"Not much. He keeps to himself, which is not unusual around here. He seems like a stable guy though, he's well thought of around town, he's really turned the restaurant around since he got here. And he tolerates Tom, the owner, pretty well."

"The guy who won the poker game? I've never met him."

"Ah, the poker game. Yes, that is a local legend and it's true. You might not have officially met Tom, but I bet you've seen him. Kinda beefy guy, very quiet. Dirty hat he never takes off. Big angry scowl. Tom glares at the world."

"That describes a bunch of guys, but I think I know who you mean. He's in the restaurant two or three times a week, and sometimes he ties up a big table when I've got people waiting, which bugs the crap out of me. You'd think as the owner he would know better."

"Oh, no, not Tom. He's a cowboy, he knows diddlysquat about the restaurant biz, which is good for Ray, who pretty much runs the café the way he wants. But Tom is as stubborn and insensitive as they come. He is a brick wall. He is the exact opposite of Keith — and maybe I'm biased, but I'm just sayin'. Tom was the original strong-silent-type cowboy until it all went sideways for him during the BSE. It has always amazed me that he has such a sweet loving wife — and you've probably never seen her in the café or anywhere, she's very shy. They definitely will not be at the dance. Tom won't show up because he's too proud about what he's lost, and Marta won't come because... well, just because."

"BSE, what's that? What has he lost?"

"You don't know about BSE?" Amanda seems a bit incredulous, but Lucie simply shrugs.

"Ah well, that's a long story for some other time," Amanda says, standing. "I've got chores to do. We have a table booked at the dance, but I think there's still room for you and Ray, unless he has other ideas." And with a pointed wink, Amanda takes up the coffee pot and cups and goes indoors, leaving Lucie to watch the grazing horses.

Lucie spends the day relaxing, a rare treat. She visits horses in the pasture, offering chunks of carrot to their soft probing lips. She walks along the fence in brilliant sunshine, swatting flies and inhaling the sweet, dusty, pungent tickle of ripening hay. She takes a long bath and even has time for a brief afternoon nap before Ray arrives. Obeying his guidance, she wears jeans and a plain black shirt, the closest thing to 'Western' in her wardrobe. Before Ray arrives, Lucie joins Amanda in the kitchen. She tries not to show her anxiety but can't stop herself from pacing restlessly. Amanda doesn't comment.

Ray knocks at the back door and is already stepping inside as Amanda calls, "Hello." They stand in the kitchen chatting until Ray says, "OK, Luce, let's get there and grab a good table."

Ray drives a battered Toyota of indeterminate age and colour — blue, sort of, decorated with blooms of rust. Lucie settles into the uncomfortably low and hard passenger seat. She considers commenting that even her own poor excuse for a car has better seats, but she's distracted by the clean scent of his freshly laundered shirt and something minty, maybe toothpaste or shampoo. No cologne, no aftershave, no artificial scent. His hair is fluffy, a halo of reddish curls.

I'm such a sucker for red-blond hair. So cheerful. And freckles, who doesn't love freckles?

They barrel south down the highway to the community hall in the next town. Lucie gazes out the grimy window, watching fields, fences, and houses hurtling by. She laughs aloud as they zoom past a long fence where every post is decorated with a ball cap. "Do all those hats belong to one guy?" she asks.

"Nope. It's all kinda donated. He started it, nailing his old hats to the posts, then people caught on, and they've been hammering their hats onto the fence posts for years. You'd be amazed about the competition. When a hat blows off, right away there are six guys ready to put theirs on the post. I've heard of people actually arguing about who got there first."

"Jeez. Small town life, eh? So," she turns toward Ray, "you seem to know a lot about people here, for a guy who hasn't been around all that long."

"I do my best," he says, glancing away from the road to give her a big happy grin. "You're right, I'm a newcomer, which around here seems to mean anyone whose great-grandparents weren't born here. And maybe I do know a bit, for a newcomer. The restaurant is great for that; I learn things by listening. Even though I spend most of my time in the kitchen, I try to get out front and talk to people. You do that too, Lucie, you connect with people. I've seen you talking to the Mounties and the 'ladies who lunch' as I call them, you know who I mean. And I'm sure you've met Tom, our owner."

"Actually, I haven't met him officially, but I think I've seen him. Never takes off that awful hat of his, looks like a cowboy but he's kinda not a cowboy. All the other cowboys are skinny and strong, and he looks like he hasn't been on a horse for years."

"That's Tom all right." Ray pulls into the parking lot, his small car lost amid the giant pickup trucks already lined up outside the community hall.

"So what's his story?" she asks, slamming the car door.

"Tell you later." They walk side-by-side toward the hall. The air is sweet with grass and sage. He opens the door and steps back so she can enter the bright, noisy, crowded room.

Ah, the dance.

The dance is like nothing Lucie has ever seen. It is utterly unlike the slick, glamorous dinners and parties of her city life. Those were about fashion, about gossip, about image. Though Lucie was a willing participant in the many social gatherings that decorated her previous life, she always harboured anxiety and suspicion, worrying about what people thought of her pale skin and odd appearance, wondering what women said about her when they made their trips to the restroom or outside for a smoke. And she was constantly on edge about whatever unpredictable thing her lover *du jour* might say or do, wondering what apology she might have to make the next day on his behalf. In truth, it had been terrible. Exhausting.

But this, the firefighter's ball, is a different cat altogether.

Nobody is wearing only black, nobody has lacquered fingernails or skin-tight leather pants or three-inch heels. Instead, as Ray told her, virtually all the men and half the women wear jeans, mostly frayed and faded. Striped and plaid shirts are everywhere, cowboy hats and boots. Some of the women are a bit dressier. Lucie spots a number of long full skirts and several very nice jackets, embroidered, fringed, or decorated with sequins.

Ray leads her to a table of eight. The circle of unfamiliar faces overwhelms Lucie for a while. Throughout the day she'd fretted about what she could possibly have in common with ranchers and small-town residents, what she would find to talk about. But tonight they put her at ease, asking about how she came to be in Sweetgrass, about her work at the café, one woman even queries her about good restaurants in Vancouver. Lucie in turn asks about family, about horses. They mention weather, and it's not just small talk. Laughing and trading jokes, her apprehension disappears.

Besides, several people at the table are familiar to her after all. One of the Mounties who regularly stop by the café is seated next to Ray. He introduces himself as "Sergeant Charles Donovan, proud member of the Royal Canadian Mounted Police. But tonight I'm off duty, so you can call me Donny, which everybody does anyway, whether I'm wearing my stripes or not." Another is the redoubtable Bob MacDonnell, mechanic and mayor. He greets her with a nod and asks, "How's that little beauty of yours running, Missy?"

Not for the first time she wonders whether he's being sarcastic about her car, but she only nods and says, "Good, Bob, thanks to you and Jake."

Seated next to him is a tall, white-haired woman with square shoulders and warm hazel eyes, graceful as long grass. "Agnes," the woman says, leaning across the table to offer a solid handshake.

Although Lucie is an outsider in Sweetgrass — and if Ray's observation is correct, it takes generations to become truly part of the community — these acquaintances welcome her, joke with her, even dance with her. Tomorrow they might come to the café and only nod a passing hello, but tonight they are open and ready for a good time, their cares and animosities parked elsewhere.

Lucie lets herself be drawn into the energy of it. The dinner is simple: sliced beef on a bun, baked beans, tubs of salad that's largely shredded iceberg lettuce, purple cabbage, carrot and cucumber slices. The buffet table also sports huge plastic bottles of ketchup, mustard, and several kinds of gloppy salad dressing, all of which people squirt onto their food with abandon. There are plates of brownies and cookies for dessert, plus tall pots of terrible, bitter coffee. The cash bar is doing a brisk business.

Where has this food come from, who has prepared it? Who is staffing the bar? She has no idea and doesn't ask, but simply loads her paper plate and eats the meal. Goes back for seconds.

Everyone is relaxed, enjoying the food, the music, the excuse for a night of good plain fun, nothing serious about it. Lucie makes her way through a beer or two, then notices a rancher across the table pouring shots of whisky into Styrofoam cups from a bottle concealed in a paper bag, placed beneath his chair when not in play. "Rye," he says, catching her eye and raising the bottle toward her. "Want some?"

"Sure, thanks," she replies without hesitation, despite never having tasted rye whisky before.

"Alberta's finest," he says, pouring a generous tot and passing it to her across the table.

She swirls and sniffs the clear, rich, gold liquid, getting a nose full of smoky caramel. Takes a goodly swallow. "Sweeter than Scotch," she comments. "And a bit spicy."

He nods approval. "Breakfast of champions," he says, and winks at her, to which she grins and raises her cup and takes another sip.

The rye is also dangerously smooth. Initially she dislikes its sweetness, but when she notices the paper bag making a round of the table — while Donny is out on the dance floor — she pours herself another share. Ray meanwhile, who's nursed a single beer through dinner, has switched to water, which he pours from a clear plastic pitcher he's brought to the table. Others use the pitcher too, for watering their rye.

Lucie leans over to Ray and asks, "Are these guys all cowboys? None of them look like what I thought they would."

"And what does a cowboy look like?" Delivered without any sarcasm or judgment, just a curious question.

She shrugs. "I dunno... Tall, skinny. But it's not so much the physical appearance as attitude. I expected swagger. Cocky, you know?"

"Yeah, I do know. And some of them are like that. They can look like rock stars, with scruffy beards and shades. But they are still the real deal. If you can't ride, rope, or hold up your end when it comes to cowboy work, you get dismissed pretty fast. But then there are the old guys. See that fella over there, glasses and red plaid shirt? Looks like an accountant, yes? He's one of the toughest yet most gentle guys you'll find on the range. He doesn't have a university degree — though lots of ranchers do, these days — but he's got a lifetime of experience and he shares it. He mentors young guys. Everyone around here asks his opinion about all kinds of ranch stuff. His name is Allen Rogers, he's a pillar of the community in more ways than one."

"Yeah, he does look like an accountant. Glasses and paunch and all."

"Don't be fooled by appearances. Every person here, women and men, they are tough and smart and have a lot to say and share. And they all sit horses like they were born to it, which mostly they are. Lucie, do not judge people around here until you know them. There's more beneath what you see on the surface. Always."

Lucie and Ray dance a few times. Contrary to his assertion, there is no square dancing. The not-so-practiced country band — the Hay City Rollers — are as relaxed as the crowd. They make mistakes, occasionally they halt mid-song, regroup and start again. Nobody's fussed. On the tiny dance floor, Ray leads adeptly, turning and twirling her, and Lucie follows as best she can. She's never been one to dance in public, thinking it both too suggestive and too silly. Ray doesn't seem to mind. After each dance he says with a sincere smile, "Thanks, that was fun."

Between dances they re-join the others at the table. When the talk turns to cattle management, Lucie absently gazes around the room and fixes on a vaguely familiar man at another table. At first she thinks it's Tom, the restaurant owner. She's about to nudge Ray and tell him their boss has attended after all. But no, it's not Tom.

Agnes leans over. "Know who that is?"

Lucie replies softly, "I feel like I should know him, but I don't."

"That's Ian Tyson."

Ian Tyson. Ian Tyson. I know that name. "The singer?"

"Yes. He lives just down the road from here. Raises cutting horses."

"But he's famous! Shouldn't he live in Hollywood or New York or Nashville? Or even Toronto?"

"Well, I guess he still tours quite a bit," Agnes says. "But he lives here. He's one of us."

Lucie suddenly remembers why she faintly recollected the name Sweetgrass on the day she drove into town: she's heard it for years, if only on the ragged edge of awareness, as the home of Ian Tyson, fabled Canadian folk and cowboy singer. Now memory and knowledge click together in her mind like jigsaw pieces. It's almost a physical sensation, this connection-making.

The dance is over before she knows, before she's ready. And now, here are Lucie and Ray driving home, car windows down to admit grass-scented night air that cools and refreshes them after the stuffy hall. They both smell of beer and sweat, and Lucie's head swims from several helpings of rye.

"I saw Ian Tyson at the dance," she ventures, speaking loudly over the rush of wind from the open windows.

"He comes to all the local events — dances, suppers, whatever. Supports all the local causes. Turns up at The Sow's Ear sometimes."

"Like I said, you know a lot about this place."

He just chuckles. "I'm not really a local, though. It takes years to be accepted here. Or it takes some significant event, like if you rescue someone from a burning barn or something. Besides, I don't get out much. Most days after work I'm too beat to do anything but go home and sleep."

They hurtle northward. Lucie is increasingly apprehensive. The car spears through the dark, headlights fanning the highway ahead. Insects blaze in the light and thunk against the windshield. Smack smack smack.

What does Ray want from her?

For that matter, what does she want from Ray?

I need this job, I have to work with you. What if you want more from me than I can give? That would really make a mess of this perfectly comfortable situation. Don't mess this up, buddy.

Ray turns off the main road, and drives through silent Sweetgrass with its streetlights casting cones of dust-filtered light onto empty streets. He picks up speed again as they leave the town westbound, headed to the ranch. She fidgets, lacing her fingers, unlacing, and then she quietly picks and worries a ragged fingernail.

Ray pulls his sad little car into the circular drive at Amanda's house. He does not turn off the engine, to Lucie's relief. He does not get out of the car. He only leans over quickly, unexpectedly, and kisses her cheek. "Thanks, I hope you had fun," he says. "See you tomorrow. Business as usual."

She giggles nervously. "I might be nursing a hangover, just so you know. I don't get two days off in a row?"

"Nope."

And that's it. He sits as upright as possible given the terrible condition of the car's seats, both hands on the wheel, looking straight ahead, clearly eager to get home to sleep. She creaks her door open and with some difficulty heaves herself out of the low seat and slams the door. He pulls the car away, slowly, without a wave of his hand or blink of his lights.

She's almost disappointed. *Lucie you idiot. Rye whisky is not your friend. Neither is Ray.*

—)///(—

Sunday. The café is quiet as a library. Ray theorizes that everyone's hung over, but Lucie suspects the day's steady rain has more to do with the dearth of customers. Then, late in the dripping, dreary afternoon, the door swings open to admit the black-hatted cowboy whom Lucie believes to be Tom, the owner. He walks hunched forward as if he's headed into a fierce wind, eyes cast down, occasionally flicking his gaze up in an angry, don't-mess-with-me way that reminds Lucie of her mother.

With Ray in the kitchen prepping for the evening meal, Lucie says hello to Tom, bids him to take a seat wherever he wants, and asks whether he'd like a cup of coffee.

"Yep," is all he says. He stomps across the room to the farthest table by the window, heedlessly tracking mud and rainwater as he goes. Lucie half considers retrieving the mop and handing it to him, but decides on a different tactic. Placing a mug on Tom's table, she says as she pours the coffee, "I think you're the owner here, right? You're Tom? My name's Lucie."

"I know that," he replies gruffly.

"You do? How's that? I don't think we've met."

"We haven't."

She fills his mug but doesn't leave the table; she waits instead to see whether he'll continue speaking.

I can push as hard as you, cowboy. Don't mess with me.

He takes a long, slow, full drink of hot coffee and stares pointedly out the window, ignoring her. Finally he says, "Ray told me about you. That you wound up here by accident, and now you're a server." He neither smiles nor looks at her.

"Yes, all true," she says pleasantly, turning away. Over her shoulder she adds, "Want anything to eat?"

"Pie."

"Coming up." She doesn't go to the kitchen pass-through window but walks into the kitchen itself through the swinging door, letting it rock noisily to convey her presence to busy Ray. "Yikes, he is a piece of work," she comments, making no effort to keep her voice down.

Ray looks up. "Who's that?"

"Boss man came in for coffee and pie."

"He comes by his attitude honestly, you know. Don't judge him. The past few years have been tough for him and Marta. There's half a peach pie left, check the fridge."

"You should let me in on his story, don't you think?" she says, adding, "and you should let me do the baking, instead of buying pies from the market."

"Should I? Why is that?"

"Because I can," she replies, placing an extra-large slice of pie onto a plate. "Do you think he'd like ice cream with this?"

"Not if he didn't ask for it. Don't do him any favours. He won't thank you, he'll just think you're wasting stuff on him that customers would pay for."

"Got it. Clearly everyone in town but me knows his story, and cuts him some slack because of it. Too much slack, in my opinion."

"Calm down, I'll tell ya later."

Tom says not another word, makes no acknowledgment when Lucie places the plate and fork on his table, and offers no nod of thanks as she refills his cup. He has removed neither his hat nor his battered sheepskin jacket, its shoulders damp and dark from the rain. He eats the pie in wolfish bites, but he doesn't really seem to enjoy the flaky crust and sweet filling, he just chews and swallows and drinks his coffee, eyes locked on the window. The street outside is buzzing with traffic swishing through town, splashing up dirty water. The room remains empty.

Come on, buddy, would a smile or thank you be too much to ask?

He bangs his empty cup on the tabletop, a hollow and forlorn sound. It seems a customary movement, as though he punctuates the end of every meal in such a way. He stands and adjusts his hat — or was that a curt touch of his fingers to the brim as some stingy appreciation for the food and service? — then stomps loudly across the floor, flings open the door, and steps out into the wet.

When Lucie turns, Ray is standing by the bar watching this silent play with a sardonic smile. "Come back to the kitchen and keep me company while I get dinner going, and I'll fill you in. Lock the door. It's pouring, nobody's going to show up this afternoon."

The kitchen is humid and pungent with browning onion and garlic and meat. It's a comfortable smell, homey.

"I'm not kidding about baking," she says, leaning against a counter. "My mother was a professional baker. I learned from her. Like you learned from your grandmother. I learned bread, buns, pastry, pies. Cakes, even wedding cakes."

"Not on the menu," he points out.

"So? Let me try, we could become as famous for pastry and bread as for lamb shanks and marrow." Once again she doesn't notice her use of the word 'we'.

"Are you that good?"

"I'm out of practice, but yeah, I think so. Let me try."

He says nothing.

She continues, "OK what about this: do you ever cater? Or maybe I could put a sign in the window for made-to-order wedding or birthday cakes."

"You could. But Tom would want a percentage. You'd be using his kitchen and supplies, so he'd be entitled to a piece of the action."

"So is he broke or what?"

Ray doesn't look at her but she notices a shift in his shoulders. A tightening. "Do you drive around the countryside much?" he asks as he heats olive oil to grassy fragrance and starts searing the large pork chops piled beside the stove.

"Um, no, not really. Back and forth between here and the ranch. I haven't even made a trip to Calgary since I've been here. Too many ways to spend money there."

"So you haven't noticed how empty the fields are."

"And what would be my reference? How would I know an empty field? They all look empty to me. I'm from Vancouver, remember? Does this have something to do with Tom?"

"Ever hear of the BSE crisis?"

She expresses her exasperation with raised hands and a credible growl.

"This used to be cattle country," he says. He pauses, considering. Continues, "OK, so most of this happened before I got here. I didn't live through it, and I don't have first-hand experience, but I know farmers here and elsewhere so I understand how terrible BSE was, how destructive. So — here's the local story as I know it. This part of the world is famous for cattle ranching and cowboys — the real deal, people who understand the life, how to raise good beef, how to take care of their cows and land and water, how the work moves with the seasons. They are born to it, a tradition more than 100 years old, 200 maybe. Branding, round-ups, tough winters, country dances, everything. Before BSE, it was a good living and this was a prosperous town. Every field had a herd of Herefords or Black Angus or Charolais. But then came BSE. You probably know it as mad cow disease."

"Heard of it. But I'm not much of a beef eater, at least not 'til I came here. And until recently, I lived a long way from the nearest farm."

"Fair enough, but it was all over the national news, for months."

"I don't really listen to the news, either."

He glances at her with disdain, she thinks, but he makes no comment. He continues recounting the devastation that resulted from the discovery of a terrible brain-wasting disease in a few individual cows that were widely dispersed across Alberta. Not an epidemic by any standard. Nonetheless, overnight a previously profitable and well-regarded product — Canadian beef — was barred from export to virtually everywhere.

"Even though the meat from that handful of infected cows never made it to any butcher shop or supermarket or even a tin of dog food, suddenly every place in the world put a ban on Canadian beef. So imagine," Ray says, "having a hundred or more cows and calves ready to sell but suddenly the market disappears and nobody is buying. Winter is coming. You've got bills to pay and, as you've always done, you counted on a big paycheque in the fall when you sold your cattle. But there's no pay coming and you've got all these extra animals to feed that you hadn't planned on. You've got to buy more hay. But you've also got to put gas in the truck and food on the table. Pay the vet. Pay the mortgage. Buy schoolbooks and clothes for the kids. You're broke and there's no help coming. And you're not alone. Every beef producer in Canada has exactly the same problem. The price of beef tanks overnight and the only market is local. And even though Albertans eat a lot of beef, it's a tiny market compared with the rest of the world."

"But why all that fuss over a few sick cows, what's the big deal?"

"Fear. It's possible that BSE could be transferred from cows to humans through contaminated beef. I forget the name of the human disease. It's rare and I think the actual connection between contaminated food and people getting the disease is not proven, or maybe the chances of actually getting the disease are beyond miniscule. Anyway, it was all about perception. The diseased meat never got near a market, science proved all the beef was safe, but none of that mattered. Countries didn't want the risk no matter how small, so they stopped importing Canadian beef in any form. Frozen, packaged, on the hoof, didn't matter. Nada. Zero. No sale."

"So what happened around here?"

"Everything. From guys turning their herds onto public grazing land and not bothering to round them up again, to guys selling what they could — at a loss — to guys shooting cattle because they couldn't feed them and they couldn't sell them. Leaving carcasses in the fields, wolves and coyotes had a bonanza. But it didn't affect everyone. Some people managed to keep their herds and weathered it out because they had off-ranch income. For the most part, those are the herds you see today in the fields, few and far between. Every field used to be thick with cattle. Now, the fields are empty."

"That's terrible."

"It got worse. The international ban on Canadian beef lasted for years. A lot of people went broke, lost their homes and land. That's what happened to Tom and Marta."

"Ouch... "

"Ouch, no kidding, ouch." Ray has forgotten his work; he's facing Lucie and waving the knife as he talks. "Think about this, Luce. You've told me a bit about what you went through when you lost your job and your condo — you say your friends weren't there for you. It was like that here, only it touched almost everyone. It was huge, like people had the plague or something, or so I've heard. It was an avalanche of hardship and money trouble. Tsunami. People would pass each other on the street, but nobody could look their friends in the eye. Even among the people who were suffering, there was no solidarity — too much pride. Some people still had income; lots of guys work in the oil patch or drive logging trucks or whatever to keep the ranch going, and lots of ranch wives have town jobs, like Amanda at the hotel. They couldn't talk to their neighbours, their friends who were going broke. And then the land sales started. That, I'm told, was terrible."

Lucie nods for him to continue, wraps her arms around herself. Chilled.

"Families around here who held land for a century or more were forced to sell, and there was so much land on the market it was going cheap. But not cheap enough. Kids who always thought they would inherit their parents' ranches and continue the cowboy life and tradition suddenly had to *buy* the land from their parents, and they couldn't afford it. So a lot of land was sold to developers who had visions of rural condos or estate developments or, God help us, golf courses. Lucky for this community, not many of those developments have actually been approved because there's not enough water around here to support them, so proposals are hung up in water rights and development appeals. But it's coming. The landscape has already changed, and it's going to change more. The fields are empty because the companies that own the land — well, they just own the land. Nobody lives there, nobody is managing the pastures. No cows, no cowboys."

"And what happened to Tom?"

"He has his own spin on what happened. His official story, which you might hear around town, is that he was bucked off a horse or maybe kicked, depends on who you talk to. Basically his line is that some big accident ended his ranching career, and he had to sell and move into town due to a sudden disability. And it's true he does have a limp, though I think it's arthritis. But that story is his pride talking. In fact, he was part of that whole BSE storm." Ray puts down the knife and wiggles his fingers in the air, pantomiming rain. "Tom's family was on that land for three generations, and he lost it to the bank — he was mortgaged to the hilt because he'd built a new house and barn and bought equipment for haying — a swather and baler and such. The bank foreclosed. He and Marta had to auction their farm equipment, their horses, their house. He lost everything, including himself. He used to be a cowboy, and he knew how to do that. He thought it would be his entire life and suddenly, through no fault of his, it was all gone. He was a proud and independent guy to begin with, and now he's bitter, too. And who could blame him?"

Lucie shifts from one foot to the other, wishing she had a glass of Scotch to help soak up this sad tale.

"Then one night in the back room at the hotel, with a bunch of big drinkers and oil guys, high-stakes land developers, he plays a few hands of poker. And who knows what he might have bet, his house maybe? But he wins ownership of the restaurant. Fair and square — after the game, the old owner and Tom drew up the transfer of ownership, no questions asked, no 'gimme a break it was only a card game.' And here he is: our owner. This place is his only income now. I'm trying to do my best for him. I'm doing OK; we get a lot of traffic from around here and the city. But it bugs me when he comes in on a rainy day like today, looks around, and the place is empty. You can bet that tomorrow I'll get a phone call. Plus he drinks too much." Ray turns back to the pan of meat he's searing. Says, "You know, I don't think we'll be serving anyone tonight. It's terrible weather outside. Nobody will be coming out here from the city. No reservations in the book, right?"

"I'll check," she says softly, heading out to the bar, "but I think you're right, no reservations tonight."

"We'll close up then." Ray wraps the half-prepared meat, stacks it in the fridge, and packs up the kitchen, while Lucie wipes tables and readies the café for tomorrow. She turns off the lights, shuts off the coffee maker, and dumps the dregs. She's shrugging into her jacket, ready to head back to her room at Amanda's, when Ray comes up behind her and places a warm hand on her shoulder. "Let's have a burger at the hotel."

"OK," she says wearily. "I'm not going to be the best company though. I'm tired, and yes, I am hung over. And just so ya know, that story has pretty much eaten up any fun that might have been left in this day."

"Yeah, it's a sad story. And you're right, Tom is a piece of work. But he lets me run this place the way I want. Next to Gran, he's pretty much the only person in my life who's ever believed in me, even if it's for his own reasons. He needs this place to pay for itself. Maybe he has no choice because I make money for him, but I like to think it's because he sees some talent, some initiative in me. Something."

She glances over her shoulder to catch Ray's eye, but he has released his light touch on her; she only sees his retreating back. "Grab your car, see you at the hotel," he says.

It's cold, the rain is pelting. Two people huddle warily between the hotel's Dumpster and the building's back wall, taking minimal shelter from the streaming downpour.

Rain soaks his jacket, his hoodie, his hair, and trickles down his back. Still he waits, shoulders hunched. Through the open window above he hears the shouts and clatter of the hotel's harried kitchen staff, the smell of deep frying, and occasional puffs of steam. The window's glass is opaque with moisture and grease.

Another hooded figure approaches. Stops in the shadows.

"Gimme that." Jason's hand reaches, index and middle fingers splayed to receive a glowing and very sizeable joint. The newcomer's hand stretches from the shadow and places the fat spliff between Jason's grasping fingers. Eagerly, swiftly, Jason draws a long, sweet toke into his starving lungs. He holds holds holds, and exhales with exquisite slowness, blue smoke filtering up toward the open window.

"Careful," says the seller. His breath makes ghosts in the frigid air.

"Relax," mutters Jason. His hand shakes as he takes another hit, the cherry end of the joint glowing. He hears the roar of trucks on the nearby road as they brake for the four-way stop, lurch around the corner, gear up, and roll on.

"What else do ya got besides weed?"

"That depends on your cash situation."

Jason's laugh swiftly escalates to choking guffaws until he can't breathe. He leans hard against the iron-cold side of the garbage bin, slides down until his butt collides with the pavement. "You crack me up. Cash situation. I don't get paid 'til Friday. I don't got a *cash* situation."

"Gimme that back."

The joint changes hands. Jason fails to notice that the seller does not take a hit. "I got maybe some crack. Maybe some fun pills. How much cash on ya, Jason?"

The whisper of a nylon sleeve rubbing against his jacket as Jason's hand dives into a grimy pocket. He fingers a tight, too-small wad of bills. "Maybe fifty bucks."

Now the seller snorts. "That all?"

"I don't get paid 'til Friday."

"Then you got a long dry spell in front of you."

"Yeah, I guess. What ya got?"

"Fun pills."

"Ecstasy?" The word comes out slurred, "eksussee."

"Oxy. Two hits, fifty bucks."

"Yer kiddin' me..." A deep breath. "Gimme that back." The joint changes hands. Jason tokes, holds — not so long this time — exhales quickly, noisily. "OK."

"Let's see the cash."

Jason fumbles in his pocket, produces a twenty dollar bill, a ten, another twenty.

"You got more in that pocket."

"Gotta put gas in my truck."

"How responsible."

The seller snatches the cash and his fisted hand extends into the pool of light, palm down, fingers curled around his hidden prize. Jason drops the joint into a puddle where it fizzes briefly, extends his cupped hands just as the seller opens his fingers to let two pills drop. One falls into Jason's palm but the other bounces away. The seller pockets the cash, strides away quickly.

"*Fuck you,*" Jason hisses as he kneels, cold-numbed fingers feeling the pavement, scrabbling for the pill before it dissolves in a puddle of rain.

"Quiet, ya fuckin zitface," says Jason's companion, who's been silent throughout the transaction.

The hotel bar is bright but devoid of customers. Lucie and Ray order beers and burgers. Lucie grins and greets the servers she knows from her stint as a hotel resident, although being seen with Ray makes her nervous.

Last thing I need is gossip. I wish Amanda was on shift tonight; she'd keep the rumour mill in check. Assuming there is a local rumour mill.

Lucie avoids commenting on Ray's earlier remark about nobody believing in him except his grandmother and Tom. Not that she's incurious about Ray's story, but she's wary. He might misinterpret any further questions about his past, get the impression she's interested in him, interested in more than a job. It would be so easy for her to ask a few questions, make eye contact and flash her famous smile, maybe untie her hair and fluff it over her shoulders. But for once, Lucie holds back.

The last thing I want. The last thing I need. I'm in Sweetgrass to straighten out my life, not tie it into more knots. He's cute and funny and a good cook. But he's exactly the wrong choice right now. Exactly, precisely, entirely wrong.

Instead they talk about the café, about staffing and menu choices. She again suggests she could bake for the restaurant. "I'll start small, put a little sign in the window advertising special-order birthday or wedding cakes. And I'll practice baking some different breads and maybe cookies. I want to make sure I can turn out consistent product. I'll practice at Amanda's for now. I can bake, but I'm rusty."

"OK, but I can't pay you any more," he says.

"Fine. I get that, and now I understand why. It's about convincing Tom that this is another revenue stream."

"Yep... but listen to yourself, City Girl. If you ever say the words 'revenue stream' to him, he will walk out on you faster than you can say 'do you want fries with that?' Let me handle Tom. You can do whatever you want — make cakes or bread or anything. And yeah, practice at Amanda's to start. Just tell me what you need, and I'll buy the supplies. And I'll talk to Tom."

"OK, got it. Say ten per cent for Tom?"

"More. Twenty-five. Remember his situation. He needs the money more than you."

They finish, pay, and push out into the wet and chilly night to stand on the sidewalk facing each other. It's cold. When they speak, their breath puffs clouds into the night.

Jeez, it's August, right? Not November? Now people will whine about how cold it is.

But she only says, "Thanks for telling me about Tom. All of it, the official and unofficial. I feel like I'm at least a tiny part of the grapevine now."

Ray says nothing. Leans forward quickly, kisses her lips, and turns away. She doesn't have time to respond, she doesn't kiss him back, not even a small pucker. "See ya," he calls without looking back at her.

What the hell was that? What just happened?

She stands, rooted. Confused. Elated. Disappointed. Not a coherent thought in her head as she watches him walk up the sidewalk. Then she turns away too, in case he looks back at her with those sky-blue eyes and that open freckled face of his. She rounds the corner and walks toward the ever-faithful Agememnon, stuffing her damp, chilly hands into her pockets and shrugging deeper into her jacket.

Ahead she sees a dark shape. Or two? Yes, two people seem to be prowling the cars parked along the street, including hers. "Hey!" she shouts.

One of the hooded shapes —clearly a young man in bulky dark clothing, with hood pulled forward to conceal his face — turns toward her. At first he approaches, one hand in a pocket, the other slightly raised, but his companion spits in a low voice, "No, Jason! Gotta go." Both the dark shapes turn and move away from her, heavy-footed, splashing through pooled rainwater, and lumbering as if they're drunk.

"Hey!" she shouts again. She knows better than to chase them on foot — big city life has taught her that much street savvy. They duck away, perhaps up the alley, she's not sure. She reaches her car and finds no damage, nothing amiss. She quickly unlocks the door, slides inside, and locks the door again. Starts the car with no problem. Turns on the headlights, and before she even considers the implications, she wheels into the alley where she thinks the two hooded boys have gone. But the car's white beams reveal nothing except driving rain. She guns her car down the gravel alleyway, spraying water and stones, emerging into the next street. She sees no movement. She waits, watches, and then turns toward the ranch and home.

I guess there's trouble everywhere. Whether you see it or not. Small town, big city.

It's September. How did that happen? Lucie has spent two full months in Sweetgrass. Summer came and vanished like a thunderstorm that gathered, poured, and whirled away.

"Tempest fugit, that's what I remember from high school Shakespeare. Or maybe something else, I dunno. And would that be 'fuj-it' or 'fug-it?' Or something else entirely?" Ray has said this more than once over the summer, meaning, 'Whoa, that storm is moving really fast.' She's coming to anticipate his jokes and word play. He's funny and more clever than she expected. Like the unexpected words she hears all the time from Keith, she's continually surprised by sophisticated vocabulary from Ray.

Her work has settled into something approaching routine. Some mornings she dashes to the arena for a riding lesson, other days she enjoys coffee on the back deck with cats, early light, scenery, and sometimes Amanda for company. Some mornings, she experiments in Amanda's kitchen with bread, pastry, cake, cookies, or whatever comes to mind.

On the café's lunch-only weekdays, once Ray closes up at mid-afternoon, she usually goes back to the ranch and tries to spend time browsing the Internet for interesting recipes. But the big wide landscape distracts her, calls her to come outside to play, so she walks around the ranch's paddocks and pastures, hearing birds and the wind rattling leaves, and taking deep breaths of cool, pure air. She pauses and takes time to look carefully, observing the slowly ripening autumn grass changing from green to champagne, the subtle colour shift of leaves from full, rich green to olive, and then slowly shading to yellow. The atmosphere is so clear, it's like a fine pencil line has been drawn around every object. That sharpness is a dramatic shift from the summer's blurry haze, yet it's a shift that has come about so slowly she's only just noticed.

Stop and smell the roses, how often have I heard that? I've never understood what it meant until now. It literally means stop walking, look around, hold your breath to listen, then breathe deep and slow. When have I ever done such a thing before? Only I'm not smelling roses, I'm smelling horses and grass and trees and maybe winter coming up. Ach, Lucie. Such a wild imagination, just like Ma used to say. She was right. Only she used to say 'you have a wild imagination' like someone would say 'you have a contagious disease.' Like it was terrible. Like nobody could possibly want a wild imagination.

Over the summer, Lucie's face has lost its pallor, replaced by a rosy pinkness. She sleeps well in the muffled quiet of her basement room, and she rises early and buzzes with energy. Her smile is quick and honest, and she laughs often. The knots in her back and shoulders have eased.

She's barely spared a thought for Vancouver. So distant. It's all so far away in time, in spirit. Even if she did want to call someone other than Judith, it would be hard to explain where she is now, what she's doing. Her story seems bigger than 'I'm working in a restaurant and renting a room in a ranch house,' yet if she stops to think about it — which she doesn't — that simple sentence is in fact the sum total of Lucie's current situation. But there's an undercurrent to her life in Sweetgrass — the people, land, air, light, and horses. Baking. She is living in the moment, looking back not at all, looking forward only occasionally. How would she explain this to Gwen, Patrick? Even Judith? Anyone?

Lucie is beginning to think she might spend the winter here. But that's months away, no need to make a decision now. It's only September.

Besides, there are the horses.

What a revelation.

Unlike her childhood friends who read *Black Beauty* and *My Friend Flicka*, Lucie, the thoroughly urban kid, was never enamoured with horses. Her friends' fantasies harboured what Lucie considered weird dreams about some crazy, inaccessible country life and the unlikely companionship of a noble horse. "Come on," Lucie reasoned, "we live in Toronto!" So how could any of those dreams find a footing? She was never bitten by the equine bug. Until now.

At first a glorious diversion, riding has become an obsession. She loves her morning lessons — which, depending on Keith's mood and schedule, can be anything from fifteen minutes on how to tack a horse to well over an hour of detailed instruction. Occasionally they ride across a pasture or along a fenceline. In between, she is taking every opportunity to practice with one of the two horses Keith has been using for her lessons. She is brave enough to saddle up and ride around the arena on her own, concentrating on balance, hand position, using her knees and subtle shifts of weight to cue the horse. Riding has become a release, a recreation like no other. She's hooked.

In fact, in the immediate moment she is consumed with riding because she's decided to undertake a new adventure.

In the lazy warmth of this early September afternoon, Lucie stands beside Quincy, the small dappled-grey mare. The mare flicks her ears and tail calmly. Lucie, however, is anything but calm. Although Keith has been patiently teaching her the essentials of tacking and basic riding skills, this is the first time Lucie has decided to saddle up for a solo ride outdoors. Her shaky confidence has already leaked away like ink from a faulty pen. Keith challenged her last night over dinner, saying, "It's about time for you to fly solo. Try it. You'll like it." He clearly meant for her to ride through one of the ranch's pastures, but not being one to back down from a dare, she has another plan entirely.

Throughout her sessions with Keith, his main advice has been simple and consistent. "Just keep the horse between you and the ground. Everything else is detail."

Ha, cowboy humour.

Lucie checks the cinch for the tenth time, takes a ragged breath, puts her left foot in the stirrup, and lifts herself into the saddle — now an easy and accustomed movement. The mare takes a step to steady the weight on her back, then stands quietly while Lucie settles herself and surveys the open pasture from her vantage point. Lucie takes up the reins as Keith has shown her. She balances, putting weight equally on her feet and seat. The saddle creaks, and the mare's ears flick back attentively as Lucie readies, then moves the reins forward while squeezing the mare's sides with her knees. "Walk on," Lucie says softly.

Quincy steps forward.

OK. Good start.

They walk across the meadow, headed toward the far fence where there's a gate and a path that leads uphill. It's steep and Lucie leans forward, bearing weight on her feet, and lifting out of the saddle as the horse powers up the slope. With each stride Lucie matches her weight to the horse's rhythm. She relaxes and forgets to be nervous. Gaining the ridge top, she guides Quincy along the wide path. Lucie is now sufficiently tranquil to glance over her left shoulder, to the mountains rising smoky-blue, purple, and grey against the incredibly clear cobalt sky. Not a cloud in sight.

"The mountains seem so close here," Lucie had commented to Amanda one evening after dinner.

"The Rockies have quite a strong eastward slant," Amanda answered, complete with hand motion indicating how the mountain range angles in a northwest-to-southeast orientation. As Lucie has come to expect, Amanda spoke with no hint of lecturing, simply happy to share her love and knowledge without condescending. She continued, "When you're in Calgary, the mountains seem a long way off, and that's actually true — it takes an hour to drive west from the city until you're surrounded by mountains. But from here? Twenty minutes and boom, you're there."

Lucie and Quincy continue over the ridge crest to the east side, where a narrow, enclosed valley shelters a ranch that has a half-mile racetrack. Keith and Lucie rode here once, it's where Lucie learned to sit a trot after much embarrassing bounce and thrash and a sore butt the next day. Today, she's headed to that track again, but she envisions more than a trot. She wants to take a tale of triumph back to Keith tonight, an answer to his 'fly solo' challenge.

Today she means to gallop for the first time. How hard can it be? She's learned that riding is about balance and being in rhythm with the horse. She's cantered around the arena at the ranch. She's got that experience: the rhythm, the muscle memory. Gallop around the track? No problem. What could go wrong?

The path leads down from the ridge through a grove of poplars that swish noisily in the breeze. As horse and rider descend the slope, faithful to Keith's teaching, Lucie leans back in the saddle to help the horse balance and bear her weight.

Reaching the bottom, she moves Quincy along to the barn where she finds one of the ranch hands.

"Hi," Lucie says, trying to recall the man's name.

"Hi there. Fine day."

"Extra fine! This is my first solo ride without Keith, and I'm having a blast."

"She's a good little mare, that one."

Right. It's all about the horse. "So I'm going up to the track, OK?"

"Sure," he says. "Nobody's training there right now. Take your time."

"Thanks. See ya."

The track is a short ride away and within sight of the barn and paddocks. If she falls, people will know right away. If they spot a riderless horse, they'll come looking for her. No need to be anxious.

As Lucie approaches the track entrance, Quincy begins to hop and dance unexpectedly. This didn't happen last time. Lucie has no idea how to calm the mare, how to make her walk placidly onto the smooth sandy track as she did previously in Keith's company. Lucie's plan was to trot around the track once, then move Quincy into a canter, a slow rocking gait, gradually gaining speed.

They enter the track, and without warning the horse explodes into a full gallop. The mare lunges forward and begins to stride, stroking ahead in a rapid waltzing rhythm, one-two-three, one-two-three. The horse's front legs grab the ground while her hindquarters push push push, driving forward.

Lucie has not one instant to think through Keith's lessons. She doesn't stop the mare's run by pulling on the reins or sitting her weight back in the saddle. She doesn't even have time to scream. She only catches the saddle horn in her left hand and tries not to bang bang bang onto the saddle with each forward thrust the horse takes. After a number of strides Lucie regains some presence of mind and stands slightly in the stirrups, then starts to move her own weight in concert with the horse. By the end of the first straight section, Lucie is, if not comfortable, at least keeping her balance, her black hair streaming and tossing like the mare's own silver-grey mane. They round the top turn and head into the back straightaway. The mare's head is down, and she drives with purpose and energy, every stride a declaration of freedom and spirit. Lucie keeps pace, moving hips and back and arms to stay centered. One-two-three, one-two-three.

She lets go of the saddle horn, her anchor. Now it's about balance and working with the striding horse. Now it's about flying.

The mare keeps thrusting forward, a running machine, stride stride stride. Lucie balances, leaning over Quincy's neck. The second corner approaches. She feels the mare tiring under her, pace slowing. As they enter the second turn, Lucie takes up the reins and sits back in the saddle.

The mare slows to a canter, and then a bouncy trot that Lucie is not prepared for. She pulls the reins back again and Quincy slows to a walk, breathing heavily.

Lucie tips her head back and laughs outrageously. She comes to a halt, drops the reins and raises both arms to the sky, feeling the mare's sides heaving between her own shaking legs.

Ohmygod ohmygod ohmygod… How did I live through that?

Horse and rider make another circuit of the track at a walk. Their breathing slows. Quincy walks placidly, showing no sign that ten minutes ago she charged around the track at full speed. The feisty breeze cools them. There is no acknowledgment of any kind, from any quarter, that Lucie has just done something remarkable. There's only wind and sky and the horse moving beneath her.

Rounding the far turn, Lucie spots an odd clump atop one of the tall, whitewashed fence posts. As they approach, Lucie realizes it's an enormous bird. Dark head, white breast and underparts. Unmoving. The wind tickles up feathers from the bird's head and shoulders.

It's huge, nearly a metre from its clawed feet that grip the post to the top of its motionless head. It's clearly a bird of prey: curved talons and hooked beak. An unnerving, unwavering, pale-yellow gaze regards Lucie and Quincy as they approach, pass, move on.

"What is that, Quince? An eagle? What *is* that?"

Lucie rides back to the barn but nobody is there. So much for her theory that somebody would notice should anything go awry with her ride on the track. She turns Quincy up the hill, along the ridge, and down the west side. Arriving at the barn, she dismounts unsteadily, stows her saddle and gives Quincy a thorough brush-down before turning the mare into the pasture. "Thanks, girlfriend. What an adventure." Quincy walks away and rolls in the grass, as if ridding herself of the day's ride.

That night over dinner, Lucie tries to recount her experience. "So. I did it," she says to Keith.

"At last," he says laconically, raising an eyebrow slightly, making her blush.

"Um. I mean a solo ride."

He sits back from the table and smiles ever so slightly. "Good."

"Don't you want details?"

"Up to you."

She's instantly annoyed. Back in Vancouver, her friends would crave every detail of a new adventure tale and ask for more, but

Keith doesn't seem to care about his student's accomplishment.

"No, whatever. It went well. Just thought I'd let you know," she says curtly.

"OK good. So I can depend on you for the fall gather." A tiny uplift on his lips.

Is he teasing? Lucie can't tell. "Sure." *Whatever that is.*

Amanda says nothing until the two women are in the kitchen, cleaning up after dinner. Then she asks, "So — what exactly did you do today?"

Lucie gives her best defensive don't-mess-with-me shrug, something she's never done with Amanda. "Nothing."

Amanda stops washing and touches Lucie's arm with a soapy hand. "Listen, there's something you need to know about living here, and I don't even know if I can explain it." Amanda sweeps hair from her brow, leaving a trail of dishwater and suds across her forehead. "Around here, there's a certain way to tell people that you've done something you want them to notice. And it's less about telling them and more about showing them. Or maybe coming at it sideways. It's like... I get that you had a good ride today, your first solo ride and that's a big deal for you. But you can't *tell* anyone that. Because around here, a solo ride is something kids do when they're, I don't know, maybe six years old or less. It's a rite of passage, but not for someone your age. I understand that you're new here, and it's important to you. But... oh, I'm sorry. It *is* a big thing, learning to trust yourself as a rider. But around here nobody thinks it's remarkable. It's kinda like learning to ride a bike."

Lucie, dishtowel over her shoulder, looks at the floor. "It felt like flying," she says, "although it scared the crap out of me and I don't know when I might be brave enough to do it again."

"So tell me about it. And I'll tell him."

Lucie looks out the kitchen window. The sky is full of pink and peach light. She relates her adventure to Amanda, including Quincy's unexpected headlong gallop and sighting the enormous bird. "In my entire city girl life I've never done any such thing. I was freaked right out."

"Yeah, Quincy does that. She likes to run. You've got to watch her. I'm surprised Keith didn't mention it. And I don't suppose you were wearing a helmet?"

Sheepish, Lucie shakes her head. "I don't use one in the arena so it never occurred to me. Dumb, yeah?" Amanda nods. They return to washing dishes.

"Any ideas on what that bird might have been? I've seen bald eagles but this was different."

"Probably a red-tailed hawk. They are big. And that *is* something you could talk about: seeing a hawk up close, or a moose. Or bear. If that happens again, remember what you saw. Or if you spot some cow in distress in a pasture. Or a herd of elk on the ridge. It's never about you, Lucie. Just so you know."

"But — *it felt like flying*. And Keith is a good teacher so I thought he'd like to know that I paid attention to all that stuff he taught me, and I figured it out more or less."

"Oh my God, yeah. Being on a galloping horse is fantastic. And I can tell you every cowboy around here, including Keith, agrees with you: riding a free-running horse is one of life's great pleasures. But you will never hear anyone around here say that. Except maybe over a beer some time, if they really trust you. Meanwhile," Amanda grabs both Lucie's hands in her own warm, wet embrace, "I know, Lucie, I know. It's so great, and it's such a sense of 'I did it!' But be careful, horses are dangerous. Never lose your wariness. You need to have that edge. Watch them, always. Even a horse you trust can surprise you. Just like Quincy did today. It turned out OK, but that was actually a dangerous situation. You need to be watching and aware, always. And wear a helmet."

"Don't worry, I don't think I'll ever be sure about myself around horses. Anyway, what's a fall gather?"

Amanda laughs out loud. "It's the round up. Coming some time in October-ish. And you don't want any part of it, except maybe in the kitchen."

"Because?"

"Everyone gets together to round up cattle from the common grazing ranges where the cows have been all summer, and believe me those cows are wild. People who have cows on the public range need help to round up and separate them. It's a big deal and a lot of hard work, and you have to actually *help*, there's no watching or taking pictures or whatever. The gather is hard, tough, dirty, dangerous cowboy work.

"We used to host fall gather because we have lots of corrals here, but we don't do it any more; there are better places farther west, closer to the summer range. We don't use the grazing range, we've got enough land to graze our own cows. We're actually thinking we'll get out of the cow biz completely because there's more money in horses these days. But we still help out with fall gather because that's what you do. At least, Keith helps, with the round up and whatever other rodeo happens. I mostly don't want to know what he does. Me, I'm in the kitchen. Safer. Generally speaking you're unlikely to lose teeth or break bones in the kitchen."

"So what do I say to him? Was he actually asking me to help? It seemed like teasing, but I can't read him."

Amanda grins. "He was totally teasing and if you showed up at the gather ready to work in the saddle, he would say 'thanks but no thanks' and send you away, and there's no shame in that. Don't even mention it to him. He was having a laugh at your expense, and I will speak to him about that."

"Oh, please don't. I get that I'm a newcomer, but you don't need to protect me. It's not like I would show up at a rodeo ready to rope and ride. But — Keith knows that about me, right? I'm confused about my ride today and what he thinks I could possibly do."

"Forget it. He's teasing. You have to get used to cowboy humour. They will set you up to fail. You have to protect yourself from that. You have to prove yourself. It's their idea of fun."

"Set me up to fail, I can't believe you just said that. Like we're in some big corporation."

"We all have past lives," Amanda says.

TWO PARTS COOL, ONE PART STRANGE

Another crisp morning. Southern Alberta is wearing her party dress: poplar leaves are brilliant yellow, with cranberry and russet and flame-orange in the underbrush, the display continuing unusually late in the year according to Amanda.

Revolving seasons have never previously grabbed Lucie's attention to any great extent. In Vancouver, fall colours were pretty, lasted for a while, and then leaves fell and autumn rains arrived. The city turned soggy and grey, a condition that persisted throughout the winter — although even winter was punctuated with hardy bright flowers in planters and gardens, and occasional startlingly warm days. She barely recalls the brilliant fireworks of autumn in Ontario. The complete sweep of seasonal change—harvest, celebration, shorter days, the appearance of different stars — she's had no previous experience in closely observing any of those patterns. Instead, in her urban lives she's mainly responded to changing seasons through a shift from bright summer clothes to sombre winter shades: from cotton and silk to wool and fleece, sandals to shoes to boots. For Lucie, fall and winter were heralded by new footwear more than anything.

This fine autumn morning she is restless. She doesn't have time to catch and saddle a horse, and she doesn't feel like baking. She considers going to The Sow's Ear early, but she's already spending more time at the café than Ray can pay her for. She needs something else to do.

After coffee, she decides to walk along the river, which she's been meaning to do all summer. She fills a Thermos with tea, drives to one of the two local bridges, and laces up her hiking boots, giving a passing thanks to Judith and their long-ago Vancouver shopping trip for outdoor gear. She picks her way cautiously down through rocks, bush, and fallen timber to the gravel-scattered riverbank. It's low water now compared with the boisterous flow when she arrived in Sweetgrass. The river rattles cheerfully over stones in the shallows. The morning is calm and warm. Lucie chooses her way carefully, headed upstream.

She comes to a bend where the water is wide and oh so clear. She can see pebbles and stones under the surface, and thinks she spots the quick flash of small fish. She sits, knees up, arms folded around her legs, and back against a poplar trunk that's warm from the morning sun. She sips the fall-scented air, sharp like rosemary, pine, citrus, drops her cheek onto her knees. It's so quiet, only the sound of chuckling water. She dozes.

A crackle of twigs and crunching gravel snaps her awake, momentarily disoriented. She holds perfectly still, listening. Yes there are footsteps, someone is making their way down to the river, picking their path carefully. She stands, ready for she's not sure what.

A blue-clad figure emerges from the bush and pauses to look downstream, away from Lucie. A small person, not much taller than a child. Lucie relaxes but does not reveal herself. The person turns toward her. It's an older woman, silvery hair peeking from beneath a hooded jacket that's clearly too large for her. Her face is vaguely familiar.

She spots Lucie and waves. "Hello!"

"Hi," Lucie responds uncertainly.

The woman steps toward her. "I am looking for colour leafs," she says, speaking with a definite accent. "My granddaughter in the city says to me, 'Nana, I am doing school art and I need colour leafs. But not city leafs. I want leafs from wild trees.' So here I am, the good grandma, getting leafs from wild trees. I hope these wild trees don't eat me!" The woman smiles broadly, revealing crowded, crooked teeth.

'I hope deess vild treess don't eet me.' What is that accent? German maybe? Dutch?

Lucie smiles in return.

The hooded woman approaches, extending a hand in greeting. "I am Marta," she says. "I think you are from the café? My husband Tom is owner."

Yes that's why I know you.

Marta carries a plastic bag full of her bounty of colourful fall leaves. "I see you've been successful in trapping wild leaves," Lucie ventures.

"Ja, good hunting," Marta responds, grinning. In Lucie's experience, most adults would be self-conscious about wandering the woods plucking leaves, but Marta doesn't appear to be embarrassed in the least.

"Would you like some tea?" Lucie asks.

"Sure." Marta plunks herself onto a large rock. Lucie pours a cupful and passes it over. Marta pushes her hood back, revealing a thick mop of white hair, a round, open face that's surprisingly unlined, and deep brown eyes at once curious and guarded.

"You're right, I'm the new server at the café," Lucie says.

"And your name again?"

"Lucie. And how did you know me?"

Marta sips tea and does not offer the cup back, clearly intending to enjoy the entire serving. "Tom, he tells me about you. 'There is a new girl in the café,' he says. 'She is better than the others, she is smart and has energy. She has nice smile but very white skin, and black hair like wild pony,' he says. And I have been to café once when I see you there, so I think you are new girl."

'She iss better... I haff not seen you... I tink you are new...' Where are you from Marta? You're a newcomer too. I know you've been here for years. But maybe not long enough. Maybe you're still a stranger. Like me.

"That's nice of Tom to say those things," Lucie says. "He comes in often, but he never talks, just has a coffee and sometimes some pie. I guess he's watching the goings-on, and then he leaves. I'm surprised he's noticed so much about me."

"He is cowboy," Marta replies by way of explanation. She doesn't elaborate.

"Sorry, meaning?"

"Cowboys, they watch. They see everything. Not too much talk. Just watch. See."

"He must really miss the ranch," Lucie says thoughtlessly, instantly regretting her remark. But Marta only smiles, a warm, open smile. "Ja, he miss everything. His dogs, his horses, all those darn cows. Me, not so much. It was sad to lose our house, but I save some precious things, plus I bring our cats to town. So I am not so lonely as Tom. I already make a big move in my life, another move not so big heartbreak for me."

"You're from Europe somewhere?"

"Vienna."

"I've never been there. I hear it's beautiful."

"I don't know. It was beautiful when I left but so many years now, who knows?"

"You've never gone home?"

"This is home," Marta says, turning her gaze to the sparkling, noisy river. "My parents are gone now, my sister is... what is the word? Demented?"

"Dementia?"

"Ja. She is much older than me; we were not close. So when I leave home to see the world, I never expect to return. And I meet a cowboy, marry him, have my kids, make my home. This is home. Ranch, town. I only need a house and my cats, a place to knit and bake and keep warm in winter. Tom, he needs big fields and long days away from home. He needs sky. Horses. Ja, he miss it all."

They sit in silence for a moment, then Marta continues. "Ranch is good place to raise kids, lots for them to do, hard work keep them busy, horses to ride, cows to raise for 4-H Club, chickens and eggs. For me as wife, not so good sometimes. Hard, lonely. Always work, always cook or clean or look after kids. Hard to visit or get to town, I don't drive. I think when Tom said, 'Let's get married and move to the farm' — he says *farm* and I think about pretty little house with chickens and flowers. Well," she chuckles, "we sure did have chickens. Many chickens! Too many chickens. I make good money from eggs and then every fall we kill them, burn off the feathers, ach, what a smell. Sell frozen chickens to make more money. Sometimes that is all the money we have, egg and chicken money." She laughs softly. "Ja, I got my wish for chickens. I do not miss *them*," she says in a conspiratorial whisper, handing the empty cup back to Lucie. Big warm smile, but her eyes slide away.

"More tea?"

Marta shakes her head. "No, I must continue to hunt for wild leafs." She rises stiffly, straightens slowly to her full height, such as it is. She barely comes to Lucie's shoulder, and Lucie herself isn't tall.

So you would be what, five feet tall, if that? You are an elf.

Marta begins to walk away downstream but stops, and turns back to face Lucie. "Ach, where are my manners? Lucie, you are so welcome for coffee at my house, any time. Please come visit me. I don't get much company. I am home most times, except when leaf hunting."

"Sure, thank you."

"OK, see you." Marta turns abruptly and shuffles carefully across the loose gravel along the water, heading for a grove of bright-orange bushes. She plucks a handful of leaves, drops them into the bag, and then begins her ascent of the steep bank and is lost to view amid the willows and poplars.

Only when Lucie can no longer hear Marta's footsteps does she realize she has no clue where Marta and Tom live. Never mind, Ray will know. Or Amanda.

Lucie pours more tea, which is still hot and minty. Sipping, she thinks about Marta. Chickens, cows, kids. Hard work, isolation. Not the life Marta contemplated. But who *does* get the life of their dreams? Lucie herself certainly never imagined being a refugee from her urban life, waiting tables in a tiny ranch town, but here she is — and so far, it's not bad. Not her dream, but not bad.

But what *is* her dream now?

Ah, yes, the great change-your-life quest. Where am I going, who do I want to be? Maybe I've arrived. Watching the river run by, sunshine, nowhere to go. Life could be worse. Has been worse. Much worse.

Lucie feels comforted after her conversation with Marta. A new friend, another connection in this community that seems so open, yet is really only welcoming to a point. Increasingly she's learning this is a town that holds its cards close to the chest. Polite enough, but it keeps a poker face.

Guess that's how you win a restaurant.

Back at home later, Lucie showers and dresses quickly, ties back her massive mane of hair, and then drives into town. "I met Mrs. Tom this morning," she recounts to Ray.

"Marta, really? Where?"

"I was walking along the river and ran into her. I had a Thermos of tea so gave her some and we sat and chatted for a bit. She's nice."

"Yes, she's really sweet. And she's the local nature expert. She knows every bush and flower and bird by its first name, plus its mom, dad, siblings, and second cousins. The way some people know the roots of words or something. But she's so shy, I'm surprised she talked to you."

"She invited me to her house for coffee."

Ray fixes Lucie with an incredulous look. "Seriously?"

Lucie only gazes back calmly, shrugs, nods slowly. No big deal.

"Wow, that is something," he says, resuming his task. "I have never been invited to their house. I don't even know where they live."

Lucie laughs out loud. "Well that makes two of us. Never mind, I'll figure it out. She said to come by any time. So I will do that, soon as I figure out where I'm going."

"By the way, there's a phone message for you. Someone looking for a birthday cake and probably catering a dinner as well. You up for that?"

"Totally."

The order proves to be fairly easy: a decorated cake for a fiftieth birthday, plus a simple lunch of wraps, vegetables and dip, bowls of flavoured popcorn. "Not much imagination," Lucie grumbles.

"Hey, take it easy," Ray says. "Walk before you run."

"Yeah, yeah. You're right of course. And how much do we owe Tom for this extra-curricular activity?"

"Dunno, I haven't talked to him yet. Let's just do it, and I'll mention to him next time he's in. And you should make the cake at Amanda's instead of here. Just tell me what you need, and I'll buy it."

Next weekend, Lucie delivers the cake and lunch to a house in town. The customer, a downtrodden-looking woman, pays cash and hustles Lucie away quickly, it being a surprise party. "Don't want anyone to see you," says the woman. Lucie pockets the money and divides it once she's back at the café, a third for herself, a third for Ray — who prepared the lunch — and the remainder for Tom. When she hands him the small wad of bills, Ray slips the cash into his back pocket.

"Ray's back pocket bank. This might just be our little secret for a while," he says, and actually winks.

"You're the boss. I'm cool with not paying a commission to Tom if I don't have to. But I thought you were committed to helping him out of his hole?"

"Yep, plenty of time for that. It's a long-term plan."

Whatever — you do the books. Seems strange but it's none of my business, really.

That first success is the incentive she needs to start baking in earnest. Although it means cutting back on riding, her weekday mornings are now energized with bread, cakes, cookies, the best of which she takes to The Sow's Ear for sale, the rest she serves to Amanda and Keith at dinner. "You'll make me fat," Amanda complains with a grin.

Keith just smiles and digs in, often taking seconds — once, a third helping of brownies. Ray advises, "Don't put your cakes or cookies on the menu board, just tell people we have house-made desserts. But be careful if Tom's in." She doesn't ask about the arrangement, and the extra cash continues to go straight to her pocket and Ray's. Lucie feels a bit odd about the situation, but attributes Ray's management of the baking income and his reluctance to put baked goods on the menu to the fact that she still needs to prove she can produce consistent bread and pastries, day in and out. Plus, Ray doesn't know whether Lucie will be sticking around for the winter, so why would he promote her baking only to lose it when she leaves for new horizons?

Fair enough. I need to make a decision.

So she does. On the last day of September, she drives to a mall in the city and buys a winter coat, boots, sweaters, and other warm clothes. A fuzzy blue toque with a tassel. Mittens, an item of clothing she hasn't owned since she left Ontario.

"Thus begins my first real winter in years," she says to Agememnon as she drives home, noting a new bright touch of snow in the mountains visible over her right shoulder. "Yippee. Can't wait."

It's decidedly frosty this October morning, and decidedly dark at this early hour, as the days shorten and the season slides toward winter. There's now serious snow on the not-so-distant peaks. Many trees are bare of leaves already, but others are still flecked in brilliance, and when the sun shines, they are luminous. Fields once green have faded to soft yellow or ochre, roadside ditches offer dry grasses of caramel and gold, and brilliant flashes of lemon yellow, cranberry red, and butterscotch dun. It's like living in a candy jar.

Lucie is now in the habit of setting her alarm to rise at six o'clock — *six o'clock!* — dressing quickly and hurrying to the café to bake, having outgrown Amanda's kitchen. She's remembering the stretchy feel of firm dough under her hands, the bubble and tang of yeast, she's adjusting her recipes to account for bigger, restaurant-sized batches. She's experimenting with gluten-free recipes and seasonal ingredients. She's having a ball. Last night she even called her mother to check on some half-forgotten techniques.

"You're *where?*" her mother asked. "What happened to Vancouver?"

"Oh, Ma. It's such a long story. I just needed to leave the city for a while, and I guess I'll be here for the winter."

"It's going to be bloody cold you know. You don't know how cold. You're not used to it. You have no idea. Winter is awful there."

Yeah, thanks for that positive outlook. Never a good word from you. Never.

"I know, Ma. I bought myself a good winter coat. Boots, mitts. Even put a block heater in the car. Ma, I now know what a block heater is."

"And what about your condo? And your job? You can't work in a restaurant for the rest of your life. What are you *doing* Lucie?"

Oh, Ma. "It's a long story, I said. The condo is gone. So is my job. Never mind right now. Listen, Ma—I might be home for Christmas, so I can tell you the whole story."

Why did I just say that?

A longish pause. "Well I was thinking of going to Florida to see your aunt."

Whew, dodged that bullet. Lucie barely stops herself from emitting an audible sigh of relief.

"Oh. OK, yes, you should do that. Actually, I don't even know why I said that Ma. I'm making a decent wage and tips are good, but I probably can't afford a flight to Ontario for Christmas. Maybe later, in the spring or something. But Ma — I'm really getting back into baking, remember the way we used to bake on weekends when I was little?"

Another pause. Longer. "I'm thinking about moving to Florida."

It's all about you. No baking tips. No fond memories. Fine.

"Oh. Well that would be good for you, Ma. Warm all the time, right? Beach. No winters, great shopping, what a treat. We'll talk, OK? Soon. I need to go now. Love you, Ma."

Do I? Love her? Argh, so move to Florida already. A place I'll never, never go. Good. Goodbye. Good riddance. Oh I don't know.

This morning in her chilly bedroom, Lucie shrugs into a sweater, pulls on heavy socks, dashes up to the ranch house kitchen for a quick snack, and then bolts for her car. The air feels weighty on her shoulders. A half moon leans over the western horizon, and it's still dark enough to see stars overhead, though the eastern horizon is bright. A coyote sings in the distance as Lucie fires up her mighty car and drives the ten minutes into town. She unlocks the café's back door and steps inside, flicking on kitchen lights.

Hears the scrabbling of claws. Freezes. She's familiar with that sound. Occasionally, mice find their way into Amanda's basement — once, Lucie awoke at night to the feathery scratchy sound of a rodent right in her room. Amanda gave her an old-fashioned wooden spring trap, baited with peanut butter. The next night, just as Lucie was settling into sleep, she was jolted by the crack of the trap's killing blow, and the next morning she was faced with the disposal of a furry, beady-eyed corpse.

But this sound in the early-morning kitchen is bigger. That was no mouse. Lucie remains still and eventually she's rewarded by the sight of a nut-brown snout that cautiously advances from beneath the stove, then withdraws.

Ohmygod, what is that? She plucks her cell phone from her pocket and dials Ray. The phone rings rings rings.

Finally he answers. Surly. "This is Ray…"

"I'm at the café, and there is an *animal* in my kitchen."

A longish pause that reminds Lucie of the conversation with her mother. It occurs to her that he might be trying to figure out who's calling him.

"An animal."

"Yeah. Like, a rodent. Only bigger."

"A moose?"

"Ha ha, I said *rodent*."

"A beaver?"

"Ray I am *serious*, there is some kind of creepy animal thing...
Oh, there it goes! Ugh!"

"Since when is it *your* kitchen?"

"I'm in it right now and that makes it *my* kitchen, buddy. And
there's a rodent in here."

"OK, offer it a coffee. I'll be right there."

Lucie, treading carefully for fear the critter will nibble her toes
or dart up her leg, starts her baking routine. Indirect daylight
gradually suffuses the kitchen windows. Ray arrives in due course
but the creature, which he suspects to be a gopher or squirrel, does
not reappear. He teases her about making up a tale to get him out
of bed early. "You just wanted to see me," he says.

She rolls her eyes. "You wish."

"Yeah, I do."

She wheels around to confront that remark, but he's moved
away to open the freezer and pull out assorted items to thaw for
the evening meal service.

What the hell was that about?

They continue working with no further conversation. The offend-
ing animal remains hidden.

"So what are you going to do about it?" she finally asks.

"Well, I might offer to cook you dinner."

"What? I mean the *rodent*."

"Traps work."

"So you know it's Thanksgiving weekend coming up, right?"
Ray asks. "What you don't know is, I do a big dinner on Sunday,

two sittings at six and eight. A harvest dinner, it's a celebration. It means a lot of prep and work, but it's fun to see people enjoying themselves. Lots of kids. Then after the weekend, I change to winter hours. So we need to hit the farmer's market tomorrow morning to buy a bunch of stuff for the dinner."

"We? Who's minding the store if we're both out doing retail?"

"Nobody. We'll put a sign on the door, 'closed 'til dinner.' You could also put a note on the website please. We'll only serve dinner on Saturday and by rez only for the harvest dinner on Sunday. The market opens at eight on Saturday, but I like to get there early, so we'll have time to shop and get back here to get prepped and open for dinner. OK? You in?"

"Sure. So, um — winter hours?"

"We'll only be open four days a week. Lunch on Wednesday and Thursday, lunch plus dinner on Friday and Saturday. Closed Sunday, Monday, Tuesday. It's what the market dictates, as you city folks say. My first year here, I kept summer hours all year, but in winter the revenue didn't cover costs. Even Sunday brunch in winter, you'd think there would be a bit of business, but on some Sundays not one person came through the door. So I started a new winter schedule. Tom is not really on board, I had to convince him that it doesn't pay to stay open on the chance somebody might drop in. Being closed seems like a bad idea to him. Locals don't like it, or so he says."

"*I* don't like it. I'll get fewer hours."

"Yeah, I know, sorry. If you can't afford to stay, I'd be sorry to lose you, but I'd understand why you have to move on. However, I live in hope." He gives her a forlorn look, like a puppy that's done something it knows is wrong.

Hope, yeah I've been there. Hope for what? Do you want me to stay or leave?

"I'll think about it," she says in a flippant tone, then decides to give him the truth, waves her hands in the air. Surrenders. Takes a deep breath. *Why is it so hard for me to tell you this?*

"Actually Ray, I *have* thought about it. I've decided to spend the winter here. Even bought warm clothes and boots, mitts, scarf, the entire ensemble. Maybe I'll head back to Vancouver in the spring, I don't know. I don't have a plan at the moment. But for now, for winter at least, Sweetgrass is home."

Whatever he thinks of this news, she can't tell. He only nods and says, "Well here's a plan: I'll pick you up at six-thirty on Saturday morning, and we'll zip over to the market."

"Yep, that's a plan all right."

And here they are on a frosty morning, sun blushing the horizon but not in sight yet. They're buying seasonal treats from squash to apples, potatoes, kale, carrots and more. They are so early that most vendors are still setting up their booths, yet everyone is eager to pause, talk to Ray, show him their best produce despite the annoyance of interrupting their set-up to accommodate him.

For his part, Ray is a master of sincerity and appreciation. "Hiya, Bruce!" He shakes hands with a local garlic seller. "Sorry, you're in the middle of your set-up, but I need a bunch of good garlic for my season finale dinner tomorrow. And you know I won't use anyone else's garlic for my mashed spuds. People would notice. They'd *complain*." He gives Bruce his huge freckly grin.

The vendor smiles and hands over a bag full of plump garlic heads. "Thanks for your business Ray," is all he says. "Another great summer behind us. No pay this week, it's on the house."

And it's the same at every booth Ray and Lucie visit. People are trying to get their displays in order, but they seem happy to help Ray choose the best of this or that.

"How do you do it?" Lucie asks. "I mean, they are trying to get stuff ready for the day, and you just stroll in and screw things up for them, but you get what you want, sometimes *gratis*, and nobody seems pissed about it."

Ray stops walking to face her. "It's about respect," he replies.

"What is respectful about disrupting their routine?"

"Respect for their product," he says, turning again to stroll along the booths. "I come here every weekend, you know that. And they all know me. They know what I want and that I promote their products whenever I can. Through the menu or the website. Haven't you noticed? I tie a lot of our menu items to a specific grower or producer. I make a point to promote Gary's lamb and Felix's chicken and Caroline's cheese. And Bruce's garlic. I'm not kidding, people would actually notice and complain if the garlic was different."

She stops walking. He does likewise and faces her.

"I have noticed that you include a farm or producer's name on the board. But honestly, until this minute I never got the connection. I just thought it was about them paying you to promote them, that's what would happen in my Vancouver world. Everyone's looking for an angle."

He shrugs. "Collectively they are the reason we are a success. I might have good recipes and ideas, but you've got to start with good product. You have to look after your sources, Lucie."

"Yeah, I get that now."

"It's about buying where you live. It's about supporting people. Like Tom and Marta."

"Yeah. Got it."

He takes her elbow and turns her around. They continue walking up the alley of booths. He bends his arm, she slips her hand under his elbow. "Lead me on," she says cheerfully.

"OK..."

She doesn't catch the irony in his voice.

They meander slowly, arm-in-arm, absorbing the ever-warming morning air, the market activity, the displays of bright fruit, flowers, hand-crafted pottery, and knitwear. Fresh bread, pies, jars of jam, pickles, local dandelion or wildflower honey. He is barely taller than Lucie, but Ray guides her confidently with only a slight push or pull, leading her through the market as he led her at the firefighter's dance. Once again she feels included in his circle, the vendors and suppliers whom he knows.

Loaded with fresh produce including two giant pumpkins, they hustle back to the café and start preparing tonight's dinner and the next day's harvest feast. The phone rings all afternoon with people seeking reservations for this special celebration. Between taking phone and online reservations, Lucie helps Ray prep vegetables. She peels apples and makes piecrust. As the afternoon darkens toward evening, the restaurant fills with the sweet sticky scent of baking bread, the tang of homemade cranberry sauce bubbling quietly on a back burner, the bass notes of frying onions and pork as Ray readies stuffing for tomorrow's turkeys.

"How many turkeys are we doing?"

"Twelve."

"Jeez."

"And we'll sell out. In case you were hoping for turkey sandwiches the next day, forget it."

Fortunately, Saturday's dinner at the café is slow, only two tables. "I guess people are saving up for tomorrow," she observes.

"It's become a big deal, this harvest dinner, which makes me feel really good. Like I'm putting on a party for the town," he replies. "Most people around here can only afford a night out once in awhile. Yeah, they are saving up for an event."

"What time do you start roasting?"

"About ten."

"OK, I'll be here by eight. I've got bread started already, and I'll do more pies and cakes. Plus I can stuff turkeys with the best."

Overnight, clouds sneak over the town and softly drop a thin white layer of downy snow that sticks to trees and fields and roofs but not roads. When Lucie awakens she is chilled, the tile floor in her room is icy under her bare feet. She takes a hot shower, dresses, and hurries upstairs. Amanda has coffee on. "Fresh muffins in a couple of minutes," she says.

"Are you coming to dinner tonight?" Lucie asks.

"Yes. We're on the second shift."

Lucie gazes out the window as she gratefully sips hot coffee, cupping the mug to warm her hands. "I'm such a stranger to winter," she comments. "Everything looks so different with snow. Softer. Prettier, with the trees all decked out like a Christmas card. But not as welcoming, somehow. Colder, and I don't mean temperature."

"I know," Amanda replies, tucking a strand of hair behind her ear, a gesture Lucie has come to think of as meditative, something Amanda does when she's considering her words. " And this is nothing, this little sprinkle of snow — once the sun comes out it will all melt. But it's a taste of things to come. And I *do* mean temperature." She giggles a bit. " I guess I'm saying all this because I want to make sure *you're* sure about staying the winter."

" So far, but I guess I'll find out. Maybe by Christmas I'll be fed up and want to trade snowshoes for rain boots and move back to the coast. But I don't think so. I'm feeling OK about being here, I'm even looking forward to the cold — it'll be an adventure. Amazing for an alien who dropped in from some random planet, eh? But honestly, Amanda, I can't picture myself anyplace else right now. Unless of course you need to turf me out of your basement. If you and Keith want your house back, just say so."

"Nothing doing. You stay as long as you want. And keep up with the baking. Keith is missing it now that you're baking at the café instead of here."

"Ha, you only love me for my cookies. OK, gotta go. Ray's expecting help to stuff the birds and who-knows-what else to get ready for dinner."

"See you later."

To Lucie's surprise, she is first to arrive at the café's back door. Without Ray to direct her, she's at a loss about what to do, so she hauls out a bag of potatoes and starts peeling. Ray arrives a bit breathless and seems anxious. He makes sure the back door is locked and glances frequently out the window. He snaps on the ovens, yanks a turkey from the cooler and gets to work stuffing and trussing, but impatience gets the better of him and he actually curses softly.

"What's up with you?" Lucie asks.

"Nothing." A pause. "Everything." He sighs, and turns toward her, scowling. "It's a long story. I thought I'd left some trouble behind when I came here, but it might have followed me, thanks to my sister. Then again, it was my mistake in the first place, so I'm as pissed with myself as with her."

Ray has never volunteered much about himself and she hasn't asked. Always when they're working together they are fully occupied, not a moment for talk. Now she's uncertain how to respond, so merely offers a slice of her own life. "Yeah, I understand family trouble. I couldn't wait to leave home, I ran away from a terrible situation. It was just my mom and me, and that was one person too many."

He only shrugs and turns his attention back to the turkey. "What's that saying, 'you can pick your friends but you're stuck with your family.' Too true."

They labour on. They spend hours side-by-side, sliding past each other with trays of peelings or bowls piled high with readied vegetables. They do-si-do around each other, never touching. Their kitchen dance, although unrehearsed, is easy and natural. Not once do they collide or interrupt each other's flow of chopping, rinsing, stirring, ferrying, ovens open, ovens closed, sinks full, coolers and fridges open, fresh produce on the counter, dishwasher loaded and operating. She isn't thinking about where he is in the space, where she is, or how they need to balance and move. They just do.

But she's watching.

Throughout the afternoon, Lucie watches Ray as she never has before. Sometimes directly while he's focused on a particular task, head bent, knife in play. She watches how he holds the blade, how quickly he dispatches onions or garlic or carrots, how he often raises an ingredient to his nose, inhaling its scent and character, rubbing herbs to crush them lightly and release their scent. He continually tastes and tests, adjusting, nuancing.

Sometimes she watches peripherally, when they stand next to each other at the counter. She notices the powerful curve of his shoulders and back, the quick motion of hands, the soft curl of red-blond hair over his ears and forehead. That galaxy of freckles. Once he glances up and catches her gaze. The clarity of his sky-blue eyes surprises her again, just like the first day she stumbled into the café. His sudden smile actually makes her blush.

"What are *you* lookin' at?"

"You've got carrot peel in your hair," she lies, reaching to pick an imaginary shred from above his ear. His hair under her brief touch is soft yet springy.

She also notices that he continues to take furtive looks out the window to the back lot where their cars are parked. She assumes he's watching for the first wave of customers, but there's no time to ask.

The turkeys are roasting and the entire café fills with the rich, comforting home-smell of them, turkey and onion, pork, garlic and sage. Lucie readies her breads and pies — "Pop them in soon as the birds come out," Ray instructs — then she returns to peeling and boiling potatoes. Ray peels and roasts garlic, leaves a heaping bowlful of soft golden cloves ready by the stove for making garlic mashed potatoes. They both work on preparing Brussels sprouts, green beans, beets, yams. Amid the rhythm and ritual of cooking, Ray seems calmer, his motions more regular and rhythmic, though he doesn't speak except to ask Lucie for assistance. "Better get pots of coffee going," he says as the clock nears 5:30. "And let's get more white wine into the fridge. Some rosé too, if we have any. And can you get the menu on the blackboard, please? And did you carve the pumpkins?"

"Argh, no, forgot them. I'm on it right now." She grabs the two huge pumpkins, each one tall as her knees, and tries to think of an appropriate design for their jack o' lantern faces. She's done this before in Vancouver but always for parties, always the faces have been ghouls or perhaps a likeness of the party's host. Or both.

She's temporarily at a loss about how to create a cute yet cunning pumpkin face, until she thinks about Marta's open smile.

OK, let's see if I can do that.

Lucie grabs a marker from a drawer beneath the bar and scribbles on one of the pumpkin skins. She considers. Bad work. Too sinister. She continues drawing on the pumpkin skin, then hefts it in her arms and carries it into the kitchen. "Yo, boss!" she cries. "What do you think of our mascot?"

Ray flicks a look up from his work. "Good," he says, and goes back to cooking.

"Did you even look?"

He says in a brotherly tone, " Luce. I trust you to do certain things, and this is one of them. I'm entirely behind you as long as you haven't created some kind of Goth face. And I know you haven't done that because I know you get what this restaurant is about. Family, community, food. So just do it, I trust you. Go, Pumpkin Girl."

She nods, and to her surprise doesn't feel patronized as she would have done in the past. Instead, she feels like he's just hugged her. Smiling to herself, she starts hacking out innards and seeds, then she carefully sculpts the faces. They are happy faces, warm and welcoming. She sets the pumpkins on the steps outside, places candles inside, lights them.

No spooks here tonight.

In the café's restroom, Lucie changes into a fresh shirt and spritzes a bit of cologne on her wrists, unties her hair, fluffs and sweeps it back from her face, and re-ties the ribbon.

Ready. Set. Go.

Customers for the first sitting start to arrive. She greets people at the door, walks them to pre-arranged tables, and takes drink orders. She chats with those she knows. The room fills with talk and laughter, voices of kids, the odd baby cry. Lucie busily carries drinks and wine bottles to tables, popping corks and filling glasses, crunching bottles into waiting ice-filled buckets on rickety stands. The menu is simple — turkey — but people have a choice of side dishes. Turkey with garlic mashed potatoes and Brussels sprouts. Turkey with sweet potato fries, spinach, and kale. Turkey with salad and charred sweet peppers. Her orders are complicated and the kitchen is busy. Ray's helpers have arrived, and Lucie also has front-side help from Melissa, a sweet local high-school girl who's clueless about attentive table service but energetic and takes direction well. Never mind, she's putting plates where they should go. The café hums.

"Can I bring you more cranberry sauce?" Lucie asks. " Let me pour that wine for you. How about another bowl of spuds for the table?"

The room overflows with laughter and talk. It's loud with families, and Lucie makes a point of taking a jack o' lantern to each table with kids. "It's not Hallowe'en yet," yells one little boy, to which Lucie responds, "So do you have your costume idea? Maybe I should save this pumpkin for you?" The boy laughs, his parents laugh. The mom leans to Lucie and says, "No joke, they're great faces. Save one for me, I'll pick it up next week."

Gradually the first sitting leaves. Lucie and Melissa quickly clean tables, and the second sitting starts. An older crowd, no kids. For a moment, Ray stands by the bar watching, arms folded defensively across his chest. "This is the crowd we need to impress," he whispers to Lucie as she gets people settled. She nods, hurries on. He dives back into the kitchen.

Tables fill. Keith and Amanda arrive, joining Bob and Agnes. Other familiar faces gradually populate the room. Here is Donny, the Mountie, with a pert brunette woman Lucie vaguely recognizes, and here comes George, the backwoods wonder, accompanied by a tall woman with luscious, long, chestnut hair.

Tom and Marta appear at the door. "Hello!" Lucie says merrily. Marta gives her a big smile. Tom ignores her and scans the room.

How many seats. How much revenue. Like you're looking over a herd of cows. Buddy you need to relax for one night.

"Please follow me." Lucie strides into the room, leading them to their tiny, isolated table. Unlike the other couples she's guided to their tables, where the man has placed a guiding hand on his wife's back or shoulder, Tom strides ahead in Lucie's wake, leaving Marta to trail along. Tom and Marta specifically wanted the corner table where Lucie herself sat the first day she set foot in The Sow's Ear. Tom faces the room, his back to the window. Marta faces the corner with no view of anything except the wall, the dark window, and Tom.

We should hang local art on the walls, if for no other reason than to give Marta something to look at while dining with her charming husband.

Lucie takes drink orders around the room. This is a hard-core drinking crowd, full wine bottles at every table, and who knows, perhaps a concealed bottle of rye or two on the floor. The customers seem less jolly, more intent on drinking, less laughing and more talk. Lucie and Melissa take appetizer plates to each table, a bonus for the second sitting, the appetizer is seared scallops with a coulis of local sweet peppers. More wine. A few beer orders. Lucie notices that Marta drinks a glass of wine, only one throughout their dinner, while Tom orders beer upon beer, at least four. Tom shuns his scallop appetizer. Marta sneaks her fork across the abyss of their tiny table to snag a few extra morsels. Lucie clears their plates and cannot stop herself from fixing Tom with what she hopes is a stern look, and says — a statement, not a question — "You didn't like the scallops."

He gives her back a steady, no-nonsense gaze. "No ocean around here."

Lucie takes her time to look pointedly around the room, gathering evidence. "Looks to me like everyone else enjoyed it." Tom glares at her with a look that could cut sheet metal. She smiles amicably at him and removes their plates.

Lucie and Melissa serve dinner. Gradually, as plates hit tables, the volume of talk increases. People seem to be enjoying their food; they are smiling and laughing as the wine takes effect. Lucie opens more bottles, and the cheerful sound of popping corks seems to inspire other diners to order yet more wine. More beer. She clears dinner plates, serves dessert. Coffee. After-dinner special drinks that she mixes with care, having little experience in the realm of Spanish coffee or blueberry tea. "Whatever," Ray says in her ear as the kitchen orders slow, and he emerges for a few minutes by the bar. "Make it up. They don't really know what they're drinking. Just keep track of what you pour. And if Tom asks, we bought those pies at the market." Lucie frowns, then simply shrugs.

Ray dons clean whites and visits each table, thanking people for coming. He approaches Tom and Marta, but Tom curtly nods and waves him away.

On a side street, while Sow's Ear diners are revelling in their turkey and spuds and vegetables and company, another adventure is unfolding.

A shadow hisses, "Jason! This one."

Two stumbling figures in dark clothing, hoods pulled up and ball caps pulled low, open the door of an unlocked pickup truck and scrabble in the glove box, behind and under seats, looking for something, anything of value. They find nothing and run away as passing traffic approaches, leaving the truck's doors open.

Inside, Lucie says to a lingering guest, "Oh gosh, I'm sorry. I'll get you the right pie, you ordered apple not peach. Just give me a minute." The customers are patient but because of Lucie's mistake it takes them a few minutes longer to complete their meal. They order another round of drinks. Nobody is fussed.

Eventually people go home. They leave big tips: $50 and $100 bills are slipped under glasses and plates for Lucie to find. The room is quiet. Tom and Marta are still at their table. Lucie rushes over. "Oh my goodness, I am so sorry. It's been so busy, I have not been giving you good service."

"Not at all," Marta replies. "We have been happy to watch. You have been giving very good service to this whole place this whole night, and we are very pleased." Marta looks over to Tom for validation. He nods.

And how would you know, little elf? You're facing the wall.

Marta looks up to Lucie. "You have done good work here tonight. We are so happy. We hope you will stay. Winter is coming, yes? What will you do?"

Lucie stands away from the table so she can see both Marta and Tom at once. Announces, "I plan to stay in Sweetgrass for the winter."

She is rewarded by Marta's huge smile and a gesture that might indicate a hug, except that Marta is snugged against the table. "Good," Marta says. "That is very good."

'Goot. Fairy goot.' Thank you, little elf.

"And do not forget you should come for coffee to my house."

"I have not forgotten, but I don't know where you live."

Marta laughs and provides directions. Tom sits stone-faced, as if daring Lucie to actually darken his door. Marta and Tom stand to leave, Tom stalking across the floor ahead of his wife, not looking back at her. Certainly not holding the door for her. And no backward glance or thanks to Ray, Lucie, or any of the staff.

I'll consider that a personal challenge to visit your home. Don't you dare dismiss me, cowboy. Don't you dare ignore me. Your wife might not stand up to you, but I will.

At last at last the room has emptied. Everyone seems to have had

---

a great time. The food was terrific, and the service, if Lucie does say so herself, was pretty good overall. She clears tables, stacking dishes and toting tableware to load the dishwasher. She carts the two jack o' lanterns into the kitchen, uncertain what to do with them, but then she recalls that someone has asked to retrieve one, so she places them carefully on the counter. Ray glances over his shoulder. "Thanks, Pumpkin Girl. You did a great job tonight."

Back in the main room, someone comes through the door as Lucie is busy with the mop. She hardly looks up. "Sorry," she says, "we're done."

"I know," says the man standing at the door. "But would you call the police please? My truck was vandalized."

Lucie looks up immediately. Sees a heavyset man in blue jeans and a yellow shirt. Nobody she recognizes, so she suspects he's a city guy out for a good meal in the country. "Right away," she says. "Please take a seat."

Donny answers her call. "Hi Donny, this is Lucie at The Sow's Ear. I think we have a car break-in. Can you come over?"

"Sure."

The officer arrives in two minutes — the station is just up the street — and takes over, questioning the man, his wife and friends, all of whom have come back into the restaurant. Lucie continues to clear tables and helps Ray in the back while Donny talks to the crime victims, then goes outside with them to review the damage. Finally everyone leaves. Donny comes back inside and walks into the kitchen.

"What's the story?" Ray asks.

"Car prowling. But I think the owner left his truck unlocked, so it will be hard to press charges even if we ever catch someone. Kinda typical of city people, they come out here thinking it's safe and quiet. Mostly they're right, but not always. We have some druggie kids in town who are always looking for an easy break and enter or car prowl. Just because it's a small town doesn't mean we don't have problems."

Ray gently punches the Mountie's shoulder. "You guys are the best. Thanks for coming over."

"I doubt we'll ever catch them," Donny says. "I have a good idea who they are, mostly a couple of 'youth at risk' as we call them now. What chance do they have? They're on the wrong road. We try, but..."

"And too bad for those city people, kinda spoiled their evening and their impression of our fair town," Lucie adds.

"That too," says Donny as he leaves, firmly closing the door behind him.

Ray and Lucie continue clearing, cleaning, dumping coffee. Her lower back aches from long hours on her feet, and Ray actually groans as he bends to slide trays of leftovers into the cooler. "I'm beat," he says. "I love doing these dinners but man, they're a ton of work."

"Me, too," she replies, loading the dishwasher. "And you lied, you said there wouldn't be leftovers. What do you do with them?"

"Depends. I can re-purpose stuff that's never been out of the kitchen. But if it's been on a customer's plate, it's done, even if they didn't touch it. However," he looks up at her with a big grin, "I also lied about turkey sandwiches."

"Oh?"

"I now have several turkey carcasses in various stages of undress. I'll make soup stock from the bones but there's tons of meat scraps. Did you eat anything tonight?"

"I nibbled a bit. I'm good."

"But you haven't had a proper Thanksgiving meal. So it would be my pleasure to cook for you tomorrow night. Leftovers, just so you know." He accompanies his invitation with a low courtly bow that doesn't strike her as self-conscious in the least, only cheeky.

She regards him from across the kitchen and grins. "Oh, yeah. Turkey sandwiches. Turkey anything. I am so in."

"OK," he says. Grabs a napkin, writes his address, and hands it to her.

—⟩⟩⟨⟨—

Lucie squeezes Agememnon into a difficult parking spot on the street where Ray lives. For a small town, Sweetgrass seems to have a lot of vehicles, big ones at that. Her tiny car is a minnow in the company of whales.

It's not an especially prosperous-looking street. The trucks parked in front of virtually every house are not new and not clean. Yards are neat but small, likewise the houses. It's a cool evening, nobody is outside, nobody walking, no kids playing. A tired, puffy breeze pushes its way through a dense stand of tall spruce behind the row of houses. Clearly, this is the last street in town.

"Beyond here be dragons," she mutters as she walks up the sidewalk, checking house numbers.

This might just be the worst decision you've made since getting together with Brad. You ought to be smarter by now. But no, here you are going to Ray's for dinner. Then again, you are probably making too much of this. This guy has invited you for leftover turkey sandwiches. How romantic. A reward for your hard work and no Thanksgiving dinner.

"OK, relax," she tells herself as she finds the house she's looking for. Ray lives on the second floor; his door is around the side. She regards the house critically. It's tall and narrow, unlike the other squat bungalows lining the street. The house's windows, doors, and siding suggest it's a newer building than its neighbours, but the dry grass in the front yard is overgrown, and the house looks neglected. Instead of curtains, the lower-floor front windows sport bedsheets pegged up to keep the world at bay.

"This is not promising. Still, a turkey sandwich is a turkey sandwich." She walks around to the side door, nearly tripping on the uneven sidewalk blocks. To her surprise, the side door is painted a deep marine blue and the trim, a buttery yellow, is also fresh and bright. There's a clean doormat, and a sticker on the window that bids welcome in several languages. She presses the buzzer but hears nothing, and wonders whether it's broken. She's about to try again when the door swings open. There stands Ray in clean jeans and a plaid shirt, wiping his hands on a striped cloth.

"C'mon in, Pumpkin Girl," he says and stands back to let her enter. There's not much space inside, just a landing where several jackets hang neatly and his boots and shoes are lined against the wall. A steep staircase. He indicates that she should precede him up the stairs, which she does, arriving in the top-floor suite amid a delicious warm aroma that envelops her in welcome.

That is no turkey sandwich.

"Sorry, I should have taken your coat," he says, taking instead the bottle of wine she offers.

She says, "I'll keep my coat on for a few minutes, I'm cold. I was riding in Keith's arena this afternoon, and I haven't managed to warm up yet."

"Yep, it's that time of year. Shorter days, colder nights. Do you think you made the right decision to stick around here all winter?"

"Guess I'll find out."

There follows a stilted silence. She stands in the living room, coat on, arms dangling at her sides with nothing to do, as if having delivered the wine she might change her mind and leave. He stands between the living room and the kitchen. "So," she says decisively. "We're talking about the weather like we don't know each other and don't know what else to say." She sits in one of the green side chairs. It surrounds her like a protective hug.

Ray nods. "Yep, you're right. I'm not nervous, exactly. But I want you to like my dinner."

"All right, here's a safe topic," she says, and she unzips her coat and fixes him with a smile she hopes is sincerely warm yet distant, even discouraging. "I think we need to invite local artists to hang their stuff on our walls at the café. And I think we need to have a daily wine even if we actually only change it up once a week. We could call it 'Whine du jour', and see who gets the joke."

He raises his gaze and rewards her with a grin. "Whoa, ideas.

You are full of ideas, City Girl. Maybe let's have some wine *du jour* and talk about it." He pulls a bottle from the fridge, uncorks it, and pours two generous glasses of perfectly chilled white wine. "To fresh ideas."

They clink and drink, but Ray barely wets his lips while Lucie takes a good long draught. She nests into the green chair and swivels. After a moment she shoulders her coat off and folds it over the back of the chair. "Yum, what is this wine?" she asks.

He offers the bottle, and she reads the label while he steps into the galley kitchen to tend pots and pans on the stove. Lucie puts the bottle on the coffee table that separates a plush, deep-blue loveseat from the two wide bucket chairs of pea-green, one of which she occupies. "This dinner looks and smells like way more than left-over turkey sandwiches."

"You are correct," he says, stirring the contents of a saucepan, "but you'll have to wait to see what's on tonight's menu. It does involve turkey, but not sandwiches. Meanwhile," he lifts a couple of lids and adjusts burner temperatures, "let's just sit for a bit while it's cooking. How was your day, what did you do? Riding, you said?"

"I saddled a horse and rode around the arena because I'm too chicken to ride outside."

"And why is that?" Ray takes a seat opposite Lucie, reclining on the sofa. He spreads his arms like wings, or maybe fences, along the sofa's back.

"Because a while ago, I thought I was brave enough to do a solo ride, and I got a big surprise: my horse bolted. I loved it, but it really scared me. I guess I learned my limits."

He smiles and says affably, "Bullshit."

She sets her wineglass down with a sharp click on the table. "No, not bullshit. That ride scared the crap out of me. I'm not as brave as I think around horses. I need to be more aware. Smarter."

"With horses, maybe. I couldn't say, it's been years since I've been on a horse. But I think there's a parallel between learning to deal with horses and dealing with people. And from what I've seen, you've got the people side covered."

She picks up her glass again and drinks, saying nothing.

"So, to illustrate," he continues, "when the Mounties come in, you know they're in a hurry and you get them served and out the door in good time. But Donny says they never feel rushed, they just know you're looking after them. Ditto the lunch ladies, they say you pay attention to them when they want service but you leave them alone when they want to talk, and you never push them to finish up and leave. Even that guy whose vehicle was broken into last night phoned to say how much he appreciated your help. Plus there's George. He is opinionated and probably as difficult a person as you're likely to get at The Sow's Ear, but you made an impression."

She laughs. "As if. We hated each other on sight."

"Not so. You've earned some fans, and that's not easy in this town. But there's more." He takes a sip of wine. "Tom and Marta really like you."

She sets her glass down again. It's nearly empty — she's drinking way too fast. "That's good, I guess," she says with her best *who cares* shrug. "But, let me get this straight. The owner dude who knows nothing about the restaurant business, who's actually a jerk and treats his lovely wife like a piece of furniture, is happy that I..."

Ray holds up stop-sign hands. "Whoa. I don't want to get into a discussion about Tom, his ethics, or his values. He is who he is, and I can't change that. You can't either. And look, Tom and Marta have survived each other for, I dunno, forty years? Is it our place to criticize?"

She regards him for a moment and then shakes her head. "You're right. It's a lot like my mother's life. I've offered her ideas and options on how she could make things better, but nothing sticks, we only argue. I tell her she has choices, she tells me who she blames for her current predicament, whatever it is. Tom is kinda the same. He's a proud guy so he blames everyone except the person he sees in the mirror. He was a victim of circumstance like everyone else.

But still, he could be nicer to Marta, to everyone for that matter, including you and me. What good does it do to walk around with all that anger?"

Ray reaches to refill Lucie's empty glass. "I guess that's what I'm getting at. Tom could give lessons on being proud and stubborn. But I bet he's carrying a ton of guilt about losing his ranch, and you're right, he's pretty much wallowing in it. I think he doesn't move on because he doesn't want to or maybe he doesn't know how, so he just stays grumpy all the time. It's his excuse to drink too much. But it's not up to us to straighten him out."

"Was Tom different before he lost the ranch?"

"I can't say, that was before I got here. But you're changing the subject on me. What I want you to know is: people notice you, they come into the café, and I hear from them at the bank or wherever. They like you."

"Well, I'm happy to be an asset to the team."

"I'm trying to give you a compliment."

"I'm trying not to let it go to my head."

"Man, you are chippy, always the tough girl," but he's grinning at her. He stands and heads into the kitchen to check on dinner. "Anyway, you've made an impression," he says over his shoulder as he lifts lids, stirring, tasting. "And I, for one, am happy that you're sticking around for the winter." He turns off burners and produces warmed plates from the oven. "Find yourself a spot," he directs, as if the table will be crowded. "Dinner is upon us."

Lucie seats herself, feeling fuzzy-headed already. Ray brings a plate from the kitchen and sets it before her. "Turkey curry, and a bunch of other stuff." She inhales the exotic and remarkably rich, spicy scent.

He sits opposite her and somehow her wine glass is full again, this time with rosé. He offers his glass for a toast. "To leftovers."

"Cin cin."

They dig in to their meals and for a few moments neither speaks. Lucie rolls the flavours over her tongue, enjoying the chewiness of turkey and the sharp crunch of sweet peppers, celery, broccoli, the satisfying stickiness of rice. "So," she says finally, looking up at Ray. "You know a lot about people and the community here, but you never go out — you keep to yourself, you don't socialize except sometimes you have a coffee with someone in the café when it's not busy. But you don't, you know, *mix*. What's that about?"

He stops eating and takes a long, slow sip of wine, the most he's had all evening. Pensive, lips pressed together. Considering. Eyes lidded, not looking at her. "Maybe I'm shy," he says.

"Now it's my turn to call bullshit."

He laughs and sets his glass down, rotating the stem so the liquid whirls in the glass. "Two things. One, I'm not a very social person to begin with. Not shy, but I'm kind of a recluse. And two, the restaurant business is intense and relentless, as I've discovered, so when the café is closed I'm happy to be at home alone, decompress by myself. Kind of like therapy, I can breathe and relax. I'm not a trained chef. Everything I'm doing at Sow's Ear is based on what I learned from my grandma, plus what I pick up day-to-day. Trial by fire, you might say. So I spend a lot of time on the Internet, looking for interesting recipes I might be able to copy or adapt, or going through cookbooks from the library. And then I play around in my own kitchen. I experiment all the time with stuff I might be able to add to our menu."

She nods, drinking more wine. *Jeez, slow down, girl. You're drinking like you're nervous or something.* She says, "I've watched you in the kitchen. You smell things, taste, touch, clearly you're thinking about what's going into the meals you create. It's fun for you, yeah? Finding new ways to use ingredients or discovering techniques you didn't know. I like that about baking, too."

"I love cooking, it is so cool, it's tremendous fun to take what you know and build on it, add new ingredients, or find something unexpected. Or find a new cookbook, it's like a whole new roadmap. Cooking, Lucie... I guess it's like painting, like composing music. But," he says, carefully placing his glass on the table, "it also means spending a lot of time doing research and playing with recipes, with no audience. I don't have a social life and that suits me fine."

"Understood. But if you don't like going out, why did you take me to the firefighter's dance?"

Instead of answering, he stands and starts to clear the table, loads the dishwasher. "Dessert?"

"I'm stuffed, I can't even finish this glass of wine at the moment. It was all delicious, thank you."

"We could go for a walk, work off dinner," Ray offers.

Despite her words, she drains the glass. *OK, so I am nervous.* "Fresh air, good idea."

Outside in the insistently sharp, cold air, he tucks her arm through his. She lags at first, but he pulls her along energetically as she looks around, seeing again the dark wall of spruce over her right shoulder. "You didn't answer my question about going to the dance."

"I'm not sure you'll like the answer. I wanted to spend some time with you away from the restaurant, see what you're really like."

"And?"

He grins. "You got a dinner invitation, didn't you?"

Ah, where is this going? Do I run right now? Should I bolt like Quincy?

They continue walking west through the gathering dusk. She feels the rhythm of their steps, the heat of him even through sweaters and jackets. The breeze riffles through her hair like caressing fingers, the air is soft and sweet as a ukulele chord. The pale, fresh skin of her throat is exposed. She shivers and zips her jacket higher as a vee of geese streaks overhead, yakking to each other. Twenty, thirty of them. Getting ready to migrate away south.

"We had lots of little pothole sloughs on the farm. I've always loved geese and how they talk to each other," he says, stopping to watch the chattering flock. "They're so noisy in the spring when they're looking for a place to nest. Then they're quiet all summer when they've got kids — you'd never know there are geese all over the place. And now they're getting ready to head south, they practice flying in formation and calling to each other, and they're noisy again."

"I'm learning to pay attention to things like that," she says quietly, almost talking to herself. "Geese calling and the colour of leaves and fields... the difference between wolves and coyotes. Who knew?"

They've walked up the block and around the corner. He's pointing out homes of people she knows. "Jake, the mechanic, lives there. And that sweet little house with the great garden? Agnes and Bob-His-Mayorship."

"Seriously? He doesn't have the biggest house in town?"

"No. But he's probably got the biggest heart in town."

They find themselves facing each other, almost eye to eye.

"You know," she says. "I've had my head up my own ass for so long I am only now learning to look around, to see what's beyond me. To see — really *see* — light, and smell things, and pay attention to which way the wind is blowing. And it's not just the air and land and birds or whatever — it's people too. I don't know, there are so many things in my head now that weren't there before. I feel like I'm finally paying attention? Waking up? I don't even know how to describe this. And maybe I don't know what I'm talking about right now. I've had a lot of wine for one thing."

You certainly have, and it's making you babble. Then again, he's easy to talk to, wine or no wine. I don't think he'll turn it inside out or criticize me for being so ignorant about so many things. He seems kinder than that. OK, relax. Just relax.

He steps forward, wraps her in a hug, and says, "Good for you."

For a moment she's stunned, her arms remain straight at her sides like a tin soldier's, then slowly she raises them, gives him a tentative hug back.

He releases her. "So maybe dessert now?"

Crap, what was that about? "Sure."

They walk back to his house. But before opening his door, he grabs her hand and says, "Something I want to show you." He leads her to the back of the house where there's a thin, scrappy lawn and a gravel pad where he parks his sorry car. But snug against the house are raised garden beds. They're mostly empty now in autumn, the soil flat and sad, but a few robust-looking plants remain — rosemary bushes, pots of oregano, and other leafy things she doesn't recognize. "I had sage and basil, but we used it all for Thanksgiving dinner," he says. "Plus carrots and two kinds of spuds, turnips. I buy most of what I need at the farmer's market or in the city, but I like to grow some stuff of my own. Keeps me busy and connected to real food."

"I know zero about gardening," she admits, pocketing her cold hands. "I am a total city girl, I wouldn't know a potato plant if I fell over it. What's this stuff?"

"Kale. It's hardy, can stand some cold. Parsnips too, over there — they get sweeter with a bit of frost. Come on, you're freezing. Let's go in, I'll serve you some nice cold ice cream." She laughs as he quickly walks around his car, checking that the doors are locked. He leads her back to his door, firmly throwing the deadbolt into place once they're inside, and turning out the lights while she mounts the stairs. Upstairs, he glances out the front and steps out onto the tiny deck that's tucked into an alcove on the east-facing side of the house. He gazes up and down the street, and then comes back inside.

She notices his behaviour but is too tipsy to question or think it odd.

Apparently satisfied, he returns to the kitchen to scoop ice cream into bowls, pouring on maple syrup and adding a handful of black-berries. Lucie reclaims her seat, once again leaving her coat on. She makes her way through the rich, creamy bowlful, even the berries that are just on the edge of thaw: tasty and juicy but still icy at the core. "Yum," she says, nodding.

After they're finished, Ray clears the table and pours modest shots of Scotch. Warm at last, she pulls her coat off, and folds it over the sofa's back within easy reach. It's nearly time to leave. She wanders over to the window to gaze out at the street.

"Tell me about Tom and Marta at dinner last night," he says, joining her there. "I'm curious because they never come to the Thanksgiving dinner."

They sip their whisky and watch as the widely spaced street-lights blink on. The sky releases stars into the dark, and then a quarter moon rises above the rooftops. The room is dim, lit only by bounced light from the streetlights and the tiny moon's glow.

"I did my best for them," she says. "I tried to make their meal special, I wanted them to have a good time. And I didn't charge them, I figured they probably should eat free, but if you don't agree, I'm happy to pay for their meals. It was my idea." She glances at him, but his expression is unfocused, drifting, as if he's not paying attention.

She gazes out the window and settles on the line of parked cars including her faithful Agememnon. She sighs. "You did a great job and I do think Tom was happy, though of course he didn't bother to say so. Sorry, I'm rattling on and you're tired. Me too."

He focuses on her as if she's just appeared in his field of view. "No, part of me is listening."

"And the other part is thinking, 'How am I gonna get rid of her?' Because, may I remind you, we both have to work tomorrow. Or maybe we don't? I forget, it's winter hours now. I'm confused and it's not just the wine. Are we closed tomorrow?"

He sets his glass deliberately onto the windowsill and faces her, but it's so dark, she only sees white highlights on his face. "The other part of me is wondering what it would be like to kiss you."

She barks a sharp laugh so forcefully her body rocks forward. She steadies, folds her arms around herself, and to her surprise she shrugs and says into the darkness, "Well, I guess you could... um... find out." Looks up at his shadow.

He steps forward and his hands alight above her ears, fingers threading into her hair. He tips her head up and his lips caress her forehead at the hairline. Soft, so soft. His lips move to her cheeks, her closed eyelids, the tip of her nose. Quick brushes, the touch of petals or feathers. At last he takes her upper lip between his own. So tender. So sweet.

She is melting. Her hands fist against his shoulders but not in a combative or defensive way, only intense and blissful. He lets go her upper lip and takes her lower lip between his own, again so gentle. Searching, asking. He releases his kiss, looks up. She leans into him. His arms fold around her, he rests his chin on her shoulder. They stand like that for a long quiet while, until Lucie says, "Ever read *Oliver Twist*?"

He leans back and looks at her quizzically. "Dickens? Nope, why?" She feels his voice vibrating in his chest.

"There's a famous scene in the orphanage when Oliver goes to the awful headmaster, holds up his empty bowl and says," she pauses to make sure Ray catches her meaning, "'Please, sir. I want some more'."

Ray laughs, a resonant, genuine laugh. He kisses her again, this time full on the mouth and long long long. Lucie rubs her hands over his chest, and then her arms encircle him. Again he leans back to look at her. "How *much* more, Oliver?"

"Oh, quite a lot. All of it, in fact."

"I want you to know this was not my plan."

She grins, shakes her head. "Sure. First you take me to a dance to check me out, then you invite me for dinner and feed me a bunch of good food and wine. Don't tell me that wasn't a plan." Her last word is smothered as he kisses her again and starts to unbutton her shirt.

Her whole body smiles.

She is floating, lifted, cradled, rocking. She is hungry. He slows her down and she rises...he gentles her again and again like she's a colt, nervous, anxious, full of energy, curious. Where has this craving come from? Hungry. She is so hungry.

Light, warm as milky tea, seeps through her eyelids, but she's cold. She's crunched into a ball under a too-light blanket. Where's her duvet, has she kicked it to the floor? The mattress is hard. Her head aches. And why is it so bright? This is not her dark, cozy cave at the ranch. Where is she?

Lucie groans loudly, every muscle joining the choir as she rolls upright and regards the unfamiliar scene around her. Shakes her head as memory asserts itself.

Right. In Ray's bed. Idiot.

Her clothes are scattered. Jeans and shirt, bra and underwear, all on the floor, socks who-knows-where. She notices his fleecy sweatpants and a hoodie neatly folded on a nearby chair. A hint: 'Put this on.'

Better than nothing. Way better than nothing.

She pulls on his clothes — only slightly too long for her — and pushes the sleeves up past her elbows. There's no mirror to reflect what puffy face or mass of fractious hair she might be presenting to whomever might be waiting. Her feet are icy. Where are those socks? She bends stiffly to peer under the bed. No luck.

She shuffles out to the living room, to find morning in full blaze: sun rising across a perfect cobalt sky above the neighbouring roof-tops. Pure crisp light flies in through remarkably clean windows.

How does he do that? This is the second floor. Cleaning those windows would take one big-ass ladder. It's the most coherent thought she can cobble together.

There's no man in sight but she smells coffee and heads to the tiny deck where she finds Ray, a cookbook balanced on his knees. She sees the back of his head, bushy hair even wilder than usual, mad corkscrews spiking every which way. She closes the door

softly and steps toward the other chair. He reaches for the cof-
feepot and fills a cup for her. "Sleep OK?"

"Not bad. Chilly though. And it's about that futon. Excuse me for
complaining, but it's like sleeping on frozen ground. Every bone in
me is sore." She stretches before sitting down. "Not that I would
know anything about sleeping on frozen ground."

He grins. "I'd like to think you're sore because... hmm, never
mind. How's your head?"

"Fine. Ah, actually *not* fine. I feel like my face is on crooked. How
much did I drink, anyway?"

"There are two empty wine bottles on the kitchen counter. You
didn't do that alone, though. And again I say, it was not my plot to
feed you a bunch of wine and get you into bed."

She yawns. *You say. But that's what happened. Stupid me.*

The cotton cushion beneath her is sun-warm. She tips her head
back to the sun's full force. It's surprisingly hot and straight into
her face. She closes her eyes, gropes for her cup, and takes a deep
swallow. "You make the best coffee."

"Long years of practice. And I use a local roaster."

"Of *course* you do." Pause. "I'm sorry, that sounded crabby. What
I meant was, I'm not surprised because it's *what* you do — find
good quality, local stuff." Eyes squeezed against the dazzle, she
takes a long, slow breath. Makes a point of expanding her ribs
without groaning.

Just breathe. It'll keep you from babbling.

She relaxes into the morning in spite of herself. She breathes
slowly, deeply, her clenched back muscles gradually releasing.
"Smells great, doesn't it?" she says dreamily, almost musing to
herself. "In Vancouver, the smell of the air was maybe the one and
only natural thing I noticed. Even downtown you can smell rain and
ocean and wet ground. Cedar. Especially cedar. There's a certain
freshness but something deeper too, almost a smell of rot, not bad
or foul, just the smell of things regenerating, earthy. I'm sure the
Native people smelled that same thing, hundreds and thousands

of years ago. But the air here is fresh in a totally different way. Sharp and clean, like air nobody's breathed before. Woodsy, like pine, but grassy too. Maybe it's the smell of stone, of mountains, glaciers, rivers."

I thought you were supposed to be breathing not babbling.

"What else?" he asks gently.

"What else can I smell?"

"Or hear. Whatever you notice. You said you're learning to pay attention."

She listens with care. The fitful breeze flaps the few remaining leaves into soft applause and then dies away. A distant motor, perhaps a tractor, hums a bass note. The rumble of a passing truck on the street rises and falls. Sporadic chirps from unseen birds, interrupted by a raucous grating cry like the hard swing of a rusty gate. "What's that?"

"Blue jay."

Her face feels happy, caressed to the tip of her perpetually cold nose by such delicious heat. Even her bare feet, stretched out before her to gather the sunshine, are now comfortably warm. He pours more coffee: rich, bitter, and spicy. She murmurs, "I never really noticed birds either, except seagulls."

A bee lumbers around her head and moves off as she flails her hand. They cease talking, instead they sip, listen. Breeze, birds, sunshine. The shapeless ache in her head dissipates. She stretches arms and legs, and arches her back to rid the stiffness. Her body is easing but her mind is ticking.

What have I done? Damn. He is sweet and smart and undemanding, but I can't do this. I have to work with him. I need this job. This is such a mistake. Leave, Lucie. Just leave. Now.

High in the scaly, grey, ossified branches of a dead spruce in the neighbouring yard, a squirrel starts chattering and doesn't stop for at least a minute.

You sound like my brain, buddy. Rattling like a wind-up toy. Lucie, go already. Just say what you need to say, and go.

"I named that tree Ray Charles," he says.

She giggles. "Because?"

"I'm a big fan. Never saw him live but I used to see him on TV sometimes. He had a weird way of moving, rocking left to right like his spine was fused. Or maybe he did that on purpose so he would know exactly where his hands were on the piano, since he couldn't see. When the wind blows, that tree moves the same way. No bend, no flex, it moves back and forth like Ray Charles at the piano."

"And does it play *Hit the Road Jack?* Which is what I should do." She empties her cup and shades her eyes to look at him, all bravado as usual. "So. This feels a bit odd. Don't get me wrong, I had a lovely time with you. But if it wasn't in your plan, it wasn't in mine, either. Look, I'm staying in Sweetgrass for the winter, but after that I don't know. I work for you, I need the job. And I don't want you to misunderstand..."

Ray sets his cup on the deck, stands, and holds out his hands to her. Without thinking, she puts her own cup down, and lets him draw her up. He wraps her in a firm hug and kisses her sun-warm forehead. "Stop. Just listen to me."

Inside his embrace, she tries to shrug.

He speaks slowly as if he's considering each word, mapping what he wants to say. "I had a good time too. I like being with you. You're organized at work, you make things run a lot smoother, and you've got lots of ideas. But aside from work, Pumpkin, you're funny and easy to be with. I don't care if you're here for a week or a year. I like you and I'm pretty sure the feeling is mutual. I'm not asking for anything, Lucie. I get that you have things to sort out. Me too. So, let's enjoy each other and see what happens. I won't hurt you, I promise. Why would I? You're fun and special and the best thing that's walked into my life for a really long time. Maybe ever."

He releases her and stands back to see her face contort, as though she's trying not to sneeze. "What?" he says.

Don't cry don't cry don't you dare cry don't don't don't...

She folds into a misery that takes her by complete surprise. She is annoyed with herself but unable to stop the sudden onslaught from years of accumulated disappointment in her various lovers and liaisons, her wariness, her fear of being hurt, emotionally and physically. Maybe Ray is a safe harbour, maybe not. But his kindness, his sincerity have wormed through some crack in her shell. His words are entirely different from those any man has said to her before, and he's poked a hole clear through the dam that's taken her whole life to build.

And maybe Judith is right, maybe she needs to trust someone. Maybe Ray. But there's such danger, such potential for betrayal and disappointment. She is afraid. Unbidden, unrestrained, her past pours out of her. It feels like she's tipping over the lip of an enormous waterfall. She is bereft, powerless, swept away.

Lucie sinks back into the chair and covers her face with shaking hands. "I haven't told you everything. My boyfriend — the latest one in a long long long string of losers... *hit* me..." She begins to sob in rolling, full-body gusts. She is astonished, helpless. The anxiety, the daily exhausting need to hold so much history in check for so long, dissolves her and she crumbles like a sandcastle, undermined by this hurricane of grief and frustration. He's gripping her hands and murmuring her name over and over. Kneels before her as she bends her head to her knees. Between crying and shivering, words fly from her like hurled stones. A torrent.

She tells him everything. Brad's abuse, his betrayal with Lucie's own friend. "He *bragged* about how he was fucking her *in our bed* — he made damn sure to tell me that — and then he hit me *he hit me!* I swore I'd never let that happen again..." She cries so hard she can hardly breathe. "And then he ran out on me and all my worst fears came true... everything I've always been afraid of." She finally takes a deep long breath. "He took away every shred of my life and my confidence, and now I'm so angry, and I don't know who I'm angry with — him, or me, or my mother, or I don't know, maybe the whole fucked-up world.

"And my friend Jude says I need to grow up and get a grip on my life but I have no idea how to do that. I live in this shell that I've been carrying around for *years*, like a crab, like I'm some slimy thing with no skin. I *need* this shell! And now I'm trying to figure out who I am, but I don't know how to do that either, I don't know what I want. I'm just broken. So broken."

All this delivered with her face bent to her knees, hands covering her face, fingers threaded through her hair. Ray holds her head gently between his palms, and absorbs her torrent of rage without comment. He rocks her for a long time until she stops crying and her breathing slows. The breeze picks up. She becomes aware of birds chirping and the sun warming her back.

"Then let's put you back together," he whispers into the back of her head.

Lucie starts shaking like tall grass in the wind, quivering in waves, her teeth chatter. He finally succeeds in prying her upright and presses her face gently into his shoulder as she cries again, pauses, and cries again. His shirt soaks up her sorrow. He cradles her shuddering shoulders, he rubs the back of her neck, he combs her copious hair.

At last she is empty. He kisses her cheeks, her forehead, her mouth.

"Oh don't, fergodssake. I'm a mess, you'll get snot all over yourself."

"I'm a farm boy, remember? Had worse stuff on me than snot. Let's go inside and get some food into you, your teeth are chattering."

They stand together for a moment.

"Lucie, I won't hurt you. And I sure as hell won't hit you."

She takes a hot shower, cursing herself, feeling skinless and exposed in every possible way. But when she turns off the water, she stands in the steam and lets her shoulders relax, tips her head back, stretches her neck, her back. Feels taller. Quieter. The stone in her gut, the fist around her heart — she didn't know they were there, but now they're notable by their absence. She weeps again, and then impatiently scrubs her face with her wet hands, steps from the shower, and gives herself a fierce towelling as if trying to remove the shards of a crusted, shattered old shell.

She retrieves her clothes and gets dressed, stuffing several tissues into the pockets of her jeans, anticipating more crying jags. Feeling uncertain and transparent — and still unable to find her socks — she drifts into the living room.

Ray has pans in play on the stove. The radio is broadcasting cheerful country music into the sun-bright room. The windows are wide open. The breeze has a catchy scent of fall leaves and dry grass.

"More coffee?" he asks.

"Oh yeah."

He flips scrambled eggs onto waiting plates. The toaster pops. He slices tomatoes with the firm quick movement of a practiced chef and points his knife at a chair. "Sit."

She complies. They munch through the meal without much talk. Then, gathering plates and cutlery, he says, "I think you need to get out of your head today, do something different. Want to go for a hike?"

"A hike? I'm not saying no, but you need to know I've only done two hikes in my entire life. I am not up for climbing Everest."

"How about Volcano Ridge?"

"Sounds like Everest to me." For the first time that morning she gives him a genuine if wan smile. "Sure, a hike, why not? I'll have to get my boots and stuff at Amanda's. And, Ray — where are my socks?"

He tips his head back and laughs hugely. "Don't you remember playing sock puppets last night? No? Never mind. I'll find them for you."

She drives back to the ranch, Ray following. She darts into the house, expecting that she'll have to explain her absence last night, but nobody is home. Instead, she finds a note on the kitchen counter:

Hiya Lucie—didn't get a chance to say we are going to visit family in BC. Sorry to spring this on you, it came up fast. You are welcome to all the food in the fridge. We'll be gone for a week, maybe a bit longer. The horses are fine, Gary will come to feed them, you don't need to do a thing except please feed the cats and dogs and don't have any wild parties (haha). Cheers, A

Lucie grabs boots, backpack, water bottle, and new socks — after much searching, Ray could not produce her missing footwear — along with a couple of granola bars from the snack basket on Amanda's kitchen counter. She tosses her gear into the back of Ray's questionable car, and they head west. The day is remarkably warm and the sky pristine but for a few wisps of mare's tail cloud. Poplars shed their remaining leaves like bright coins into the light breeze. Shrubs and grasses along the roadside are cranberry and russet, the fields are champagne and dun. Ahead, the hills rise dark green with their groves of spruce and pine, and the mountains behind are soft, smoky blue and most are tipped with snow. Lucie kicks off her boots and places both feet on the dashboard.

The highway becomes ever more rough and potholed. Ray slows and finally turns onto a gravel road that climbs steeply as it follows a deep gorge where Lucie glimpses the white foam of a busy little creek far below. Ray parks the car, and they sling packs over shoulders. He leads her along a narrow path, overgrown but not difficult to discern as it climbs slowly through open woodland. At last they emerge from the trees and begin to ascend in earnest.

"Thought you said this wouldn't be hard."

"I said no such thing. Besides, no pain, no view."

"Ha. Hiker humour."

"Yeah, you might call it the bait and switchback."

She rolls her eyes and rewards him with a full round belly laugh.

Walking is rhythmic and calming, meditative. Her thoughts drift but then coalesce around the nugget of an idea. She explores it from several angles, worrying it the way a tongue can't stay away from a chipped tooth.

All the times I failed before, was it because I always had to be a hero and a fixer for the men in my life? All that rescuing and saving and nagging and believing I could make them turn out OK, but it never worked out like that, not with Brad and not with any of the others. And he knew it, he knew I was trying to reform him, and he threw it back at me, made me see how stupid I am, how stupid it is to try changing somebody. He made me feel so small. Fixing somebody, what was I thinking? Is that my task in life? Hell, no. What an idiot.

But I've made that same mistake over and over. I pick gorgeous guys who have lots of money, they're all flash and bling, but turns out they are totally immature or insecure or something. Their mothers hated them. Their dads drank. Their puppies rejected them. Whatever. There's a million stories and I swear I've heard them all. And I always think I can save them, make them whole and beautiful human beings. And I think they will thank me, love me, worship me, their saviour. They'll be grateful ever after, stay with me forever.

Christ, I'm actually my mother. To the core.

They toil upward, puffing, not talking. From time to time they stop to rest, drink water, and munch a handful of nuts and chocolate chips from a bag Ray pulls out of his backpack. The breeze is stiffer, cooler. Lucie shivers and wishes she'd brought a sweater.

"You're quiet," he says. "You OK?"

"Yes. Just thinking things over."

"Want to talk?"

She shakes her head. "Not yet. But I expect you'll hear it all eventually. Long winter coming up." She smiles at him, he grins back. "So, how much farther?"

"Not long now. And it's worth the effort." He is right about that. Cresting the ridge, their reward is a panorama of valleys and peaks rolling into the purple distance like ocean waves. If they had hoped for a rest and picnic here, the now-insistent wind dissuades them.

Lucie takes a few pictures with her cell phone — far, far out of any service range — reminding herself to send some photos to Judith. Chilled but energized by the flinty bright sunshine and rushing breeze, Lucie follows as Ray leads back down the trail until they reach a sheltered spot. "Want a snack?" he asks.

"I grabbed some granola bars."

He grins at her. "Pumpkin, you gotta do better than that." Taking a seat on a large flat rock, he opens his pack and extracts a cutting board and Swiss army knife, sausage, cheese, sliced tomatoes left over from breakfast, carrots, a bag of cookies. A Thermos bottle. "Pour yourself a drink."

The liquid she pours is not tea or coffee, but rosé. "Are you trying to get me drunk again?"

"Do I need to?"

She takes a long sip. The wine is fruity but not as sweet as she'd feared. She regards Ray for a long time, her lips pressed together, before she answers. "I don't know, Ray, I don't think so. But, what are we now? We work together and occasionally — OK, once so far — we attend dances and once so far, we sleep together, assuming last night was the first in a series. So what does that make us?"

"Two people who enjoy each other in a variety of locations and positions. Here, hand over that wine and don't worry. We'll figure it out, OK?"

She nods, mouth full of cheese and another quick sip of wine. The tangy scent of pine resin fills her head. She reaches to stroke his cheek, which makes him smile. He swiftly captures her hand in his, kisses her palm.

Lucie is alone in Amanda's big house. It's oppressively quiet. Time to go somewhere, do something.

Hope you're home, Marta. It's your turn today.

She grabs a warm jacket. Her destination is outside of the main town, in a small enclave of older houses next to the community golf course. The street is isolated and hard to find, but eventually Lucie thinks she's located the correct house, surrounded by a high hedge that forbids observation from the street. She walks through the opening to see a small cottage and neat yard. There are front steps, of course, and a wide wooden door with frosted glass inserts, but she has a hunch this is not the usual entrance. She walks around to the back, skirting a rain barrel and side garden, both mostly empty now. Upon reaching the back of the house, Lucie mounts three steps onto a broad deck populated with a table and chairs, a workbench, gardening tools. She knocks loudly on the screen door.

"Ja, I am coming," calls Marta from somewhere inside. Footsteps. Then Marta appears and breaks into a huge grin when she sees Lucie. "Hello, you came to see me. So good. Welcome, welcome, come in."

Lucie steps into a narrow space occupied by a cabinet and shelving, coats and jackets, a stool. Marta beckons her to step farther into the house. "Sorry, I hope this isn't a bad time," Lucie says, bending to kick off her shoes.

"No. There is no bad time. My door is always open. Please come in." Marta ushers Lucie into the kitchen, which is busy with what seems to be several projects on the go. There's bread dough rising in the corner, covered by a checkered cloth. The sink is occupied by a colander filled with peeled vegetables. And there's a chicken, oiled, trussed, and ready for roasting, beside the stove. Marta rustles, moves items in the fridge to make room, and pops the chicken inside. She then fills the kettle, puts it on to boil, and busies herself with getting cups from the cupboard. Asks over her shoulder, "Coffee or tea?" to which Lucie says, "Coffee would be great but either, really, don't trouble."

"No trouble. We have coffee."

And here they are, seated at the kitchen table with windows open wide, watching late-season golfers shoot and putt and swear.

"I don't get golf," Lucie comments. "Why play something that makes you angry and frustrated? Being mad, is that a good way to spend a gorgeous fall day?"

Marta laughs and nods. "Yes, is strange game. We buy this house because it needs fixing, so it costs not so much. Tom does fixes and now is much better. But golf, we do not golf. Who does golf, it is costing so much! But is good to live here because winter is quiet — just deer come and winter birds and foxes and coyotes. Sometimes moose, I love when moose come, like a big black ghost. Indians say moose is sign of survival. Good news if moose come, you will be OK, plenty of meat and hide and antler and bone. And in winter, I step out my back door with skis and off across golf course, no golfers, ha, just me. Easy ski, it is mostly flat. But also some fun, a steep hill down to the river. Sometimes too much fun, I break my ankle last winter."

"Oh, no. That's not good."

"Not good, you are right. Maybe I cannot ski this winter, I will see. But I still walk. That is my favourite, I love to walk. Any weather. Sometimes under the moon."

"I used to live in Vancouver, I walked to work and sometimes I would walk along the beaches with my friends, or walk along the Seawall—that's a long, paved path around a point of land. It's very nice, but it's busy, many skaters and bikes and dogs, not like walking here where you can be alone with the wind and birds. Before I came here, I never really did that. Walking I mean, just for the joy of it. You are so right, it's amazing to be outside, on foot."

Lucie is astounded that she's spoken so freely. But Marta is tiny and unthreatening, she seems to invite such confidences. And she is nodding, nodding and smiling with a warmth Lucie finds deeply charming and reassuring.

"Ja. Walk, that is best. You see, you hear. Flowers, trees, good air. Sometimes cars, trucks — gas and diesel, even sometimes skunk, not so nice. But part of where we live. Ja, walking is good way to learn. Would you like something to eat?"

Lucie shakes her head. "No, but thank you. I just came for a quick visit. I loved our first meeting on the river when you were hunting for wild leaves. And — forgive me, but I'm curious, and if you don't want to tell me it's fine, of course — but how did you come to be *here*, of all places? You told me about Vienna. But—Vienna to Sweetgrass? How did that happen?"

Marta pours more coffee. "So. I tell you some of my story that day at the river, I think. Here is more: I was making adventure for myself in Canada in 1970s, young girl with a backpack and friends, we come to Banff. I meet Tom, a cowboy, so romantic. I am young girl, looking for new and different life, maybe Canada. There is nothing to pull me back home. My father is shoemaker, work in leather, he makes bags and boots and shoes. Today that is good living but then, not so. My mother is doing baking and laundry. We are poor at home. I want better, I dream about a pretty farm and show my mother I can do well by myself. So I marry Tom and stay in Canada. My mother, she cry on the phone, she cannot see my wedding. Too much money to come here, so far away.

"I dream about a Europe farm, but I get a Canada ranch, not pretty house and barn and flowers, instead I get cold winter and wind. So many cows and hard life, sometimes dangerous. Then we have kids and we make a life, the kids grow up good. Not my dream but not bad. Better, always I think, better than Austria. I never see my mother again, so much money for her to come here, she could not, and she is gone now." Marta pauses to take a long sip of coffee. Sets her cup down gently.

We have some common ground, you and me. You wanted something but got something else. And your mom was a baker. And even Banff, land of discovery, except the only thing I discovered there was a traffic jam.

"How many kids?" Lucie asks.

Marta grins. "Three. I will show you pictures but not right now, my picture box is hard to get from the closet. I do not have phone pictures. So. We have Shay, oldest boy, he lives now in Red Deer and he is mechanic, two babies, I see them sometimes. Middle child is Chase, he is travelling now, like his mama looking for something, new life maybe. And Corrine, our girl," Marta laughs merrily. "Not a girl any more. She is woman, strong-minded. Two kids, one boy, one girl. I was looking for colour leafs for the girl, Emily. She is sweet, and she loves books. I have much good time with her, we read together. Sometimes I visit for weekends, they are in Calgary, not so far away." Marta stops to take a thoughtful sip of coffee. She peers into the mug.

In the quiet, Lucie is very aware of a ticking clock somewhere, perhaps a mantel clock or wall clock in the living room. It's loud, yet sounds forlorn — it's the only sound in the house.

Marta picks up her story. "Then we lose the ranch because we cannot sell beef. So strange to me. No help, not from the government and our friends, they are all like us. Nobody can sell beef."

"Yes, I know. Ray explained to me what happened, with the BSE. People lost everything."

Marta regards her, the first time she's made eye contact. Lucie feels she's being judged, assessed, and apparently found worthy because Marta continues, "Ja, just so. We lose everything. Land, house. That story I tell you on the river is true. And I tell you all the rest of the true story because I trust you. Tom, he has different story." Marta looks down as if ashamed. "He is proud and sad. He trust nobody. His story is not so true."

"And what is his story?" Lucie asks, softly.

"He has many. Maybe he get bucked off. Maybe he get kicked. Maybe he has back pain, maybe his eyes don't work. But he never say, 'I cannot sell my calves. I am victim, I am helpless.' No cowboy says that." Her delicate fingers tap and fiddle and worry each other along the mug's handle, moving moving moving. Marta looks up again and fixes Lucie with a gaze that is at once fierce and lost.

"Oh," Lucie says. "I am so sorry. I don't know what to say. I'm just learning about what it's like to live in a small town, and what the history is here. But I've learned there was so much loss with BSE. And — what's left for you, what is your life now? I mean, Tom owns the restaurant. I know Ray is doing his best to provide some income for you. And you have this lovely house — you have a roof, a garden, it's not a ranch, but it's fine. I'm sorry, I don't mean to judge you. I do too much of that."

"No, no, you are not judging. We think the same, you and me. I have nice house, we have money from the café. Ray, he work so hard for us, and he is doing good. You, too. But here is my trouble: Tom, he start to drink when we lose the ranch and now he drinks too much." Again Marta drops her gaze.

Lucie reaches across the table, touches Marta's hand gently. Withdraws.

Marta's voice is almost inaudible. She's talking to herself, not to Lucie. "Tom, he drink so much now. He likes too much the pool hall at the hotel, every day. Beer, whisky. Too much. He comes home but no talk, just sleep like dead because of whisky. He is asleep now and look, the day is half done. He will get up, have dinner with me maybe but no talk, then he will go out. I don't see him until late and maybe I give up and go to bed before him, then he sleep downstairs so he doesn't wake me up. Some days he feels not so good, stays home with TV or goes to the café to look around, have coffee maybe. It is sad for me, and I think for him too. We do not talk because we do not see each other. I am day, he is night. I do not know how to help, how to get my cowboy back." Marta bends forward to hide her tears.

Lucie is frozen, then tentatively places her hand on Marta's shoulder, squeezes. In a startling heartbeat, Marta sits up. "I am so sorry. This is not your story. Not for you to worry. Please, do not tell this. I am... Tom is, we are... No need to tell. Anyone. OK? Understand? OK?"

"Yes. I understand. It's not my place to tell your story. But I promise you, as long as I'm here in Sweetgrass I'll do my best to help Ray make the café pay. That's how I can help you. And — let's walk. Let's make a date, let's be outdoors together. I want to learn from you. About birds and flowers and whatever else you can show me. I can be your student. And," Lucie takes a deep breath, "I am your friend." Marta nods and Lucie continues, "Here's another idea. I'm a baker too, I learned from my mother, same as you. I would love to bake with you, to learn from you. I want to do some special baking for the café. I've been doing some experimenting already but, ah..."

Lucie suddenly remembers Tom doesn't know about her special baking or catering. "Um, I'm just trying things right now, nothing definite, just ideas. I'm used to making small batches, not restaurant-sized, so I need to figure out how to double or triple quantities. So, ah, I have ideas, and I'm trying to remember what I learned from my mom, but that was a long time ago, I'm not sure how well I'm doing yet."

Shut up. That was close, way too close.

Marta gestures to the kitchen counter. "I bake, I give all away." She sighs. "No kids at home, no one to wait for fresh hot cookies, nobody to roll dough, lick icing. I bake — cakes, cookies, pies, bread. Give it all away, every crumb. The sweetness of life." She turns to regard Lucie briefly and then drops her gaze to her hands, folded calmly now on the table. "Ja, OK, we will have fun to bake together." She nods and closes her eyes, her breathing deep and regular, almost seeming to doze.

Uncertain how to respond, Lucie stands and says gently, "Shouldn't you get that chicken into the oven?"

"You are right, I think our visit is now done. I am so happy that you come to see me. Please come again. Please. You do good work in the café. Thank you." She stands and extends a hand. Lucie grasps. Marta's grip is firm and strong, surprising for such a frail person.

With cooler weather and shorter days, and fewer hours at the café to regulate her schedule, Lucie becomes somewhat aimless. She's resumed riding some mornings, but her evenings at the ranch are quiet. She tries to read or watch the occasional movie, but can't concentrate. Somehow the plots don't make sense — she loses the thread. She's restless and more than a little worried that the coming winter will prove to be long and lonely. If there's one thing she misses about city living, it's easy distraction. Filling time? Simple. Make a phone call.

She's also become listless and tired, even though she's usually in bed and asleep by 10 p.m. and sleeps late except when she goes to the café early to bake. Her bread, pies, cakes, and pastries are now in high demand, albeit never listed on the menu board, so two or three mornings each week she's busy in The Sow's Ear kitchen creating treats to meet the demand and trying to keep her mind on her work. But once she's finished, she drifts back to the ranch and finds it hard to generate the energy for even a walk. Lucie wonders whether she's catching a cold or flu, but suspects her lethargy isn't physical but emotional. Her thoughts are constantly in a tangle. She can't stop thinking about Ray, and it's exhausting.

Since their first night together more than two weeks ago now, there's been no repeat performance. At work there are no tender looks over his shoulder and certainly no quick caresses or clandestine kisses, all of which is such a departure from her previous liaisons. At the outset of a new romance, she's accustomed to being with a new lover at every chance, supplemented by phone calls and texts: constant contact. Then again, never before has she slept with someone she's also working with. To give Ray the benefit of the doubt, perhaps he's just being cautious about staff and customers getting a glimpse of something he clearly wants to keep private.

Besides, it's not like he *never* glances her way, never smiles at her. In the course of a shift at the café, he frequently meets her gaze with his arresting cobalt eyes. But their conversation is always about the café, it's business as usual. Perhaps he's waiting for her to make the next move, to show him she remains interested? Which she is.

Ray might not be studiously watching her, but Lucie is not shy about studying him whenever she gets the chance. She can't get enough of him. In fact, it's her main recreation, her chief source of enjoyment. He moves so easily, he is solid and self-possessed. For someone who doesn't spend any time at the local gym, let alone hiking regularly or playing some sport like hockey, he is in fine shape and always seems to have energy to spare.

On days when the restaurant is closed, she doesn't see him, even when she's in the kitchen baking and hoping the back door will open and he'll step inside. His absence makes her crankier than ever. Is she missing something? Her mind ticks and ticks like a demented wind-up toy. She tries not to be sullen — but really, what is going on?

Was that a one-time event? Or do you think you can just call me up whenever you need a romp? I hope not, but buddy you're not giving me anything to go on. Did you not have a good time with me? Or did my big outburst scare you after all? Maybe you're having second thoughts, decided it's too complicated.

She sighs as she rolls out pie dough.

Stop obsessing. If he's changed his mind, fine, no skin off my nose. We can just go back to what we were all summer. He's just a guy, and this is not the first time I've had one night and walked away.

She slides unbaked pie crusts into the fridge, ready for filling later before the café opens for dinner.

But you were so sincere, so sweet. Those things you said to me, I don't think you were lying, and I am not going to give up on you. So what's up, Ray? What. Is. Up?

Ting ting ting.

The days are cold, but there's no snow yet. At the café, virtually every customer remarks on the lack of snowfall so far. Some are in favour of bare, dry roads and snow-free pastures where cattle find enough feed for themselves. Others worry about the lack of soil moisture, which bodes ill for next year's hay crop. It's all just talk to Lucie, who passes along whatever she's learned from listening to her customers. At some tables she celebrates, at other tables she commiserates. But it's irritating, this constant dissecting of the weather.

It will snow, or it won't. Whatever. Find another topic please everyone.

"People here do nothing but complain about the weather," she barks one night as she brings dirty plates and cutlery to the kitchen.

It's been slow and Ray has let the other staff go home early. He wipes hands on his apron, and she notices an uncharacteristic sag to his shoulders as he leans against the counter, looking defeated and tired.

"Don't be too hard on them," he says. "They work outdoors, mostly. The weather is their constant companion, it affects everything they do, every day... What? Lucie? You look like you just swallowed a pin or something."

Lucie's expression has shifted from quizzical surprise to a look of shock before a jolt of pain. She says, "Ray, I have to stop judging people. Why can't I break this habit? I have to stop being my mother."

To her further surprise, he takes two rapid steps across the floor and wraps his arms around her. She responds with a fierce kiss.

"Where the hell have you been?" she demands.

"Right here, Luce, I'm right here. I'm sorry for ignoring you. I've been preoccupied lately; I'm having a fight with Tom. He actually threatened to fire me, and I guess he's not wrong. He's figured out that we're generating extra money from your baking but not passing it on to him. I suppose it was only a matter of time until he put the pieces together."

"How did he find out?"

"He was in the café one day and saw a few orders of cake coming out of the kitchen, and customers were complimenting you on it. Carrot cake, I think."

Lucie gives her forehead a smack. "Oh, no. I'm sorry, I'm so sorry, that was completely my fault. I know exactly what day that was. He sat by himself at the table for four by the south wall, even though we were really busy—you never even made it out of the back that day, remember? I brought his usual coffee and then ignored him. But you're right, I served a bunch, we went through two whole cakes." She gives him a sheepish look. " What did you tell him?"

"I said we're still experimenting with baking, which is true, but he's not happy. I have to start giving him his fair share. But Luce, seriously, you have to be really careful."

"OK, yes. But... *why* have you not been giving him a share? I thought..."

"Because we *are* still experimenting, right?"

"I guess..."

I guess buying winter clothes isn't enough proof that I'm planning to stick around. Then again, I keep saying I might change my mind. So, yeah, I get it. You're still not convinced. Guess that makes two of us.

He stands back, still holding her hands, and giving her a long look that makes her glance away, cheeks flushing. He drops her hands and turns toward the still-cluttered counter. Panicked, she follows him across the floor and hugs him from behind. Under the cloth of his shirt, his back is firm and warm against the cheek she rubs there. He rewards her with a sweet smile over his shoulder, then twists to face her, folding her in his arms. "Come home with me tonight."

"Oh, yeah."

He doesn't forsake her again. As October drifts into November, she begins spending a night or two each week at Ray's apartment: happy times of jokes and laughter, good food, lots of wine, the comfort of talk, and his slow, tender, careful loving, and waking up to a smile and a cuddle. She's more relieved than she wants to admit, although her liaisons with him are still episodic and unpredictable.

Soon her toothbrush and various cosmetics take up residence in his bathroom, and a small collection of her clothes piles up on a bedroom chair until finally he offers a shelf and hangers in the closet for her things.

Returning to the ranch after an unprecedented absence of two nights, Lucie finds Amanda doing laundry and says, "OK, it's only fair to tell you what's going on."

"Ha, I'm way ahead of you," Amanda says with a huge grin. "Ray's a sweet guy, good for you."

Lucie gives Amanda a wide-eyed stare.

"What? You look like a deer in the headlights."

"Amanda, it's just — I thought we were being so careful. We don't want any gossip and he's pretty shy, I think he doesn't want to damage his reputation in town. Hmm, that doesn't say much about me, does it? What I mean is, I'm pretty sure he doesn't want Tom to know, though I'm not really sure why. But you've figured it out. Is that OK with you?"

Amanda laughs. "Oh, my friend. You are an adult, and I am not your chaperone. Come and go, do what you do. You are welcome to live here as long as you want. We love your company and hey, if you and Ray wind up here some nights, that's fine, although you know Keith will have some winks and comments for you in the morning." She slams the dryer door and pushes a button. As the machine begins to tumble, she turns to Lucie. "There's something else, though. Remember the fall gather that Keith mentioned? It's next weekend. If you can help with the food, there will be lots to do. We'll be at the community hall, miles away from the action. While the fellas do the hard work figuring out which cows belong to who, we'll be cooking to feed the hungry masses."

The day arrives, damp and foggy, sleet gradually turning to hard pellets of snow, but luckily there's little wind for now. It's Sunday, the café is closed, and Lucie is grateful for something novel to do. As she's come to expect, Ray declined to participate, opting instead to spend the day going over the café's accounts. "Come for dinner afterward if you want," he says. "I'm making chili."

"That is exactly what I'll be cooking all day for those hard-working cowboys."

"Mine's better."

"Says you. I'll call you if I'm coming over, OK? But I hear it will be a long day, I might just head home for a hot bath and three days' sleep."

"Only two. We're open on Wednesday."

"Ha. Chef humour."

"Pretty *sharp*, eh?"

Amanda pilots her enormous truck to the town's ancient community hall — smaller and more frayed than the hall where Lucie attended the firefighter's dance. Amanda and Lucie carry groceries inside, joining at least a dozen women already chopping vegetables, frying onions and ground beef, and talking talking talking as though they were seeing one another for the first time in years. Two young girls, each armed with a can opener, nudge and giggle in a corner of the kitchen. Their job appears to be taking the tops from a collection of cans — tomatoes, corn, beans — but mostly they are whispering and laughing. A horde of kids from toddlers to teens ranges around in the huge empty hall, occasionally scolded by a mother who yells at her offspring through the large pass-through serving window. Numerous folding chairs lean against one wall, while folded tables are stacked along another. Mounted high on the wall above is an electronic bingo board, currently black and silent. Underfoot, the springy wooden floor creaks and protests as the kids run around.

The fall gather itself is happening elsewhere, and in fact has been going on for two or three days already. Although she has no desire to mount a horse and join the action, Lucie does want to witness the actual event. Amanda says, "About mid-afternoon, some of the ladies will take coffee and sandwiches out. You could go with them and see a little of what goes on. And," delivered with a knowing grin, "you'll appreciate what I'm telling you about avoiding the whole business. There are no nice jobs out there."

Lucie has volunteered to make dinner rolls as her contribution to the communal meal. She's already mixed, kneaded, and proofed the dough — last night, every surface in Amanda's kitchen was occupied by trays of slowly rising rolls covered with tea towels, the room filled with the scent of working yeast. Now Lucie starts bringing tray after tray from the truck into the hall, lining them up on a counter near the giggling girls. She borrows Amanda's keys to return home for a second round of trays. She hauls herself into the truck and, with no small amount of trepidation, adjusts the seat so she can reach the pedals, and she fiddles with the mirrors. Finally she takes a deep breath and starts the engine, which roars to life, then murmurs quietly as Lucie eases into reverse.

It feels like she's steering an ocean freighter, long and bulky, wallowing. But the hall's parking lot is expansive and relatively empty, and there's no traffic as she pulls onto the street. It's a short drive back to the ranch. She's careful to swing wide around right turns to avoid mounting the curb, and she never attains anything near highway speed even when she heads west of town. Despite the oncoming snow and wet, sloppy roads, she gets to the ranch without mishap, loads the remaining trays, and drives back to the hall feeling like the Queen of Sheba on her river barge.

"Maybe I've had my adventure for the day after all, driving your monster truck." Lucie remarks as she hands the keys back to Amanda.

"Ha. Wait until we get you on the hay swather next summer."

"You think I'll be around that long?"

Amanda only glances away and says, "Hey, here's someone you need to meet. My friend Tash, best hairdresser in town. Natasha, ya old boot, this is Lucie, my renter and buddy and ace baker."

"Amy, ya bag of dirt!" cries the imposing woman who embraces Amanda with a grin and several hearty slaps on Amanda's back.

Amy? Who calls you Amy? And who calls you a bag of dirt? Nobody I know. So how special is this woman?

"Natasha? That's your name, really?" Lucie grins and shakes hands with a woman completely unlike anyone whom she has started to characterize as 'local.'

Typically judgmental, Lucie has slotted the women she sees in the café into three basic types: the hard cases, real ranch women from hardscrabble farms and ranches, their faces pinched with worry; the local leaders, stately and relaxed elder women from ranch or town, who have clearly weathered storms beyond counting and now possess immense calm, grace, and humour; and the newbies, city transplants seeking their country dream, well-meaning and ready to volunteer, but misfits who wear their furs to the grocery store or showy jewellery to The Sow's Ear for coffee.

Natasha is none of these. Facing Lucie is a tall, big-boned woman with a curtain of extravagantly thick silver hair, shiny as satin. Even here in this dreary community hall kitchen, with its harsh, blue-white fluorescent light that compliments nobody, this woman is entirely elegant despite her considerable size. Her jeans fit perfectly, and her paisley shirt drapes gracefully from her substantial shoulders — the fabric is clearly expensive. Her makeup is impeccable, expertly showing off indigo eyes, prominent cheekbones, perfectly arched brows, and a flawless complexion. Tash sports flamboyantly large earrings, two necklaces, and several rings, yet she seems to fit comfortably into the kitchen's hustle. She is her own private party, but the other women accept her as is. No prima donna this Tash, but a hard working, if exotically stunning, member of the fall gather team.

"Yeah, *Natasha*, what a name," she jokes. "I mean, if you look at me do you see Russian nobility? I think not! Call me Tash, that will do just fine, and Tash sounds more like a local name. Tash the Slash!" Her handshake is confident and firm, like so many handshakes Lucie has experienced in Sweetgrass. Tash says, "Think I saw you at the dance last month. You were with Ray the chef, right?"

"Wow, nothing gets past anyone here," Lucie laughs. "Yes that was me, but I don't remember you from the dance. Sorry, that was my first local event. I don't remember half the people I met. Plus I was drinking rye."

"Ah, the local witch's brew. It sneaks up on you, rye. So, pardon me, we've just met but — I could do some fun things with your hair." Tash boldly runs her fingers though Lucie's silky but tangled mass. "Super short and shaped, tamed a bit with good product, maybe some funky colour too, what do you think? Could be more maintenance than this style though. How often do you trim?"

"Not very, just enough to keep split ends under control. I found one of those cheap shops in the city where they just do a bit of clip and shape, you know?"

Tash nods. "I could do better. Not that long hair is a bad look for you — most women can't carry it, but you can because you're skinny and your hair's nice. But if you're ever interested in something different, we could have some fun."

Lucie laughs enormously. "If you can believe it, I've had this style since high school. It's my look, my persona. In my previous life I had a corporate job so I couldn't get too edgy. But now — here I am in Sweetgrass, and my life has changed. Yeah, maybe. Thank you."

Tash turns back to the counter and continues slicing tomatoes. Lucie, who's waiting for the buns to finish rising, looks around for something to do. But before she can step away and find a task, Tash continues. "You have gorgeous skin too, so delicate. And your eyes! It's great to see someone so different. Most of my clients want hair that looks OK when they take off their cowboy hat or ball cap. Such is my life." Delivered with a wry grin and eyes rolled to the ceiling.

Lucie ventures, "So... what's with the nicknames? Amy? Bag of dirt? Nobody I know calls Amanda by anything but her full name. Including me, and I live in her house."

Now Tash laughs enormously as she reaches for a cucumber and starts slicing. "We got into that at a book club one night, if you can believe it — name calling. The subject came up, and we started calling each other the worst things we could think of without profanity. And it stuck for some of us. So she's 'Bag of Dirt' and I get to be 'Old Boot.' I'm good with that."

Lucie nods, continues, "So are you a local girl? Or a city slicker like me?"

Tash fixes Lucie with a direct, honest gaze. "City. I lived in Calgary forever. Born and raised. I worked for the CBC, I was in radio. Then I met a cowboy, and he blew me away."

To which Lucie mutters, "Yeah, men around here have a knack for that."

Tash doesn't notice Lucie's remark and continues, "Now I live on a ranch and run my own salon business here in town. I'm living the dream, and it *is* a dream. I've been in Sweetgrass for, oh, five years... no, more than that, now — and I could not have imagined this life when I lived in the city. I love love love it here. It all just fell into place. Seems to me this is what I was supposed to be doing all along. Good karma, you know? I've jumped in with both feet. Hook, line, and Smithbilt."

"Is that a truck?"

"No, Honey, it's a brand of cowboy hat, made in Calgary. Don't make the mistake of saying 'Stetson' unless you really mean it, because that's a hat made in Texas, I think. And the difference is important around here. Just so ya know."

"Words to live by. Thanks, coach. So, were you here for the BSE thing?"

"Not really. Besides, we have a unique product that saved us."

"Unique how?"

"Ever seen a Highland cow? Those crazy-ass cattle with long red hair and big horns? Texas longhorn meets Irish setter. Highland beef is the sweetest, most tender beef you'll ever eat, in my not-too-humble opinion. And we raise them grass-fed only — no grain, no hormones or antibiotics, no feed that we don't control. We sell our product direct to restaurants and certain butcher shops in the city. They never gave up on us, so we survived BSE all right. But hey, is it time to get those buns of yours into the oven?"

"I am such a beginner at all this," Lucie says. "About cows. About everything."

"It comes to you. If you're open to it." Tash flashes Lucie a conspiratorial glance. Equal to equal.

Lucie flips tea towels from atop the rising buns, which are white and puffy. The oven is ready. She slides several trays inside. Someone says, "Let's get the pots going," and everyone jumps into action. First, onions and garlic that have been gently browning on the stove's six burners are tipped into several huge stock pots, along with contents of the giggly girls' cans of tomatoes and beans, all mixed together with great long-handled wooden spoons. Enter the browned ground beef, again there's much stirring and mixing. Then spices, shaken from commercial-sized containers of chili powder, pepper, salt, and then squeezes of juice from a quantity of limes. The big pots are hefted back onto the stovetop.

"This oven is hot, the buns are baking pretty fast," Lucie says, peering through the oven window. "But this is the first of maybe five or six batches."

"We've got some time," Amanda answers. "These chili pots take a while to heat through. Maybe turn the oven down a notch." While the chili warms, a crew of knife-wielding women chops salad and slices pans of brownies and date squares. Others set cookies on plates and cover them with cling wrap. Amanda says, "Lucie, can you help get sandwiches and stuff ready for the field lunch? But don't neglect what's in the oven. Nobody else is watching."

Lucie hurries to take her place in the assembly line: building sandwiches, wrapping them, and putting them into big boxes along with jars of pickles, plastic bags full of sliced tomatoes and cukes, stacks of napkins, containers filled with cookies, and Thermos bottles of coffee and tea. Lunch is assembled and loaded into waiting trucks, ready for transport to where the cowboys are working. Lucie occasionally steps away to check on her baking. She opens the oven door, sending gusts of heat into the already over-warm kitchen. "Heads up, hot stuff!" she yells, pulling out trays loaded with the tanned and toasted dinner buns. One load out, another in, she returns to the sandwich line.

Their trucks loaded with lunch, many of the women and children drive off to deliver the midday meal. The hall is suddenly and cavernously quiet. Lucie, who's decided not to go out to the rodeo after all — "It's really getting to be a miserable day out there," she says to Amanda — pulls her final trays from the oven. Other hands have tossed cooled buns into large bowls. By some miracle Lucie hasn't had time to notice, tables have been set up in long rows and covered with white and black cloths, chairs in place. Bowls full of buns are set upon the tables along with salt and pepper, tubs of margarine, and bottles of ketchup and hot sauce. Tall metal containers are full of knives and forks and spoons. There are stacks of paper napkins.

Tash is now standing by the sink, a towel flipped over her shoulder, clearly not fussed about getting her fancy blouse damp. Lucie stacks her baking trays for washing. Says shyly, "So, to pick up on our conversation — I've only been here since last summer. I've met a few people and learned a few things, although I'm a long way from being part of the scenery. But how long does it take? And — *what* does it take? You seem pretty smart about life here. You're *in*." Lucie waves her hand toward the hall. "But even five years isn't very long, is it? I mean, for some people it takes a lifetime. Maybe never, no matter what they do."

"Ah, thereby hangs a tale," Tash says, washing dishes. "Like I said, I was in radio. I think that's been my ticket into this community. After twenty years of live-to-air interviews, I learned how to talk to people but more to the point, I learned how to listen. Then I found out that doing hair and nails and such is another business where you have to listen. And here's what I know: people love it when someone truly listens to them. I suppose that's how I earned my place here. When I'm cutting hair people tell me stuff that they probably shouldn't, then realize they have to be nice to me so I don't go blabbing their secrets." Tash grins over her shoulder.

Rinsing and stacking dishes fast and noisily, she continues, "Maybe I do know something about this town, the people, the life, because I absorb stuff like a sponge. I tell my mom I have three jobs now: salon, ranch, trivia. Thanks to a lifetime of listening to people, there's so much crap in my brain I need a neck brace to hold my head up. So, to answer your question, I'd say my claim to fame is: I'm a good listener."

Lucie has been laughing throughout this discourse. "I'll remember that. Clearly you're someone to know in this town."

"*Clearly*. And phone me for a haircut, here's my card." Tash fishes a business card from her back pocket.

Prepared for any opportunity. Good girl.

Presently the lunch brigade returns, and the hall is again full of noise and kids. Lunch dishes and containers need washing, the great pots of chili need tending. At last, as the daylight fails and snow swirls around the hall's windows, bowls of salad make their way to the long tables. Gradually the hall fills with men and women from the various round-up sites, who are chilled, tired, dirty, hungry, wanting nothing more than the comfort of hot food. People take their places at the long tables — couples, families, groups of single cowboys. Chili is spooned into serving bowls and ferried to the hall room, to be passed from hand to hand along the tables. Bowls of salad and Lucie's dinner buns make the rounds along the tables, and then the squares and cookies. Women with carafes of hot coffee make their way along, filling mugs, while others circulate with hot water and tea bags. No beer is in evidence tonight, certainly no rye.

To Lucie's surprise, the group is not loud and boisterous like the firefighter's dance. Instead the conversation is quiet, punctuated with laughter and occasional yelps of a few young kids running around. As people finish eating, they bring dishes to the kitchen window. Tash and other women are waiting, washing, still others are drying, putting things away. They change jobs occasionally. The flow of dishes and cutlery continues until everything has been collected from the tables. Now it's time to scrape out the chili pots and clean them, time to dump out the coffee grounds. Someone furls the tablecloths, others fold the tables and stack the chairs.

"No whisky under the tables," Lucie remarks to Amanda.

"Nope. Tonight is a reward for getting the job done. Not a party."

It's late. Lucie calls Ray to say she's on her way over, adding that she needs a hot bath and long sleep, not a night of sex, which makes him chuckle and answer, "We'll see." She is disappointed that she's utterly missed the event she wanted to see — the real, honest, true-to-life round up. But today's kitchen swirl has been terrific in its own right. She's met Tash, and she has been part of a community event. It's been a connection, a means for Lucie to show up as a trustworthy volunteer.

And what does all this say about Ray, who decided to stay home and not be part of the event at all? Surely doing the café's books, which he does regularly, wouldn't have taken him all day? And there's plenty of other opportunity for research and recipes and paperwork in support of the café. With these thoughts distracting her, she rings his doorbell and stamps wet snow from her boots, waiting for him to let her inside.

A week later, Sunday morning. An amazing anomaly at this time of year — the day is warm and clear and bright, flirty clouds are kicking up their skirts. In fact, the sun is hot. *Hot.* It draws her outside like a wasp to jam. Ray is deeply asleep as Lucie slides out of bed and pulls on jeans, a shirt, and her bright orange fleece hoodie. She quietly lets herself out, making sure the door doesn't lock behind her, and strides up the street. She waves to Mayor Bob, who even at this early hour is on his deck installing Christmas lights.

She heads south and then west, making for a street that dead-ends at the top of a steep slope, affording an unobstructed view of the mountains. At the viewpoint, wind sings through her loose hair. Wiry tall grasses, aggressively saffron against the white background of softening snow, poke stubbornly from the thin crust to rustle and sigh in the breeze. In the middle ground, sunlight shines from snow-coated hillsides with a honey glow. The foothills rise behind, and then the blue mountains in ever diminishing waves. Overhead, ravens surf on the updrafts.

She grins at them. *You are having fun, and you know it. Welcome to your new life, Peter Pan.*

She walks on, now heading toward the river. Both banks are lined with shelf ice, but there's also open water, black and glassy as it slides over the gravel bars. The woods are full of birds. Chickadees, siskins, magpies, she knows their chatter and whistle now thanks to the occasional stroll with Marta, who has pointed out bird calls and shown Lucie how to recognize them. She stops walking and raises her hand, palm up. A chickadee flutters and lands on her fingers, leans over and pecks her palm, searching for a seed. Finding nothing, the bird flicks away. It's all over in an instant that leaves Lucie breathless, her arm extended. A welcome.

She carries on. The sun's warmth soaks into her and makes her unzip her fleece jacket. She stands tall, shoulders down, chest forward. She looks ahead, breathes fully, pulls her hands from her pockets, and swings her arms above her head. Her pace quickens but also broadens. Bigger, more forceful steps.

Big steps. Big breaths. Face forward. Smile. Breathe. It's a big world.

Everything seems lit from within. She sees bright red rose hips still clinging to needled branches, green-white wolf willow berries, all positively glowing. Halfway across the river bridge, she stops to look again west to the mountains. There they are, close enough to touch. She reaches out her arm and wiggles her fingers as if to tickle the peaks.

I can feel you, I can touch you.

She holds her breath, the better to hear the surrounding subtle sounds: wind rattling long dry grass, the river chattering to itself over its stones and gravel bars. A few leaves still hang on, rustling in the breeze and whispering their stories. She's aware of her own heartbeat. Distantly, the buzz of a small plane. But no traffic, no voices.

She shakes her head, breathes and laughs.

Keep your shoulders away from your ears, as they say in yoga. Focus on your inner voice. Breathe. Oh yeah. No problem there. In, out... Drink it in....

For so many years, Lucie's inner voice has been yelling, badgering, insisting, saying, 'You're not good enough, Lucie. Your hair's a rat's nest, and you have the face of a ghost. You're too stupid to recognize a loser boyfriend when you see one. You ran away from your mother like a spoiled kid...'

Self-doubt and second-guessing have been her constant companions. Always the high-pitched zing in her ears, like some tiny anvil in her head upon which a demented blacksmith relentlessly hammers. But right now, right here, overlooking this talkative little river on a November morning in this oddly intense sunshine, that insistent, critical hum is gone. It's *so* gone. And in its place is... not a damn thing.

Lucie spreads her arms wide and starts to twirl. She is alone on a pathway above a tiny river in a small town. Nobody knows where she is. And that's the thing. She twirls, she laughs, she's dizzy. Sunshine has soaked into her, making her silly. It's November, and she's warm and dry and outside and loving... what? Loving here. Loving now.

Look where I live.

"Ah!" Her spinning stops. She is facing west to the mountains, arms still outstretched. In any previous life she would have been too embarrassed, too cool for such behaviour. But here she is alone in the great wide West, her arms open to the sky. She tips her head back and yells a big full-throated cowboy yell.

The birds chirp, the wind blows, the ravens soar. Nothing has changed.

Everything has changed.

Lucie stuffs her hands into her pockets and turns away from the climbing sun, treading back up the hill to town and Ray's house, where she hopes he'll be sizzling bacon and waiting for her. He'll smile and fold her into his arms, he'll ask about the new light in her eyes. Ray, of all the men she's known, will notice something different about her, recognize that something has transformed her.

On a whim, she pulls her cell phone from her back pocket and dials Judith, heedless of the time difference between Sweetgrass and Vancouver.

"Hello?"

"Jude, it's me, your long-lost buddy out here in cowboy land."

"OhmygodIthoughtyouweredead. Lucifer, what's up? You sound... I'm not sure what I'm hearing. Are you OK?"

Lucie laughs so loudly she moves the phone away from her mouth to avoid blasting Judith's ear with her jubilation. "I am so so so OK. I don't think I've ever been more OK."

A pause. "Seriously?" Another pause. "What is up with you? Luce, what time is it there, because let me tell you it's not even coffee hour here. Are you still drunk from last night or something?"

Another huge Lucie laugh. "No, no. But, listen, Jude — I want you to see this place. How would you like to come out here for Christmas? An all-expense-paid trip to beautiful downtown Sweetgrass, courtesy of yours truly."

Yet another pause. "Sure, except how about New Year's instead? I need to see my mom at Christmas."

"Done. New Year's it is."

"Lucie, Hon, I'm still not getting it. What's up with you?"

Lucie takes a deep breath. Clearly her enthusiasm for the day is not translating well. "I'm fine. But Jude, it's an incredible warm day here, and I'm in the middle of a long walk, and I guess I've had some kind of revelation this morning. I feel so relaxed, so... I don't know, *free*? This place has really grown on me, it's under my skin I guess. Maybe Peter Pan has landed. I'd like you to see it. And," she pauses for dramatic effect, "I'd like you to meet my new guy."

"That would be terrific." Lucie doesn't catch the sceptical tone in Judith's reply. "Are you sure you can afford to buy me a plane ticket?"

"I'm making a decent wage and good tips. You make the reservation, I'll pay you back," Lucie says. "Just let me know your flight dates, and leave the rest to me. Jude? Hello?" The connection ends abruptly and Lucie doesn't attempt to call again.

Instead, Lucie continues her hike back to Ray's apartment. It's a fair distance. By the time she returns to his house, she's damp with sweat and looking forward to a hot shower and delicious breakfast. To her chagrin, however, she finds his door is locked. She rings the doorbell, her good mood evaporating.

Ray comes to the door and swings it wide, but there's scant welcome in his eyes. "Hi," he says. "Nice walk?"

She pauses, considering whether to step inside or turn on her heel and walk away. "Really nice," she says, but her response is curt. "It's so warm out, amazing."

He steps back from the door and she enters, just like her very first visit. In some ways, nothing has changed since then. He's still largely a stranger to her. He closes and locks the door as she peels off her hoodie, which he takes from her, and hangs on a hook.

Before she can start climbing the stairs, he grabs her shoulders, and turns her roughly to face him. "Please don't ever do that."

"Take a walk alone?"

"Leave the door unlocked."

It makes no sense to her, this overblown caution of his. Ray is all about locking doors and watching from windows no matter where he is, as if they live in some sketchy city neighbourhood. When they walk together, he always glances around warily. It makes her nervous and irritated.

She means to ask him about it, get to the bottom — but the sun is so warm, the day so fine, she lacks the energy for such probing and maybe provoking an argument.

Some other time. I'm curious but I'll ask you... sometime.

After breakfast and copious coffee — and no further word from him about her apparent crime of not locking the door — Ray and Lucie drive west from town as far as they can, reaching the gate where the road is blocked for the season to protect winter range for wildlife. His anxiety seems to have melted. They walk hand in hand, crunching through scant snow, talking and joking, occasionally encountering families out for a sunny-day stroll complete with dogs and kids and even a stroller or two.

The afternoon cools, she's shivering. "Let's call it a day," he says, and they return to his car. He drives east to town as the sky darkens. The days are so short now. He takes her home to the ranch, says, "I've got the month-end books to do tonight." He leans to kiss her slowly, deeply, dissolving her disappointment that she'll be spending tonight alone in her basement room. "Sorry I yelled at you about the door," he says.

DEEP AND CRISP AND EVEN

'Bleak' is the word that enters Lucie's head every time she looks out a window. The snow has finally arrived, creating a monochrome world of stark white and grey and black. Every last thing is drained of colour, even brightly painted houses appear muted. Trees are skeletal. The sky is featureless, like a sheet of white paper. And it's cold, so much so that Lucie has called a halt to her riding lessons. Even in Keith's indoor arena the air is frigid, turning her fingers and toes to ice, reddening her nose. Much to her chagrin, Sweetgrass is living up to her mother's prediction from a few months ago — Lucie is indeed unprepared for the cold, and she's not liking it one bit. She is always chilled, despite buying wool leggings, scarves, any number of fluffy sweaters. At each day's end, she can't wait to dive under her weighty down-filled duvet — or to snuggle with Ray, easing her icicle feet, hands, and nose against his perpetually warm skin.

"There's no bad weather, just bad clothes," he says.

"Yeah, right, and would you be helping to finance an enhanced winter wardrobe for me? I've bought the right clothes or so I thought. One thing I've learned, good winter clothes are expensive. I've done the best I know how but I'm still freezing."

"Pumpkin, this isn't even real cold yet."

"Brrrrr," she says, planting her frigid feet against him.

With the cold weather and snowy roads, even Tom comes to the café less frequently. "Guess you smoothed things with him?" Lucie asks Ray.

"We have an agreement," he says, which seems evasive to her but she doesn't pursue the topic.

Maybe you're not giving him much extra cash because you know he'll just drink it away.

If her outdoor world has lost its charm, her indoor world is merry and cheerful. Increasingly, Ray is more relaxed. He still makes sure the café's back door is locked at all times — and why wouldn't he, she reasons, as they keep the cash box under the bar until he has time to make a bank deposit, and often the box contains thousands of dollars. It wouldn't be difficult for someone to slip in the back door, down the hall, grab the cash and be gone in an instant. But for the most part he's ceased his habit of glancing out the window every minute or two.

And he jokes with her, all day long: silly puns and wordplay, funny songs. "At first I *lobster*, but then I *flounder*," he sings to her one day in the kitchen. Or he riddles, "What did the rancher say when he won the lottery? 'Guess I'll keep ranching 'til it's all gone.' How do you make a million dollars in ranching? Start with two million."

As Lucie departs the café one afternoon, headed to the bank to make a deposit, she calls over her shoulder, "I'll be back," to which he responds, "I'll be Beethoven."

One busy evening, Lucie gathers a huge, precarious armload of dishes from a large table, carefully stacking plates and bowls on her arm, then walking the load steadily if slowly back to the kitchen. Ray looks up and says with admiration, "Wow. Made the *trip* without a *drip*."

She gives it right back. She notices him preparing a new dish and questions him about the meat. "What do you think it is?" he asks.

"No idea. Zebra?"

"Ha, good guess! So when you put it on the menu board, make sure it's at the very end of the list. Alpha-beta you know."

"Ha, alphabet humour. What is this meat, really?"

"Giraffe."

It turned out to be goat meat. "Good luck selling that," she said.

To which Ray replied, "It's all about marketing. Make them think it's the best thing ever. As in, 'If you like goat cheese, you're gonna love this...' It's worked before. Have you noticed how fast we sell out of brisket or marrow?"

One day, she says, "I learned something fun on the radio the other day, see if you know this: a group of crows is a murder, a group of lions is a pride, what do you call a group of rats?"

"Parliament," he says. She laughs so hard she has to stumble out of the kitchen.

She tells him about a conversation she's had in the café, talking to a young boy about his exotic pet, a chameleon.

"I had one once," Ray quips, "but if you put the damn things down they change colour, and you can't find them again."

I laugh all the time now, don't think I've ever done that before. Enjoyed someone's company like this. He's easy, easy.

On a frigid, dreary afternoon, a weary young man in heavy overalls comes into the restaurant for a bowl of hot soup. It's a quiet day, Ray sits at the bar adding up receipts, so Lucie fills the simple order herself. When the customer leaves, Ray and Lucie watch him cross the icy street and climb into a truck hauling a battered trailer piled high with used tires. "No wonder that guy is so *tired*," Ray says, grinning. "*Spare* me," she retorts.

He reaches to rub her back, squeeze her shoulder. Touching her is something else he seems to be more relaxed about, though he's still careful not to do so in front of customers or staff. Never mind. Ray matches her puns, her jokes. He knows the news, local and beyond, he pays attention to what customers are talking about. He's curious about food, a good mentor to his young sous-chef and even to Lucie, helping match her ideas for bread and pastry to complement his own menu. He's gentle and kind, his eyes twinkle. Physically he has a secure presence, a confidence in himself but without swagger, the like of which she's never encountered before.

He treats her as an equal, in every way. Yet she's aware of a shifting geometry of who they are together — the shape, the volume, the angles. Now this, now that. She's still not sure they've found their stride.

"You're the first guy I've known who doesn't need reforming," she tells him one evening as they curl on his couch, flipping through a new cookbook he's purchased.

"Well thank you for _that_, Pumpkin." He ruffles her hair.

"Honestly, that says more about me than about you, because I am starting to see that probably _none_ of the men in my previous life really needed reforming or rescuing or whatever the hell I thought I was doing. But you? You're perfect."

He only ruffles her hair again.

Happy landing, Lucifer. Let's see what happens.

A Monday morning. Lazy. Quiet.

"Pumpkin?"

"Mmm?"

"We don't, um...," he moves away from her slightly, lying back on his pillow so he can look at her. She hears concern in his voice, and she is seized with anxiety. Perhaps there's a problem with the café, maybe Tom has fired Ray after all? Or Ray has decided, without consulting her, they cannot continue as lovers. But he only says, "I've been meaning to talk about this. We don't want to make a baby."

She smiles, relieved. This is something entirely under control, so much that she hasn't spared a thought for it all winter. "No, we don't. And we won't. I have an IUD, I've had it for years."

"And it works?" He seems doubtful.

She sits up and draws the duvet to her chin. "It hasn't failed me yet, and — this is not news to you — I've been around the block a few times, but I've had exactly zero issues with the IUD. So no pills for me, no condoms for you, unless you want to. I've done that before. One of my pretty boys was so paranoid about it, said he didn't trust something he couldn't see so we used condoms. It's up to you, I'm not crazy about condoms, but if it means you won't worry, then fine, let's do that."

He plays with a tangle of hair that tumbles over her shoulders. "I'll think about it, but if I decide to, I'll buy them in the city. If I bought condoms from Tracey at the pharmacy, it would be all over town in ten minutes flat."

"Ah, yeah, small towns and gossip."

"Depends," he says, also sitting up and fluffing the pillow behind his back. "You have to know who you can trust here. That's the trick about protecting your privacy in a small town. Some people are likely to spread rumours for fun; for them it's the local spectator sport — and it can do a lot of damage if it gets out of hand. You have to be careful about what you say, what you do. But most people want their privacy, too. It's a case of 'do unto others'. If you respect people, generally they'll return the favour."

"I'm pretty sure there was gossip about me in Vancouver. I don't think small towns have a monopoly on it."

"Yep, it's everywhere. I'm a farm kid, went to a tiny country school. Not a one-roomer but close: four teachers and maybe fifty kids. I didn't get into town much until high school, which had three hundred kids. And then gossip hit me full in the face, and in the gut too I guess. Besides the whole cooking thing with me, which kids thought was weird, there was a divide between townies and farmies. Every farm boy wanted to date a town girl — they were so *sophisticated*." He leans his head back, smiling. "Who was good enough to date who... that was the number-one source of talk, along with who was taking drugs."

"Really, drugs? Like what, in a small town? I'm amazed."

"Drugs are everywhere, Pumpkin. Any damn thing you want, you can get it. Mostly weed, but some kids were into harder stuff, and they had no problem finding it: LSD, heroin, whatever pills at the time. Cocaine."

"Here, too? In Sweetgrass?"

"Sure. Like Donny said, there are a couple of kids in town who have gone down that path. Yeah, drugs, just like gossip. Here, there, anywhere."

"But you didn't do that? Drugs, I mean?"

"Never got the hang of smoking cigarettes or anything else. The rest just seemed like too much trouble, and I had enough trouble already. I had so many strikes against me. Farm kid. Not into sports. Short hair, even."

"So kids bullied you?"

He nods.

"What did you do?"

"At first, the way I dealt with it was to beat the crap out of anybody who had something to say about me. I was a spark plug."

"I can't picture you as a fighter. Although now I think about it, the first time I saw you, you were pissed off and had a knife in your hand."

He grins and nods. "Yeah, I was in a knife fight one time, that's where the scar on my arm came from — you know the one I mean."

She nods.

"That nearly landed me in juvenile court. Eventually I got tired of sending guys home with bloody noses and then getting called to the principal's office for it, so I quit fighting. When I stopped reacting to them, I wasn't fun for them any more, and they moved on to other targets. And I've pretty much stuck to that approach ever since. I ignore malicious talk, try to be a good person, behave in a decent way I think, help when I can. That's how you make your way in a small town. Or anywhere, I guess."

Oh, Jude, if you could hear this. Words to live by. Or reshape my life by.

He slides his arm around her shoulders, under her mane of hair, and draws her to him. "Lucie, you don't need to be afraid of small-town gossip, and you must know by now there are people you can absolutely trust here. Keith and Amanda, Bob and Agnes. Donny, the cop. George, although I know you don't believe me. A number of others you probably haven't met yet. They'll have your back, no matter what. But you still need to be careful. There are still some topics I wouldn't share with any of them. And I'd definitely buy condoms someplace else."

Despite Ray's affection, Lucie remains confused about the logistics of their relationship. He steadfastly refuses to take her out anywhere, except for a very occasional beer at the hotel bar or a stroll around his neighbourhood if the weather's not too cold for her. She doesn't really mind staying indoors with him, but she doesn't know how to describe this connection. Where is this going, is there room for progression — and what would 'progression' be, anyway? He's sweet and easy, smart and funny. They enjoy warm nights, terrific sex. At the café they work together seamlessly: they're efficient, comfortable, mutually respectful. The business thrives.

Something nags at her, a small and ever-present disquiet she can't quite identify or define. Uncharacteristically, Lucie decides to put her worry aside. For the moment she's content to ride this deeply pleasant wave, even with its uncertain edges. Besides, she's preoccupied, getting busy with pre-Christmas baking. Ray has agreed to let her make special cookies for sale at the café. To that end, she's purchased a collection of cute little boxes, quantities of wrap and ribbon, and she's enlisted Marta. Three weekends in a row Lucie has gone to Marta's house with its cozy kitchen, to make batch after batch of shortbread, pepper cookies, jam-filled thimble cookies, chocolate truffles. They laugh and joke together, Marta tells stories of her ranch life: "Oh we had good times, I play with my kids like I was a kid too. Tag and ball catch and kick the can, hide and find, so much laughing. Tom, he never play like that but he was good teacher, show the kids how to ride, how to look after horses and animals. And all those crazy chickens."

They share tips — "My mother used icing sugar in her shortbread instead of brown sugar. It doesn't give that rich traditional taste, but it makes a light, fluffy cookie," Lucie says. Marta's little house fills with the satisfying scent of baking.

Lucie never sees Tom, she's not sure whether he's even in the house. Marta makes no effort to speak softly, and her laugh is remarkably boisterous; it seems she's unconcerned about possibly waking her slumbering husband. Lucie suspects Tom is lurking in the den or downstairs or even in the garage, perhaps tinkering with a small appliance or something that needs fixing, only too happy for an excuse to avoid these two loud, laughing women. Or, more likely, he's out at the hotel bar or the town's pool hall. But that's only conjecture on her part. Tom never appears.

Lucie leaves with bags full of cookies she takes to the café to be boxed and wrapped. She piles the boxes on the bar with a sign: Assorted Christmas Cookies, $10 per Box. Business is brisk. After buying a box each, two of the ladies-who-lunch return the next day. "I couldn't help myself, I opened the box to see what you had in there and damned if my husband didn't eat the whole thing," says one, grinning. Lucie grins back.

Your husband, as if. Your secret is safe with me.

Lucie is also baking up a storm of stollen, cinnamon buns, pecan pies. She attempts almond roca but isn't pleased with the result. Ray no longer cautions her against listing special items on the menu board, so she chalks in her pies, cakes, cookies, and seasonal treats. Lucie assumes Ray and Tom have resolved their argument, and Ray is paying additional revenue from her baking and desserts.

As Christmas approaches, the café is constantly full and people seem cheerful — they're certainly going through plenty of food. The kitchen is always chaotic; Ray and his two helpers are continually rushed. It takes hours to clean up and re-organize once the café's doors are closed for the day.

Time hurtles toward Christmas. It's mid-month already. Lucie hasn't had two moments to think about shopping or what she might purchase as gifts for Amanda, Keith, Marta, even Judith, and ·

especially Ray. Ray... oh, she has no idea what he might like. He's so self-sufficient. He has all the clothing he needs, so a sweater or new shirt seems redundant. She considers buying herself some racy lingerie. After all, that trick has worked for her before, though this time it seems a bit unimaginative and self-serving.

It's Saturday night and The Sow's Ear is packed. Lucie is on the run, taking orders, delivering meals to tables, opening wine, clearing plates, pouring coffee, and slicing cake and pie. Suddenly there's a commotion at the door and a dozen or so people step in, gusting cold air inside with them. They cluster by the door, stamping snow from their boots, removing mitts and hats, unzipping coats. Lucie looks on in dismay, wondering how she can possibly seat such a large group, when they start singing.

Carollers.

Everyone in the café stops eating, stops talking, and listens. The choir starts with *Silent Night*, then *Hark the Herald Angels Sing*, then *Good King Wenceslas* — the entire restaurant lustily joins the choir to sing the line "Bring me flesh and bring me wine," laughing outrageously. They finish with *We Wish You a Merry Christmas*, to much applause and shouts of "Merry Christmas," and "Toby, I didn't think you could *remember* all the words, let alone sing them." The room takes on a heightened jolly liveliness as the singers depart. Lucie, tears in her eyes, turns to see Ray and the kitchen staff standing by the bar, laughing and applauding.

Later, Ray sends the staff home, and he and Lucie finish cleaning up. They are quiet and companionable, until he says, "I need a favour."

"OK."

"Don't say 'OK' until you know what it is." He stops loading the dishwasher and turns toward her. His hands dangle, he seems forlorn. She snaps to attention, instantly apprehensive.

Ray says, "I have to go see my sister for Christmas, and I need a ride to the bus depot. I leave next week, on the twenty-second, and I'll be back on the twenty-eighth."

Her short temper rears up, hiding her intense disappointment that he'll be away over Christmas and he's not chosen to tell her until now. She snaps, "So you need me to turn out pork hocks and beef tongue while you're away? Sure, no problem."

Come on, it's not like you've made any plans to spend Christmas together. He may be easy and sweet, but he's also his own man with his own family and history. Get over it. Pumpkin.

"The café is closed from the twenty-first until January second. But that's not my point. The weather's supposed to be good next week so it should be OK to drive me to the bus. But you might not want to pick me up after Christmas, the weather might change, the highway could be awful."

She considers. He's right, she is unaccustomed to driving in ice and snow. So far this winter, she's not been confronted with any truly difficult situation. But Judith is coming December twenty-ninth — not that Lucie has had time to make any arrangements beyond asking Amanda whether Judith could have the upstairs guest bedroom for a few nights — and she was counting on introducing Judith and Ray to one another. In fact, that was her main purpose for inviting Judith to Sweetgrass.

And then there's Christmas.

"OK, tell you what," Lucie says, calmly she hopes. "Yes, I'll take you to the bus, and I'll plan to pick you up, but if the weather turns crappy I'll ask Keith to drive in to get you after Christmas. And here's the favour I need from you in return: my friend Judith from Vancouver is coming out for New Year, she arrives the twenty-ninth. So..."

He grins. "You got it. We'll go get her. I'll be back in time. And I can't wait to meet her."

"Seriously? Most guys are so bored by 'Meet my best girlfriend, the one who already knows all about you because we talk about you endlessly.'" He laughs, so she presses on. "OK, yet another favour: take me to the town festival tomorrow night. I keep hearing about all the fun stuff that happens: the concert and hay rides and a big street party. I've never in my life been on a hay ride."

"You get hay all over yourself, it gets under your clothes and scratches like hell."

"That doesn't sound like yes."

He regards her solemnly for a moment and crosses his arms over his barrel of a chest. She's certain he's about to refuse, reluctant as usual to be seen in public. But he nods. "Sure," he says, "let's do that." He turns back to the dishwasher.

Yikes, a date. Be grateful for small miracles.

"Why would you take the bus to go home for Christmas?" she asks. "It's faster to fly."

"I don't mind," he says, "it's cheap and right now I have more time than money, so it's the bus for me. I settle in with a book and my iPod, the miles go by, and next thing I know there's my sis and it's Christmas. Besides, I'm going to North Battleford, in deepest Saskatchewan." He closes the dishwasher and turns the machine on.

He glances over to see her troubled, sad face. "Listen, Pumpkin. I know you're disappointed. Me too. This is not what I wanted for our first Christmas, and I'm sorry, but I have to go. Family business to take care of. Plus I'm looking forward to seeing my sis and her family, haven't seen my nieces and nephews for a long time. But," he places his warm, sure hands on her shoulders, "never mind, we'll have a rip-roaring great New Year with your buddy, and we'll make our own Christmas, maybe before, maybe after. Which reminds me, what are you doing tonight?"

"As if you don't know."

The next evening, Sweetgrass is buzzing with light and energy. Main Street sidewalks are zipping with families, restaurants selling snacks, retailers' tables of merchandise and racks of clothing on the sidewalks, ice carving in front of the art gallery, and an Elvis impersonator in front of the burger joint. Crowds circulate, everyone cradling Styrofoam cups of hot chocolate, terrible coffee, or mulled wine. Kids, so excited, scream and run, jump and collide. The street is blocked to traffic so people freely cross and wander, or meet in the middle to talk, laugh, hug. A choir, mostly the same carollers who visited The Sow's Ear yesterday, stands at one end of the street singing lustily if not entirely tunefully, sending puffs of breath into the night. Every shop and business is open, all decorated with lights and garlands and music. Occasionally a team of steaming heavy horses hauling a wagon piled with hay and children slowly jogs up and down the street, bells jingling, as revellers jump on and off the wagon.

It's a festival of all ages and all people. Lucie has come to realize Sweetgrass is a pretty white-bread place, but she knows there are Asian and Pakistani and other families in town. And here they all are, their kids giddy with excitement, the adults meeting and talking and laughing. All together.

Holding hands, Lucie and Ray stroll along the street. Lucie says, "So why do we not participate as a business in all this?"

"Because I'd rather not," Ray says, which is no kind of definitive answer. He doesn't elaborate.

Just as Lucie forms another question, Amanda and Keith step up to greet them. "Are you going to the bar?" Amanda asks. "I'm so happy I'm not working tonight. We alternate. This year I'm off, so I can enjoy the dance." Amanda throws her head back to laugh extravagantly, so unlike her — but such is the Christmas effect.

Eventually Ray and Lucie make their way to the hotel bar, where indeed the band is pounding out vintage rock tunes and the floor is crowded with townsfolk of all ages, wearing their party dress — jeans with fancy stitching, denim jackets studded and beaded, bright scarves and shawls, boots of richly tooled leather or downy soft suede.

Ray and Lucie dance, so differently from the firefighter's fundraiser dance. This time, they twirl slowly, he leads her confidently, they lock eyes and smile, they move in tandem. They dance as a couple, not as two uncertain strangers discovering each other.

"This is great, I am really not a dancer. You are magic, you sweep me off my feet. Or at least you sweep my feet along with you," she says.

Ray rewards her with the endearing smile she adores, the big happy smile that lights his eyes, his whole round, pleasant face. "Let's hop on the hay wagon," he says. "Then we'll go home."

They shrug into their jackets and stand shivering on the sidewalk, waiting for the hay wagon to come by. The team of heavy horses labours up the street, blowing from their bright red nostrils, steam rising from their dark, damp backs. As the wagon approaches, Lucie and Ray dash to climb on board, hauled up by those already on the wagon, and greeted with a thorough dousing of fragrant hay. They ride along and laugh, throwing hay onto people on the street. As the wagon turns around, Ray jumps off and pulls Lucie behind him. He wraps his arm around her, and they stride away from the party, headed home.

It's a long walk, and Lucie is thoroughly chilled once they achieve Ray's apartment. She quickly sheds her clothing and jumps into the shower to warm up. Coming back to the bedroom, she finds Ray ready to greet her. "Thanks," she says, mounting him, leaning forward as he cups her breasts. "I had fun tonight."

"Party's not over."

December twenty-second arrives, and she's driving Ray to the bus depot. City traffic is intense and requires all her concentration, so there's no conversation between them. At last she finds her way to the parking lot. Ray hefts his luggage from the back, and they enter the dreary, busy depot. He buys his ticket — she's surprised he hasn't pre-purchased a reserved seat — and then they stand awkwardly in the dank, brick-lined, and echoing waiting area.

"This is not what I wanted," he says, placing his arm around her shoulders. There's no warmth in his embrace, encased as they both are in heavy winter garments. "But I did get you a little present. You can't open this 'til Christmas day." He retrieves a small, pretty bag from his coat pocket. She reaches for it, but he pulls it away. "Promise?"

She smiles. "OK, no cheating." He relinquishes the bag. "And I have nothing for you," she says. "I honestly have not had time to think about a proper gift. But by the time you get back I'll have solved that problem."

"Pumpkin, you *are* my gift," he says as the loud speaker announces his departure. "Merry Christmas. See you soon." He folds her in a clumsy, parka-clad embrace, but his kiss is deep and warm and honest. He releases her, picks up his bag, and disappears through the doors.

Roughly she smears tears from her face as she turns away.

Lucie spends Christmas morning with Amanda and Keith, opening gifts — she purchased a painting for them from the local gallery — and drinking coffee liberally laced with rum. The Christmas tree sparkles, late morning daylight spears through the windows bright and clear, and the fire in the huge hearth pops and crackles.

Amanda's gift to Lucie is a luscious, soft winter sweater, ivory in colour, and a clutch of shower gels and bath soaps. Keith hands her an envelope from which Lucie withdraws the photo of a lightweight black saddle, its colourful skirt patterned with blue, purple, pink and black zigzags. "Jeez, Keith," Lucie says. "What is this about? Don't get me wrong, this is a terrific gift — but a saddle, really?"

As usual for him, Keith only gives her the slightest of smiles, but his eyes twinkle. "You've earned your stripes. And this saddle is a perfect fit for Quincy, just so you know."

After their gift exchange, the three get busy with meal

preparation. Amanda has invited several friends for dinner. Lucie prepares a pie and helps with salad. Keith stuffs the turkey. They work seamlessly in the kitchen, just as Lucie and Ray work in the café. By mid-afternoon, the turkey is roasting and nothing, for the moment, needs doing.

"I'm taking a nap," Lucie declares. Once in her room, she retrieves the gift bag Ray gave her at the depot. She inhales, fidgets, and then unties the bag and pulls out a tiny envelope. This she opens, shaking out a sterling silver ring with filigree whorled around a dazzling pale blue stone. There's also a note, which reads:

> *City Girl — this is blue topaz, it reminds me of your eyes. It's pretty and I thought you might like it. Hope so, hope it fits. Merry Christmas, me*

The ring is too large for her ring finger, so Lucie pushes it onto her middle finger, left hand. It's snug over her knuckle but once on, it's not a bad fit. She moves her hand to catch the light and make the gem flash. She grabs her cell phone and taps his number, but he doesn't answer. After a few more tries, she gives up with an exasperated sigh.

She thinks about Ray's open smile, his warm embraces, his searching kisses. She is undone and overwhelmed. He is familiar yet foreign territory to her. What is this — trust, friendship? Love? She has no idea. And despite his absence on this special day, she both smiles and cries as she twirls the ring.

Thank you. For more than you know. Merry Christmas, my sweet man.

"Judith will adore this room," Lucie says aloud as she arranges a bouquet of flowers on the dresser and Amanda places two fluffy orange bath towels on the bed. "It's bright, the view is great, and what's not to love about the steam shower? And I hope you'll like her, too. Jude is my best friend. She knows me up and down and seems to love me anyway."

"We all need a friend like that."

December twenty-eighth arrives with no significant weather, and Lucie is ready to pick up Ray at the depot. But her problem is not the road condition: her head is pounding, her eyes itch, and she can't stop sneezing as she drives into the city to retrieve him. His arrival is delayed, and she paces the sterile waiting room, sniffling and blowing her nose until the bus arrives and at last he comes through the sliding doors.

He spots her immediately, and rewards her with a quiet smile and bear hug, swaying her side to side. "I am so happy to see you, Pumpkin. I thought about you every day. I can't believe I forgot my cell phone at home, how dumb of me, I couldn't even tell you how much I was missing you, every damn day." He kisses her on each cheek, then full and long and sweet on her mouth. Winks at her while they trundle out to the car with his luggage. "So, a guy might be hoping his girl doesn't have plans for tonight?"

In response, she holds up the hand sporting his ring. "Ha, as a matter of fact I have a date with a box of Kleenex and a mittful of headache pills. Meanwhile — oh, Ray, this ring is gorgeous, thank you. I like it, but I don't know what it means. Rings _mean_ stuff, you know?"

He walks to the driver's side of the car. "I'm driving, right? Pumpkin, it means I saw a gorgeous bright stone the exact colour of your eyes. Maybe I should find one for myself with that same stone, to remind me of you. Anyway, I'm glad you like it. And what's up with the head cold?"

There's no further discussion about the ring, though she's dissatisfied with his answer. Instead, she asks about his time away. He says, "I have two nieces and two nephews. I was worried I'd be in a house full of yelling, overexcited kids but they're not so little any more, in fact they're teenagers. Been a long time since I've seen then. Mostly it was better than I thought it would be. And besides my sis and her family, I got to see a few aunts and uncles and cousins. I haven't seen them in the past few years, and that doesn't sit well with them. But nobody complained or bitched at me. It was just a good family time."

"I have no idea what that's like," she says, clutching a damp tissue and gazing out her car window to the passing streets, houses, traffic. "When I was little, Christmas with my mom was bleak to say the least. I see now that she was doing her best, and I admire that, in hindsight. But you know, this year was my favourite Christmas ever, with Amanda and Keith and their friends who came for dinner. Except, I remember one year in Vancouver when I was first there, I was friends with some college students who couldn't afford to go home so we had an 'orphan's Christmas' together, that was fun. But this year at the ranch was better by far. It felt genuine, peaceful, all about celebrating the moment, like Christmas is supposed to be. Dinner was great, we laughed and put on silly party hats, we even sang carols. I've never done that."

"I'm sorry I wasn't there." He looks over to her.

She meets his eyes, smiles, tickles his thigh. "No need to apologize, you've got family and right now I've got — *me*. I was disappointed that you weren't around, but you know, Christmas is just a day and everyone attaches a whole lot of freight to it."

He gives a small snort and says, "Freight, no kidding," as he pilots the car through the streets. At last they're out of the city and they turn west. The sky is blue-black and free from the glow of streetlights. They continue away from the city and she gazes idly across the dark fields. Over her shoulder, something in the sky is glowing, not with the sulphurous orange distant city but with an eerie, pulsating greenish-white light.

"Jeez, what's *that*?"

"Northern lights."

"No way, really? Stop the car. I'm not kidding. *Stop* the car."

He pulls onto a side road, tires grinding into the gravel. Even before the car has fully stopped, her door is open and she flings herself out. He cuts the engine and turns on the flashing hazard lights. Slowly he gets out of the car himself and comes to join her as highway traffic hurtles by. "Never seen them before?"

She shakes her head, still gazing skyward.

I'm from some big-ass city that's spitting distance from the U.S. border. When would I have seen northern lights? For that matter, when did I even bother to look at the sky?

Ray says, "When I was a kid on the farm, I was maybe six or seven, one night my mom woke us up because the lights were all over the sky. Amazing colours: green, red, purple, white, I can't even describe it, there's no word for 'dark cherry-red that you can see stars through.' The whole sky was alive, except when you looked straight up, you could see a dark patch of sky. It was like being in a teepee of light. I've seen northern lights many times, but never anything like that. It was one of those life moments, you know?"

She grabs his hand.

They watch without speaking as the lights shimmer and wiggle and dance, long shafts dart upward, intense spots spread into soft curtains that undulate against the densely dark sky, then fade. In a heartbeat, the aurora seems to evaporate, the show is over. They stand shivering for a few minutes longer until Ray says, "Let's get you home."

As they arrive in Sweetgrass, he turns to her. "So, where do you want to go?"

"Your bed, where do you think? Head cold or not, I haven't seen you in a week. Besides, I haven't figured out a gift for you yet. Maybe we could share this cold?"

"The gift that keeps on giving. Merry Christmas."

Late the next afternoon as the rapidly setting sun skirts the southern horizon, Ray drops Lucie at the airport's arrivals area.

"You are as wound up as a kid on Christmas morning." He gives her long ponytail a light tug.

"I'll text you when we've got her luggage. Meet you right at this door, OK?" she says. She sends him off to a nearby mall with a shopping list of cold remedies for her before he returns to wait in the airport's cell phone parking lot. Meanwhile, Lucie darts into the terminal building to await Judith's arrival.

Judith's flight is on time but there's such a crush of holiday travellers it seems hours before she finally appears at the top of the escalator. When Lucie sees her friend, she gives a somewhat abbreviated and congested cowboy yell, waves both hands, hopping and dancing. By the time Judith steps off the escalator into Lucie's waiting arms, both women are crying and laughing, and Lucie has broken a sweat inside her parka and turtleneck sweater. They hug and kiss and hug again. "Ohmygod onhmygod ohmygod," is all Judith can manage.

Finally they realize they're blocking the escalator. Linking arms, they walk to the luggage carousel where Judith collects two bags. "One is nearly empty, I figured we could do a day of shopping," she explains. "But Sweet Pea, you're sick. When did that start?"

"Two days ago, wouldn't you know it? I have us lined up for a New Year's Eve party but I may be having a party of my own by that time. I'm experimenting with an entire pharmacy's worth of cold and flu drugs."

"Think of the money you'll save on alcohol," Judith says, touching Lucie's parka-clad arm. "Listen. I'm happy to sit on the couch and trade stories for five days, and drink wine of course, cold drugs notwithstanding. And I must say, apart from your shiny red nose you look terrific, Rudolph."

The two friends wait by the appointed airport door. After their uproarious greeting, Lucie and Judith are now quiet, almost shy. They stand close but speechless, watching. "Agememnon!" Judith cries as the redoubtable silver Civic rolls into view. A grinning Ray hops out, gives Judith a hug and kisses both her cheeks.

"Hi I'm Ray. How do you like me so far?"

"Jude, you should sit up front," Lucie instructs, as she clambers into the back seat. "You've been to Calgary before, yes?" Judith nods as Ray pulls into traffic. "But it's not the city that I want you to see," Lucie continues. "The best is beyond Calgary. The land and sky and river and countryside where I live now. And it's such a perfect day today, getting dark already though. But it's so clear, you'll see at least a bit of what I love about this place."

"Wow, you're a living, breathing travel brochure," Judith teases.

"Living, maybe. Breathing, not so much," Lucie says, sneezing.

As they reach the city limits and turn west, Ray glances over his shoulder to see Lucie in the back seat, fast asleep. "I guess her getting sick was inevitable," he comments to Judith. "Lucie works hard at the café, then she puts in extra hours baking, and the run-up to Christmas was really busy. I know she's bought good winter clothes, but if you're not used to the cold, chances are you're going to catch a chill eventually."

"She phoned me one day back in November," Judith says. "She was out for a walk and having a glorious time, I guess it was unusually warm and she was up to her eyeballs in sunshine and scenery, in love with the place. I was shocked, I've never heard such enthusiasm in her voice. Lucie is not one to embrace the great outdoors."

"How long have you known her?"

"Ten years, hmm… actually, it's been twelve years now. She arrived in Vancouver from Ontario determined to escape her mother, and she didn't know a soul. I met her at a women's networking event and I liked her the moment I met her, though I can't say why, exactly. She's independent, sassy, and tough, and it's hard to penetrate that rock-hard shell. My nickname for her is 'Lucifer.' The fallen angel, which is a bit blunt and not really accurate." Judith looks away, watches the passing countryside from her passenger window.

"Because?"

Judith murmurs, "Well, to be a fallen angel you'd have to be an actual angel in the first place. Lucie is my best friend, but I would hardly describe her as angelic. Although you might beg to differ."

"Nope," is all he says, with a chuckle.

Overhead the sky is now dark enough to show early stars, though the twilight horizon to the west is still pale blue shading to teal and yellow behind the ragged black outline of the mountains. On either side of the road, snow-clad fields of deep cobalt blue stretch away, lines of trees are black in relief, farmhouses and fences are lively with Christmas lights. "Warm enough?" Ray asks, reaching to turn down the heat as Judith nods. "So you've been to Calgary before?"

"Years ago. I had a client here, so I've been to the city itself but never out here. It's gorgeous, at least what I can see right now. And where are you from?"

They trade histories, to a point — Ray talking about farm life in Saskatchewan, Judith about her Vancouver childhood. She says, "My parents were rich, I grew up in a huge house two blocks from the beach, and I thought that was normal. But my dad made some bad investments and lost an unthinkable amount of money, so we moved into smaller and smaller places. Eventually my parents found a little house on Vancouver Island. My dad is gone now, and my mom is frail. She's fine but she's not living the life she thought. Hmm. Funny about the choices we make. Which brings me back to Lucie."

Ray says, "She's told me about her Vancouver life, and a bit about growing up in Toronto. I guess she had a rough time with her mother, grew up fast, and now she doesn't trust anybody. You're so right, she's a tough nut sometimes, like a wild horse — just when you think you're making progress, something happens to scare her off."

"Lucie has some trust issues, no doubt about it. But she is totally worth the effort."

"I know. I can't believe she arrived in my restaurant one day and turned out to be the best thing that's ever walked into my life. I don't want to blow it. I'm afraid of accidentally doing something that could ruin everything because I don't know enough about her." He glances quickly at Judith. "She's tough and chippy, but she's got a good heart and I want to keep her in my life if I can."

Judith turns to see Ray's boyish, freckled face illuminated by the ghostly green dashboard lights. "Over the years Lucifer and I have seen each other at our worst and our best — and I would say her 'best' has changed recently. I'm amazed at what's happened to her since she's been out here. She hasn't called me much since leaving Vancouver, I know she's been busy with her café job — and you, I guess. But when she calls, there's been something in her voice I've never heard before. I'm looking forward to learning more about the life she's making here, because I have to tell you, from what I've been able to piece together it's like nothing else. She's re-inventing herself out here. It's exactly what I hoped would happen, exactly what I wanted for her. It's a transformation."

"Yeah, Sweetgrass seems to be good for that."

The car radio plays softly as Ray pulls up in front of Amanda's house. Lucie groggily heaves herself from the back seat. "I'm so sorry, girlfriend. I'll get you settled, then I really need to sleep. I'll be better tomorrow, I promise." She stumbles toward the open door where Amanda is waiting. "I can't believe how awful I feel," she whispers as she enters, then turns as Judith and Ray step inside, Ray hefting Judith's considerable luggage. "Amanda, this is my best gal pal Judith. Jude, this is Amanda, queen of the ranch, the bar, Keith, and keeper of much local wisdom," which makes Amanda grin and duck her face behind her hand.

"Jeez Sweet Pea, go to bed, you're babbling," Judith says, as she gives Amanda a hug. "Amanda, thanks so much for having me here."

Just as she'd done months before when Lucie arrived at the Sweetgrass hotel, Amanda grabs Judith's luggage and starts down the hall. "I'm glad you're here, a friend of Lucie's is a friend of mine. C'mon, here's your room."

Judith follows along the hallway, leaving Lucie and Ray at

the door.

"Thank you," Lucie says, giving him a limp hug. "I'm sure the two of you got acquainted and solved all my problems while I was asleep. You can tell me in the morning."

"Get some rest, Pumpkin." He kisses her cheek and turns to leave. "I'm taking your car, OK?"

"Sure, I'll call you tomorrow."

"Just get better." He steps out into the moonless night.

The next morning, Ray drives Lucie's car back to the ranch, leaves the keys on Amanda's kitchen table — the ranch house door is never locked — then hitchhikes back to Sweetgrass to spend a few hours cleaning and organizing the café's kitchen, readying to re-open after the holidays.

Later, Lucie barely surfaces. Upon waking her throat is clogged, her head and sinuses throb. She takes a hot shower and greets Judith in the kitchen, they share coffee and several of Lucie's soft, chewy oatmeal cookies for breakfast.

"You're not any better," Judith says. "Should we get you a doctor?"

Lucie shakes her head. "You know me, I didn't have a regular doc in Vancouver and I don't have one here, either. I guess we could go to one of the crawl-in clinics, but those are for *sick* people. I just have a cold, although I'll admit it's a doozey."

"Well then, are you taking a good decongestant at least?"

"Yes and it works for draining my head and drying out my sinuses but it dries out everything — eyes, lips, mouth — so I'm trying to cut back until I really need a shot. Besides, it makes me ineligible for Olympic competition, clearly I have to consider that."

"Clearly." Judith laughs and strokes Lucie's cheek fondly. "You crack me up, you know. I always wonder where this stuff comes from, the funniest things come out of your mouth." They talk a while, catching up on Vancouver news. "Gwen is pregnant," Judith confides, to which Lucie responds, "That is great, I'm happy for them. And I need to send Gwen and Patrick some news, let them know I'm still alive, more or less. They have been good to me, and they're still paying to store my furniture, I need to get that straightened out. But I never seem to have time to call or email or anything. Shame on me."

"I phone them with an update whenever I hear from you. Plus they have more money than some small countries; you know that. Storing your stuff is what they want to do to help, it's no burden for them."

"Maybe not, but it means a lot to me."

"Then what stops you from just saying, 'Here I am, here's what I'm doing, thanks for your help'? A phone call, an email to them? Would that be such a huge effort on your part?"

"Maybe I'm scared of being judged. I mean, look at my life now. I'm a waitress in a little café in a little town, period. What would they make of that?"

"Why do you care?"

Ah, sweet friend, not now. I'm too tired and sick for this conversation.

Lucie, dressed in black leggings and her new downy sweater, her damp hair a snarled jungle around her head, leans back on the couch. Her face is even more pale than usual but for her tortured nose, which is red and raw, likewise the bright-red rims around her eyes. She gazes past Judith out the west-facing windows to see snowy fields, dark trees, and the remarkably bold, clear sky. "I don't know, Jude. Why can't I just be who I am, why do I feel some need to prove something? I guess I want to measure up. That's my mother speaking."

"And what makes you think that contributing to a local restaurant business, finding a good man and good friends, being happy in your own skin — what part of that is not success, not measuring up? Fuck your mother."

"This sounds like several conversations we've had. Hundreds, maybe."

"A few things have changed since then."

"Oh, girlfriend. *Everything*. Every last thing has changed." Lucie drains her coffee, stands unsteadily. "And, yes, you were one hundred per cent right that day when I nearly doused you with coffee, about me needing to get a grip on my life and grow up. I think I'm on that path here in lovely Sweetgrass. My life is better in many ways, but overall it's just as uncertain as the day I left Vancouver...Jude, I'm so sorry but I really need to sleep again. I'm sick and so tired. What do you want to do now that we've had coffee? My car keys are on the kitchen counter, you can drive into Calgary if you want to shop and fill that empty suitcase, or you can explore Sweetgrass. In fact, I'd love it if you would walk around town, see for yourself what my life looks like now. That's why I wanted you to come here. We have cute stores here, a really good art gallery, restaurants, it's a fun town for the size of it, and I'm sorry The Sow's Ear isn't open right now because you would love the food we serve. My point is, you're on your own today and I'm so sorry about that. Ugh, when was the last time I had a cold this bad?"

Lucie goes back to bed. Judith takes her time getting ready for the day, eventually driving into Sweetgrass. True to Lucie's assessment, the town is home to shops offering funky clothing, interesting jewellery, and antiques, and an exceptional art gallery. Judith visits the local butcher where she buys sausages, and she buys sourdough bread at the bakery, intending to contribute these purchases to the ranch's table. She passes The Sow's Ear and tries to peer inside but the blinds are lowered. Judith even visits the library with its impressive display of local quilts hanging from the walls. Finally she heads back to the ranch, spending the balance of the day on the couch with a book and pot of tea.

Lucie rouses in late afternoon and warms soup for dinner. Amanda is working at the bar and Keith is still out working horses, so Lucie and Judith share soup and sourdough bread, then head downstairs to curl up on the couch and watch movies. "I don't even have popcorn or a bag of chips," Lucie laments. "Jude, this is not what I wanted for your visit."

"Sweet Pea, sick is sick. You don't have any control over that."

The movie doesn't captivate either of them, so halfway through they start chatting. Eventually Judith turns the video off. The sudden silence is a bit disconcerting, but they pick up their conversation.

"He seems sweet, and I don't know... authentic? Genuine?" Judith says of Ray. "Gentle, respectful. He adores you, as if you didn't know. So — I'm just saying, because I know what you're like — nothing about him needs, um, fixing?"

Lucie shakes her head emphatically. "Nope, and even if I thought so, I've learned it's not my place to criticize someone or mould then into what I think they should be. I know," she laughs, seeing Judith's sceptical expression, "that is such a departure for me. Although..."

Judith rolls her eyes. "Although *what?*"

Lucie continues, "I have to say he does some weird things."

"Such as...?"

Lucie describes Ray's odd vigilance. "It's strange, but it's not bad enough for me to start needling him about it. Besides, I can hardly criticize him for such a small thing because he knows much more about me. I spilled it all, the morning after our first night together."

"Oh, brilliant, good job. You had a great night together then you unloaded your whole terrible story?" Judith grins and rises. "I think we need a bottle, where would I find such a thing?" Lucie instructs, Judith returns with wine, corkscrew, glasses. She pulls the cork with a festive pop. "OK, time to tell me what's going on," Judith says. "He's an adorable, huggable, teddy-bear guy, but I suspect there's much more to this picture. I have to say, Sweet Pea, he's not your usual type. I'm all ears."

Lucie starts, "I tried so hard not to get involved with him. But how can you resist a man who is sweet and kind? He is all that and more. He is like nobody I've ever known. That morning I had a meltdown like never before. It was unbelievable, a surprise to me and I'm sure to him. But... He was so gentle and considerate. No verdict, no sentence. And it's continued like that, he's... *kind.* So now we're... whatever we are, it's only been since Thanksgiving. Then again, I'm still undecided about my own future here so I don't want to make promises I can't keep. Not like me, eh?"

"But he's worth all this new-found patience of yours?"

"I think so. I *am* happy in the moment. Content. Whoa, there's a word I've never applied to my own life before, *content*." They clink glasses but Lucie doesn't drink, instead she sets her half-emptied glass on the table. "I'm so sorry, Jude, I need to sleep again. But, did you have a good day? Did you have the Sweetgrass experience?"

"I did. You're right, this is a cute and quirky town, plus the scenery is gorgeous."

"That's not all, in fact that's the smallest part," Lucie says, wobbling as she stands up. "It's the people, Jude. You've met Amanda and Keith and Ray, everyone I've met here is great. Except Tom. He's the most ornery person I've met in years."

"*Ornery*. That's not in your Vancouver vocabulary. You are turning into a cowboy, girlfriend." Which makes Lucie grin broadly as she staggers off to bed.

New Year's Eve morning finds Lucie and Judith at the table with Amanda, Keith, and Ray, who arrived to cook a breakfast of blueberry pancakes, oven-crisped bacon, and creamy scrambled eggs. Judith asks, "Ever thought of doing brunch at the café?"

"Tried it, didn't like it," Ray responds emphatically, pouring more coffee all around. "Breakfast is a lot of work, it's a whole other game. Besides, I don't like getting up that early, especially on weekends." Lucie, who knows otherwise, frowns at him but Ray doesn't notice.

"So who's coming to the New Year's dance at the hotel?" Amanda asks, looking around the table. "Lucie, how are you feeling?"

"Better. We might turn up tonight, but I likely won't make it through to midnight. Besides, we have to get this girl to the airport early, right?"

"I leave at eight-thirty tomorrow morning, the only flight I could find," Judith says apologetically.

Ray shrugs. "No worries, I'll get you there. But we'll have to leave here by six. Earlier, maybe."

Lucie and Judith groan, which makes Keith laugh softly and say, "I'll wake you up at five when I feed the horses." They groan again, louder.

"Did I mention there are some drawbacks to country life?" Lucie says to Judith.

Ray stays through the afternoon, urging Lucie to take a short walk for fresh air, and she finally agrees. The day is bright, the sky spotless, the air sharp, clear, crackling dry, stunningly cold. The winter sun is brilliant but brittle, as though the light itself could shatter.

They bundle up — Amanda arms Judith with her own parka — and wade through the snowy pasture as horses crowd around, looking for treats. Judith is nervous but Keith takes her arm, shows her how to hold a chunk of carrot flat on her palm to be nibbled up by the horses' soft lips, which tickles and makes Judith laugh. Quincy sidles up and lays her head on Lucie's shoulder. Lucie herself is surprised but, true to Keith's teaching and what she's learned about being around horses, she remains calm, simply stroking the mare's nose and neck as though this happens every day.

"Wow, look at that! Is this is your horse?" Judith inquires.

"Hard not to be jealous of that horse," Ray interjects softly, laughing.

Lucie laughs too. "My horse? Ha. This little mare is Quincy. She's sweet and gentle, so I ride her, mostly." She scratches the mare's ears as the horse jerks her head from Lucie's shoulder and backs a step away. "And when Keith thinks I need a challenge, I ride Banjo, that pinto over there. The others are too big for me."

"You do fine with the big horses too," Keith responds.

As Quincy turns away, Lucie leans on Ray and shields her eyes against the glare of full sun on snow, says, "Hey, I want to check out my new saddle, I haven't even seen it yet." They make their way to the barn, where Keith snaps on the lights and opens the tack room, and there's Lucie's Christmas gift hanging on a saddle rack. It's a lightweight affair made from nylon instead of leather.

"It's sturdy enough for lessons and for trail riding," Keith explains. "If you want to do more intense riding you should invest in a leather saddle. But this saddle is like the ones the chuckwagon outriders use at Stampede. If it works for them, it will work for you." Lucie only smiles at Keith and nods, knowing a bigger reaction would embarrass him. They step back outside.

"I love these sparkly days," Lucie says. "Jude, look around. Stars on the snow, in the trees, sometimes in the air. Blue shadows. It's magical. This is exactly what I wanted you to see."

"But it can change so fast when a chinook blows in," Ray says.

"And what is that, exactly?" Judith asks.

Ray says, "When there's a big storm on the west coast, the weather moves east, drops rain and snow over the mountains but keeps the heat, or so I understand. And then it comes roaring over the foothills here with a big, warm wind that melts snow and sucks up moisture. Sometimes the temperature changes from ten below to ten above in a few hours. Or faster."

"Come on," Judith says.

"No lie," Keith responds, hands in his pockets, squinting at Judith against the brilliant light as they leave the barn. "The Native people call it 'Snow Eater,' because that's exactly what happens. The arch rolls over, the wind picks up, and in the middle of winter we get weather born in Hawaii."

"The arch?"

"Chinook arch, a dark, solid cloud with a sharp edge that reaches across the sky. It might hang in place without moving for hours, but eventually it comes over us, the wind blows, and bingo the thermometer goes up."

"You've never mentioned this miracle," Judith says to Lucie.

"I haven't had the pleasure."

"Not one chinook yet this winter, it's been odd," says Ray.

Keith, hands still in his pockets, replies, "I guess it will come when it's ready."

They wander back to the house, which is toasty and welcoming. Lucie stretches her arms over her head and admits, "I'm not so sure I want to go dancing." She glances at Ray, who nods and says, "Fine with me, Dumpling. Why don't I run to the café and grab something from the freezer I can fix for dinner, then we'll call it an early night?"

Judith laughs. "Ray, you are a true chef. Your endearments are all about food."

"Yeah, he also calls me 'Fruitcake' and 'Nutbar,' for the record," Lucie says.

Ray returns from the café with bags and containers, sets to work fixing a meal while Judith and Lucie doze and talk on the couch. Keith and Amanda depart for the dinner and dance at the hotel. "I likely won't see you," Amanda says, giving Judith a hug. "Please come again in the summer, we'll get you on a horse."

"Oh no you won't," Judith says, hugging back. "Thank you for hosting me. And thank you for providing a home for my crazy friend." Amanda giggles. Judith relinquishes her hug to look Amanda full in the face with a full, sincere smile. "Happy New Year."

The remaining trio enjoys a quiet meal, without so much as a bottle of sparkling water. Again Lucie apologizes and goes early to her bedroom. "Sorry, I'm so very done, Happy New Year," she says, hugging them and leaving Judith and Ray to stoke the fire and ring in the year's passing.

In the amber firelight, Judith settles into the worn leather couch, snuggles under a crocheted blanket, and says, "Well, the verdict is in: you are officially the best thing that's happened to Lucie since she discovered the joys of wine, and you might even top that."

The enormous, butter-coloured leather armchair squeaks like a saddle as Ray settles in. He doesn't answer right away. Instead he takes a nip from the snifter of Scotch warming in his hand and gazes at the fire thoughtfully.

Eventually he says, "I'm sure you can tell I am crazy about her. I believe that feeling is mutual, but she can be so hard to read, sometimes she's all about that big chip on her shoulder, and I'm confused about what she wants from me. That's not a complaint, mind you. She is who she is, she's got her reasons, and I think I'm up to the challenge of peeling away her tough layers. But," he places his glass on the coffee table, "I don't want to screw this up. I don't want to make some big mistake and piss her off, chase her away. She's precious. Special."

He stands to stir the logs, throws on two more, and waits until they catch and the flames roar up. Looking at the fire, he says, "She's told me about her life in Vancouver. Sounds like it was great on the surface. But seems to me she was never really happy there."

Judith grins sardonically. "So true. I gave her a big fat lecture one day, I felt terrible afterward. I told her to get out of town and do some growing up, then wondered whether I'd ever see her again. She was so angry." She peers deep into the flickering depths of the fire and tips the glass to her lips for a good long swallow. "But look at her now. It's a revolution. I'm so happy for her. I miss her, but I think this is where she's meant to be. And, for the record, you are the best — by far — of any man she's ever hooked up with. Hmm, maybe that's too much information?"

"Nothing I don't already know, including the guy who hit her. And I've been around, too. I'm no angel. Fallen or otherwise."

They watch the popping, hissing flames. After a few minutes, Judith continues — speaking softly, almost musing to herself. "And I'm happy for *you*, Ray. You are right, she's got a hard shell; she'll show you that tough girl whenever she feels threatened. Ach, listen to me, the all-knowing Jude, ha. But… I've known her a long time, and I can tell you she is totally worth the effort. And when she's got your back, you never have to think twice, you can count on her entirely. Like... when my dad died, she held me up when I couldn't think straight, she supported me in ways I can't even describe. Hell, I wish I'd known Lucie in high school when I came out to my parents, she'd have been awesome."

"Came out?" He smiles. "Not that it matters to me, but she's never said that about you. I had no idea."

Judith just shakes her head. "Whatever. I'm kind of surprised. Luce and I share everything, I thought she might have told you. Because, Ray, I probably know more about you than you'd like. But I'm guessing it never occurred to her to tell you about me. And it doesn't matter."

"Maybe she forgets what she's said to who. Or maybe I should have absorbed that information somehow, paid better attention. She talks about you all the time."

"Ach, no. Don't think it's something you should have done, or paid attention to. Ray, don't second-guess yourself. You understand Lucie better than you think — to the extent that anyone can understand her."

They pause.

She muses, "And about the talking. Lucie talks talks talks. She is a blatherskite."

He rewards her remark with the full, round belly laugh that Lucie cherishes.

"My gran used to say that. 'Blatherskite.' I haven't heard that word in years. Thank you for bringing it back to life. And you're right. Lucie talks and analyzes everything. And that's good for me, I don't do that enough. She's about thought, insight, paying attention. How could I not appreciate that? It's part of her, who she is. It's what I *love*."

Judith does not remark his use of that particular precious word. She's tired, and she's had plenty of rich food and whisky. The moment passes, followed by another long, pleasant, comfortable pause. The fire wanes but still provides some surprisingly loud and energetic pops.

Ray raises his glass to Judith with a warm smile. "I truly want to keep her in my life, but I also think she wants to go back in Vancouver. I'm not about to stand in her way. I live and work here in Sweetgrass, I'm not going anywhere — sure as hell not Vancouver. I would be so sad to lose her but I'm OK with being someone who helps her move forward, in whatever way she needs to move. I promised not to hurt her, and I mean to keep that promise." He sips again and turns back to the diminishing fire.

"You are a saint."

He laughs again, his voice echoing from the high ceiling. "As if," he says. He checks his glass: it's empty.

They remain quiet for some time as the blaze subsides to intense coals that pulse and fade. At last Judith says, "It's nearing the zero hour. If you're not going to open a bottle of bubbly, I'm done."

"I need to drive home," Ray responds.

"So the party's over," she says, standing. They hug.

"I'll be here at six to pick you up."

BLOW ON, CHILLY WIND

Perhaps predictably, Lucie's head cold clears up right after Judith's departure. The Sow's Ear re-opens after the holidays, and Lucie's daily routine gets back to what passes for normal: baking at the café three or four early mornings a week, assisting Ray in the kitchen, and serving tables when the café is open. Otherwise she returns to the ranch without much to keep her occupied. She still finds it too cold for riding, so her Christmas saddle remains in the tack room, untried.

"You need something to get you out of the house besides the café," Amanda comments one day. "There's a gym in town, you know."

Lucie shakes her head. "I never could get interested in weights or aerobics, though I did yoga ages ago, back in one of my Vancouver incarnations."

"I'm pretty sure they have yoga classes at the gym in town. Not that I'm trying to manage your life. But you seem a bit lost."

"I have exactly zero motivation. Lately it's all I can do to drag my sorry ass to work and back."

"I know what you mean. It might be the daylight. Those short days in November and December kill my energy, and it's taking some time to revive. But have you noticed, the days are already getting longer? More daylight makes such a difference at this time of year. I watch for every extra minute of light."

"I have noticed. Especially in the evenings, it's still light at five instead of dark at four like in December. And daylight is coming earlier in the morning, too; I notice that when I'm baking early at the café. Yeah, daylight could be my problem. But mostly, I'm cold," Lucie admits. "I love walking outside on those gorgeous days when the light is brilliant and sparkly and incredible. But Amanda, I just can't warm up."

"So I guess skating and curling are out of the question?"

Lucie laughs. "I'm not very sporty, you've probably figured that out. I mean, yoga is one thing, but... ugh, team sport. Nope. Plus for me it's about going out into the cold. I just can't."

"You don't have to practice downward dog in the snow," Amanda points out. "And we do have an indoor skating rink — heated, may I point out, at great expense to the community. Anyway, you're not alone, Lucie. A lot of people around here hibernate all winter; they pretty much stay home from November 'til March. Or they go south — Mexico, Arizona. Phoenix is the second home for lots of people around here. I understand why they go there. If you don't like the cold, you don't, and that's that. But there are tricks to staying warm through winter here, and it really is worth the effort to gear up and get outside. Winter lasts a long time — seven or eight months, some years — you might as well enjoy it."

"I bought a honking huge parka, I thought that would do the trick."

"Try layering. Usually a bunch of layers works better than one heavy coat."

"OK, you're right," Lucie says. "I do need to get out. Maybe yoga would be a good start, I need to broaden my horizons. Plus I haven't seen Marta since before Christmas. Time to get moving."

The local gym does indeed offer yoga. Two nights each week Lucie dons tights and a close-fitting top and forces herself to drive through the frigid evening to Sweetgrass, dashing into the gym to spend an hour bending and stretching. The yoga classes are accompanied by the sound of soft surf and chanting, inducing Lucie to meditate about travel and faraway, imagined places.

She soon feels better. Physical engagement serves her well. Her usual snap and energy return.

"Hey, Pumpkin, what's got into you?" Ray teases one night after some unusually playful sex. "I'm not complaining, just curious. You taking vitamins or something?"

She's also noticed a poster on the gym's bulletin board, a local hiking group seeking new members. "They're doing a snowshoe trip next Sunday, think I'd like to give it a try if the weather's not too cold," she tells Ray. "Want to go?"

He shakes his head. "Doing some research that afternoon — we need to change up the menu pretty soon. But I'll cook you something special when you get back."

Guess if I'm going to discover the Great White North, I'm doing it on my own.

"What is it with you — how do you stay in such good shape, anyway?" she asks. "Maybe you actually have another girlfriend."

"Ha. One woman keeps me busy. Two women would kill me. The guy who rents the main floor suite in this house has cardio and weight equipment in the basement; he lets me use it in exchange for keeping an eye on his place. He's a surveyor, he's away a lot." He kisses her with the long, slow caress that always undermines whatever chagrin she might be holding. His every kiss melts her.

Besides, she's been enjoying the results of his time spent alone at home, his researching and experimenting with new food ideas, new recipes. Whenever she's at Ray's apartment, he gives her something different to eat: Scotch egg, rabbit pie — made with Lucie's pastry — crispy deep-fried chicken feet, lamb shanks, salmon skin chips. True to The Sow's Ear theme, he's trying to make good use of off-cuts and the material many chefs would throw away. When experimenting with food and recipes, he always asks her opinion. He's genuinely interested in what she says and never takes criticism personally. Lucie makes a sincere effort to be thoughtful and honest when offering a critique.

"That pastry is too sweet for a savoury pie, let me change up the recipe," she tells him when they're sampling a beef and kidney pie. Or, "You know Ray, you can use mashed potato to thicken soup, instead of flour. I forget where I learned that, maybe from my mother though it seems unlikely — she was all about flour." They collaborate and finesse his creations. "Ugh chicken feet again, are you kidding me?" she teases, as he tweaks and adjusts seasoning and sauce until he achieves consistent results and adds a new item to the café menu.

This late January Sunday dawns with the sparkling clarity she's come to love. It will be a tremendous day for snowshoeing. Ray makes a hearty breakfast and sends her out with a flask of hot tea and snacks for lunch. "Have fun, Pumpkin," he smiles. "I'll give your regards to my other girlfriend."

"Yeah, you do that."

Lucie drives to the meeting place, the local bank's parking lot. In her eagerness, she's arrived too early and sits in Agememnon waiting, second-guessing herself.

Are you out of your mind? What do you know about snowshoeing? Why do you even want to do this? They're probably all like that Kevin guy you met in Lake Louise last spring, all super-fit backcountry experts. They'll leave you in the dust, Lucie, or in a snowdrift. Go home right now before anyone else shows up.

She's about to turn the ignition and escape unseen when a none-too-sturdy Volkswagen van pulls into the lot and three people jump out. One is an athletic man whose appearance confirms Lucie's misgivings, but the other two are petite women: one older, the other a snippet of a teenager. Reluctantly, Lucie clambers from her car and walks over to introduce herself. She's greeted warmly by Kurt, Janet, and Daisy.

Daisy, really? That's a hillbilly hippie kid name if ever there was one.

Lucie explains to the trio that she's new to this endeavour and doesn't have her own pair of snowshoes. "We don't either, we borrow them from the library," Janet explains. "They have an outdoor program; they organize summer hiking and winter snow-shoe and ski trips, and they even have telescopes you can sign out. Once everyone gets here, we'll figure out how many snowshoes we need and Kurt will get them, he's got a key to the library."

That's crazy, the library rents snowshoes.

The parking lot quickly fills with vehicles. People greet one another with hugs and handshakes. Finally Kurt calls everyone into a circle and says, "Who needs snowshoes?"

Lucie and five others raise their hands. Kurt jogs across the street to the library and returns with the required equipment. The group organizes carpools and Lucie finds herself in Kurt's van, seated next to Daisy, mom Janet, and Kelly, a family friend. They chat as Kurt pilots the rattling vehicle westward toward the mountains.

"You're from the restaurant, right?" Kelly asks.

Lucie nods and jokes, "I drove into Sweetgrass last summer and my car broke down. Found a job and I've been here ever since."

"Kinda sounds like something from *The Twilight Zone*," Kelly responds. "Remember that TV show? Some weird thing happens... seems normal but soon you're trapped. Yikes, I've just dated myself. In my defense, I was a kid at the time *Twilight Zone* was on TV."

"Or *Hotel California*," Lucie muses. "'You can check out any time you like...'"

The convoy arrives at a substantial metal gate blocking further westward progress, which Kurt explains to Lucie is a means to protect winter wildlife habitat by preventing vehicle access. Everyone hops out and straps on snowshoes. Janet shows Lucie how to walk in snowshoes by swinging her feet wide around each other to avoid tripping, and lends Lucie a pair of ski poles for balance. In twos and threes, the group sets off along the untracked and unplowed road west of the barrier gate. On this easy, flat terrain, Lucie gets the hang of snowshoes, building her confidence until she sees the group leaving the wide road surface to take up a wooded trail. Fortunately, the trail is well packed and poses little challenge, even as the slope steepens. "You could pretty much walk this in hiking boots," she comments to Janet, who is puffing but striding along gamely.

"Yes," Janet says, "hardly any snow right now. Other years, if you didn't have snowshoes or skis you would sink out of sight even on a packed trail. It's early yet, though. We usually get a lot of snow in March. And April and May, for that matter."

The group ascends through tall trees, the stillness punctuated by the chatter of chickadees and squirrels. The hikers spread out and straggle along the trail. Lucie pushes upward, working hard, determined to not be the last person to make it to wherever they're going. The trail emerges from the woods, traverses a steep slope, and then switches back and keeps climbing. Topping the ridge, Lucie pauses with Janet and Daisy, who have stopped to rest.

The ridge top offers a view down the valley where they've come from, and westward to blue and purple peaks candied with crusty snow. "Funny year," Janet comments, taking a handful of raisins and nuts from the bag Lucie passes around. "Not much snow yet but no chinooks either."

"It's global warming, Mom," Daisy says.

Janet waves her hand — dismissively, Lucie thinks, but Janet says — "I don't know, Daze. If you talk to Sweet Water Woman, she'll say this winter is not unusual. That's why the bighorn sheep and elk herds graze here, because usually there's not much snow cover whether there are chinooks or not. I'm not saying there's no climate change effect, but I think it's hard to tell what's normal and what's not, in a place like this where the weather is so variable."

"Sweet Water Woman?" Lucie asks.

"She's a Blackfoot elder, she lives with her husband and kids in the hills northwest of Sweetgrass. Her English name is Elizabeth but nobody around here calls her that, not if you know her anyway."

"She's amazing," Daisy adds breathlessly. "She knows so much about what plants are food or medicine, legends and stories about the animals and the 'Old Ways,' that's the Native word for 'history' she says. She gave me a spirit name as a present on my sixteenth birthday. My spirit guide is Owl. My spirit name is a secret until I'm ready to tell it. Sweet Water Woman — you should meet her. She is totally cool."

"If you ever want to go foraging with her, let me know," Janet says. "Especially mushrooms. You don't want to take a chance, the ones that'll kill you look exactly like the ones that won't. She'll teach you the difference."

"I'd love that," Lucie says.

They keep going up the ridge. To Lucie's alarm, rounding a corner she sees an even steeper and more daunting slope. Daisy says. "Go, get to the top. It'll be the lunch break. You'll be amazed."

Daisy is right but it's not the view that amazes Lucie, although the vista is gorgeous. Her surprise is what happens at lunch. Everyone steps out of their snowshoes and spreads tarps or cushions on the snow surface, where they sit and pull pouches of food from their backpacks. They munch on sandwiches and pour tea, soup, coffee, they pass around bags of chocolate, cookies, cups of wine and whisky.

"Oh, I recognize this evil brew," Lucie says, taking a sip of buttery rye.

I should have brought cookies or banana loaf or something. Next time I'll know better. So I guess there will be a next time. Ah, Lucie. Welcome to another door. Another world.

Kurt pulls a book from his pack, stands and flips to the page he wants, and starts reading poetry. When he's done, someone else sings a few lines from an Ian Tyson song most people seem to know. They join the chorus.

"I'm chilly," someone says, and the group packs up. "Some people will keep going but most will head back down," Janet says to Lucie. "Kurt will be in the 'keep going' group, but I've had enough, Daisy too. You're welcome to do whatever you want. If you come back down with us, just know that we'll be sitting in the van for a while 'til Kurt gets back, or you can probably find a ride to town with someone else."

Lucie elects to descend with Janet, Daisy, and a goodly portion of the group. Back at the barrier gate, she hugs Janet and Daisy, and then finds a spot in someone's truck headed to town. Soon she's back again at the parking lot, seated in Agememnon with the heater going full blast.

Ah, ah, ah. Look where I live. Look who else lives here. People who love this place. People willing to share what they know. People with crazy names like Daisy.

She forgets the snowshoes don't belong to her until she's parked in front of Ray's house. "Damn, what do I do with these? Take them back to the library, I guess."

Trust. That's what this town is built on.

Clouds have seeped over the mountains and slowly thickened like pouring milk into coffee, and now it's snowing lightly. Shivering, she stands at Ray's door and rings the bell, wondering yet again why he won't give her a key. The porch light over her head blinks on, and she hears his footsteps on the stairs. He swings the door wide, she steps inside.

"You look exhausted," he says.

"Yes, but it's the best kind of tired," she replies. "There's the beaten-down tired from stress or whatever, but there's a different kind of tired from stretching your physical self. Ohmygod, what a day! Ray, I met great people and hiked up to this high ridge, I don't even know where we were. They were all so kind, so helpful, they truly, honestly wanted to share this place. Plus I've had amazing chocolate and a few sips of terrific whisky. What a day! Ah, look where I live. Look where I started, look where I am now. I'm so happy to be here."

He folds her in a hug that's snug and warm as a sleeping bag, kisses her forehead, her cheeks. "I'm so happy, Pumpkin. You want to learn about where you are, who lives here, how amazing this place is. And you're doing that. Good, good, good."

Ha, fine words from someone who never goes out.

But Lucie refrains from speaking her doubt, instead she says, "I really need a hot bath. And by the way, do you know someone called Sweet Water Woman? An elder, I think?"

"No, but if you get any possible connection to a Native person, you should follow it. They have forgotten more wisdom about this place than us newcomers will ever know."

She runs hot water, lights candles, and drops a lavender bath bomb into the tub, then immerses herself in divine bubbling heat and scent. When she emerges, rosy and relaxed, the apartment is redolent with cooking. The rich scent is something familiar she can't quite place. Wrapped in a bathrobe, she stretches on the couch while Ray readies the meal. He says, "It's liver and onions, just so ya know."

Oh yeah, liver. A blast from my frugal mother's past. Yum, can't wait.

"Is this a test for the restaurant?"

"No, I had some cheap beef liver in the freezer so I'm feeding you crap I would never give anyone else." He glances over to see her frown. "Ha, I'm kidding. Come on, you know I always need to practice." He lifts a lid, giving the pan's contents a quick stir. "Yes, Fruitcake, this is a test. If I'm going to serve something as ordinary as liver and onions at the café, it's got to be the best damn liver and onions ever."

"Maybe we should stick to stuff nobody's tasted before. Working on the theory that if we're first, we're best. By the way, I want to add good local cheese to our menu as dessert — put together a cheese board."

"You do the research, I'm fine with that idea," he says. "Just keep in mind what Tom will say. If it generates cost and not cash, he'll squash it. It's all about food cost. If it makes money — go."

"And what about getting local artists to show their stuff on our walls?"

"Fine as long as it costs nothing."

"And what about house-made ice cream?"

"Whoa. Talk to me in July."

Two weeks later, Lucie is once again in the bank's parking lot early on a Sunday morning, shivering as she waits for everyone to turn up. The day is overcast with snow in the forecast. As people arrive, she's disappointed that Janet and her family don't show. But Kelly, whom Lucie met on the previous trip, is among the group that assembles for today's adventure.

They seem less jolly than last time, perhaps because of the grey skies and chilly wind. They drive westward and park at the same barrier gate. This time, Lucie takes her own car so she can go home when she's ready. She's already borrowed snowshoes and ski poles from the library and heeded Amanda's advice about dressing in layers. Pulling her woolly toque firmly over her ears, Lucie joins the rest as they start off.

There's been no new snow since the last trip. The walking is easy, but there's little conversation. They all seem hunkered into their own thoughts.

Instead of trekking west along the unplowed road, the group turns south along a secondary and equally snow-covered road. They trek past a large campground that's closed for the winter and onward to find a steep descent into the river valley. As the group trudges on, snow starts falling in large, wet flakes. The snowfall soon thickens and lends a festive appearance to the surrounding forest, quickly building on limbs, branches, and the walkers' heads and shoulders.

After nearly an hour, the group reaches the frozen river where they stop to discuss their destination and various routes. Apparently there are a number of choices, some easier than others. But as Lucie catches her breath and sips hot tea from her flask, she says, "I'm worried about driving in heavy snow, think I'll call it a day and head back to town."

A few others agree, so Lucie and a handful of companions start the arduous toil up from the river valley and back to the parking area. It's a steady, tough climb. By the time she attains the top, Lucie's skin beneath her many layers of clothing is slick with sweat, and she's breathing hard. At the parking lot, she quickly kicks out of her snowshoes and starts Agememnon, quivering with cold as she brushes snow from the windshield and roof and waits for the engine to warm so she can turn on the car's heater.

Snow is funnelling down fast and thick. She waves to the others and turns for home, driving slowly, windshield wipers barely keeping pace with the snow. With relief, she finally pulls into a space across the street from Ray's house and dashes to his door, but there's no response when she rings the bell. She rings again and pounds on the door, but he doesn't come to let her in.

She recalls what he said about gym equipment in the house's basement, which he's welcome to use. She assumes the basement access must be from within the main-floor suite. There are no basement windows, except on the far side of the house, and she's unwilling to wade through the deepening snow to see whether she could knock on one of those windows to summon Ray. Instead she goes to the front of the house and knocks firmly on the door, but can't tell whether anyone is inside. If Ray is there, it seems he can't hear her. Cold and frustrated, she goes back to her car and tries calling his cell phone with no response.

OK, I get it. You really do have another girlfriend, ha ha. Seriously, where the hell are you? And why won't you give me a house key?

Angrily, she snaps on the car's radio and pulls off her wet toque and mitts. She sits, arms crossed, with the heat blasting. After what feels like hours, but is really just twenty minutes, she watches as Ray emerges from the house's front door. He doesn't notice her car as he carefully locks up and walks around the side to his own apartment door.

Lucie quickly turns off the car, slams the door, and runs after him.

Hearing rapid footsteps behind him, Ray wheels. To her amazement, he raises a fist as if to fight whomever is approaching. His face is grim, his eyes narrow. But seeing Lucie he lowers his hands and his face relaxes into a look of surprise and relief. "You're back early."

"It's snowing hard, so I bailed."

They stand facing each other as snow gathers in their hair, on their shoulders. He's biting his lower lip, and his face is full of pain. He looks as though he'd just stepped on a nail.

"Ray, what's going on?"

He closes his eyes, turns to unlock the door, and stands back to let Lucie enter before him. "I have something to tell you. Do you want a hot bath first?"

"Hell, no."

"You should at least get out of your wet clothes." He follows her into the bedroom and sits on the end of the bed while she peels off layer after layer and pulls on warm dry leggings and her downy cream sweater.

Ray is at first pensive, lips pressed together, eyes half closed, not looking at her. "I have some debts," he begins. He sighs heavily and leans forward, elbows on his knees. She can only see the powerful curve of his spine, the fluffy red-gold curls on the back of his head. He speaks to the floor. She has to listen intently to hear him.

"Some of this you know already. Some of what I've told you has been... a story. But Pumpkin, here is the truth. My parents divorced when I was young and my mom left the farm. My dad's parents moved in to help us. My gran was awesome; she shaped my life, and yes, I did learn to cook from her. They're both gone now, my grandparents. Dad died a few years back, and my uncle got title to the farm. He wanted to sell it for the money, but it was a bad time to be selling land — prices were down. Me and my brothers and sister were all against him. We didn't want to sell, but we were powerless because Dad willed the farm to his brother, not his kids, so we could only try to persuade him. That didn't work — he just wanted to sell. No question, no argument.

"Then I decided to buy the farm from him myself. My uncle just wanted money; he didn't care whether it came from me or some random buyer. I was completely desperate, but I had no money, of course. My brothers tried really hard to help. All of them had long since left the farm, but they still pulled together $100,000 between them — still it wasn't enough. So, I was, um... on a cliff, about to fall off. I did not want to lose our farm.

"I knew some guys from high school. They'd gone on to become big-time drug dealers. Bad guys, but they had money. I thought they could help me. I thought they would cut me a deal because I knew them back in the day. So I lined up some financing from those characters and gave my uncle a down payment. He took the money and cleared out. Then I thought I could pay off both my uncle and my debt to the drug guys through farming — every year I'd make a bit from the farm, sell some calves, some grain and hay, whatever, pay them a little at a time. Like paying a bank loan. Stupid me."

She leans against the dresser, facing him, but he's still bent forward, looking at his knees. "And?"

"Let's just say that's not the finance plan they have in mind."

Pause.

"And?"

He shrugs and finally looks at her. "Right now, I am a fugitive. I lost the farm after all. We had a few bad years because of drought, and I couldn't keep up my payments to the druggies, never mind my uncle and taxes and whatever. Eventually my family found out what I did, and now they're pissed with me, as well they should be. In hindsight, it was a stupid, desperate thing to do. And now some very determined guys are after me to get their investment back.

"So I keep moving, doing different things. Five years ago I was a mechanic in Saskatoon, where they tracked me down. I moved on, did a few other things. Now I manage a restaurant in Sweetgrass, Alberta. And often as I can, I make a payment through my sister, which is much against my better judgment, but she's willing and it's the only way I can think of to give the drug guys money without them finding out where I am. I'm not running away from my debt. I'm paying the druggies back bit by bit because it's the only way I know to get them away from me. But now I'm hiding from dudes who want to beat me up. And what good would that do? If I'm in the hospital, or dead, how can I repay them? But for them, it's all about punishment, revenge, intimidation. I get it. I'm intimidated, already."

She is riveted. Whispers, "How much money, Ray?"

He sags down again, his head bowed. He takes such a deep breath that his back rises substantially, but his words are so soft she can barely hear him. "One hundred fifty thousand. Of which I've paid back about half. Right now I can pay about five thousand a month. The restaurant has been good to me. As for paying back my brothers... well, that may never happen. But I'm going to try."

A long pause while she thinks about it. "And what happens when they find you here? Because they will, right?"

He sits up again and gives her a tight-lipped, joyless smile. "I'll move, fast. But I've been in Sweetgrass three years, the longest I've been anyplace since this all started. I'm making good money, and I've been able to give them some sizeable payments. Maybe they've given up, or realize they're going to get their money back eventually, or maybe my trail has gone cold because I don't have a credit card or a bank account. My sister holds my cell phone account, and she owns my car. I'm hard to trace, or so I believe. Even this apartment — I rented it furnished, I pay cash. Except for my clothes I don't own a thing in here, right down to the dishes. Basically I'm a shadow. A shell. I'm nobody. Nowhere."

Christ, buddy. You fell off that cliff anyway and now your whole damn life needs fixing.

But she doesn't know what to say or where she could possibly begin. In the face of his enormous sorrow and fear and regret, for once Lucie has no advice, no smart remark or instant fix to offer. Instead, she melts to her knees before him and reaches to take his head gently between her hands. She threads her cold fingers through his curls and massages his temples with her thumbs, caressing and comforting just as he did for her on their first morning together.

"Then let's put you back together," she says softly, looking straight into his brimming eyes. "You're not alone any more. My sweet man, if you've got my back — and I know you do — then I've got yours."

He leans forward to lightly nuzzle the top of her head.

"You can't help me, though. Lucie, I'm serious. I appreciate that you want to help. But you can't get involved because it's dangerous. I know that sounds like a movie plot, but it's true. And — I'm sure I don't need to tell you this — it's not a story for sharing, with anyone. Nobody knows this, Lucie. Not Tom, not George. Not Donny. Nobody."

" So except for your sister, your family doesn't know where you are?"

He closes his eyes, sighs and shrugs. She's never seen a face so full of sadness. "Right. I send money to her — another crazy thing, I mail cash — and she arranges payment through someone she knows, who happens to be the girlfriend of one of the drug guys. I made a mistake just before Thanksgiving. I was in a hurry and mailed the money from here instead of from Calgary or someplace else, so the envelope had a cancellation stamp from the Sweetgrass post office. My sister didn't notice until she was about to hand over the envelope, but she grabbed it back and did some fast talking. The girlfriend might have seen the postmark, maybe told her boyfriend. I have no idea, but I've been pretty nervous since then.

"As for the rest of my family, I love them and I miss them, but I don't keep in touch. I can't, it would put them in danger. If my family knows where I am, the thugs will threaten them, too. It was nice to see some of them at Christmas and by now they know better than to ask too many questions. Maybe my sis has filled them in, I don't know. The bottom line is — oh, Luce..." his voice cracks, he almost sobs, "my farm is gone and it's my fault. I couldn't keep it, even with shady financing. And I guess that's why I try so hard for Tom. I completely understand his situation. Desperation. I understand that."

She pauses and breathes intently for a moment. Her mind is going in a thousand directions.

OK, slow down. Think of something concrete, because everything else just became vapour.

"So... don't get me wrong, I'm not fussed but... now I get why you never told Tom about the extra money from my cakes and desserts and such, until he figured it out. Really, it was going to your debt repayment plan, yes?"

"Still is, though I am giving Tom some of the baking money now. But Lucie, I'm not running away from anything. I will make it all right. Once I have the druggies paid off, a couple of years from now at most, I'll repay Tom. I don't mean to steal from him, but I guess that's what I'm doing. I've never admitted that to myself because I have every intention of making things right for everyone. Besides, Tom's not likely to land me in the hospital."

Lucie has nothing judgmental to say about Ray's robbing-Peter-to-pay-Paul thinking. She only says, "OK, I get that. And — please forgive me, but I need to know — is Ray even your real name?"

"Don't ask me that." He gazes straight at her with a look so piercing and sad she feels tears sting the corners of her eyes. "Pumpkin, the less you know about me, the better. If I have to leave, I'll be gone in a hurry, and you can't know where I am because that would be dangerous for you. It sounds crazy, but it's true."

They are both weeping. Ray's tears are a slow leak, but Lucie is dissolving. She can't keep eye contact with him. This is all too sad, too huge. She drops her gaze. Says, "But, seriously, I can help. I *want* to help. I can do more baking, I can push the catering idea, I could get another job..." She's grasping at ideas, looking for some path out of this dark maze he's described. "Surely we can do this. Together."

Ray wraps his arms around her and pulls her to him. She feels his damp cheek against her neck as he rocks her. But she also feels him shaking his head. "No," he says, simply but emphatically. "No, Pumpkin, you can't help, and I won't let you. This is up to me. Thank you. But... no. I can't take that risk. Neither can you."

Presently, he releases her and once again they look straight into one another's eyes.

"I'll get through it, Luce. You just have to be patient with me. That's what you can do. Just please be patient." He stands and pulls her gently to her feet. "Go take a hot bath, you're shaking. I'll start dinner. And Lucie?" He tips her face up. They lock eyes again. "I'm so sorry. I should have told you, but I could never find the right time. I never meant to lie to you. I *didn't* lie, I just didn't tell you the whole story. I need you to trust me."

"I'm still here," she says. "And I'm not going anywhere."

Ray fixes a light dinner, uncomplicated by his standards: a melange of potatoes, onions, carrots, turnips, parsnips and chicken, all drizzled with olive oil and simply grilled in the oven. It's delicious, of course, but Lucie has no appetite and only eats dutifully to please him. She drinks glass after glass of dry white wine. They don't talk much. He is quiet but not in an angry way — he simply seems exhausted, drained. After they've eaten, Lucie cleans up while Ray takes a long, hot shower, then he says, "Going to bed," as she finishes tidying the kitchen.

But before retiring, he looks out each window and says, "Man, I really wish I had a back window so I could check on the car."

"You don't think it will start in the morning? It's not really cold out, it's just snowy."

He gives her another sad smile. "No, Dumpling. The first thing they'll do is smash my car or slash the tires, so I can't get away. I check the downstairs door locks every night, and I'd also like to check the car without going outside, but none of these windows face the back. So I don't go out, I just trust that the car's OK."

She only looks at him and nods her new understanding.

The story unfolds.

She's finished washing dishes. In the dark bedroom, she removes her clothes and eases into bed, unsure whether Ray is already asleep. She folds herself against him, but he doesn't respond.

Although she lies quietly, Lucie's mind is racing. She believes his story — nobody could falsely conjure such pain and anxiety — but... her old self-interest is calling. What does all this mean for their future together? Or the logistics of their present life, for that matter? And what if... what if it's all some elaborate ruse to keep her at arm's length?

You know — if all this is true, you need to think about talking to Donny. And if this is a tall tale, you're building, you're doing a good job, you are spooking me entirely.

It's such a confusing puzzle, but one thought solidifies from her whirling uncertainty. More than ever, Lucie is convinced she needs a key to this apartment. Now she understands the need for diligence and caution, she also reasons that it would actually be safer for her to have a key.

I could come and go, no need to stand outside the door for someone to see me. And of course I'd be careful, lock up always.

She says as much the next morning. "It might make things easier," she observes. "I could come and go as needed, no more worries about me leaving the door unlocked."

He shakes his head. "Pumpkin, I've been thinking about it. I don't know yet. Please be patient, Luce. I have serious reservations about giving you a key because if they ever caught you here alone, they wouldn't hesitate to beat you up, or worse. I'm not joking. If they hurt you, raped you, kidnapped you... I can't even think about what they might do, and they're capable of all that. I could never forgive myself. If I gave you a key, you'd have to always, *always* watch your back. I can't say that enough. So maybe it's best if you don't have a key. I don't want to turn you into me. Paranoia is no way to live."

She gives him what she hopes is a flirty smile, trying to lighten his mood. "OK, no key for now. But consider this: if you gave me a key, you might come home after a supply run to the city and find someone dressed in black waiting for you. Black lace, that is. But only if I have a key, I'm not going to lurk behind the fence in fancy lingerie."

He grins at last, but there's a shadow in his smile.

Midwinter wears on, and although the daylight is ever longer, snow has arrived with a ferocity that matches Lucie's volatile mood. Storm after storm sweep over Sweetgrass: snowdrifts accumulate, highway ploughs work overtime, people shovel their walks and driveways only to see more snow within a few days. Repeat.

For her part, Lucie feels wayward. Ray's story certainly explains his odd behaviour: his constant watchfulness, his reluctance to be seen in public, even his caution about not revealing her baking to Tom. But is it the truth, or some wild invention to keep her at arm's length, to avoid commitment? Despite his kindness and respect for her, his quiet humour and easygoing nature, and despite the evidence of his affection embodied — she believes — in the ring he gave her and the loving nights they spend together, she is reverting to confusion and even suspicion. She knows she's slipping into old habits — her propensity to judge first and beg forgiveness second, if forgiveness would even be possible.

Sometimes she shrugs away her doubt, but with each passing snowstorm her mood darkens, her misgivings mount. She's increasingly irritable and nothing dispels her sour frame of mind. Activity makes her feel better temporarily, but she quickly sinks back into emotional squalls. She spends fewer nights with Ray, finding she needs to watch her words when she's with him, stepping carefully around what she really wants to say — instead, she chatters about new recipes she's working on or arranging for a local artist to hang paintings in the café. Everything she says seems so trivial now.

Ray also seems distant, wary of her, a reaction that frightens her as much as her own turmoil vexes her.

Ah, I can't stand this. We've only been a couple since Thanksgiving. How can we have hit this roadblock so soon? Don't let this fall apart, Lucie. Don't be your usual self, you have to trust him, believe him. You have to.

But does she?

At the ranch one evening, she gloomily goes to bed early with the ominous beginnings of a headache. In her youth, under her mother's constant harangue, Lucie frequently developed terrible headaches she suspected were born of stress, though her mother insisted — on the few occasions Lucie complained about the pain — that Lucie was trying to avoid a difficult exam or shirking her household chores. Tonight though, she takes a double dose of pain-killers and wonders whether her stress headaches are making a comeback courtesy of her current anxiety.

Maybe I should just tell him what's on my mind. But I don't want him to think I don't trust him, even though I'm not sure I do. What if it's true? He's said not many people believe in him. The poor guy needs support, not someone who doesn't have faith in him. After all, he sure enough has faith in me.

She rolls and rotates in bed, tangling herself in the sheet. Throws off the duvet, then retrieves it, then tosses it aside again.

I miss him. Bottom line, end of story. I absolutely have to get over this doubt, let it go. Either that or I have to quit, leave town, and forget the whole thing, and that is too ugly to even contemplate. He's the best thing in my life, right now and maybe ever. I am not giving up. Not. Giving. Up.

Impatiently she sits up, scraping a mass of snarled hair away from her hot face. "I wonder if it's too late to phone Jude?" She's motionless for a moment, considering whether to find her cell phone, when she notices the insistent rattling of her room's high windows, being pushed and pestered by the wind.

"Great, another blizzard." She flings away the damp bedding, pulls on a pair of thick socks, and exits her room to look outside and check the weather and make a mug of tea. Ascending the stairs, she becomes aware of an odd sound like the rolling of distant thunder. Once on the main floor, she realizes the house is being battered by a gale unlike anything she's ever experienced. Every window and door shakes and wheezes as punishing gusts slam against the building. She flicks on the porch light but sees no snow whizzing through the air. She rubs her temples. The painkillers have had no effect. She drifts back to her room with a mug of tea.

Yes, it is too late for a call. But I'll phone Jude this weekend. I cannot figure my way out of this alone.

Then she groans. "What am I thinking? How can I tell Jude what's going on without giving away the whole story, which he specifically asked me not to do? Agh! I can't even ask my best girlfriend for advice." She turns out the light and slumps into her pillow.

A restive night later, Lucie rises and immediately notices the unusual rosy light suffusing the thin white drapes of her room. The window continues to rattle and shake. She yanks her hair back — her head is still pounding — ties a hasty ribbon around her mane, grabs the half-full mug of cold tea, and heads upstairs to find Amanda gazing out the kitchen window at a marvellous sunrise. The sky is mostly hidden by a slab of oyster-grey cloud, which is slowly being lit from beneath as the sun, still unseen, approaches the horizon. Pink. Peach. The colour intensifies, revealing whorls and ridges and feathers on the cloud's underside, until the entire spread is a brilliant blaze of marigold and blood orange and fuchsia. This is not the first glorious sunrise Lucie's seen here, but it's the most spectacular by far.

"Proof that God is a woman," Amanda remarks, not turning from the spectacle.

"How do you figure?"

"Who else would take hot pink lipstick and scribble it across the whole sky?"

"It's awesome, I've never seen anything like it. And the wind is still howling." Entranced by the rapidly evolving light show, Lucie doesn't notice the snow's surface is softening and puddles are forming along the drive. She doesn't hear the gush of meltwater in the house's downspouts.

"A chinook at last."

"Really? This is a chinook?"

Amanda finally looks over at her friend and sees Lucie's red-rimmed eyes and the furrows of pain creasing her forehead. "Oh, Lucie, you're not well. You have a serious headache, right?"

Lucie nods.

"Yeah, that's a thing about chinooks, some people get migraines from the pressure change, I guess. I get those headaches sometimes too, so I've got just the thing to fix you right up. Are you supposed to work today?"

Lucie nods again.

"You should phone in sick because these pills will cure your head, but they'll knock you on your butt. No way should you be driving or pouring hot coffee. How bad is it?"

"Pretty bad. I used to get what I called 'stress head' when I was a kid, but this is different. And much worse."

"Oh, dear," Amanda says, gently massaging Lucie's temples. "I'll find those pills for you, and I'll call Ray."

Lucie nods yet again.

Amanda returns from her bedroom with a handful of tiny yellow pills. "These have codeine, are you OK with that? They will do the job for sure but don't take too many."

Lucie responds by plucking a pill from Amanda's palm and swallowing it with a gulp of water. "Thanks so much. This is like no headache I've ever had. It's a serious cramp, but I also feel dizzy. Not like I'm going to fall, more like my head is stuffed with cotton. I can't see straight."

"Get yourself back to bed and drink lots of water when you wake up," Amanda advises. "But before you do that, let's go out to the deck. If you've never been through a chinook before, you won't believe how warm it is right now."

Amanda pushes hard against the wind that buffets the west-facing door, then grabs the handle to keep the door from swinging and slamming as the two women step outside. True to Amanda's words, Lucie is more than surprised by what she feels. The physical impact for one thing — the barrelling banshee wind is screaming and swirling around the house. But the air is incredibly warm, a complete transformation from the glacial cold of only a few hours ago. A blessing and a curse.

Lucie exclaims, "What do you think the wind speed is? This is amazing, exactly like Keith described it when Jude was here. She didn't believe him. I'll have to tell her it's true."

I'll have to tell Jude a lot more than that.

"It is a wonder of nature for sure," Amanda says loudly to be heard above the roar. "It might be gusting up to 100 kilometres or more right now, enough to break trees and rip off shingles. Incredible, eh? This could last for days, or it might be over in a few hours, but it's a blast of summer in the middle of winter."

"How bizarre. Everything's melting."

Including my stupid, judgmental heart. Oh, I need to figure out how I'm going to swallow this crazy story and get my sweet man back. I need to apologize. I need to sleep.

The wind and warm spell persist for three days, turning streets into creeks and sidewalks into opaque puddles that conceal treacherous patches of ice underneath. Swatches of brown lawn appear in town, pastures turn from white to yellow and dun as the accumulated snow is sucked away by the near-tropical wind. The air holds the subtle but pervasive smell of mud. Kids splash and play on their way home from school. They use sticks to guide tiny ice floes into the streaming meltwater in every gutter. Lucie, whose headache subsided after the first day, opens her bedroom window for the first time in weeks to admit a rush of precious warm air.

Her migraine might be gone, but she still feels oddly disoriented, wakes frequently at night, and she's lost her appetite — all of which make her pallid complexion even more ghostly. Her halo of dark hair seems even blacker in contrast. She applies eyeliner, mascara, shiny-blue eye shadow, and vibrant dark cherry lipstick, all in an effort to draw attention away from her almost translucent skin, but it actually achieves the opposite effect. When she arrives at the café, she looks almost cadaverous.

"Are you sure you feel OK?" Ray asks as she enters the café's kitchen and pulls off her coat with definite effort. "I can call one of the girls to come in."

"I'm fine. I didn't sleep much, but I don't feel bad, just kind of wobbly, like I've been drinking. Without the fun."

But halfway through the dinner shift, he puts a gentle hand on her shoulder and says, "Go home and don't come back 'til you've had a decent sleep." She notices sadly that he doesn't offer to take her into his own warm bed. Shakily she nods and heads for the door.

The parking area behind the café is currently a swamp, so she's parked Agememnon up the block. It's well past sunset and the street is dim and shadowy. Head down, face shrouded by her loose hair, she trudges through the deepening twilight, concentrating on dodging puddles and ice. She doesn't see the hooded figure heading toward her until they almost collide.

"Fuckin' watch where yer going."

"Watch yourself," she replies, snapping her head up, but the man's hood is pulled forward, and she cannot see his face. He is tall and big-boned but stands in an oddly lazy, loose-limbed way — he might be drunk, or high on something. She pauses, waiting for him to move aside to let her pass, but instead he takes an awkward step back, slipping and barely catching his balance with a slop and splash of meltwater. They face each other. Lucie stuffs her fists into her pockets, squares her shoulders, and lifts her chin. Her heavy curtain of hair falls away from her milky face, which reflects the whitish light from a nearby streetlight that's just flickered on. Her dark lipstick looks black.

He stares at her. "Yer a freak. A fuckin' zombie. Are you even *alive*?"

"Fuck right off."

"Zombie," he whispers in a slurred, indistinct way, then speaks louder. "Yer a fuckin' zombie. A zombie! I didn' know we had zombies here, but I am lookin' at one right now," delivered with a cracked, dry laugh that quickly disintegrates into hoarse coughing. His hood slips away, and she sees a large nose, doughy, lightly stubbled cheeks that drag his mouth down in a pout that Lucie suspects would require a supreme effort to fold into a smile, and hairy brows that meet in the middle to create a single dark caterpillar over his eyes.

"Get outa my way or I'll bite your head off." Lucie growls. She considers baring her teeth, but instead she plunges into the soggy snowdrift beside the sidewalk, counting that the man is too unsteady on his feet to approach or grab her. With three long strides she's around him, back on the sidewalk, and heading quickly to her car.

He doesn't follow, but his voice rings along the street, surprisingly loud and now taunting, "Zom-bee, zom-bee!" His childish tone makes her realize he's younger than she'd first thought, in fact he's just a kid. Swiftly she unlocks the car door, slides in, and locks it behind her, but when she glances up, she sees he has continued away, still singing "Zombie, zombie."

I know who you are. You're the kid I caught car prowling that rainy night last fall. And you probably broke into that guy's truck during the harvest dinner. Ray is right, if you want trouble, you can find it anywhere.

She starts the car, but the encounter has left her shaking. It's a good five minutes before she's calm enough to drive.

The next morning, Lucie phones Tash the hairdresser and makes an appointment. Arriving at the salon that afternoon, she takes a seat and says with determination, "Cut it off, Tash. All of it, I'm not kidding. I never want long hair again."

"Really? That's a big step. But if that's what you want, I can have some fun — do a wedge, give it a flip at the back."

"Go crazy."

Lucie squeezes her eyes shut as Tash starts from the bottom, lopping off Lucie's bushy hair six-inch lengths at a time. But, intrigued by the process, Lucie opens her eyes and watches in the mirror as mounds of her black hair drift to the floor. Tash makes quick work of eliminating length, and then begins to meticulously shape and feather Lucie's unruly curls. The sound of scissors clipping so close to her ears and neck is something Lucie has never experienced. She tells herself more than once to relax. At one point, when Tash pauses for a sip of water, Lucie sighs and makes a conscious effort to flex her shoulders.

"Kinda like being in a dentist's chair," Tash quips.

"Ha, too right. Dentistry, that's something else I've been neglecting. Honestly, Tash, I've been in town for months, but I've been sort of underground, concentrating on my job." She nearly adds, 'Plus spending time with Ray,' but changes her mind. "Anyway, I never go out, I feel like I've met exactly six people. OK, maybe seven — Amanda's been trying to expand my social network lately, she chased me out to the gym. I've been doing yoga and Sunday snowshoe trips with a bunch of really fun people. But it's not like I see any of them except on Sundays, I wouldn't say I've developed friendships with any of them. And by the way, you are so right about this chair being some kind of confessional. I can't believe I'm telling you all this."

Tash laughs and forks her practiced fingers through what remains of Lucie's hair. "I can recommend a good dentist in the city," she remarks absently, and then sets to work again. A few more snips, then she continues, "I'm going to give you some shape and lift, but this style will require upkeep, way more than you're used to—a trim maybe once a month, depending on how fast your hair grows."

"Great, I'll be here a lot. More social contact."

Tash laughs again. "Yeah, and the stuff you'll find out here will curl your hair, as if your hair needs curling." Snip, comb, snip, spritz, snip. "What about going to the volunteer fair that's coming up?"

"Don't know a thing about it."

"A couple of local ladies organize it every year, Germaine Chow and Tanya Hiller, you may have seen them around or in the café."

Lucie shrugs.

"It's at the community hall, like a trade show of groups looking for volunteers. People set up tables and hand out information on what their group does — fundraising or making meals for seniors or driving the library bookmobile, springtime river clean-up, even the volunteer firefighters."

"Sounds like speed dating. Which I've done."

"Exactly. You meet a lot of folks in a short time, and you figure out what might fit into your life or schedule or whatever, and you sign up. Some commit to more than one thing, I know women who are out every night and every weekend; volunteering is their entire life. Most of them are retired, so they have more time than most of us, but still — they are the engine, they keep things moving around here."

"I don't think I knew a single person in Vancouver who volunteered for anything, except my buddy Jude who volunteers for the folk music festival. But she does it because she likes to hang with musicians backstage, so there's some personal motivation beyond doing a good deed."

"Well, we have a concert series here, you could meet musicians and hear great music for the price of setting up chairs or putting up posters." Comb, snip, comb, snip. "The thing is, nothing happens in a small town without volunteers. It's not an expectation, of course. I know just as many people who never volunteer for anything, like you said. We all have our reasons. But in a little place like this, there are too many needs and not enough hands unless people step up."

I guess that's the way things work here. For every fucked-up kid or bitter drunken cowboy, there's at least one person picking up roadside garbage or driving the bookmobile.

Her task finished at last, Tash gives a hand mirror to Lucie and swivels the chair. In the reflection, Lucie sees her previously massive black mane is now a well-trimmed and shapely flip. Seeing the back of her own neck makes her feel publicly naked, but as she steps outdoors into the sweet breeze she also feels remarkably light. She shakes her head, making curls bounce around her ears — a new and notable sensation.

Farewell, zombie.

She considers going straight to Ray's but decides to drive to Marta's instead. She raps loudly on the back door, but hears nothing inside the house, so opens the door and shouts "Hello?"

The silence lasts long enough that she's ready to call out again, when suddenly Tom appears from around the corner. He looks haggard, his face has a greyish cast, and his shirt hangs outside his ill-fitting jeans. Even his socks are bulky and loose.

You look so lost, like she doesn't take care of you. Or you don't let her.

Tom says nothing. Finally Lucie says, more politely than she feels, "Hi, Tom. Sorry to drop in like this, thought I'd see if Marta is home."

"Nope."

Fine, buddy. Don't make any effort to grease the wheels of sociability.

"OK, please tell her I dropped by."

He glares as Lucie turns away, stomping loudly as she can down the porch's wooden steps.

Whatever Marta saw in you back in the day, all that romance, where did it go? You've buried it in bitterness and all your damaged pride. You are such a fucking cowboy. Lucie is certain Tom is watching her from his front windows as she walks away.

For the first time in months, she feels a stab of nostalgia for big city life. She'd like a diversion right now — a long beach walk, a talk with girlfriends to order lunch, drink wine, and dissect the state of their lives. But she's nowhere near a beach. Instead of getting into her car and spitting wet gravel from under her wheels as she revs away, she confounds Tom's following eyes by turning to stroll up the street, hands in her back pockets.

She passes modest houses, each with their unique character. Some yards and homes are sprightly with painted front fences and well-tended gardens emerging from the snow banks. Others sport funky wood sculptures in the front yard, and still others host barking dogs large and small behind wire fences. One house, which resembles a hip-roofed barn, has a rabbit hutch and a trampoline in the generous side yard, while another's unpainted siding is dark and weathered, testament to many winters and battering chinooks. Above her, the sky is spotless and the wind has subsided. The air retains its spring-like warmth. Lucie paces up the roadway, pauses, and turns.

Lucie, you idiot, give your head a shake. Look where you live. Mountains over my shoulder, pure sweet air warm enough to turn snow into rivers, in the middle of winter no less. Sky so clear at night you can see northern lights and stars, stars, so many stars. I'm not walking on a beach right now, so what? I'm walking outdoors, it's the middle of winter, and it's not freezing or pouring rain fergodssake. I have a fine place to live, a few good friends, a lover who makes me laugh and feel special, respected. Not like those two, Tom and Marta — when was the last time she felt respected? It's sad and I don't like it one bit, and I'll do everything I can to let her know I think the world of her.

She drives to Ray's house, not sure whether he'll be home although the café is closed today, so he's likely in his kitchen experimenting with some new recipe or other. She knocks loudly and hears rapid footsteps on the stairs like he's been expecting her — what happened to his usual caution? He swings the door open and immediately an appreciative smile crinkles his eyes as he sees her newly shorn hair. "Look at you."

She enters, grinning broadly. "I've had enough of the hippie look, or whatever that was. Time to grow up, move on, you know?" Upstairs, the suite is rich with the scent of good food. "Whatcha cooking?" she asks.

He actually bounces on his toes once or twice, he's so eager to talk about what he's making for dinner. "This is just for us," he says. "Empanadas. They are fun but so much work, we could never do this at the restaurant, too much labour. But for you—savoury dumplings for my sweet dumpling." He flits from counter to stovetop, meanwhile pouring wine and setting the table. "You know, Luce, I know you think I don't get out enough and maybe you're right, but I never get tired of doing this. I've said this before, but, Luce… cooking is the coolest thing, I'm so lucky to have stumbled into it. I *love* it. Cooking is creative, and you nourish people, there's a connection to community or family or whatever. And it was such an accident."

"Sometimes accidents are the best things in life."

He doesn't take up that remark, instead he says, "Cooking involves all your senses, it's so absorbing, like a mini-holiday. I play with food. I play with fire, every day. In more ways than one," he looks at her with a sly smile.

It's only then she notices the ruff of hair on his face. "Are you growing a beard?"

"It's the great cosmic hair shuffle. Less hair on you, more hair on me."

After dinner, he's affectionate and cuddly, he hugs and rubs and starts to remove her clothes, but she's stiff and reluctant, resisting him, until he takes a deep breath and sends six words straight to her heart. "You don't believe me, do you?"

Half undressed, she stands beside his bed, unsure whether now is the right time for the conversation she's been craving and dreading for weeks. But he's opened a door so she's going to walk through it. She raises her bird-bone delicate hands, drops them to her thighs with a frustrated clap, and says, "I don't know. *I don't know.* It's such a bizarre story." She presses her lips together, suppressing her usual quick anger.

No, don't do that. I've got to get through this, we have to come to some place we can both agree on. I cannot take another day of avoiding each other, not talking about what we need to talk about.

Feeling her way through a jungle of emotion, searching for the right words, she continues tentatively, "Whether I believe you or not doesn't matter…"

"Of course it matters." He steps back, regarding her with an expression that's stunningly sad. She sees no guile in his freckled face, open and boyish even with the beginnings of a beard. "Lucie, I said I won't hurt you, I meant it then, and I mean it now. I'm not making up some lie to keep you away. I would like nothing more than to have a normal life, we could even think about living together. But I can't offer that right now. I am trying to pay these guys and get them off my back so I can get on with my life, but it's going to take time."

"What about going to the police?"

"To say what? I made a bad decision by accepting money from people I had no business dealing with, and now I live like a hermit so the goons can't find me? The police will want names, Luce. I know those names, but I can't turn them in because they have connections everywhere. If I snitch on three guys, then thirty more will be on my tail, not to mention the harm they could inflict on my family. Or you, or anyone else in my life. Going to the cops would actually make it worse."

She only nods.

"Pumpkin, what you see is what you get, and I don't know how long this might last, though I really think it's a couple of years at most. I won't blame you if you can't carry on this way. I would be very sad to lose you, but you have to decide what's right for yourself. Still — don't you think we could just keep enjoying the time we have? What's wrong with living in the moment?"

She is drained, she wants to sink to the floor and stay there. Instead, she looks straight into his remarkable blue eyes and sees tears leaking onto his cheeks. "I'm not going anywhere. I've said that before and I mean it. I've been twisting myself into knots for weeks — first I believe you, then I don't, then I'm second-guess-ing, jumping to conclusions, judging, thinking the whole thing is ridiculous. There was a time when I would have gone to the police myself." She raises a finger to dispel his look of alarm. "Don't worry, I'll do no such thing. What I need to say is — ah, this is so not like me. Ray, my sweet man, I will, *I do,* accept things as they are. You have always been so kind, so generous — from that very first day, you've accepted me, you've never judged or criticized me. It's like nothing I've ever known, and I want to hang on, keep going. So if living day-to-day and not making plans for the future is the price of staying together, that's fine with me. That's why I say it doesn't matter whether I believe you, it matters more that I can, and I *do,* put all my usual junk aside. So yes. Let's enjoy what we have, in a variety of locations and positions if I recall correctly."

He steps to her, laces his fingers through her newly cropped hair, and kisses her forehead, cheeks, lips, her throat, his touch soft as spring rain.

"Hey, you're cute with a beard."

"I'm cute anyway."

In the morning he wakes early and says, "I forgot to take stuff out of the freezer, I have to get to the café. See you later." Sleepily she rolls over and hugs blankets over her head, distantly aware of him moving around the room, quietly dressing, making breakfast, and descending the stairs. When she wakes later, it's full daylight, time to get herself to The Sow's Ear. She showers, towelling her hair dry — and she says to her reflection in the foggy mirror, "This is a first, dry hair in ten minutes" — pulls on yesterday's jeans and a clean shirt from the stash of clothes she keeps in Ray's closet. She feels dancey, light-hearted, lightheaded, liberated.

In the kitchen, she opens the fridge and bends to retrieve yogurt from a low shelf, feeling the sharp jab of something in her pocket. She stands and withdraws a piece of paper, folded tightly. As she unwraps the package, an object slips out and pings onto the floor tiles, coming to rest in a patch of sunlight. It glints and shines. She grins enormously.

It's a house key.

COMFORT AND JOY

Spring edges cautiously toward Sweetgrass, but it's a tedious waltz — one step up, two steps back. Days are noticeably longer but nights remain chilly. The wind is often icy, and people warn Lucie about spring blizzards. "Don't get cocky," Amanda cautions. "No putting away your winter clothes and don't even think about taking the snow tires off your car. Winter ain't over."

She delivers this lecture as she and Lucie toil through ice-crusted, knee-deep drifts at the base of the hillside above the ranch house. They are headed to the hilltop, which is snowless and may offer early spring flowers. It's a passably warm although breezy day — they both sport woolly toques and scarves coiled high around their necks. They toil up the slope, puffing, not speaking. The wind has scoured the ground bare of snow to show faint traces of green sprouts poking up from rattling bunches of dead, dry grass. "Let's hike up and see if there are crocuses out yet," Amanda said earlier that morning over coffee — all the invitation Lucie needed to don her boots and parka, and get outside.

"You have to look carefully, crocuses are tiny and hard to spot. But it's so great to find them, a sure sign of spring," Amanda says, breathing heavily as they reach the ridge crest. Both women stand facing west to where the mountains rise, steel blue and still caked with snow. "It will be June or early July before snow's all gone in the high country," Amanda comments, and then she looks at the brittle brown grass around their feet. "Oh, Lucie, here's some flowers. Look how cute and fuzzy they are. Like little cuddly toys."

Lucie, expecting the delicate, bright yellow crocuses on slender stalks she's seen in Vancouver, at first doesn't understand what Amanda is pointing to. Then she notices a clutch of greyish-purple flowers with sunny yellow centres, cupped by fleshy, hairy leaves. The crocuses are low to the ground, barely discernible amid last year's grass. She takes off her mitten and gently rubs a crocus petal with her fingers, feeling its downy softness. "Marta says they're fuzzy to keep them from drying out in the wind," Amanda says.

Lucie straightens. "I haven't seen Marta much since Christmas. I keep meaning to visit, but I'm not exactly keen, in case she's not home and I get the stink-eye from Tom again. He is so rude, so awful to everyone, including her."

"I know. I don't like it either, the way he treats her. But she's figured out how to get away from him and all his negativeness, if that's even a word. I know she takes a long walk pretty much every day even when it's crazy cold or pouring rain. Plus she volunteers at the library and a number of other things; she gardens in the summer, and she's a terrific baker as you know, and she knits, she's part of a group of women who spin and dye yarn. I think she spends quite a lot of time in the city with her grandkids, too. Which is something Tom never does that I'm aware of, he never sees those little kids. They are growing up without knowing their granddad."

"Hmm, maybe not such a bad thing considering what an ass he is."

"Don't you think, though, that spending time with his grandkids would get him out of the funk he's in? Kids are full of life and energy, they're all about the future. Maybe that would cure him. Or help, at least."

"Or he'd yell at them to sit still and be quiet so he could get on with being mad at the world." Lucie turns and gazes downhill toward the house. "Speaking of volunteering, I signed up for the river clean-up at that trade fair a while back."

Amanda nods. "Good for you. That's a long hard day, pulling garbage out of the river and collecting it from the banks. And I probably shouldn't say this, but two weeks later you'll wonder whether you did any good; it's amazing how the wind blows garbage around. People don't think twice about tossing stuff out of their cars. Anyway, good on ya." Amanda locates a few more crocus patches and affirms that spring is, in fact, underway. "All we need now is a robin sighting."

They start down the steep slope, skidding on the damp dirt. "It's still frozen underneath," Lucie observes.

"It's only March, but the equinox is this week, and then the days will really start to get longer, but not necessarily warmer. Hey, stop. Hear that?"

They pause, listening. For a moment, Lucie hears nothing except the wind whirling past her ears, and her own breathing, but then she grins and says, "Geese."

Sure enough, the women are rewarded by the sight of a distant flock of geese winging powerfully from south to north, keeping up a continual conversation with one another as they fly.

"One thing to keep in mind if you're out walking now, even in town: watch for bears," Amanda says. "They'll be coming out of hibernation, and they are ravenous. They have food on the brain, and you do not want to surprise a hungry bear. Or get between a mama and her cubs, the worst possible situation. Best to sing or talk to yourself, *loud*, especially if you're walking along the creek or in bush, or if it's windy."

"Chinooks, geese, bears. Look where I live. Danger at every hand."

"And skunks, did I mention skunks? Porcupines?"

"It's enough to make a girl stay home."

"Ha, as if. Between the café and Ray, we never see you any more. Your saddle misses you."

"Time you started riding again," Keith says in his low, quiet voice. "You've got a saddle to break in."

Right on cue. Have you been talking to your lovely wife?

Lucie knows she's forgotten much of what she learned last fall, but she is eager to try the saddle that's been hanging patiently in the tack room since Christmas. She bundles up, catches Quincy from the pasture, and spends a long time brushing the mare, getting re-acquainted. Finally Lucie hefts the saddle — constructed mostly of synthetic material and fabric, it's far lighter than even the small leather saddle she was using previously. She adjusts the saddle on the mare's back, then Keith shows her how to attach the chest strap, which he calls a breast collar. "You won't need this in the arena, but when we get out trail riding in the mountains, it's a good thing to have, keeps the saddle from slipping back when you're going uphill."

Lucie mounts stiffly, realizing how long it's been since the last time she rode a horse. Keith has to patiently remind her about hand position, body position, weight, leg aids, as Lucie and the grey mare circle the arena at a walk, trot, and lope, then the other direction, and then figure eights. After what seems like ten minutes, Keith says, "That's about enough for today. You should walk the mare a bit to cool her before you send her back outside." To Lucie's surprise, she's been riding for more than an hour.

"Easy to lose track of time, you get so involved with the horse," she says, leading Quincy around the arena while Keith works another horse. He only nods an acknowledgment with his usual calm smile, never breaking his focus on the young horse he's schooling.

The cowboy way. Amanda was so right, these guys never give up a thing — what's on their minds. They never seem impressed. No 'congratulations' or 'atta girl' for a job well done, any job. But say something they agree with and you get that famous smile. They all do it. Except Tom, of course, who's forgotten how to smile and shows no signs of wanting to recapture that skill.

"So, morning lessons again?" Keith asks, to which Lucie nods and practices her own version of the cowboy smile.

"Jude? Hi, it's me." The cell phone connection is tenuous. Lucie paces her bedroom, trying to improve the signal, finally settling on the corner of her bed.

"OhmygodIthoughtyouweredead."

" Yeah, yeah, I know, so sue me. I have much to tell. Got a glass going?"

"No, but start talking, and I'll start pouring."

Lucie tells Judith about early spring in the foothills, the advancing daylight, her weekend snowshoe excursions, the weather, the blast of chinook warmth, and her associated headache. With a giggle, she tells Judith, "I've learned that 'winter' is a verb around here, so is 'trailer.' As in, 'I wintered my cows in the home pasture and now I'm gonna trailer 'em up to the mountains.' And there's a local grapevine that works amazingly fast — if somebody's cows get outside their fence, everyone calls everyone until they're safely back behind four strands of barbed wire."

"Your inner cowgirl is emerging. So," Judith says finally, "you've told me everything and nothing. I get that the scenery's great and the people are fun and the wind makes your head hurt. That's nice to know, but it's not what I *want* to know, and I don't think it's why you called."

"How did you get to be so smart?"

"Long ears of practice. You should see how long these ears are now." Lucie laughs. Judith continues, "What's up, really?"

Lucie takes a deep breath, knowing she's about to break a promise. "It's about Ray, and it's the strangest story ever." Despite his entreaty to guard his secret, Lucie tells Judith much of his story about the ill-advised loan gone wrong and his current status as a fugitive. "He asked me not to tell anyone, but Jude, I need help here. I don't know what to do with this, or how I feel about this totally bizarre story. Or how to help. Notice I said 'help' not 'fix.'

"I think you're far enough away from this drama, though I guess if the drug guys are smart — and he says they are — they could find you through me. I don't think so but — argh, I'm sorry, I'm just realizing this — now I understand his paranoia, how he feels about not telling me too much, because it occurs to me I might be putting you in harm's way. And that's a ripple effect I hadn't even considered until this moment."

"OK, thanks for *that*, girlfriend." Judith is laughing. "I don't think it's going to keep me up at night, I'm a long reach from you and Ray. But, Lucie, listen, this story is insane. Do you believe him?"

Lucie sighs and wonders whether Judith herself is taking the story seriously. But she says emphatically, "*Yes*, I do believe him. He's a credible, honest person, as you know, and this story explains his weird behaviour. And the look on his face when he told me, Jude — so terrible and sad. I don't think he's playing me. But it casts a certain shadow over whatever my future with him might be. His whole life is a lie. Oh, Jude — I don't know what to do with this."

Judith says gently, "Let it go, Lucie. It's a weird story for sure, but if you believe him, trust him."

"Am I a fool, am I crazy? Do you believe his story?"

"Not for me to say, it's for you to decide. But, for the record — yeah, I believe it."

Lucie sighs deeply, astonished by how relieved she feels to have someone else support Ray's tale. "Yeah, OK. Me too."

Lucie eventually tracks down Marta at home one afternoon, finding — to her surprise and some disappointment — that Marta has company.

"Come in, Lucie. Meet my friend Delores."

Lucie greets a singular woman, remarkable because she is entirely grey. Hair, eyes, even her skin have a greyish pall. Her shirt is a nondescript shade, not grey exactly, but certainly not vibrant blue or green or anything, for that matter. The only colour is provided by stains that might be ketchup on the lower right side of the woman's shirt, where she appears to have rubbed her hand while cooking, leaving streaks of red that have turned dark and rusty. It seems her shirt has not experienced the inside of a washing machine for some time.

Delores seems vaguely familiar but Lucie doesn't make a connection until the woman says, "You're from the café. You made a birthday cake for me last fall."

"Ah, you were my very first catering customer," Lucie responds.

"What I wouldn't give to go back to that time." Delores sighs, turning her eyes down to stare into her half-empty coffee cup.

"Delores has troubles," says Marta sadly. "Her boy is having bad times."

"I'm sorry to hear that," Lucie says distantly, wondering how she can politely cut her visit short.

I'm not in the mood to listen to the troubles of somebody I don't know. Especially somebody who kinda looks like a fish. That's heartless and not neighbourly in the least, but there you go.

Nonetheless, Lucie accepts coffee and a muffin from Marta and listens half-heartedly, picking up details about this person who's come into her orbit. She learns the woman's oldest son and grandchildren live in Montana, but she hasn't seen them for some time — years, in fact. And now the son is ill or has had some kind of accident and can't work, and the family could use help from Delores but she is unable to make the trip.

"I used to be scared of long road trips by myself, but you just have to get behind the wheel and go," Lucie offers helpfully.

"Can't," the woman says curtly, eyeing Marta instead of Lucie, with something like accusation in her eyes. She turns to face Lucie, pouring coffee into her own cup at the same time, and then swings the pot to pour for Lucie. "Can't cross the border. Criminal record. Drunk driving, wilful damage of public property."

"Oh."

"In a Zamboni. You might have heard of me, I was a national joke."

Without looking at Lucie's cup, the woman stops pouring in the nick of time and then looks up, glares at Lucie, who's at a loss and says nothing.

But Lucie does recall the story, a woman convicted of drunk driving while operating the ice-cleaning machine in a small-town arena. She was wheeling the vehicle erratically around the ice surface, bumping into the sideboards and damaging the machine, and then she came to a halt in the middle of the rink and passed out. Police found an empty vodka bottle beside her. Lucie and her friends had laughed until they cried, made so many jokes. And now here she is, this newsworthy woman with her weary face and dirty shirt, pouring coffee at Marta's table.

"Delores and Henry lose their farm too," Marta says. As if that explains everything, which it does.

Lucie nods and munches chunks of delicious orange-and-ginger scented muffin, not making eye contact with her companions, and not willing to engage further in this sad story.

I'm sure there's more to your story, Delores. You don't swig vodka at work in the hockey arena for no reason. The thing is, we all have stuff that confronts us. Take Marta. Or Ray, someone with good reason to drown himself in alcohol, but he doesn't. So what's the difference? Some people dream, others drown.

At last Marta says, "So Lucie, spring is here, some days anyway. We should go walking, ja?"

"I'd love that. I'll have to figure out a day though, because we're going to start summer hours at the café soon. Can I phone you?"

"Sure, sure, you tell me. I walk every day. Get my feet wet, still so much snow to melt and big puddles, but I find spring everywhere, flowers and birds, I want to show you. And I will plant my garden soon, I have many little sprouts started. Lucie do you have garden? I always have too many sprouts, I can give you some. Carrot, radish, potato, other things. Beans, peas."

"I don't think Amanda has a garden patch at the ranch. But Ray has a garden behind his house, he grows stuff for the café — herbs and such, mostly. I'll ask what he might want, thank you. And," she says, standing, "speaking of the café, it's time for me to mosey back to town."

"You can give Delores a ride?"

Ugh. "Yes, of course I can."

Driving into Sweetgrass, Lucie cannot think of a single thing to say, and it appears Delores feels the same — the silence in the car is dense. Finally, and against her instincts, Lucie asks, "Where was your farm? And it's funny but that's something I've never asked Marta."

"She and Tom were our neighbours, south and west of here." No further illumination.

Clearly that was the wrong question, and chagrin brings out Lucie's judgmental streak. "Marta seems to have found new things to sustain her life," she remarks with acidity she can taste.

Pause.

"Marta is a saint. Turn left here."

I know where you live, I've been there.

Without further instruction, Lucie pulls up in front of the house she remembers from delivering the birthday cake, what seems a lifetime ago. Delores heaves herself from the low-slung car, mumbles "Thanks," and slams the door with considerable energy.

Lucie doesn't immediately pull away. Instead she watches the heavyset woman's plodding progress up the front walk. The house appears even more rundown than Lucie remembers; it's as drab as Delores herself. Then Lucie catches the flick of the front window's ill-hung curtain, and she's astonished to see the tall, lanky youth who called her a zombie a few weeks ago. Before he has time to recognize her, Lucie drives off.

Her boy is having bad times. Which boy were you talking about? The one in Montana or the one in Sweetgrass?

True to Amanda's warning, and the collective local wisdom, cold weather returns. By April, everyone in town is well and truly fed up with winter, but winter is not done with Sweetgrass. The daylight may be lengthening, but the washy, tepid sunshine is a joke with no warmth or welcome. Stubborn clots of snow remain everywhere, piled against buildings and shovelled into heaps on lawns: dense, landlocked icebergs that refuse to melt. On occasional warmish days, the gutters run with filthy water, yet the drifts never seem to diminish. The air has an iron smell like blood, and the sky is frequently obscured by sodden, grey hanks of cloud that look like spools of wet wool. Spring hesitates, as if trying to decide whether to abandon the whole business and go elsewhere.

But, increasingly there are birds, always and everywhere. It's astonishing to Lucie that an annual event of such enormity — the grand northward migration — has previously escaped her notice. It's spring and birds return, that's a fact she's known since she was six. She's never paid much attention until now, but suddenly the returned birds are inescapable. She can't get enough of them.

She bundles into her winter coat to sit on the ranch house's back deck in the evenings to simply listen to the chorus of bird song. Or she and Ray occasionally stroll the town's quiet streets. He tries to name the birds he hears — she tries to remember the names. Her favourites are chickadees, which stay through the winter and actually sing, "chicka-dee-dee-dee," but now have a new three-note spring song that Ray describes as, "I'll... find you," or maybe, "Come... get me," delivered with his teasing grin and a rib tickle she squirms to avoid.

One afternoon, she joins Marta for a damp and difficult trek along the muddy, snowy banks of the river, which is still largely covered by layers of stubborn ice. Wherever she goes, birdsong fills her ears. The noise is everywhere; from rowdy, rasping crows, to cheerful, chattering sparrows; from the whistling wings of ducks and snipes, to the territorial songs of robins, wrens, warblers, woodpeckers drumming on trees and posts, and flickers laughing with their distinctive "ack-ack-ack." Noise noise noise. "But it's not like traffic, sirens, and stereos — not city noise that gets on your nerves," she comments to Marta.

"Ja, we do not have loud city noise here, so we hear other things. But I will say, crows do get on my nerves. They come in March just when days start to get longer. They start their yapping before sunrise and go all day and do not even have babies yet. It's 'ka-ka-ka' all day, and it gets worse when babies hatch."

"Yep, I'll give you that. A pair of crows is building a nest in a big dead spruce next to Ray's apartment, and you're right, they never shut up." Lucie neglects to notice how frequently she speaks about Ray's apartment. Although she doesn't deliberately tell anyone she and Ray are a couple of some sort, still she's become careless about keeping a cloak on their relationship, simply assuming others have noticed, accepted, and chosen not to comment. Or, more accurately, she's not thinking about it at all.

Lucie also loves the fluting trill of newly arrived red-winged blackbirds. "They have cousins, yellow-head blackbirds," Marta says, "but yellow-head's song is like somebody cutting tin. 'Scrape scrape scrape.' Awful sound for such pretty birds."

"Just wait 'til hummingbirds show up," Ray says one afternoon. "Their wings move so fast they buzz like huge bugs, but they also make weird and amazingly loud chirps for such tiny creatures. And they're fun to watch. They're bullies."

"People around town are complaining about what a cold spring this is, but for me it's the best spring I can remember," Lucie replies. "I'm loving all of it: the birds, the mud, today it's cold, tomorrow it's warm. Up, down, sunny, not — whatever. I feel so... I don't know, energized...connected. I can't even describe how great this is. If there were cherry trees and daffodils like in Vancouver, this place would be spot-on perfect."

"We'll have lilacs and other stuff eventually," he says. "Though I have to tell you, the smell of lilacs reminds me of going to an outhouse. On the farm, we had indoor plumbing, but if the pump failed, we had to use the outhouse, which was surrounded by lilac bushes. The original air freshener."

"Lovely memory, thanks for sharing."

Spring advances and the sun traces an ever-higher arc over the town. As never before, Lucie notices the transition, how morning light seeps into her basement bedroom, how much earlier the sun tops the high ridge east of the ranch house. It's a surge, a revolution that propels her forward.

Even the approach of her fortieth birthday doesn't cause consternation. Always ambivalent about birthdays, perhaps another result of her mother's constant penny-pinching and a childhood devoid of parties or celebrations, Lucie has no intention of announcing the impeding milestone or acknowledging it in any way. The day arrives and passes, like the moon fattens and ebbs. It simply *is*, it's routine and there's no point in marking the occasion.

Ray offers his own take on the changing seasons. Coming back to the café after a supply run to the city, he says, "You know it's spring because ranchers are moving their herds to new pasture, and the roads around here are paved with cow shit."

"Yeah, I noticed that too when I was out to the farmer's market. The smell on that back road is rank. And when you're driving, it's all about dodging the chunks. But I thought you said this country is kinda vacant of cows?"

He shrugs. "It never ceases to amaze me how so few cows can create so much, um, fallout."

Eventually the snow disappears, all in a rush, thanks to an extended warm spell that once again turns streets and sidewalks into flowing creeks, and lawns into swamps. Then all the surface water suddenly dries up, and the town's maintenance crew sweeps winter's gravel from the streets. At long last, grass is greening and buds on the slender swaying aspens break with audible pops to unfurl tiny, bright gold-green leaves. Ditches and fields are festooned with dandelions and wildflowers. Around town, flowering shrubs and trees are everywhere — pink blossoms, white, mauve. The air is fragrant with flowers and grass and new leaves.

One morning before going to the café, Lucie rises early without waking Ray, and leaves a note on his kitchen counter — 'Gone for a walk, see you @ café' — and drives down to the river. She hasn't been here for several weeks, not since she and Marta picked their muddy way cautiously along the bank still strewn with chunks of thick ice some time ago. Today, Lucie plans to walk along the bank, perhaps wade out to a mid-stream gravel bar, but as soon as she gets out of her car and looks across the river, she sees that plan is impossible.

Not only are the slabs of ice gone, but the gravel bars have disappeared as well, and water is surging over the streamside footpath. The river pushes above its shallow banks and eddies into the willow bush on either side. But it's not the banks that capture her, it's the full-throated exuberant roar of the river as it springs and leaps, jubilant, liberated from its winter crust, draining the mountains of their long-held snow. The river's energy grabs her spirit. She spreads her arms wide and whirls around and around in the gravel parking area, heedless of anyone who might be watching a grown woman twirling to the rush of a foothills river in its full melt-fuelled flood.

It's such wild magic. Lucie is absorbing and revelling in all of it.

The café returns to summer hours and Lucie surges with energy, rising early — some days to ride indoors and out, some mornings to bake. Days are varied and always full. She helps Ray in the kitchen, serves meals, cleans and organizes, buys supplies and ingredients. New, fresh produce turns up each week at the farmer's markets. Lucie's life settles into a routine that is neither dull nor restricting. Instead, she feels relaxed, even joyful. She and Ray return to their joking, laughing way as they work together seamlessly, their problems pushed away for now. Their days whiz away like fishing line from a reel. They spend nearly every night together either at Ray's apartment or snuggled in Lucie's basement room at the ranch.

"You should come to my bed sometimes," she'd offered, back when snow still blanketed the ground. "It's safe and quiet at the ranch, you don't need to be on guard all the time. You said yourself Keith and Amanda are trustworthy, and besides, apparently they miss me, though I suspect they miss my baking more. Anyway, we don't have to tell them anything, they already know we're an 'item' as Jude would say, that's all they need to know. You could relax for a night, we could pretend to be normal."

Immediately she'd regretted that last remark, but he only smiled and said, "Yes, OK. That would be really nice. Not often, but sometimes. Thanks." And so they do. Not often, but sometimes.

She's so remarkably content, in such a generous mood, she's not even annoyed when George drops into the café one day and calls her 'Darlin.' or when the Mounties — almost daily — call her 'Sweetheart.' She shakes it off without thought. It's just the local cowboy way. She hums tunelessly but happily, facsimiles of *It Might As Well Be Spring, My Favourite Things, Got the World on a String*, songs she hasn't thought of for years much less brought to life with hums and whistles.

Tom, however, is another matter. Try as she might, Lucie cannot evoke even a welcoming smile when he turns up for one of his increasingly infrequent visits to the café. He sits at his usual corner table and observes her work, sizing her up with an appraising look she's sure he would have used, in his previous life, to assess livestock.

Stop looking at me like I'm your property. You don't understand the value of what I'm doing in this dining room, or what Ray's doing in the kitchen. We are producing good cash for you; it's a gold mine because this café has a big regional and maybe national reputation. You need to appreciate what you've got here, Tommy my man. I am not some commodity for you to judge. I am not a cow, or horse, or bale of hay. Ray tolerates your lack of respect. I have no idea how he does that, because it pisses me right off.

Lucie doesn't share her thoughts with Ray until one day — a fine, warm afternoon that's infused her with sunlight and warmth

— Tom hulks into the café and sees the walls hung with cheerful abstract works by a local artist. He gazes around the dining room at the bright, fanciful paintings, then grunts and stalks straight to the kitchen to speak with Ray. Hearing their voices, Lucie strides toward the kitchen intending to defend her idea for rotating art displays, but discovers the conversation is not about artwork at all. It's about money.

In the hall outside the kitchen, Lucie leans her back against the wall and tips her head up, listening to their voices, harsh and bitter but not loud. She holds her breath so she can hear them.

Tom requests extra cash. Ray initially declines, saying he needs to buy supplies and pay bills, but Tom persists. Finally Ray relents and counts out money from the cash box. Lucie quickly scrambles upright, springs to the coffee station, and makes a pretence of filling a teapot as Tom stomps behind her without a word and departs.

After the lunch rush, she says to Ray, "We've got to get a handle on Tom. You know he goes straight to the pool hall or the hotel bar and drinks it all away."

"I know exactly what he does with it. But he's the boss, and neither of us has any right to deny him or tell him how to spend his money. I *do* have a handle on him, sort of. I keep a cushion of petty cash so I can give him a little without backing us into a corner. And, just so you know, I'm still taking care of things I need to."

She remains angry. "This isn't the first time he's asked for extra?"

"Oh, Luce. This happens all the time, couple of times a month or more."

"I've never seen him come back to the kitchen before."

"He usually phones me, and I take a few bucks to wherever he is."

"*What*? You *deliver* it?"

"Like I said — he's the boss. It's the least I can do."

It's a standoff. Lucie doesn't agree, but from the stern expression on Ray's normally calm face she sees there will be no persuading him.

Besides, it's impossible to stay mad at someone who looks so cute with that curly beard. But you've got debts to take care of. Agh! The men in my life make me crazy. All of them.

Now once again on summer hours, the café is open on Sundays so Lucie's had to give up her weekend outings with the hiking group. She misses spending time outdoors. But one quiet mid-June day, Janet comes by the restaurant. "Daisy and I are going mushrooming next week with Sweet Water Woman, can you join us?"

It turns out to be a day off. So here Lucie is, pushing twigs and branches away from her face, stepping carefully over logs and avoiding spiny thistles and thorny wild roses, trying to keep up with Janet, Daisy, and a portly Native woman who moves with astonishing grace and agility through the dense bush.

Sweet Water Woman is nothing like Lucie imagined. Instead of the tall, long-haired, mystical person Lucie conjured, Sweet Water Woman is broad of face and body. She has a rock-solid presence both physical and spiritual, but speaks so softly Lucie often holds her breath to hear the words.

Sweet Water Woman clearly knows her land well, because in less than an hour she's discovered several caches of chanterelles, and each woman in the entourage now carries a bag full of the bright-orange mushrooms. Occasionally Sweet Water Woman stops to point out particular plants and talks about their medicinal properties. She is, as Daisy said last winter, totally cool. Entirely present, entirely confident not only in her knowledge but also in her place and presence. Lucie is intimidated, attracted, and utterly impressed.

The woods are dense and airless, the day is warm. Lucie is overdressed but reluctant to remove her long-sleeved jacket and expose her arms to the very plentiful and apparently ravenous mosquitoes swarming around them. Finally arriving back at the house, the women peel off layers of damp clothing while Sweet Water Woman makes tea.

Her house is a small but comfortable double-wide trailer in a remote clearing at the end of a winding gravel road — it had taken Janet two tries to find the gate, "Haven't been here for ages," Janet had muttered as she turned the car around at a dead end and tried again, to which Daisy had said, "I told you it was that gate with the blue mailbox. Mom, I've been here more than you."

Never mind, they found it eventually, and now they're here after a hot, muggy afternoon, sipping tea. The furniture is not new but comfortable, the walls are hung with quilts, blankets, and several Northwest Coast masks, even some vintage snowshoes. There's a wood-burning stove in the kitchen for cooking and another in the main room for heat, both of which are silent and cold on this humid June day.

The hot tea is remarkably refreshing even on such a sticky day. "Rain tonight. I can smell it," Sweet Water Woman says quietly, passing mugs and a plate of cookies around the table. Outside, the sky is clear, but Lucie has no doubt the prediction is accurate. The women chat quietly — most of the conversation is between Sweet Water Woman and Daisy — and sip tea while a number of dogs of varying age and provenance sniff around the table. Apart from their snuffling, the scratch of their claws on the floor, and the soft murmur of conversation, there is little other sound, indoors or out. The profound quiet is deeply comforting and peaceful, like a warm bath, like a rocking chair, like deep breathing.

As they make ready to leave, Sweet Water Woman grasps Lucie's hand and looks directly into her eyes with a gaze disconcerting but kind. The elder woman says, "You don't talk too much. You can come back," shaking Lucie's hand. Yet another surprisingly firm, confident touch.

Lucie, overwhelmed, nods, smiles, and whispers, "Thank you."

"Wow, that's an endorsement, especially on your very first visit," Janet says to Lucie as they drive away. "Just so you know, she means 'Come any time, just show up.' No appointment necessary. You should knock a couple of times, then walk in. If you stand outside waiting for her to open the door, you'll be there all day. And if nobody's home, just go in and wait. Make tea, she's not fussed. But if you want to pick mushrooms, or flowers, or walk around on the land, you need her invitation and permission. Don't ever venture beyond the house unless she knows you're there and she says it's OK."

"Even if she's not home, the door is never locked," Daisy adds. " If you really need to see her, just walk in and wait for her. She's never surprised to see someone in her house. I've done it twice, when I needed her advice on something. Just show up. She is totally cool with that."

In the back seat, Lucie nods but remains silent, huddled with her bag of fresh-caught mushrooms and humbled by the day's experience.

Every time I think I'm starting to fit in here, I meet someone who is so much more embedded in this community, this place, and it turns my head around. Town or country, men or women, farmers, ranchers, cowboys, local business people, and now a Native woman who tops them all. Lucky me. I am grateful for this experience, but right now I feel so disconnected, as if I could never really be part of this place no matter what I do or how long I live here. Seriously, would anyone miss me if I was gone? I doubt it.

Ray is suitably impressed with the bounty of mushrooms but to Lucie's disappointment he cannot serve them in the café. "This has nothing to do with my personal paranoia," he says. "It's all about the province's rules. If the food inspector caught me serving foraged food, he'd close us down. The same goes for wild-caught fish or game. Couple of years ago, a guy offered me meat from a moose he'd shot. A nice gesture, and moose meat is tasty, but it's impossible. However, you and I will have our own little chanterelle feast tonight." Which they do, to the drumming rhythm of steady rain on the roof and windows.

She was right. Never mind that the day was hot and sunny. She knew what was coming.

The next morning is brighter and fresher then usual, as though the air has been scrubbed. Rain has settled the dust, and generated a sweetness in the air that's half grass, half pine. Lucie and Ray rise early to sip coffee and nibble toast on his deck, absorbing warmth and the songs of chickadees, robins, wrens. Busy lively birdsong, a sweet foundation for the day. In her deck chair, Lucie leans her head back, eyes closed. Hears a sharp chirping she doesn't recognize.

She sits up to see the tiniest of darting shapes, a whirr of wings like the unwelcome buzz of wasps. But there are no insects around. Instead she sees an odd, extraordinary display by a hummingbird, a red-gold jewel sparkling in the sunlight. The miniscule bird lifts and dives, zooming down, then up, turning at the top of the arc to dive and lift again like some tiny, demented midway roller coaster that only the bird can see. Loop up, loop down. And again. And again.

"There's a girl hummie around," Ray says softly. "That's a courtship display, he's showing off." Ray takes a long sip of coffee. Astonished, Lucie watches the miniscule rocketing bird, then turns to Ray with her eyes wide, her lush lips parted in a truly radiant, genuine grin that wilts when she sees his wistful face, his eyes brimming with tears.

"I feel like that," he says, without looking at her. "One minute I'm full of hope. I think, 'OK, you've got this. You're dealing with everything, you'll be fine.' And the next minute I'm plummeting. Down, down. So full of stress and worry, I eat myself alive for being so stupid. I dip and dive. I think I know, then I know I don't know anything."

She reaches to grab and squeeze his hand.

She gazes into her jungle-dark coffee, as if the liquid could conjure some comfort. Says in a low, determined voice, "Don't doubt me. And don't doubt yourself. Listen, Ray. You work so hard, not just for Tom and Marta; you work hard for yourself. Paying your debt, I get that. But it's bigger, it's more. It's about getting back what you've lost. You had a farm, you had a life, a future.

Then it disappeared, and I don't think that was any fault of yours. My sweet man, it was not your fault that it didn't rain. And maybe cooking is your future. Maybe it's your life, my life — they're the same, only different, as Jude would say. And we *are* getting through this. You've told me so, over and over. Have some faith in yourself."

I can't believe I just said that. About either of us.

He nods gravely and takes a big gulp of coffee. He squeezes her hand back. But he doesn't look at her.

Janet comes to the café a few days after the mushrooming expedition. "Enjoy your chanterelles?" Lucie nods, grinning. "They were tasty, yes."

Janet says, "I'm organizing a full-moon hike tomorrow. It will be a late-evening start, so you could work the dinner shift and still make it. We'll probably leave the parking lot around nine-thirty. We don't go far, just out to Bales' ranch and walk up their ridge."

"*Bales*? Really?"

"Yeah I know, what a name, eh? Paul and Carolyn Bales. Wait 'til you meet them, they're a hoot."

Lucie mentions the outing to Ray and is astounded when he says, "I could do with a hike. Sure, let's go."

"*Really*?"

He grins. "Time for us to come clean instead of fuelling rumours. Carefully and gradually."

"Oh, sure, by hiking in the dark."

"Well, I *do* have a big flashlight," he says, to which she cocks an eyebrow. "I'm talking large equipment here," he continues blithely, which makes her giggle and turn away, her cheeks warm and pink. Despite Lucie's decades of sexual experience, somehow Ray's teasing and innuendo are so harmless, guileless, he makes her feel young and fresh, and she blushes at his every sly joke. Then again, she knows his remarks are deliberate. He knows exactly what effect his words have on her, which serves to make her even more confounded and self-conscious, as though nobody has ever spoken such things to her before.

Evening.

An unusually boisterous group assembles in the parking lot as daylight leaks away over the western horizon. They greet one another, hugging, joking, and laughing, it's already a party. "Look at this, it's past nine at night and still light in the west," someone observes. Eventually the group is more or less organized; people get into vehicles and slam doors. The convoy heads out, arriving just a few minutes later at a ranch east of town. The house is built into the side of what looks to Lucie like a dauntingly high and steep ridge silhouetted against the darkening sky. Everyone piles out of their vehicles, shoulders into backpacks and tests their flashlights. One couple makes the rounds, shaking hands, and welcoming the adventurers.

"Hi, don't think I've met you." Extending her hand to Lucie is a compact woman crowned with a tumble of fluffy, dark-gold hair. Backlit by the ranch's yard light, she resembles a dandelion and her character seems equally light and breezy. Although deep furrows divide her brow both laterally and vertically, and she speaks with forceful, no-nonsense directness, her eyes are fringed with laugh lines and her smile is ready. "I'm Carolyn Bales as in 'bales of hay.' That tall dude is my husband Paul, this is our place."

Carolyn turns to greet Ray. "Hiya, Honey, long time no see."

"Been cooking up a gourmet storm," he replies. "Time you got your butt into my fine establishment to see what I've been up to."

"I know one thing you've been up to. You're the talk of the town," she says, giving him a teasing poke in the ribs and actually winking at Lucie, who smiles a bit uncertainly and gives Ray an alarmed glance once Carolyn has turned away.

"Are we? Seriously?" she whispers.

He simply shrugs.

Gossip is looming, and you're not worried?

The group sets off, angling upward across the face of the now-dark hillside. True to his word, Ray produces a huge, bright-yellow crate of a flashlight with a handle on top and a lens as big around as a saucer. He follows closely behind Lucie, shining a broad beam of light just in front of her feet. But the path is easy to follow even without illumination because a giant, glorious lemon drop of a full moon is rising rapidly over the fields, an arresting contrast to the deep-mauve sky behind it. Couples and small groups stop frequently to watch the moon's ascent and comment on its remarkable colour and size.

Eventually the entire crew arrives atop the ridge, now bathed in extraordinarily brilliant moonlight that washes out all but the brightest of stars and actually gives the sky overhead an indigo hue. People switch off their flashlights and sit on the sparse grass, some first spreading blankets, others pulling on jackets or sweaters as the evening air rapidly cools. Lucie sits cross-legged, and Ray snugs up right behind her, wrapping his arms and legs around her.

A public display of affection, yikes, what are you doing? Isn't this contrary to all your usual caution? I don't know what to do with this. Play along, I guess.

Carolyn plunks down beside them but makes no remark about their entwined state. "Feels great to sit down for a bit. I'm so beat, we've been working hard this spring," she says with a sigh. "Too many calves. Honestly, we need to quit this business and take up desk jobs."

Or hang gliding. Ha, Jude, you would love this.

"Yeah office job, as if," Ray says. "When was the last time Paul spent more than ten minutes indoors? So, no sneaking away to Mexico this year?"

Carolyn gives a hearty laugh. "We run three hundred head. A vacation in Mexico? Honey, I can't take a vacation to the grocery store."

They pass around binoculars, chewy oatmeal cookies — Lucie's contribution — bars of bittersweet chocolate. Some have tea, others wine, a few have flasks of whisky. There's quiet conversation and laughter. Someone starts yipping and howling, and soon most of the group joins the chorus, laughing when a real coyote responds from somewhere across the fields.

Gauzy cloud, spun of spiderweb, creeps across the sky, turning the moonlight soft and milky. Lucie is chilled but reluctant to say so until Ray, who's resting his chin on her shoulder, murmurs into her ear, "You warm enough?" to which she shakes her head. "OK, let's head back." They stand. "Thanks, folks, this was terrific," Ray says, waving as he and Lucie start down the hill.

Behind them, someone calls, "Go straight home, you two. No canoodling in the back of the car."

"Ha, canoodling's for someone half my age and twice my stamina," Ray calls back, laughing. The group responds with whistles and whoops.

As they make their way back down the hill, Lucie says over her shoulder, "So, canoodling is for kids, eh? You know, I don't even know how old you are."

"Ditto, Pumpkin."

"You first."

"Forty-three. You?"

"Just turned forty in April, hence 'Avril,' my middle name."

"Lucille Avril Tanguay! How dare you have a big birthday and not tell me. I would have done something special. Baked a cake."

"Ha, that would be my job," she says, striding downhill. She takes a number of steps, then realizes he's not behind her — he's stopped walking so she stops too, looks back over her shoulder. His moonlit face looks perplexed and worried. She says, "Oh, Sweet Pea, forget it. I'm not a fan of birthdays, maybe because when I was a kid my mother never allowed any kind of celebration — too much work, cost too much money, and what was the point anyway? Besides, cakes were for paying customers. So I'm not inclined to mark birthdays or anniversaries. I just don't care. Besides, you make me feel special every day, I don't need a birthday for that."

He shakes his head and steps forward to continue their descent, now beside her on the widening path. She turns and walks on, neglecting to ask about his birth date, lost instead in memories of her own unnoticed and uncelebrated birthdays long gone.

Unexpectedly he says, "You grew up in Ontario but your name is French."

"My mom is from the Ottawa Valley. Petawawa, a town along the river west of our nation's capital. My dad is — was? I don't even know if he's still walking the earth — anyway, he was born in Montreal, but from what little I know about him, I understand his family moved around a lot. I don't know why. They ended up at the Canadian Forces base in Petawawa because his dad had work there, doing what I have no idea. So my mother, this young girl from a lonely northern town, meets this worldly, swarthy, curly-haired French dude and can't resist him. They ran away to Toronto, I guess they were in their late teens. Within a few months, she gets pregnant, has the baby — *moi*. He sticks around long enough to name me, then *poof* he's gone. She used his last name, but I don't even know if they were married. She never wore a ring. And never said a good word about him."

"Your mom didn't go back to her folks?"

"I assume they told her not to darken their door with her half-Frenchie brat and no money. I never met them. Seriously, never once. My life is devoid of grandparents. But my mom's sister kept up some kind of secret liaison. My Aunt Carol, the only person I know from Ma's side of the family. Ha, *family*. One person. And a terrible person, at that."

"That's harsh."

"It's true. My aunt and my mother are both bitter, angry people. They *are* harsh. And yes, my mother's been through a lot and yes, she raised me on her own, and I turned out more or less OK. But does that give her the right to complain about every little thing about me?"

"No clue about your dad? Ever thought of looking for him?"

"Nope, why would I? He gave me curly black hair and a French name, then split. He didn't want anything to do with me. The feeling is mutual."

"Do you ever go home, then?"

Now Lucie stops walking to give Ray a 'what-are-you-talking-about?' look. Raises her palms to the sky. "Home? That's not home. Vancouver's not home." Lowering her arms, she looks around at the landscape lit by the high overhead moon, bright as a dime. "Ha. 'Home is where your heart is.' I've heard that expression so many times, but tonight I believe it. I think maybe this is home, now."

His cheerful, round face seems almost blue in the moonlight. He smiles thoughtfully. "Maybe it is."

In his apartment, they lie back to back in bed, sharing body heat, placing the soles of their cold feet against one another. Lucie says, "All right, what was tonight about? I'm trying to be cautious, though I catch myself sometimes dropping some remark about your backyard garden or the crows nesting in the branches of the mighty Ray Charles, and maybe that's careless and stupid of me. Maybe I'm not being as careful as I think. But there you were tonight, breaking all your own rules and going out like we're some kind of ordinary. I'm confused."

He thinks for awhile, draws a long breath. "I figured it was pretty safe," he says quietly into the dark room. "I know most of those people, more or less, nobody in that crowd I don't trust. I'd have backed out if I'd seen someone new in the parking lot. I'm still not keen for going to movies or events together; I don't even like taking you to the farmer's market. Anything public like that where I don't know who's watching makes me nervous."

She sighs. There's no argument to be made. Instead she says, "How do you know Carrie and Paul? Don't think I've seen them in the café."

"Nope, they never come in. They don't have time. But she and Paul sell their beef at the farmer's market, plus they sell special stuff to me — all my marrow bones, brisket, kidneys, beef tongue, whatever. They were the first local producers I met when I got here. They are incredibly kind and generous. If you ever need help, you can call on them. You've met them now, they know who you are, and they wouldn't hesitate to help if you're in trouble."

"So are we actually the talk of the town?"

"I don't know," he says, rolling over and sliding his arms around her, remarkably unconcerned. "Even if there is a little gossip circulating, I'd like to think I've built up enough goodwill in town that if a stranger turned up and started asking questions about us, somebody would tell me. Not that anybody knows about my situation, but people around here are suspicious of nosy newcomers."

OK, your caution made me nervous before. Now your lack of caution is making me nervous. Jeez Louise. What the what is going on? I don't get it.

He nuzzles, breathes her in. "You smell good: wild and spicy like the air outside tonight. Or like the ocean. Or what I imagine the ocean smells like."

"Quit changing the subject."

He distracts her with a deep, long kiss.

After a while, she says, "What do you mean, you *imagine* what the ocean smells like?"

"I'm a prairie boy, never been west of Banff, or east of Winnipeg, never crossed the Medicine Line. The only airplane I've ever been on was a four-seat Piper that my buddy back home learned to fly. He had to build up flight hours so he was always taking short trips from the local flying club and I went with him. I was never afraid because it was so amazing. I loved flying over country I knew on the ground, seeing what it looked like from the air. Someday I'd like to get on a big plane and travel to some really far place, experience different food, walk on a beach, see a live palm tree, waves, surf. Ha, some day I'll even have a passport."

"Whoa, whoa, one thing at a time. Medicine Line? I don't know what that means."

"It's the Native name for the Canada-U.S. border. North of the Medicine Line was a place of refuge for Native people from Montana and Dakota, I guess. And quit changing the subject." Another long kiss.

She murmurs, "I've never had one, either — a passport, I mean, though I have crossed the Medicine Line. Went to New York once with some girlfriends, but that was long before you needed a passport to get into the States. As for Italy, France, Mexico — I guess we have some adventures ahead of us."

"Mmm, adventure. How about right now?"

"Maybe you're my Medicine Line."

Yet another meteorological wave sweeps over the foothills. From the bright, warm, hopeful days, late June has become a sodden mess of rain, rain, and more rain. Sometimes a patter, sometimes a downpour. Now ten days without a break. Runoff from the steady rain, combined with melt of the remaining snowpack high in the mountains, has made the river angry and swollen. It's bouncing and frothing, with rolling crests like the arched necks of a hundred kicking, bucking horses, a complete change from its usual clear, merry, shallow self. Water is surging up the banks too, washing over into places it has no business being. Not only is the river's volume vastly greater than normal, but the charging torrent also carries logs, fence posts, and debris that scour the banks and slam into bridge abutments. There's talk the authorities will close a small forestry bridge upstream, concerned the structure could be swept away. The highway between Sweetgrass and the city is awash in several low spots.

It's an early July morning. Watery light seeps through Lucie's curtains. She's alone. Her cell phone rings. It's Ray. "We'll be closed today," he says urgently.

She jerks upright in a panic, thinking he's in some kind of danger. "Why, are you OK?"

"A culvert blew out in town, and there's water rising fast around the strip mall with the grocery store and the bank, plus some houses are in danger too. Guys are organizing sandbags. I'm going over there right now."

At that moment, Amanda knocks firmly on Lucie's door and calls, "Hello, anyone home?"

"Just me, I'm talking to Ray — there's a flood?"

"Yeah, we're going to help. Can you come, too?"

"Be right there." She returns to the phone. "Sorry, did I yell in your ear? Guess we're all headed down there, too."

"OK, do whatever they need, don't look for me. I'll call later."

Keith, Amanda, and Lucie arrive in town. It's raining hard, but the gathered crowd seems oblivious, intent instead on the business of sandbagging. Water streams over raincoat-clad backs and hats, even those who are not so well prepared keep doing what they're doing. Once again, Lucie is impressed by how quickly people have organized themselves. A town truck is dumping sand — and where has this sand come from? — in a vacant lot across the street from the strip mall that houses the town's grocery, bank, dentist, and post office. A brigade armed with shovels is filling long, sturdy bags made from some kind of woven plastic — and where have these bags come from? — then handing the sand-filled bags to others who deftly knot the bags, handing them off to yet others who've set up a human chain passing filled, tied sandbags hand-to-hand across the street to still others who are stacking bags, creating a dam around the stores. Some people wear high-topped rubber boots and rain gear, others are merely clad in sneakers and jeans, already soaked. They are all wading ankle-deep in muddy, swirling water, and it's clear the depth is rapidly increasing.

Pulling her warm toque over her head, Lucie steps into a second line passing filled sandbags. The roar of water from the angry river is deafening, people shout to make themselves heard. Endlessly she swivels from side to side, first grabbing a sandbag from the person on her left, turning to hand it to the person on her right. The bags are heavy, and fast becoming even heavier as rain soaks into the sand. Still the chain continues but whenever Lucie looks toward the building it seems the sandbag wall is growing longer, but no higher. The pace picks up. She is sweating and breathing hard. More more and more people arrive — they tap the shoulders of those in the brigade saying, "Need a break?" Eventually, her arms weak, knees screaming, and her lower back in knots, Lucie nods and steps out of the line as somebody else takes her place.

"There's hot coffee over there," another volunteer tells her, pointing up the street. Wearily Lucie trudges through the cold, drenching downpour toward the town office, where indeed people are handing out Styrofoam cups of hot liquid. She accepts one and takes a sip. It's bitter and hot, could hardly be called coffee, but it's welcome just the same. She hears someone calling her name and turns to see Marta standing behind a table where she and other volunteers are handing out granola bars, bags of nuts and raisins, chocolate bars.

Lucie strides over to the table and smiles broadly at Marta. Says, "Where did these come from?"

"The grocery manager bring out boxes and boxes and say, 'Give, give, people are helping, they need food.' Not good food but is what we have right now. Soup would be better, maybe later at the hall."

Lucie looks around. "Does this flood happen every year?"

"No, no. Is first time that I see this. Is because snow, so much snow in the mountains. Is spring now, all that snow melt and push water down the mountains and out to here, in such a hurry. And now so much rain too these days. As you say Lucie, look where we live. Mostly good, sometimes hard."

"But people step up." Lucie waves her arms to indicate the present and constantly incoming crowd.

"Ja, is so good, this town. When we need help, everyone helps."

Lucie gulps the last of what passes for coffee and heads back to take her place in the brigade again. She walks along the sandbag line, but nobody needs relief at the moment so she steps away, thinking she'll go to the sandbag-filling station, when her cell phone vibrates in her pocket. She doesn't recognize the phone number but takes the call anyway. "Yes, hello? This is Lucie."

She hears a garble of words she cannot quite decipher over the roar of river and rain, but she catches an insistent tone. She says, "Sorry, I can't hear you, it's really loud here. Can you say that again?"

"Aunt Car... your ma ... hearta ... get here ...as you can."

"Auntie Carol, I don't know if you can hear me. I need to get to a quiet place, I'll call you back soon as I can." Knees shaking, Lucie disconnects and sinks to sit on sodden grass. She calls Ray, who picks up immediately. She says, "Hi, it's me. Where are you? I need to see you, right now. I know it's not a good time, but I need you. *Now.*"

Ray directs her to a spot where they can meet. She walks two blocks south to find more teams of people sandbagging houses on the low side of a street that's pouring with water. He meets her at the corner, sees her face. "What?" is all he says.

"I think my mom's in hospital in Toronto. Heart attack. My aunt called, I couldn't hear her but I think that's what she said. I have to leave, right away." She looks up at him, rain washing her face. "I came here with Amanda and Keith, I have no idea where they are. I need a car."

He pulls off a soaked glove, hands over his car keys. "I parked at the school, right by the back doors, you'll see it. Leave it at the ranch, I'll get it later." He bends to quickly kiss her cheek. "OK, go home, book a flight, let me know what you're doing and when. Oh, Pumpkin," he hugs her close, cradling her head, rocking. "Be brave, call me."

DOES YOUR MOTHER KNOW?

No sooner does Lucie leave Ray than everything starts to unfold in slow motion, as though she's pushing through some thick but transparent gelatine that resists every movement, every thought. It takes all her strength to walk three blocks to the school, find Ray's car, and drive slowly along the town's side streets to avoid the chaos near the river, until finally she's on the highway and picks up speed toward the ranch.

At home she parks Ray's car. She pulls off wet clothing and hangs everything to drip dry in the garage. In a tee shirt and underwear she sprints through the downpour from garage to house and goes immediately to the den, where she powers up Amanda's computer. Shivering and wrapped in a blanket pulled from the rocking chair, she begins the tedious business of booking a flight, a procedure with which she's utterly unfamiliar. At such short notice, every flight is already sold out or ridiculously expensive. Her only realistic option for getting to Toronto quickly is an overnight flight, which departs Calgary just before midnight and will arrive at Pearson International about six o' clock tomorrow morning, local time. The cost is more than she can afford but nothing else is even remotely suitable, so she enters her credit card number and prints the boarding pass. The whole process is exhausting and seems to take hours, but when she glances at the kitchen clock she sees it's barely past noon.

She grabs her cell phone and replies to the number her aunt called from. There's no answer. Lucie suspects her aunt is at a Toronto hospital and has turned off her phone. She leaves a message: "Hi, Auntie Carol, it's Lucie calling back. I've booked a flight, the soonest I could get is the red-eye that gets to Toronto early tomorrow morning. Call me back, I don't even know which hospital you're in."

Lucie takes a hot shower but she's afraid to sit down, lest she fall asleep. Instead she hauls a suitcase from her closet and spends a long time packing. Not that she's amassed a large wardrobe while in Sweetgrass, but she has no idea how long she'll be away, or what weather she might encounter. Or, for that matter, whether or not she'll be going to a funeral. With annoyance, she realizes she's left several good shirts and her fluffy cream sweater at Ray's. She considers going to get them but changes her mind, closes and zips the suitcase.

Upstairs, she makes a sandwich and gulps a glass of cold water, which revives her energy a little. She leaves the keys to Ray's car on the kitchen counter with a note for Amanda — 'Ray car keys' and a short explanation about what's happened. Then she puts on a hooded fleece jacket, grabs her suitcase, and dashes again through the downpour to Agememnon.

It's only early afternoon, hours until her flight, but she has nothing else to do. Sitting behind the wheel, she remembers to call Ray. He doesn't pick up — he probably wouldn't be able to hear her anyway — so she leaves a quick message. 'Hi Hon, it's about one-thirty. On my way to the airport, I fly out late tonight. I'll have a long wait, I know it's crazy to go now but I just want to get there. I'll call later. Your car is at the ranch, keys are on the kitchen counter." She leaves a similar message on Amanda's phone.

As it turns out, the rain has caused flooding in the city too. Several roads are closed, forcing Lucie to detour from the only route to the airport she knows. Agememnon may be faithful, but the mighty Honda is old and lacks built-in navigation, so twice Lucie has to pull into a parking lot to consult her cell phone for directions. In the end, it takes nearly three hours to drive from Sweetgrass to the airport, a trip that normally requires half that time. It's late afternoon when she arrives at the long-term parking lot and boards the mini-bus transport. At the air terminal she checks in for her flight and relinquishes her luggage, passes through security, and finally finally finally locates a seat at her departure gate. It's only then she realizes her aunt has not called back.

Yeah, wouldn't it be a joke on me if I got the message totally screwed up. I assumed she's in Toronto but Ma could be in Florida for all I know.

Desperate to stay awake, Lucie buys a paperback and a latte and tries to immerse herself in the novel. The airport is bright and noisy. Even so, her head bobs forward several times. She stands and paces the long corridor, making circuit after circuit, passing shops, restaurants, bars, other travellers.

Stay awake, come on, stay awake.

Ray calls at about eight-thirty, sounding utterly worn out. He tells her the sandbagging was successful. The river level crested and is now subsiding, so the stores, bank, and houses all remained more or less dry but for a bit of leakage. And it's stopped raining.

"Still pouring here," she says, "but I don't think it's affecting flights, everything seems to be coming and going on time."

They pause. She senses he'd like to finish the call and go to sleep, but she's lonely and uncertain about what's awaiting her in Toronto, reluctant to let him go even if they have little to say. She mentions that her aunt has not called back. "My Auntie Carol and I have never had much to say to each other, but you'd think she would at least call to give me an update, or tell me which hospital I'm going to. Ugh, I am not looking forward to seeing her. I am not looking forward to any of this."

"Does she come equipped with a husband? Kids?"

"Ah, another family tale. My aunt and uncle both worked in a car factory in Ontario, made sensational wages, retired early and moved to Florida, where my uncle got hit by a drunk driver within the first three or four years they lived there. No kids. So now Auntie Carol and my Ma are two peas in a pod, on the phone to each other every day to complain about their sorry lives. I haven't seen my aunt for years."

Another pause.

She continues, "OK, sorry, Hon. You are totally beat, and I'm filling time by whining about my dysfunctional family. Go to bed. I'm glad things are OK there. Everyone worked so hard. I'll call tomorrow when I know what's going on."

"Travel safe, Pumpkin."

At last the flight departure is called. Lucie finds her seat, buckles in, and is asleep before the plane leaves the ground. But she wakes frequently throughout the flight, squirming to try a new position that might be a tiny bit comfortable, dozing again.

The plane circles Toronto on its approach. She's forgotten how enormous this city is — streets, houses, buildings stretch to every horizon. She sees it now from her Sweetgrass perspective. She is appalled.

Disembarking the large plane takes a long time, but at last Lucie stands beside the luggage carousel, awaiting her suitcase. She feels dazed, grubby, and overdressed for the humid air. She pulls her phone from her pocket and turns off airplane mode to discover she has a curt message from her aunt.

"Come straight to your mom's house, Lucie. You're too late. She died last night."

A long and costly cab ride later, Lucie arrives in front of the modest Scarborough house her mother purchased after Lucie fled from their old shared apartment in her teens to begin a life of drinking and debauchery. She's only been inside this house a handful of times. Back in her party days, Lucie's mother barred her from coming to this house unless she was sober — which was rare — or unless she was willing, which was never. But once Lucie quit drinking and started classes at York University, her relationship with her mother warmed somewhat, and Lucie occasionally drifted to her mother's house for dinner or a short, tense Sunday afternoon visit. They didn't ever revive their Sunday baking sessions, which now makes Lucie a bit melancholy.

We tried, Ma, you and me. But not very hard. Maybe not enough.

Big trees that join hands over the street are in full leaf, birds are hopping and chirping. Lucie is weary to the point of blurred vision, yet incredibly it's early morning here. Kids make their way to school, hand-in-hand with parents or nannies. Even at this hour, the air is close and humid. She drags herself and her suitcase to the house's front door. Raps loudly.

Lucie hears heavy footsteps inside. Her aunt appears, swings the door open and glares balefully at Lucie, who stares back. Time has not been kind to her aunt. The woman's face and arms seem to have been boiled, or perhaps baked. It's the result, Lucie supposes, of too much sun exposure in beautiful Florida. Aunt Carol's skin appears rough, with whitish patches that look like blisters interspersed with blotches ranging from dark red to soft tan.

You could be made from crumbling old brick.

Aunt Carol holds the door open, hesitantly, like she's ready to slam it against this foreign intruder. There is no welcome in her aunt's eyes or scowling face, no sign of affection or even sympathy. "Couldn't get here sooner, eh?" is all she says by way of greeting.

Lucie only shakes her head. *Nice to see you, too.* "Did you fly up from Florida, or what?" she asks.

"I've been here for three weeks. I come up every year to see my doctors," Aunt Carol says, in a tone Lucie takes to indicate she should already know this fact, which is confirmed by her aunt's next words. "Not that you'd know, it's not like you to take time from your oh-so-busy life to call your mother. *I've* been here, Lucie. I've been doing your job, keeping your Ma company, making sure she knew somebody cared about her. Two days ago I went out for a few hours, came home to find her on the floor. Called the ambulance and they took her to the Grace. That's when I called you. They did everything they could, but then she had a stroke. She never woke up."

Lucie is still standing on the porch, wondering whether her aunt will invite her into the house. "It's good you were here, then," is all she can think to say.

Aunt Carol steps back from the door. "You'd best come in. There's plenty to be done now."

"What day is it, Auntie?"

"Eh? Monday. July eighth."

I drove into Sweetgrass exactly a year ago today. Not that I'm keeping track or anything.

There is, indeed, plenty to be done. For a start, the two women arrange a memorial service.

Lucie says, "I don't even know who to invite," to which the funeral director replies, "Just publish the obituary, you'll be surprised who turns up." But only twenty people or so from her mother's church and bridge club come to pay respects on a very hot, muggy day. Lucie feels almost embarrassed by the tiny handful of mourners. So few friends. Such a small life.

Short service, followed by tea and cookies. Lucie shakes the hands of people she's never met and thanks them for coming. Then it's over.

Lucie and Aunt Carol agree that the ashes should be scattered along the Ottawa River. Aunt Carol says she'll make the trip and take care of the ashes, though she's vague about when or how. Lucie relinquishes the box of ash without a word.

And then it's down to clearing out her mother's belongings. Her aunt has taken over the house's only spare bedroom, leaving Lucie to sleep fitfully on the living room couch — she cannot begin to imagine sleeping in her mother's vacant bed.

For days, the two women share minimal conversation as they

determine what clothes should be donated, what furniture and kitchenware should go where. Lucie's mother lived modestly and was never one to collect keepsakes. There is nothing of sentimental value to Lucie, who would be perfectly happy to simply junk everything. Aunt Carol claims a new-looking cloth coat and a selection of loose blouses, also some teacups. Lucie takes nothing, not even the few remaining baking pans.

They order packing boxes, arrange for various local charities to pick up donations. Ladies from the church arrive to pack and take away kitchen items and a number of tables, lamps, chairs, and a small desk for the church's rummage sale. As the rooms empty, Lucie scrubs the floors, dusts the windowsills, and launders curtains. She wonders whether Aunt Carol will sell the house, which is now hers, according to the will. The estate bequeaths nothing to Lucie, which is no surprise. In fact it's a relief.

The only things you gave me have nothing to do with stuff. Your legacy is about anger, judgment, and dissatisfaction. Well, Ma, I'm through with that, now more than ever. But you also gave me baking, I'm grateful for that. And resilience. OK, thanks for that, too. Will I miss you? I have no idea. I don't think so.

Since her arrival, Lucie has eaten out every night, finding local ethnic restaurants. She's busied herself observing their table service, taking note of intriguing menu items. "Research for The Sow's Ear," she tells herself. She used her phone to take pictures of menus, plates of food. It's been a welcome distraction.

It's been ten days since Lucie left Sweetgrass. Her mother's house is largely empty, though there's still the matter of disposing of medications, mattresses, and upholstered furniture that no charity wants. There are the final bills to pay and accounts to close. Aunt Carol seems to have it all well in hand and doesn't appear to want Lucie's assistance. In fact she seems to resent her niece's presence, so Lucie books a return flight and calls Ray to say she's headed home.

Anticipating an irate response, Lucie postpones giving her aunt the news of her departure. Finally she says, "Auntie, I've got to go back to work," only a few hours before her westward flight. She's already packed and ready to leave. And she's correct about Aunt Carol's reaction.

"Sure, Lucie, you just head on back to your little hayseed town. I can finish up here." For a long moment, they face each other wordlessly in the empty, echoing kitchen. "You were never a good daughter, Lucie. She was always disappointed in you. Always thought you'd do better."

Against her better judgment, Lucie breaks. She yells, "And is that supposed to be tough love? Because, Auntie, it is way too far on the 'tough' side of the equation. I grew up under her thumb, learning how to criticize and how not to trust people because that's what she did. And besides, I turned out just fine. I've got a degree and a good job. I'm *fine*, thank you very much."

Aunt Carol smirks. "Right. Waiting tables for farmers? Well done."

OK, stop right now Lucie. Do not let her hook you, because you will never win, she will never see who you've become.

Lucie raises and drops her arms. Rebel, defeated. "You're right, Ma and I were never close and that's all I have to say," she says, and turns away, leaves the conversation at that. Her aunt's words sting. But all Lucie's rage and disappointment have evaporated. It's simply not a fight she cares to take up now; there's no point. As for Lucie's own struggle with her rush to judgment — well, she's working on that.

Lucie phones for a taxi and waits on the porch, the screen door open so she can call to her aunt when her ride arrives.

The cab pulls up. "I'm going now, Auntie," Lucie says loudly through the screen.

There's no reply.

It's dusk as Lucie's flight makes a wide arc to approach Calgary's airport from the south. She gazes out her tiny window to see broad fields surrounding the city's compact downtown and spreading suburbs, the smoky-blue-mauve mountains beyond, the sun sinking behind a bank of cloud that might bring rain overnight. Even at this relatively lush time of year, the fields look drier than Ontario farms. There are far fewer trees, it's much less verdant.

Even so, the scene below makes her grin and she even softly sings, "Give me a home where the buffalo roam," which causes the man seated beside her to lean away.

It might seem barren, this landscape. There are no hardwood forests or giant freshwater lakes. It's not Ontario with its lush farmland. It's not Vancouver with its ocean and rainforests. It is what it is: rolling foothills, sere and windblown, and she can't wait to breathe the crisp, dry air she's come to love.

It's home.

"I guess it does bug me, a little." Lucie draws a deep breath, waving her wine glass, which Ray has already replenished several times. "OK, it bugs me more than I thought. I've fought with Ma all my life, so it's not like I've lost a close companion, and there's no sudden, gaping hole in the shape of my mother. Besides, I hardly told her anything. She never knew about you, for example. I barely told her that I was living in Sweetgrass. But now it feels weird to be an orphan. Apart from my aunt, who I never expect to see again, I have no blood relatives I know of, depending on what my errant dad has been up to in the last forty years.

"All my life I've battled my mother and the marks she left on me... *in* me. But the thing I now realize is that I *had* a mother, someone who knew my history even if it was through her own crazy, slanted way of looking at things. But now, my whole history is gone, it only exists in my own head. I could build any story I want, because there's no way for anyone to check what I say. I could be the child of deposed royalty, for all anybody knows," she says wistfully, wildly, amazed to be mourning her mother in this way — in any way, for that matter. "I guess you never really know what hold your past has on you, until your past becomes your present."

"Don't I know it," Ray says ironically, though she's too drunk to catch his meaning.

"What about you? Your parents are divorced, your dad's passed, but where's your mom? Do you see her?"

"She remarried and moved to Texas, of all places. No, I don't keep in touch. It was pretty clear to all of us, even my younger brothers, that she wanted nothing to do with us. I asked my gran a few times, she's the one who told me Mom was living in the U.S."

"We're both orphans. Alone in the world."

He folds her in his arms, and she's grateful for the warmth of his body, his heartbeat, his energy. He says, "But the thing is we're *not* alone, Lucie. You've got me."

"You've got me."

They stand, wrapped, for a long time. Finally he leads her to bed, where they lie clasped together. She feels like crying but can't summon the energy for tears of any kind, neither angry nor sorrowful nor regretful. Instead, she melts into Ray's warm body, his strong arms around her, his quiet words.

He's right, Lucie, you're not alone. That is all I've ever wanted from a partner. Support. Kindness, compassion, a little understanding. Ray, where have you been all my life? For that matter, where have I been? And that's all I can give to you in return. I'm here, my sweet man. I'm here.

Happy to be back on familiar ground, Lucie steps right into her routines — baking, working, riding, the occasional walk with Marta. She tends the few vegetables and herbs she and Ray managed to plant in his back garden.

But one evening during a riding lesson in the outdoor round pen, with fluffy clouds colouring pink and peach, and a light breeze brushing her cheeks, Keith stops her and steps over to Quincy. He places a hand on Lucie's knee and says, "Are you all right? Because you're not with me, and you're not with your horse. You are someplace else, and you've been there a while."

Lucie sits back in the saddle and Quincy responds by shuffling her feet to shift and balance her weight. But Keith's hand remains, in fact he grips and shakes her knee, in no way suggestive but entirely insistent. "Come on, Lucie girl. Where are you?"

She looks into his chocolate eyes, surprisingly large and wet, boyish-looking for such a sinewy, powerful and self-possessed man. She sees no challenge or rebuke there, only concern. Taking a deep breath, she says, "Thank you, for calling me out on this. I have always been the tough girl, always the one with the answers. But it's funny how my mother's death is bothering me, in ways I never anticipated. She is with me. I can't shake her. When I moved to Vancouver I thought I'd put her away, thought I'd turned into my own person and I was free from all her crap. Then my life went sideways and I wound up here. I never told my mom much about my life in Sweetgrass. Maybe I've been running from her for longer than I thought. She's been in my head, bugging and pestering me ever since I left Ontario, and that was years ago. So now maybe I need to make some kind of peace with her. Ohmygod Keith, does that sound like nutty pop psychology? Because, really, I just want her out of my head. I want her to go away."

Keith withdraws his hand and places his palm on the mare's neck, thoughtfully rubbing under Quincy's mane. He looks away from Lucie. Says, "My dad was a drunk and he hit me, my sister, especially my mom. I left home young. But later, when he straightened up and Amanda and I needed help to buy this place, he was there for us. Turns out he's proud of me for being a horse trainer, for having land, for carrying on whatever part of his life he thought I could manage. You never know about your parents, what they really think of you or how they might step up for you. Or how you might have to step up for them. It's such a swamp, family."

That is maybe the longest string of words you've ever said to me.

"You are so right. You want to do the best for your parents, make them proud. But who knows what that looks like, really? What do they actually want from you? And eventually you have to live your own life, whether they like it or not."

I can't believe I just said that. Jude's words coming out of my mouth, after all these years.

He looks up at her with his usual guarded gaze, shrouded by the brim of his hat. And maybe now she understands the source of that caution. Keith has his own demons to battle. Who knew?

"I have an idea," he says. "Maybe you need a trail ride. Get into the back country. You say how an hour's ride in the arena or the field is a vacation for you. So an overnight ride might just break up a certain headspace you're in. It works for me. Might work for you."

He turns away, leaving Lucie astride Quincy with a whirl of thoughts. She squeezes her knees against the mare, who steps forward at a walk. Lucie leans forward slightly while lifting the reins, and Quincy responds with a slow, rocking canter. That motion is fine for the round pen but it's not enough. Suddenly Lucie craves the wanton, headlong gallop she experienced last fall, with the full wind in her ears, the pounding rhythm of a horse beneath her. It's the first time since that nearly disastrous ride Lucie has felt the need for surging speed. But instead, tonight she canters sedately around the round pen, stops, reverses, dismounts, and then brushes out the mare and releases her to the pasture.

—>‖<—

The horses' hooves clatter on the rocky trail that leads steadily upward, punctuated by occasional steep climbs or descents, especially when they encounter a creek crossing. The three riders — Amanda, Keith, and Lucie — are surrounded by evergreen forest. The enclosing trees are tall and tightly spaced, the undergrowth sparse. Two dogs dash ahead exuberantly, tails waving, coming back to the horses then rushing ahead or scuttling into the bush to chase some delightful scent, returning to trot alongside the plodding horses, then running ahead again, tongues lolling. It makes Lucie tired just watching them, when she spares a thought for the dogs at all. Mostly, she's paying very close attention to herself and her horse. She is almost terrified.

The interesting thing about her new saddle is that it makes no noise. Keith and Amanda both have heavy Western saddles of tooled leather that creak pleasantly with each step their horses take, adding to the experience of riding through a warm summer day deep in the foothills. By contrast, Lucie's nylon saddle has no voice. It rests on Quincy's back, and the grey mare moves easily, but when Lucie lifts her weight onto her feet and leans forward as the mare digs into a steep slope, the saddle doesn't make a sound.

Never mind, Lucie has plenty to occupy her senses, largely the push and drive of the horse under her. The way the mare's shoulders work, the way her feet find purchase especially on the rough, steep ascents, short but intensely arresting climbs that make Lucie nervous. The other horses, both bigger and sturdier than her mount, climb and navigate the rocks, roots, the sucking mud holes without bother, but each time the group encounters a challenge, Lucie takes a deep breath to steady herself and leans forward as she's been taught, slacking the reins, letting Quincy find her own way up the incline or pushing her mare through a puddle of mud or over a tangle of tree roots.

The descents are worse. On the occasional steep downhill grade, Lucie is required to lean back in the saddle as a counterbalance to Quincy's weight. She slackens the reins and lets the mare pick her way down a rock-strewn path, usually to splash through a creek and quickly jump up the far bank. Lucie simply holds her breath and trusts her horse to find good footing and not slip. So far, so good.

Arriving at a wide creek, the horses paw and splash and drop their heads to drink, an unnerving experience for a rider because suddenly the horse's solid neck dives forward, so Lucie sees nothing between her and the rushing water. Yet again, Lucie slacks the reins to allow Quincy to bend forward into the riot of froth and spray. Lucie, meanwhile, feels like she's on top of a camel's hump with no way down.

The forest is surprisingly silent. Sometimes there's a burst of squirrel chatter or a bird call, occasionally a tree creaks as it sways in the light breeze, but for the most part, the riders continue through the heat of the day accompanied only by their own small sounds: saddles, hoofbeats, dogs panting.

The riders continue onward, climbing until finally they break out of the forest into a high alpine meadow that dances with flowers, reminding Lucie of the brilliant, flower-flecked meadow she trekked through last summer at Mount Revelstoke. She stops her mare, gazes around the bright meadow, and says to herself, "This is *gorgeous*."

Eventually they arrive in a narrow bowl surrounded by towering bald peaks with slides of rock chunks on the steeper slopes that descend into the bowl. The meadow is lush with grass, and there's a tiny meltwater-fed lake at the far side. The riders dismount, brush and water their horses, stake them to long lines, and set up camp. Lucie is largely incompetent, but Amanda and Keith give her patient direction as they set up tents, fluff out sleeping bags, and get the gas stove fired up and dinner underway. They make a simple meal of sausage, cheese and crackers, hearty soup, and Lucie's brownies. But they've brought wine for dinner, and rye whisky for sipping later.

Before sleep, Keith secures the campsite by placing their food in sturdy bags he hauls some distance from the tents. Coming back, he says to Lucie, "Beware of bears, cougars, wolverines, wolves. This place is full of predators. But if you know that, you can prepare. In an open meadow like this, no trees to hang our bags from, we put the supplies far away from our tents. The critters might get into the food, but they won't get into *us*. It's a case of mind over mind."

The sky overhead is the most intense, velvety indigo Lucie has ever seen, sparkled by many many many stars. No moon tonight, no northern lights either. They retire: Keith and Amanda to one tent, Lucie to her own.

Thank you my friends. Mission accomplished. I am now, I am here, my head is here, I am entirely engaged with this spot, this adventure. Ohmygod, the stars. And I'm tired, physically, emotionally. So — guess I'm on vacation. Horses. Stars. Sleeping on the ground, who knew?

Snuggling into her sleeping bag, she grabs her cell phone. She composes a text message to Judith: " Big news in life of L: I am camping."

She is amazed when her phone buzzes with Judith's reply, "OMG hope for us all where r u?"

" Mtn meadow, horses, friends. Call u tmro. This is my life now. LOVE"

Lucie lies back. She can feel the jab of stones beneath her sleeping bag, but she's not so uncomfortable she can't sleep. Besides, she's exhausted. It was a five-hour ride to this alpine meadow. The day's journey was intense, and of course that was Keith's point: to live in the moment, to get Lucie out of her head, her regret, her sorrow, her ambivalence about her mother. Her uncertainty about Ray. Now, relaxed in her sleeping bag, Lucie is not bothered by any of it.

Horses re-set your life. He's a smart guy, that Keith.

There's something lovely and comforting about feeling safe while falling asleep. As she drifts, Lucie has a vague and distant memory about a quiet, soft bed bathed in late evening light, in a place where evening lasted for hours — her aunt and uncle's home? Friends of her mother's? That seems unlikely... It's only an insubstantial and fleeting memory, or perhaps it's a dream as she slips into sleep.

Lucie wakes early, or so she thinks. It's the soft light through her tent walls that awakens her. But when she pushes her way out of her tent and stiffly rises and stretches, she sees Amanda and Keith are already up, they have breakfast started and Amanda approaches, offering a mug of coffee. "Sleep OK?"

"Awesome. Me and the stones and spiders. Who knew?"

Summer rolls away, once again the days are shorter, the nights cooler.

One evening after dinner at the ranch, Ray says, "Grab a jacket, let's walk up the hill." There's a light breeze that keeps the bugs at bay, and the air is rich with the dusty scent of ripening grass. The horses grazing on the hillside lift their heads to regard the hikers curiously, then resume munching grass, moving placidly in twos and threes across the slope. Arriving at the hilltop, Ray sits, cross-legged, and then leans back to lie staring up at the darkening sky, a few early stars, the sliver of a moon. Lucie does the same, reaching to hold his hand.

"I love it here," she says to the sky, then turns to look at him, grass tickling her ear and cheek. "We're all right, you and me. It's a weird life but it's OK." He squeezes her hand.

They remain there together until Lucie starts to shiver, then they pick their way down the slope in near-total darkness. Ray goes home for one of the now-infrequent nights they spend apart, and Lucie goes downstairs to find Amanda watching the late news. She seems restless and fidgety. "Anything wrong?" Lucie asks.

"It's none of my business," Amanda says, tucking a strand of hair behind her ear. "And like I've said before, it doesn't bother us that Ray comes and goes here; you're adults, what you do is none of my biz. But," she turns to look directly at Lucie, who sees genuine concern in Amanda's eyes, "are you going to get married? Or move in together? Or something? It's just — I'm worried that he's not getting on with it, which surprises me about him, but some guys are just afraid of commitment. And I don't want to see you hurt. Not that I think he would hurt you, but... OK you get my drift. Enough said."

With a vigorous headshake, Lucie says, "No, no and no. I am not moving anywhere, unless you want me to. I guess Ray and I are whatever we are, 'an item,' as Jude would say. But we're not moving in together, he can't because..." *Lucie! Shut up, right now.* "Because, um, because he's just not ready, his history with women is as bad as mine with men. We're taking it slow, one step at a time, you know?"

Amanda actually blushes. "I know you've had some terrible experiences and issues, with boyfriends or partners or whatever. I'd like things to work out for you and Ray. That's it, truthfully. It seems to me that you've found someone who's become part of your life — good for you. And, may I say, you could do a lot worse than Ray. But I take your point. Go slow, don't paint yourself into a corner. OK, I've said what I want, I'm done. And I'm sorry to be nosy."

"No worries ever, and you are right, I *have* done a lot worse," Lucie says. "I guess Ray and I will figure out where we want to go. Who knows, maybe we'll high-tail it for the coast, or move to Banff or something. We could go anywhere."

Amanda laughs, now relaxed, her agitation evaporated like the steam from her tea. "'High-tail it.' You're turning into a local, Lucie. I'm just sayin'."

Ray is late getting to the café the next morning, and when he finally arrives, his left arm is bandaged and held tightly to his body with a sling.

"What the *hell*?" she says, incredulous.

"Slipped and fell down my stairs last night."

"Why didn't you call me?"

"To say what? I drove myself to the hospital, did some fast talking about forgetting my health care card. They did an X-ray and patched me up. I was home by midnight. I don't like sleeping on my back, though. And showering is a challenge, maybe you could help me with that." Delivered with a mischievous grin that doesn't hide the pain in his eyes. "I called Bernice, asked her to come in, she'll have to take over the cooking instead of being sous-chef. She's perfectly capable, but I might need more of your help in the back for a few days."

She regards him skeptically. "You can be such a *guy*," to which he simply shrugs. She says, "Is it broken?"

"Sprained wrist. I'll be good as new in a week or so."

But the injury takes longer to heal than that. Although over the past months Ray has hired several competent people to assist in the kitchen and support Lucie in the café's front end, they are short-staffed and scrambling throughout most of September. Ray stations himself in a corner of the kitchen and offers instruction and guidance, waving his good arm like a conductor overseeing an orchestra.

For the most part they're doing just fine until Tom barges into the kitchen in the middle of a busy lunch hour. He's belligerent and seems more incoherent than usual. Lucie suspects he's already been drinking. Tom looks around the room, finally noticing Ray perched on a stool.

"Howdy, Tom," Ray says affably. Tom only makes a gesture, pointing to his palm. Ray sighs and stands to lead Tom out of the kitchen. "Lucie can you supervise please, for a few minutes?" She nods, but can't help overhearing the conversation Ray and Tom have in the hall beside the coffee station.

Ray says, "I have a few extra bills to pay right now. I can only manage a hundred today."

Tom counters, "Not enough. I lost at poker last night. I pay my debts," a remark that makes Lucie shiver and glance over her shoulder, but the two men are out of sight. She can't see Ray's face or how he's reacting.

Presently Ray returns to take up his position again, nodding his thanks to Lucie, but she can see the fury in his usually calm, open face. "How much?" she whispers. He holds up his good hand, fingers splayed. *"Five hundred?"* she whispers. "Are you serious?"

She grabs a waiting order and takes the plates out to the dining room, but as soon as she's served the orders she tears out of the café's door and follows Tom along the sidewalk. He's walking slowly, not stumbling but clearly concentrating on every step. His head is down, shoulders hunched forward as usual, shoving his way through the world. She catches up, circles around him, and stands in his way, forcing him to stop and face her. She is shaking with rage, but keeps her voice low as she confronts him.

"You think it's fine to wallow in your pride, like you're the only person who's ever lost everything. Well you're not, it happens all the time. And here's what you're supposed to do about it, Tom. You peel yourself off the ground and put one foot ahead of the other *and you figure your life out.* But not you, oh no, you're so blinded by your own pride and pain, you can't even tell there are people around who care about you, like Ray fergodssake, and what about that lovely sweet woman who lives under your roof?"

Tom fixes her with a searing glare she can barely meet. His eyes bore into her, his mouth is turned down. His shoulders hunch forward. He is a fortress. "What the hell would you know about it?"

"Plenty. I'm an expert at losing everything, from my job to my mother, and all stops in between."

He regards her for a long moment. He seems to be appraising her, the look that infuriates her. "Mind your own damn business," he snarls and steps around her.

"Cone on, Tom! *Cowboy up!*" She whirls around and stomps away, wishing she still had a mane of curls she could toss in a mass of black fury. When she returns to the restaurant, Ray doesn't ask where she's been.

Ray's wrist is finally on the mend, and not a minute too soon — he's busy buying supplies and getting ready for the annual Sow's Ear Thanksgiving dinner. Lucie has persuaded him to prepare as much of the food as possible in advance, to avoid the last-minute flurry that exhausted them the year before. Still, the days leading up to the long weekend are frantic with activity. The final push is upon them, they are preoccupied with ingredients, recipes, reservations — all this on top of their usual restaurant routine.

At last it's Friday, two days before the big event. They're up early, though neither has slept well. They're both so overwhelmed with details. "Hey do you have any cash?" she calls, pulling her jeans on as he's in the bathroom washing, the door slightly ajar. "I have to gas up the car pronto or we'll be walking to the farmer's market tomorrow."

"Sure," he says, "there's forty bucks in my wallet."

"Wallet, wallet," she mutters, scanning the dresser, the bedside table, finally remembering it's likely in the back pocket of his jeans, which are folded neatly over the chair. Yes, bingo. She withdraws the wallet, flips it open, and takes out two twenty-dollar bills. But then, she sees something else. Also tucked inside the wallet is a card that catches her eye. No photo, just a Canadian flag and a string of red numbers on a plain white background. His social insurance card.

And his name: Daniel Joseph Hnatyshyn.

Oh, Buddy, did you intend me to see this? Or did you forget it's here?

She puzzles over his odd surname, hearing his footsteps coming toward the bedroom door but making no motion to conceal her discovery. Instead, still holding the card and wallet in her hands, she turns to look up at him.

"Did you find the cash... Oh. I see you've found something else, too." He leans against the doorjamb, his muscular arms crossed over his bare chest. His expression is not angry, in fact a smile curls his mouth as he sees her bewildered expression.

"There's only one vowel in this name. It's Martian."

"No, it's Ukrainian. It's pronounced 'na-TISH-un.' The 'H' is silent." He steps to her and gently takes the card and wallet from her. "And I don't need to tell you never to call me that, right?"

"I can't even call you 'Danny' when we're alone?"

"Nope," he says decisively, wrapping his arms around her, rocking her. "Although I have to admit it sounds sweet, my name coming from you. But listen, Pumpkin, we're doing fine, you've even said so. We have to keep up this charade — all of it — until it's one hundred percent finished."

"I know, I know, you're right, we are doing fine. But it would be so nice to call you by your own name, that's all."

He murmurs, "I know. I am so sorry about this stupid way we have to live. Hang on, Pumpkin, we're getting through it. I'm paying them, there's some light ahead of us. Besides," he leans back to look at her, "I'm still the same guy no matter what you call me, right? And if you call me Ray, you don't have to remember how to spell some weird Martian name."

BIGGER THAN TROUBLE

The harvest dinner is even bigger and busier than last year, with three separate seatings, and ham on the menu in addition to turkey and all its usual companions. Coming on the heels of Ray's injury, the enormous effort to prepare and serve the dinner leaves both Lucie and Ray weary and grateful to be going back to winter hours. "Let's take a little holiday," he says as they celebrate what passes for their first anniversary on Thanksgiving Day. This year, they do have turkey sandwiches, accompanied with a bottle of Prosecco.

She's startled. "A vacation? Whoa, Sweet Pea, what a concept. Got someplace in mind?"

"Nothing too adventurous. We've only got a few days, so we're not going far, plus I seem to recall neither of us has a passport. We're not going to Mexico. But what about Banff?"

She laughs out loud. "Banff was supposed to be my destination when I left Vancouver on my voyage of self-discovery."

"You missed it by about a hundred miles."

"It was July and jammed. I drove in, drove out. Never even got out of my car."

The following Sunday finds them driving west in Agememnon, Ray having left his rattletrap vehicle at the ranch. Unlike last year's extended, glorious blaze of fall colour, this autumn is cold and blustery. It's only mid-October, but most trees have been stripped bare and a substantial accumulation of snow already decorates the peaks and encroaches into the valleys.

Ray and Lucie are unfazed. They've reserved a townhouse that has a wood-burning fireplace and a full kitchen, and they've brought wine and food and books. For the next few days they cook together, and make love on a soft blanket they spread before the fire — "I've always wanted to do this," Ray says, and she responds by curling herself around him, warming and welcoming him. Making love before a crackling fireplace is an experience she's never had, either.

It's better than I imagined, except one side is hot from the fire and the other side's freezing. Romance, meet reality.

A punishing wind makes it unpleasant to be outdoors, so they only venture into town once, braving the icy blast to browse the main street's shops and galleries. Lucie buys Ray a new shirt, commenting, "I'm tired of looking at your limited wardrobe. Besides, I still owe you a Christmas present." They have a light meal in a boisterous bistro, then scurry back to their cozy condo. What could be better than forgetting the Sow's Ear Café, their own preoccupations? They simply lose themselves in each other, such a treat, such a release.

After three days, sated and relaxed, they head back to Sweetgrass. "I still haven't really had the true Banff experience," Lucie laughs as they drive home again on Tuesday. "At least this time I got to walk around, but I'm guessing there's more to this place than I've seen. The hot pools, for instance."

"So we still have some adventures ahead of us," Ray says with a happy grin as he pilots Agememnon along the same highway Lucie remembers from her initial eastward journey, her headlong arrow into self-discovery.

And look what happened, where I've landed. Sweetgrass. A new sweet man. A job. And many good friends. I'm so far away today from where I was last time I drove this road. So very far.

The weather continues its headlong rush toward winter, and as usual, customers at the café have complaints, opinions, and local lore to share on the subject. 'If it snows before Halloween, it'll stay until May,' and 'Could be a long winter but we'll get a hot summer to make up for it,' as though the weather itself had the power to give and take, mete out justice. Snow does arrive in abundance well before month end, catching everyone off guard and messing with plans for kids' Halloween costumes, which now must accommodate heavy jackets, scarves, hats. There's a general scramble to get winter tires onto vehicles, dig out sweaters and boots and mitts, find snow shovels. And on it goes. The cold is relentless and discouraging.

One gloomy November afternoon as Lucie readies the dining room for the evening's customers, Ray comes into the dining room and says, "I think we need to freshen the place up a bit. New paint, and maybe some nice table linens. What do you think?"

"Can't hurt, and it might put people into a better mood. Does this mean I get to shop for tablecloths and napkins and such?"

"Go crazy. Well, not *too* crazy, let me know how much you want to spend first. We could buy paint next week, and I'll hire somebody to do the work. We could get it all done and looking spiffy in time for Christmas."

Jason shuffles up the street, hands stuffed into his pockets, head down, bent into the cold slap of the north wind. He steps inside the café and lets the door slam behind him. He waits in the empty dining room until Ray appears, wiping his hands on his apron. Jason smirks to see a guy wearing an apron, then quickly remembers to remove the grimace from his face. He needs money. He's drinking, but can't afford drugs. He's been living more or less in his mother's basement, sleeping on a leaky air mattress on the concrete floor. He is sore and cranky and badly in need of a fix, but that requires cash. And Ray has a job.

"Hi," Ray says, not extending his hand, eyeing up this punky-looking kid.

"Here for yer job."

Ray pauses. He knows who this kid is, a bad seed and probably the town's break-and-enter expert. The kid is a mess, stinks of beer and cigarettes, and looks like he hasn't bathed in days, his hair greasy and slicked to his head. But nobody else has answered Ray's ad in the local paper, so he says, "I need this whole room painted. That means moving furniture and using a ladder. You good with that?"

Jason rolls his head up like it's a bowling ball his neck can barely support and slowly gazes around. "Just this room?"

"Just this room. Four straight walls, but you need to be careful around the windows and such. This is a restaurant. It's got to be a neat job, and fast."

"How much?"

"I'll pay five hundred for a good job. Less if I have to fix stuff you mess up."

"OK, five hundred. You got all the paint and shi... stuff?"

"Everything. Paint, ladder, brushes, tape because you'll have to tape off the trim around the windows and door. I've got drop cloths for the floor. You have to be careful moving the chairs and tables — they're old and if you break anything, it comes out of the pay."

"Yeah, got it. When?"

"We're closed Sunday through Tuesday. So you've got three days, starting tomorrow morning."

"OK, t'morrow."

"Eight in the morning."

"Yeah, dude, I got it." Jason rotates himself, stiff as Ray Charles, and blunders his way outside.

But his work is not good. He does not use the painter's tape, so the new, light-yellow wall paint slops over the white window and door trim. He does not use the drop cloths, so spatters paint on the floor. "Three hundred bucks," says meticulous Ray, who is now faced with a day's worth of touch-up and scraping paint from the floor and trim.

"What the fuck ya talkin' about? Ya said five."

"I said five if it's a good job. This is a lousy job. And you broke a chair."

"I fuckin' did not break a fuckin' chair."

"Three hundred," Ray says, holding out the cash, "and get the hell out of my sight. Now."

Jason snatches the bills and leaves, but he does not go to the ratty sleeping bag and stash of beer in his mother's basement. Instead, he yanks open the door of his grit-coated white van and starts driving, cruising the snow-choked streets. Nobody is about except the odd person taking a dog out for a quick sniff and a pee. "Bullshit, fuckin' bullshit. Three hundred fuckin' bucks. I can't buy shit for that. I gotta get more money. Do somethin' big. I gotta rob somebody. Snatch a kid. Hey, yeah! I'm gonna grab a kid. Yeah! Grab a kid, get big cash, get outa this fuckin' town. Yeah. Five thousand. Ten thousand. Yeah. Fuck, yeah."

Ray goes back to the kitchen, fishes the cell phone from his jacket, and calls Lucie at the ranch. "Hi, can you come get me?"

"Sure. What's up, are you OK?"

"Just mad. That kid Jason did a crummy paint job, I'll have to patch it up. Guess I know how I'm spending next weekend. I paid him less that he thought. He walked away mad. Me too, I'm pissed off and I don't feel like going home. I just want to relax tonight."

"Great, you'll be terrific company." Pause. "Sweet Pea, that was a joke. It's fine, I'll be right there. Grab a bottle of wine from the bar, we'll pay it back later."

Lucie and the faithful Agememnon arrive in due course. Ray locks up the café and dumps himself into the passenger seat. Lucie has the car's heater on at full blast, so the interior is over-warm. He snaps the fan down a couple of notches. They drive back to the ranch in silence and go straight down to Lucie's room. Ray sits on the bed and peels off his clothes. She lights candles, pours wine.

"Taking a shower." He comes back smelling of soap, his skin rosy from hot water. She's already in bed. He flips up the duvet, exposing her body to the cool air—she yelps and curls up. "Sorry," he says gruffly.

"Wow, you are a bear with a sore butt."

He gives her a sheepish smile. "Listen to you, Country Girl." He sighs and lies on his back, looking at the warm flicker of candlelight on the ceiling. "That kid pissed me off."

"Have I ever told you he's the reason I cut my hair?" She relates the 'zombie' story, then says, "He seems like trouble."

"He is. I think of myself as a community-minded person. I try to respect people, try to support local farmers and such, keep money in town. I wanted to hire someone local to do a perfectly straightforward paint job. But the only guy to show up is the town druggie, and he did the crappy job I expected of him. I don't know if I'm disappointed in him specifically, or in the town as a whole. Or me, for being stupid enough to hire him."

"Know what?" she says, turning onto her side and nuzzling him. "Maybe the paint job needs fixing, but overall — it's done, right? I'll help, we'll make it right. You're not alone, remember?" Slowly she rubs her palm over his chest, his stomach. Wraps herself around him. He responds. Soon they lose themselves in each other.

The wind rises.

Jason comes across his buddy Frankie.

"Hey, get in," Jason hollers over the wind. "Ya know that guy Ray from the café?"

"Kinda."

"Know where he lives?"

"Think so."

"OK, we're goin' there. He fucked me outa two hundred bucks."

The van pulls up in front of Ray's house — "I think it's that one," Frankie says dubiously. Jason drives around to the alley and finds the back of the house, where he sees Ray's snow-covered car. Jason gets out and surveys the situation as wind whips his inadequate jacket, but his hoodie remains pulled low, hugging his face. The lane is dark, not a single overlooking window is illuminated in the fast-gathering dusk, made even darker by the storm. Wet snow quickly soaks Jason's jacket. He screeches the van's reluctant back doors open and grabs a length of wood that's been hibernating on the van's floor for months. He walks to Ray's poor dilapidated car, raises his weapon and smashes it onto the windshield, which shatters in a shower of glass fragments and snow.

"Whatthefuckareyadoin?" Frankie yells.

"Quiet, moron. It's payback time."

Jason continues to pound the windshield, then punches in the side windows, and the back window too for good measure. He tosses the lumber into the van, slams the back doors, climbs into the driver's seat, and guns his vehicle away up the alley, bald tires spinning on slush and ice.

"Jason you are one crazy fucker," Frankie says with admiration. Jason laughs, hugely.

Storm warnings are all over the radio, TV, on everyone's lips. A menacing blizzard is on the way, beginning with the heavy, wet snow that's already pelting the foothills. As the temperature cools, the snow will gradually freeze into a layer of ice on every surface, followed by more snow and lots of it. Power lines will be coated, tree branches are likely to break, roads will be ugly. Best to stock up on food and water, make sure battery-operated radios are ready to go, generators are primed for use if the power goes out. Feed the horses, bring cattle to near-home pastures and spread feed for them. Cancel trips. Cancel dinner reservations at The Sow's Ear.

It's Thursday but nobody comes for lunch. Nobody shows up for coffee and pie in the afternoon. All day the phone is busy with people calling to cancel reservations for tonight, tomorrow, the weekend. "It's no problem," Lucie tells the callers. "Bad weather, yes we completely understand. Can I rebook you?" By five o'clock the wind is hurling snow horizontally across the windows, down the street, over the fields.

Ray sits at the bar, going over the accounts. "I'd say we're done for the day," he says. "Maybe for a few days."

"Sad but true. Want a lift home? Or back to the ranch? With company...?" she asks, standing behind him, kneading his knotted shoulders.

He turns and engulfs her in a hug, and kisses her once, twice. "Pumpkin, I need some sleep. Home tonight, alone." Disappointed but understanding, she drives him to his tall, dark house. "See you tomorrow," he says wearily. She drives away as he wades through the gathering drift on the unshovelled front walk, and makes his way to his side door entrance. As is his habit, he goes to the back to check on his car.

Freezes, breathless.

His car is smashed. They've found him.

He quickly retreats, opens his door, and snaps the lights on but sees no disruption, hears nothing as he cautiously climbs the stairs, heart pounding, his breathing tight and shallow. There is no sound from the apartment. He flicks on lights in the living room and kitchen. Nobody. Shaking, he moves along the hall to the bedroom, turning on lights as he goes. Nothing. Bathroom — nothing. He opens all the closets. At last satisfied the flat is empty, he takes a deep breath. Nobody. Nothing. He locks the downstairs door.

Ray calls Lucie on Friday morning. His voice is calm. "No need to show up any time soon, Pumpkin, the weather is crazy. I'm going to put a 'closed' sign on the door and finish the month end."

"OK. I've got stuff in the fridge that needs attention. I'll get there later to take care of it."

Lucie eventually makes her way to the café. At the bar, Ray is hunched over the ledger and cash box until finally he says, "We had a good month in October. I've got cash for Tom. Could you deliver it to him?"

"Now, really? There's a blizzard going on, in case you hadn't noticed."

He gives her an exasperated look, and Lucie regrets her flippancy. He says, "You'll find him at the hotel bar, snow or no snow. Come on, it's just a short drive. It's his monthly revenue. Could you just take this to him, *please*?" Ray proffers an envelope stuffed with cash.

She grabs it and drives to the hotel, tires slithering on the snow-choked streets with their underlying layer of ice. The bar is unexpectedly noisy and busy with people who've knocked off work early because of the storm; they've come for a beer and conversation before heading home, perhaps to be marooned there for a while. The bar's lights are bright, the music loud — it's only mid-afternoon, but the usual Friday night party is already rocking. Amanda and her crew are flying around the room with trays of beer and burgers. Amanda nods and waves as Lucie comes in, stamping snow from her boots.

Lucie finds Tom in a back corner, among a cohort of drinkers whom she doesn't know. But what's this? Here's Marta, perched on the edge of a chair, sipping a glass of wine and chatting offhandedly with some of the characters around the table. She spots Lucie and grins.

"Marta! What's a nice girl like you doing in a place like this?" Lucie yells over the bar's music and hubbub.

Marta laughs like she's never heard that frayed line before — and perhaps she hasn't. "Having a drink in a warm place. Very cold outside, ja? Too soon, this is January weather in November."

"This snow reminds me of Vancouver, it's wet and heavy like cement, really slippery, and right now the wind is blowing the snow around so you can't see past the front of your car."

"Ja, is crazy. And I could ask you that question, too."

It takes Lucie a moment to remember what question she'd asked Marta. "Ha! A nice girl like me is here because Ray did the October month-end, and I have some money for Tom. But maybe," she says, glancing at Tom, whose face is ruddy with beer, his gaze bleary and unfocused, "I should give it to you instead."

Marta sighs. "Tom has been here for some time. Ja, I will take the pay, I give it to him later. With thanks to you and Ray, you work so hard for us."

Unaccountably, Tom is waving his arm in great arcs to get Lucie's attention. "Siddown," he invites. "I'm buyin'. Havva beer, meet my frens."

Lucie looks back to Marta. "Sure, sit for moment, talk to me," Marta says. Lucie complies, giving a curt salute to Tom. Pulling a chair over but not close to the table, she faces Marta instead. She declines to take one of the full glasses of draft beer that forest the table, so Tom seems to lose interest and ignores her. Lucie and Marta chat for a few minutes, then Lucie says, "I need to get back, still a few things to do at the café. We'll probably be closed all weekend. Do you want a ride home?" Marta shakes her head, but Lucie persists. "Look, Tom is in no shape to drive."

"He did not drive here. His friend Gus pick him up. Gus is not so good now too. I will ask Amanda or the bar boys. Go, go, I will get home, do not worry."

Lucie stops on her way out to have a word with Amanda. "Tom is firing on all cylinders and shows no sign of stopping. Can you get him home? And Marta?"

Amanda grimaces. "Yep, we'll figure it out. This isn't the first time. Someone sober will get them home. Maybe me."

"OK, see ya."

Back at the café, Ray is tidying the kitchen, preparing to remain closed for several days. "Can I drive you home and keep your car?" he asks. "I need to pick up some orders in the city tomorrow, but my car won't start, did I tell you that? I'll get it fixed next week, once I'm done with the painting. Funny how running a restaurant becomes every kind of odd job."

"Are you kidding me? You're going to Calgary in this weather?"

"Tomorrow will be fine. The plows will be out tonight, and the roads will be better by morning. And I only need to get to the south side market."

"OK, if you're sure. You're driving my baby, remember. Just so you know, I gave the money to Marta because Tom was loaded, looked like he's been in the bar since yesterday."

"Marta was there?"

"Apparently she had some errands in town, then she wound up at the bar. Yeah, she was having a glass of wine with the boys, who of course were ignoring her, as was her fine upstanding husband."

"Don't start."

Absently Lucie hands over her car keys. "You drive."

He carefully drives Agememnon to the ranch. Before she opens the door, he grabs her arm so she looks at him. He leans over to kiss her long and tenderly, his fingers threading through her hair. "See ya."

In the loud, bright, overheated bar, Marta finally stands. "I will go home now, Tom."

He looks up at her face, luminous in the harsh bar light. He smiles thinly and to his credit says, "I can't drive."

"I know. I'll walk, is not so far."

"Wear my coat," he says. She takes his heavy parka from the back of his chair, puts it on, and drowns in it, engulfed by bulky fabric. The garment is far too long; it reaches nearly to her knees and her hands do not emerge from the sleeves. She fusses to find her mitts and scarf from her own jacket, puts on her woollen hat, and pulls it low over her ears. Her feet are clad in inadequate bright blue boots more suitable for a child.

"Tom, get Amanda to drive you home, do you hear?" He makes no indication that he's understood her. Marta walks to the bar and places her red-mittened hands upon the smooth surface. "Amanda, drive him home later."

"Don't worry, dear. We'll find him a ride."

"I will pay you tomorrow for his beer, everything."

"Don't fuss. You know it's fine, it will all get sorted out."

Marta goes back to Tom just as he drains another glass. "See you later. You will want supper?"

He lurches forward in his chair, steadies himself with one hand on the table, uses his other hand to capture her mittened hand, and squeezes. "Don't think so, be late. You g'won home now, Missus, I'll see ya t'morrow. You have y'seff a good sleep. You needa resss." Momentarily, he focuses on her. "You are the bess thing in my life." The words run together like paint, "yerdbessingimyllyff."

She kisses the top of his head. Then she's gone, pulling the hotel's heavy door open to a rush of wind-hurled snow. She walks carefully along the slick, icy sidewalk that's already drifting in, despite a recent pass by the town's maintenance man and his snow blower. Her hard-soled boots are no match for the poor footing — she slips and catches herself from falling a dozen times before she reaches the deep snow — with better traction at the sidewalk's end.

She plows against the wind and muscles through the accumulating drifts, head down like a big old thug of a draft horse determined to push the wind aside. Determined to not think about the love of her life, the anchor of her soul, the husk of the man she left behind in the bar. Instead she thinks about Ray and Lucie working hard to make The Sow's Ear a dependable source of income for all of them. She thinks about how much whisky and beer Tom will need to forget how old and broken he is, about how much it will all cost, and where the money might come from.

She lurches on through the storm, eyes down, feet moving. The wind becomes inconsequential to her, the cold brushed aside — it's to be endured. Endured like mad cow disease, endured like the auction of her home, her possessions. Endured like this early storm that's even now bending tree limbs to the snapping point. She keeps going because what else is there to do but keep on keeping on?

A tiny vessel lurching hard against a frozen sea, she comes to the four-way stop and does not pause because there is not a moving vehicle in sight, She keeps pushing, kneeing aside the drifts. Turns up the hillside road, pushing pushing. She becomes encrusted, barely discernible from the storm itself.

A battered white van, its headlights little more than dim yellow moons in the flying blizzard, rolls to a pause at the four-way stop, jerks forward, makes a left turn, and grinds up the hill. Blearily though the driving snow and dusky light, Jason spies the toiling figure. "A kid, a kid all alone! *Fuckin' brilliant.* This is it! My ticket outa this shithole town. Better hope yer daddy's rich, kid." His vehicle labours up beside the snowbound walker. He stops, leans across to wind down the passenger-side window.

"Yawannaride?"

"What?" she calls through the gale. She turns her head but her face is obscured by the parka's gigantic hood and fur trim.

"Ride!" he bellows.

Marta labours her way to the passenger side, pries open the door — a feat that takes all her strength — and gets in. As Jason starts driving, she pulls the toque from her head, revealing her white hair.

"Yer not a kid...."

"What?"

"Never mind."

"Hi, you are Jason, ja? Son of Delores. How is your mama?"

"Yah," he spits as the van lunges forward. Her voice is sandpaper on his nerves. She's not a kid at all. This is some old lady, his mother's friend. How could he have made such a stupid mistake?

But maybe it can still work out. A rough plan forms in his beer-clouded brain. He'll take her out to Doolley's abandoned barn, find a way to tie her up, and lock her in there. Then he'll phone her old man Tom for ransom.

She looks out the side window. "Is nice of you to give me a ride."

He passes the turn to her street.

"No, Jason. We need to turn back."

He glances at her. She's looking straight ahead through the wiper-slapping, snow-heaving windshield into the bluing late afternoon. "No," he slurs, "We're goin' s'meplace else. I wanna show ya the view."

"But is no view, is blizzard."

He barrels on, sliding sideways, and does not even pause at the next stop sign but careens around the corner, the van's slick tires skating on the ice under the ever-building snow.

"Jason, stop the car."

"Nope, can't do that. We have somewhere to go."

"Jason, stop the car." Her voice is like his mother's. Telling him what to do. Nobody tells him what to do.

"Shaddup."

"Jason, you must stop this car."

"I tole ya t'shaddup!" Peering ahead into the storm, without looking at her, Jason lashes his right hand to punch her, meaning to send a message, to make her obey him and quit her yammering. His fist slams into her jaw, snapping her head back, smashing her into the van's sturdy doorframe. Above the wind's howl and the engine's grinding complaint, he does not hear the crack of her skull against the unyielding metal. After a minute, a smear of blood from a deep gash on her scalp decorates the doorjamb as her body slumps. More blood gushes onto the seat, down the door, and starts to pool on the floor. He does not see any of this. Instead he's staring through the torrent of snow. He even waves his hand before his face, mimicking the useless windshield wipers.

He drives on through the storm and gathering dark, turning onto a trackless side road. Finally, he stops in the middle, mostly because he cannot discern the road's edge, and he is afraid of tipping his van into the ditch. In the deep blue snow-flying gloom, there's no other traffic, no house or farmyard lights, only trees crying in the whipping wind and ditches filling with snow. He is disoriented and lost, can't remember how to find the abandoned barn. Never mind, this is a mistake anyway. He'll dump her out here instead, she can find her own way out of this.

He turns to his prisoner. "Wake up ya dumb bitch." He shakes her, she does not move. He flings obscenities at her, shakes and shoves her. No response. Finally he screams, his voice high-pitched in panic, "Yer dead, ya dumb bitch, yer dead *yer dead*! What the *fuck*!" Furious, he thrusts his door open against the wind, wades around the van, and hauls the passenger door open. Her body spills out.

He hoists and hurls her into the ditch.

A blanket of soft snow welcomes her as she rolls and sinks almost out of sight. He slams the passenger door with a shriek of rusted hinges, stomps back to his own side, gets in, and yanks his door shut. Drives away, mindless, into the winter blast. Within minutes, the wind skims over his tire tracks.

In the ditch, a drift begins to form. Snow accumulates hour upon hour until eventually the surface becomes smooth and crisp and even, concealing its guest perfectly.

As dusk thickens and traffic halts and pulses along the city's snow-crusted streets, a small Honda pulls into a shopping mall parking lot that's pre-Christmas busy even on such a wicked evening. The driver, exhausted after a horrific journey on the snowblown highway, cruises row after row, finally pulling into a narrow spot at a considerable distance from the mall doors. A heavily dressed figure labours to get out of the car, opens the hatchback, and pulls out an overstuffed backpack and duffle bag. Closes the door and trudges to the mall.

Inside the bright and cheerful shopping mall, alive with seasonal music and swarming with shoppers, the short man in his bulky winter coat makes his way to a store where he buys a package of large envelopes, a notebook, and marker pens. He then finds a coffee bar where he sets down his baggage and shoulders off his enormous coat. Gently setting his coffee cup on a tiny table, the man writes two letters in the notebook, then tears out the pages. He opens the package of envelopes, withdraws one. Fishes in his coat pockets and finds car keys. Places the keys, some documents, and a note into the envelope, which he seals, folds, and re-folds to create a tight, compact package that prevents the keys from rattling. He inserts this tightly folded package, and another note, into a second envelope, which he seals and addresses. He swallows what's left of the now-tepid coffee, dons his gargantuan parka, and once more hefts the pack and duffle. Abandoning his newly pur-chased stationery on the coffee shop table, he lumbers back to the store and its postal outlet. He mails the envelope, with the tightly folded envelope and car keys hidden inside.

He leaves the mall, slogging through the stormy night toward the closest light rail transit station, two blocks away. His footprints in the sodden snow mingle with those left by many other walkers who are passing this way, destinations unknown.

The bar is quieter now, most patrons having finally decided to make a break for home before roads become completely impass-able. Tom and two buddies remain at their corner table, playing cards to the extent they're able to focus, until Tom burps loudly and throws his cards to the table. "Nuff. Sh'go home." He gazes around the nearly empty room and spots Amanda, who's cleaning up behind the bar. He waves her over. "All done here, Darlin'."

"Sure, Tom. I'll round up one of the cooks to drive you home. How about you fellas, need a ride?" Both men nod.

Tom searches his pockets. "K'han fine my wallet," he slurs. "K'han pay."

"Don't worry, Tom, we'll sort it out some other time. It's late and stormy, and I'd like to go home soon. I'll take you boys home. Let me get Russ to warm up his truck for you, Tom."

Getting Tom to Russ's truck proves to be an ordeal. Tom can barely stand, and he's forgotten that Marta took his winter coat. He fusses about the missing coat until Amanda reminds him that Marta has it, and then he tries to put on Marta's tiny winter coat. Russ talks him out of it, saying, "Let's just step out to the truck, it's warmed up, you don't need a coat." Tom leans heavily on Russ, making their progress across the room and out the door awkward and wobbly. "Do you need a hand getting inside?" Russ asks, as he finally stops in front of Tom's house.

"Nah, m'good." Tom slides from the seat and staggers to his front door, which Marta always leaves unlocked for him. He blunders inside, turning on a light or two, neglecting to remove his wet boots until he's halfway across the living room. He kicks them off and collapses onto the sofa, where he quickly passes into the stone sleep of the deeply drunk.

Lucie sleeps late on Saturday. The storm has abated somewhat, or at least the wind has diminished, but the pour of snow continues — now large flakes drifting lazily, now a thick curtain as though someone has ripped open a celestial pillow and is shaking feathers all over. She takes a long hot bath, and makes a big pot of soup from ingredients she finds in the fridge: potatoes, carrots, celery, tomatoes, chunks of leftover steak.

The house is quiet. Amanda is probably at the bar, and storm or no storm, Keith is likely in the arena — horses, always horses for him. Muffled by heavy snow, the house seems to wrap itself around Lucie like a duvet. Her soup bubbles on the back burner. She settles on the downstairs couch under a fuzzy blanket, surrounded by cushions and cats, to watch a movie. But she nods and dozes, finally switching off the lamp over her shoulder. She snuggles into the soft couch and enjoys a deep, untroubled sleep. When she awakens it's dark and snow is still cascading. Keith has come in; she can hear footsteps in the kitchen above. She stands, stretches luxuriously, and heads upstairs. To her surprise, it's Amanda she finds in the kitchen. "Hi, didn't expect to see you 'til later."

"I'm sick," Amanda says. "My throat was raw yesterday, and this morning, my head was stuffed with cotton, and now I'm a snot factory. Sorry, was that too much information?" She grins, but Lucie sees her red nose, shiny face, and bleary eyes. "I'm having some tea, then going back to bed."

"I made soup, want some?"

Amanda shakes her head. "Not for me, but Keith will be hungry, he's been in the arena all day. I assume the café is closed?"

Lucie nods. "I assume so too, I haven't heard from Ray. In fact he's got my car. He had to pick up some stuff at the south side market this morning. But as of yesterday, every dinner reservation was cancelled, so he put a 'closed' sign on the door. We won't be open again for a few days at least. Hey, did Tom get home OK?"

"Yep, one of the cooks drove him home, had to practically carry him out. Gosh I hate to see him like that."

"I know, it bugs me too, but Ray keeps telling me there's nothing to be done, and I guess he's right. Anyway, get yourself to bed, girlfriend. I'll feed Keith, and the household critters as well. See you tomorrow."

Tom wakes some time on Saturday, head throbbing, gut churning. He moans, rolls over, sleeps again. The day wears away, and still he sleeps. When at last he surfaces, the house is silent. It takes him several attempts to sit up, stand, and shuffle into the dim kitchen.

"Where's my missus?" he asks the wall. "Was she goin' t' city this weekend, see kids? I f'get," he mumbles as he gets a glass from the cupboard and painfully wanders into the living room to pour a tall shot of whisky. "Hair'v th' dog," he says, toasting the television as he flips through the channels. He finishes the shot, pours another, and drifts back to sleep sitting in his armchair.

Tom resurfaces on Sunday morning, greeted by harsh white light reflecting from snow on the ground and the overcast but bright sky above. Everything outside is coated with hard, crusty snow, every branch, vehicle, and rooftop. It looks more like January than November. The house is cold and silent.

His every joint aches, his gut and mouth are sour, and he stinks of beer and clothes worn for too many days. He starts the coffee-maker, takes a shower, shaves, and even pats on cologne, a long-ago gift from Marta. Returning to the kitchen, he makes toast and pours a mug of steaming coffee. The hot liquid rouses his mind and spirits.

He still can't recall whether Marta planned to be in the city this weekend, visiting Corrine and the grandkids. "Must be," he says aloud, staring again at the snow-encrusted back yard. The window sports a line of ice along the bottom — the storm appears to be over, but clearly the outdoor temperature has plummeted.

It doesn't occur to him how unlikely it is that Marta could have found her way to Calgary in such terrible weather. He doesn't remember the storm. He doesn't remember Marta sipping wine at his table in the bar. He doesn't know how he got home.

Tom wanders around the house and finally settles in his armchair again, plunking his mug of coffee on the side table. He flips through channels again, finds a hockey game and then another, watches halfheartedly throughout the dreary afternoon.

At loose ends on Sunday, Lucie drives Amanda's gigantic truck to the café. She's annoyed that Ray has not called to invite her for a cozy night together. In fact, he hasn't even called to let her know whether he made it to the city and back without incident yesterday. Predictably, he's not at The Sow's Ear. She fusses around the café kitchen a bit, though really there's nothing to do, it's already tidy. She tries phoning him, but her call goes to his cell's voice mail just like every other time she's tried to contact him today. Reluctant to surprise him at home uninvited — he might simply be taking advantage of the restaurant's closure to sleep, after all, or perhaps he's caught the same bug Amanda has — she locks up the café and drives back to the ranch.

As dusk falls on Sunday, Tom rouses himself and dials his daughter. "Hi, Dad," she says.

He can never get used to Corrine's smart-aleck phone that tells her who's calling. "Hi Corrine. Just wondering if you're thinking of bringing Mom back home tonight. Maybe the roads are no good. I'll drive in tomorrow and pick her up."

A pause. "Mom's not here, Dad."

"No? Is she at Shay's? I thought she was visiting you this weekend."

"Shay and Joanne went to Edmonton for a birthday or something. They haven't been home all weekend. In fact I've been worried about them, with the storm and all. But you know Shay, he'll drive through anything."

Another pause, too long. Finally Tom says, "Well. I suppose Mom's mad at me and went to stay with someone in town."

"Oh, Dad, another bender? Really?"

"Don't start, Corrine. You can't say anything I haven't already heard. I imagine Mom will call when she's ready to come home. Guess I don't blame her."

Yet another pause. He can hear the sounds of Corrine making dinner. He says, "I'll let you go."

"Ask Mom to call me when she gets home."

But there's no sign of Marta, no footsteps up the front walk, no phone call. Night falls and the sky clears as the moon rises, glinting diamonds on the ice-sparkling snow, the light hard as bone. His mouth tastes of salt and iron. Tom paces, round after round, living room to kitchen to dining room to living room and again and again, peering through every window on his route, checking the kitchen clock each time he passes it.

At 10 p.m. he calls the police.

It's noon on Monday, and Lucie is stomping around the ranch house in a full-on rage.

"What is with you?" Amanda asks, still afflicted with her cold, blowing her nose vigorously.

"What is with *him*?" Lucie retorts. "Where the hell is he?"

"Take it easy. If he's got this flu, he probably doesn't want to move, much less talk to anyone, even you. Listen, I'm not going to work today, but Keith needs to run a few errands with the truck so he can drive you to town later. Relax, Lucie. There's nothing wrong."

But when Keith drops her at the café's back door, Lucie waits, pretending to fuss with her keys until his truck has rounded the corner out of sight. Then she turns and strides as briskly as she can through the drifts toward Ray's house. The day is brilliant but bone-breaking cold, so not many town residents have shovelled their walks yet. By the time she reaches Ray's house, she's out of breath from wading through deep drifts. Her cheeks and ears burn from the glacial air, and her fingers are so stiff she can hardly get her key into the lock. She swings open the door and hollers, "Hello, anybody alive in here?"

Nothing.

She heels off her boots, looking up the stairs and failing to notice Ray's jackets and shoes are absent from behind the door. She goes upstairs and shrugs off her coat, leaving it and the house key on the kitchen table. With growing astonishment, she roves from room to room. The apartment is as neat and orderly as ever, but there is no sign of its occupant. No toothbrush in the bathroom, no clothes in the bedroom closet except her own. She considers how little Ray actually owns. Everything in the kitchen is still there, every cup on the shelf, every fork in the drawer, every pot and skillet in the cupboards, the kettle shiny on the stove. She makes another circuit of the rooms, as though she thinks he'll appear if she simply walks around enough. In the bedroom she sits on the neatly made bed, her mind buzzing, her hands shaking. She stands and walks back to the living room.

A strange guy is standing at the top of the stairs. He is tall and scraggly, unshaven, with a long angry scar decorating his chin. A black cap is pulled low over his head, hiding his hair and eyebrows. His jacket is also black, so worn it's faded to grey at the cuffs. Frayed jeans. He hasn't bothered to remove his wet boots.

"Who the hell are *you*?" she demands.

He surveys her for a moment, then slowly gives her a wolfish smile. Long, nicotine-stained teeth. "You're his girlfriend."

"That's the wrong answer."

His grin twists to one side. "Feisty bitch, ain't ya?"

"I asked you a question."

He changes stance, spreads his feet, ready for a fight. "I'm looking for Danny. Know where he is? Some buddies of mine want to talk to him."

"I don't know any dude called Danny. I'm the landlord's sister and our renter just skipped on us. A girl and her kid, for your information."

I have no idea why I said that.

This inspires a rasping laugh. He withdraws a hand from his pocket to scratch his face vigorously. "Hmm, landlord's sister, yeah, maybe. I dunno about that." He glares at her, perhaps trying to judge her story. "OK, just in case you are the landlord, get this. Don't go telling the cops anything about me. But I think you're Danny's girlfriend, and I think you know where he is. So get this, too. We'll be watching you. I think he'll come back to find you. Hell, I would, you're cute." Lucie stares back at him wordlessly, which generates another throaty laugh. "Landlord's sister, that's good. You think on your feet, I like that in a woman."

He takes a step toward her, but she doesn't flinch, just fixes him with a level but electric gaze and growls, "Get. Outa. My. House." She wonders whether she could take him by surprise, suddenly ram his midsection with her head, push him backward down the stairs.

He blurts another phlegmy laugh, but turns away without a word and clomps down the stairs, two at a time. She sees him step outside and glance to his left, then he says, "Shit," and bolts toward the back yard.

Lucie takes a few steps down the stairs, intending to close the door, but her knees cave and buckle. She sits, shuddering, face in her hands, rocking, heedless of the puddles from the stranger's boots.

You told me, you told me. You are who you said. And you're not who you said. And I didn't believe this day would ever come. It's all a lie. But it's all the truth. And here it is, just like my eviction. The nightmare come true.

She hears a scuffle on the landing below and looks up, but it's not the scrappy stranger she sees. It's Donny with two constables behind him. "Who was that?" he demands.

"Don't know."

"Where's Ray?"

"Don't know."

"Do you know where your car is?"

Frustrated to tears, she yells, "I don't know that either! What's going on?"

"I'm coming in, Lucie, and so are constables Smith and Duggan. Go upstairs, please." He steps forward. She rises shakily and stumbles back up to the apartment. Once, there, she turns to face him. He says, "Your car was found abandoned at a mall in the city. Any idea how it might have got there?"

"Donny, what is going on?"

He watches her impassively, waiting for her answer, but finally relents and glances away. Then, after a lengthy pause, he says quietly, "Lucie, Marta Williston is missing. Your car turned up in Calgary with no insurance or registration papers in the vehicle. City police traced the car to you through your licence plate, and I got a call from them. I went to the ranch to talk to you, talked to Amanda instead. She told me Ray borrowed your car. And now it seems Ray's missing, too."

Lucie's jaw tightens. "What do you mean Marta is missing? I just saw her on Friday afternoon."

Donny holds up his hand. "Stop. Lucie, I have to take you in for questioning."

"*What?*"

"Do you have a key to this apartment?"

"Yeah, it's on the table."

"Leave it there and come with me, please." With that he turns, expecting her to follow down the stairs. She remains rooted. When he reaches the bottom landing, he looks up at her and says, "Lucie, don't make this harder than it needs to be."

"*Fine.*" She muscles into her coat and trails behind him.

"Will we find your fingerprints in this apartment?" he asks.

"Of course, everywhere. And my clothes. And a toothbrush." *And nothing bloody else.*

He leads her to his patrol car and opens the back door. Wordlessly she slides in, shivering violently, whether from cold or panic she's not sure. She's never been in a police cruiser before — not even during her party days back in Toronto — but the experience is lost on her. She rides the entire five minutes to the police station clenched into herself, head bowed to her chest, chewing her lower lip until she tastes blood, hands wringing in her lap.

At the RCMP office, Donny directs her into a tiny room. There is nothing on the walls. The floor is scuffed linoleum, grey with age and wear. The walls are sound-deadening concrete block, off-white, streaked with smudges and marks. A long table with chipped edges is pushed against one wall. She sits in one of two plastic chairs under the annoying flicker of an unhappy fluorescent ceiling light. She is intensely cold. She knows there's a camera watching her.

"Let's start," Donny says, closing the door behind him. "I'm Staff Sergeant Donovan. You're not under suspicion or arrest; I simply want to ask you some questions. However, I will be recording this conversation. Please state your name."

She stares at him, disbelieving. "I know who you are, Donny. And you know me."

"Staff Sergeant Donovan," he repeats. Then she understands. In his eyes there is no friendship, no sanctuary, no café customer. Instead he exhibits a wary sharpness that makes her feel dirty. "That is a closed-circuit camera equipped with microphones," he says, pointing to the upper corner of the room where a malevolent red eye beams down on them.

"Lucie Tanguay." Her breathy voice sounds timid and small in this echoless shoebox of a room.

"You're here because we want to ask you about Raymond Tucker, who is currently a person of interest in the disappearance of Marta Williston. When did you last see him?"

Tucker. I've never even heard that name, Ray. Funny how you never told me your fake last name. There's so much I don't know about you.

"He didn't do anything to Marta, Donny. You know that. I know that."

He watches her dispassionately. The silence continues, each vying to outwait the other. Deep in her coat pockets, her fingernails dig into her palms. Finally, he blinks. "Look, Lucie. I have a job to do. I need to sort this out. Just tell me what you know. When did you last see him?"

She sighs and wraps her arms around herself, now too deeply chilled to shiver, her feet numb. She's angry and intends to only answer Donny's questions with terse, sharp replies, imparting the bare minimum of what she knows. But when she starts talking, she can't stop. Words pour out of her. She is astonished, helpless, she keeps talking. The gates are opened and the flood is on.

"Ray is not his real name. He wouldn't tell me his real name, because he was trying to protect me. Ray made some enemies in Saskatchewan where he's from — and I don't know where, exactly, maybe near North Battleford." Despite her sudden eagerness to tell Ray's story, she's aware that she is choosing her words carefully. It's true Ray never deliberately revealed his real name to her, but she knows it. And she's not about to tell Donny.

"What kind of enemies?"

Lucie explains. The misguided loan, the thugs, the impending danger. Everything she knows, which turns out to be remarkably little.

She says, "Today I went to check on Ray, but his place was empty. For whatever reason, he had to run, just like he said. And then that spooky dude showed up in the apartment, said his buddies want to talk to Ray. Which proves Ray's story, right? Ohmygod Donny. There's so much I should know, but I don't," she admits. "Ray was trying to protect me. He said the less I knew the better, because the thugs wouldn't hesitate to hurt me if they thought I knew something. So he was living with a made-up name to protect himself, and me, and Tom, and whoever else, too. But Ray is a good person. He *is*. You know that, Donny, right? Come on. He had a lot of sympathy for Tom, he was making the restaurant pay... Oh. *Ohmygod.*"

"Yes?"

"On Friday. Ray did the month-end and gave me an envelope full of cash to take to Tom. He said I would find Tom at the hotel bar, which of course I did. Tom was loaded, so I gave the money to Marta. Did somebody see me hand over that money? Did some-body grab her to get the cash? *Ohmygod,*" she wails.

"Keep going. Was that the last time you saw Ray?"

She takes a tattered breath. "I talked to Marta in the bar for a while. I was so surprised to see her there. Then I offered her a ride home..." Lucie's voice trails off as she starts to cry. "But she said no, no, she could get home herself. Oh, Donny. What hap-pened to her, what do you mean she's *missing*? I should have taken her home."

"One thing at a time. Where did you go after the bar?"

Another ragged breath. "Back to the café. Ray was still there. He asked to borrow my car. He drove me home. I haven't seen him since."

"What time was that?"

"I have no idea. Late afternoon? It was kinda dark by then, but with the storm, it got dark early, snowing hard. Might have been between three and four, but that's a guess. I don't know. Five, maybe."

"Why did he want your car?"

Again she explains, realizing with every word how implausible this story is, how she's betraying Ray. Her mind is whirling, she's barely aware of what she's saying. "I guess in hindsight it's odd that he was in a rush to pick up supplies in the city when the café was closed for the weekend and the roads were crappy."

Shut up, Lucie. You just said something monumentally stupid.

"No contact from him?"

"Nothing. Unusual, but he works hard, he never gets more than a couple days off in a row, so I decided to just leave him alone. I wasn't worried."

Liar. Who are you protecting here, yourself or Ray? Step careful, girl.

"So you've had no further communication with him in any way?"

"*No,* I said. And it's a complete surprise to me that my car got ditched at a mall. I know nothing about that. Donny? *Nothing.* I swear."

And the car had no papers? Ray, did the thugs find you after all? Did they grab you, hurt you? Where are you?

Donny sighs deeply and shifts in his chair, leans forward, both elbows on the table. "Why did you go to his apartment today?"

Lucie tips her head back, gazing at the ceiling and its flickering light. "Donny, come on, give me a break. You know me. You know us, Ray and me, I know you do. So what would you do, if you hadn't heard from your, ah, *partner*, for three days? He didn't call me, I didn't know whether he actually went to the city on Saturday, and if he did — did he get home all right? I'm his *girlfriend*, for the record. I tried his cell, but every call goes to voice mail. Yeah, OK — I *was* worried, so I went to his apartment. And there he was, gone. And then that crazy guy showed up." She leans back, arms crossed. "Now you know what I know. All of it."

"Why didn't you call the police?"

"To say what? He told me going to the police would only make things worse because these guys are likely to harass his family, or me, or Tom, or anybody else Ray knows. So I didn't encourage him to call you."

They stare at each other for a century.

He blinks. "Lucie, I know this is tough for you. You're romantically involved with Ray. But he disappeared the same day Marta disappeared. I know you want to help him, but you can't protect him. You have to tell me the truth and let me — us, the police — figure out what happened. So, where do you think he may have gone?" He stops, halted by the way her face crumples. She leans over and sobs soundlessly into her hands. He looks around for a box of tissues, but the room is barren of any such compassion. She'll just have to use her sleeve, which she does.

Finally she lifts her head and regards him with whatever dignity she can still knit together. "That's all I know, Donny. He's gone. He never said anything, he just left, like he said he would when the goons found him. I haven't heard from him, and I don't know where he might be. All along I doubted he'd actually have to run.

But it's all true, what he told me. And now the thugs have found Ray, and he's running. That's it. I'm empty, Donny. I've told you all I know. So it's your turn. Tell me about Marta."

"Tom reported her missing yesterday — Sunday night. He thought she was in the city for the weekend, but he called his daughter and found out Marta wasn't there."

"That's it?"

"We think she disappeared Friday afternoon on her way home from the hotel, but we have no proof yet. How much money did you give her?'

"I don't know, the envelope was sealed. Could have been two thousand or more."

"Cash?"

Forlornly, she nods.

He finally retrieves a limp, torn tissue from a pocket, and passes it to her. Says, "I have to fingerprint you, and I'll need Ray's cell phone number. Then I'll drive you home."

"Fingerprints, are you kidding? You said I'm not under suspicion."

"You said we'd find your prints all over the apartment, so we have to discount them from whatever else we may find. You are not under suspicion."

"But Ray is."

"Yes."

Back in the station's stark lobby, just as she and Donny are ready to leave, the two constables return. "Anything?" Donny asks.

"Nothing out of place in the apartment, but the Toyota out back is smashed to pieces."

Donny turns to Lucie. "Would that be Ray's car?"

She nods, shocked.

Your car wouldn't start. Yeah right. No wonder you needed my car. But that proves my story. Your story. Just like you said, the goons smashed your car to keep you from getting away. So you took my car to Calgary and ditched it, and now you're running.

Going to the ranch in the cruiser, she sits in the front seat, as far from Donny as possible, crowding the passenger door like she wants to melt into it.

Romantically involved. Jesus.

He pulls up outside the ranch house.

"Do I get my car back?" she asks.

"Soon, I'll call you. Lucie, you are not a suspect. You can relax. And please contact me right away if you hear from Ray."

She flings open the car door, she can't get out of the cruiser fast enough.

Ha. My lover is missing and suspected of who-knows-what. Relax, my left foot.

She sticks her head back inside the overheated cruiser to ask, "Will you let me know if *you* hear from Ray? Or find Marta?"

"It's a police investigation."

She gives him a piercing look and steps back, bathed in cold blue moonlight. Slams the car door.

Inside the house, Amanda and Keith are waiting. For the second time today, Lucie recounts what she knows about Ray's story, standing in her winter coat and boots on the kitchen floor. Then she says, "Do you want me to leave?"

Keith and Amanda exchange glances. Amanda says, "No. We talked about that, and we agree, that's not what you need right now, and there's no reason for you to leave anyway. You've done nothing wrong, and we don't think Ray's done anything wrong, either. And — what a crazy story. He hid it well."

Lucie bends to rest her elbows on the kitchen counter, cradling her head in hands. She does not cry; her tears are done for now. Instead she says, "He wanted to protect himself and all of us, too." She looks up at them. "Thank you. Thank you both, so much. You are true friends."

Tuesday morning.

With nothing to do, Lucie stays in bed late, listening to the radio. But every hour the news is all about Marta's disappearance. Eventually she gets up and paces about the ranch house. She considers diverting herself and her trouble by catching a horse and riding, but she's too distracted and nervous for that. She doesn't bother to dress, remains in her leggings and tee shirt. She drifts about the house, now flipping through the newspaper, now watching TV, now gazing out the windows at the snowbound hills. The landscape is relentlessly black and white, sky overcast, and still more snow falling.

And it's cold. So very cold.

On Tuesday night, Amanda returns from work with an envelope. "This showed up in the hotel mail," she says, placing the package on the kitchen counter. "It's from Ray. There were two things inside: a note for me, and a package for you. This is my note: 'Dear Amanda, and I do mean *dear*. I trust you as a friend to deliver the enclosed package to Lucie. And I want you to know I have always valued the friendship you and Keith have shown me. All the best, Ray.' That's it. This is the package for you."

Amanda holds out a tightly folded envelope. Lucie takes it, unfolds it, dumps out her car keys, and starts to cry.

Amanda comes around the counter, hugs Lucie, and smooths damp hair from her forehead. "Lucie, it's not your fault. He had a problem, he needed to deal with it, and he did. And he had a plan to protect us. Protect *you*. Don't you think that shows he cares about you? You got caught in the crossfire."

"I know, I know, you're right. But he's my *guy*. I feel so good with him. Yet it's all been a lie, but not. He tried to tell me, he *did* tell me. Now it turns out his crazy story is true, and I'm the one left holding... nothing. He is totally, utterly gone, and what do I believe now? I don't know." Lucie takes the crumpled envelope and car keys. "Guess I need to tell Donny about this."

"Yes, he needs to know you've got your keys back, and how that happened. Be honest, Lucie. That's the only way."

Lucie nods, then says, "Don't think I want dinner. I'm done. And — again, thank you. I can't ever thank you enough."

She goes down to her chilly bedroom, car keys and envelope in hand. The folded envelope feels bulky, she knows there's something else inside. Once alone, she fingers open the crumpled envelope and withdraws the Honda's registration and insurance papers, and a note. She pries it out, unfolds and smooths it. Reads:

> *My sweet City Girl. By the time you get this, I'll be some-where else. I can't say where. You know why. Please stay in Sweetgrass so I know where to find you. I will come back for you I promise.*
>
> *You are the very best thing in my life. I love you. I have never said that to anyone ever in my life. I should have said it to you long before now, and I wish I was there to say it in person. Please please believe me.*
>
> *Love, Ray (or DJ, that's what my family calls me)*
> *Love, DJ*
>
> *PS: help Tom find another chef*

Finally in legal possession of her car, again, and with nothing else to do, on Wednesday afternoon Lucie drives to the café. The 'closed' sign is, of course, still taped to the door. The menu board lists the items Ray had ready for the previous weekend, all those precious potentially great meals now put away into fridges and freezers, never to be prepared or served. The restaurant is cold, and the walls echo hollowly as she steps from the kitchen into the dining room.

Help Tom find another chef. How the hell do I do that?

Lucie is standing in the main room, lost in thought, when pounding on the door rouses her. Annoyed, she pivots to see Tom standing outside. When she opens the door, he bursts inside. He is a ball of incandescent rage.

They haven't spoken directly to each other since Lucie confronted him on the sidewalk. A lifetime ago.

"Where the hell is Ray?"

"I don't know," she responds sharply. She steps back as he storms inside. She stands in the cold, empty café, facing Tom unflinchingly. Angry, vindictive, her mouth full of venom, she spits, "And where the hell is *Marta*?"

Tom glares at her for a moment. Then he abruptly jerks around and yanks out the nearest chair. Sits. Collapses forward, elbows on the table, face in his gnarled hands. It takes her a few moments to realize he is crying. He is silent but his shoulders heave convulsively. She is appalled. She has no idea what to do, so she pulls out the opposite chair and sits, waiting for him to look at her.

She waits a long time.

Finally she softly says, "Oh Tom, I'm so sorry, that was stupid of me. Look at me. Tom?"

"Corrine's not speaking to me. Her idea to go on TV. It'll be on the news tonight." At last he raises his head, ever so slowly. The whites of his eyes are veined, his cheeks sag, and the curve of his mouth drags downward as though he's never smiled in his life. Like he's bearing the weight of the whole stupid, unfeeling world — and perhaps he is. His firm back and squared shoulders may want to say he is a fortress, a true tough cowboy, yet he is bent and crying before her. He seems small, diminished. Utterly lost.

What's going on, Tom? Are you actually worried about Marta? You're an ass of the first degree, and I can't believe you really care about her. I think you're more worried about yourself, your sorry life, and what happens to you now. But — prove me wrong, I dare you. I'm waiting.

He talks but he's looking at the wall behind her. His voice is distant, as if he's speaking to himself. "My poor sweet missus, my golden girl. I let you down before but never like this. It *is* my fault. I was drunk, I couldn't take care of you."

He suddenly focuses his gaze on Lucie. "She's gone."

Astonished by his words, Lucie takes a deep breath. "Tom, listen to me. We all had a part of that day. I was there at the hotel, Amanda was there, other people too. Any of us could have said to her, 'I'll drive you home.' In fact, I did that, *Tom. I did*, but she refused and I let it go. We all failed her, Tom. But look, we have to talk about Ray. He has done good work for you. He respected you and Marta. You know he would never do anything to hurt either of you. He understood your situation..." this comment generates a derisive snort from Tom, and she doesn't elaborate, "but he did right by you."

Lucie realizes she has to tell Tom the truth. She says, "Tom, I have to tell you something," and she relates what she knows about Ray. As she tells this bizarre tale, her voice takes on an urgency. She wants to grab his shoulders, shake him.

"Tom, you have to believe this story. *You have to!* I know it's true, because they smashed up his car, that's why he took my car into the city. I'm guessing that after he ditched my car he got on a bus or hitched a ride to someplace where he can start again, so he can keep paying his debt, keep going until they find him. Then he'll run again."

Yeah, and why would Tom believe that? You only half-believed it yourself, Lucie. Until it all happened the way Ray said it would.

Tom suddenly sits up and looks around the room. Then he says, with fierce anger, "He lied to me. Been lying to me for years."

Lucie is taken aback. "Yes. He lied to me, too. But, listen, he had his reasons."

"Still lies." Tom stands, knocking his chair over. He turns and exits the café without another word or backward glance. The door slams.

What now? Do I find you a new chef? Do you want my help? If you do, I don't know how to help you. For that matter, I don't know how to help myself.

"It's all over the news now," Amanda says forlornly.

The police and Tom's family, led by his fierce daughter Corrine, have decided to broadcast a public appeal on TV. It's prime national news content: a peaceful small town where nothing much happens until this mysterious event — a quiet, well-liked older woman who's gone missing, and the unexplained disappearance of the chef who ran her husband's restaurant. The reporter seems to accuse Ray. The coincidence is damning. The video pans across Tom's snow-clad house and then focuses on Corrine's exhausted, angry face. She speaks a few terse words, appealing to whomever has taken her mother — implying that person is Ray — to show mercy and let her go, then appealing to anyone who may know anything about Marta's whereabouts to come forward with information. Next it's a photo of Ray on the screen, accompanied by the narrative, "Wanted for questioning is Raymond Tucker, described as five-foot seven, about 160 pounds, with red hair and blue eyes."

Lucie rolls her eyes. "I can't believe this. Truly, I cannot believe this is happening." Her voice breaks. She tries not to cry.

Amanda nods in agreement.

And where did they get a picture of him? I don't even have a picture of him.

It's snowing again.

Judith calls.

"Yeah, Jude, that's him on the national news, my sweet Ray. But he's got nothing to do with Marta—it's coincidence that he had to leave town in a hurry on the same weekend she disappeared."

"Hon, do you honestly believe that? Maybe he's actually the charming psychopath nobody suspects because he seems sweet and innocent? Maybe it's just lucky he didn't do something to you. Maybe you should come back to Vancouver and hide out with me until they find him."

"No, no, it's fine and I *do* believe him because the goons smashed his car like he said they would. And when I went to his apartment this creepy guy showed up. I don't know how I faced that dude without fainting; I have never been so scared. I'm still scared. That creep said he's watching me in case Ray comes back. Which he won't, not any time soon. He's running, and I'm so worried about him."

"So his crazy-ass story is true."

"Every word."

Over the next few days, there are occasional media updates on the story, but the rise and fall of world news takes over, and after a few days the Williston family saga disappears from the headlines.

Lucie is paralyzed. She has no clue how to find a new chef for the café, no idea whether Tom even wants to continue the business. And where is Ray? Cold and scared, homeless, sleeping in some shelter? Or worse — did they find him and force him to abandon her car? Is he a prisoner in some barn in Saskatchewan? Are they burning him with cigarettes? Are they kicking him? Worse? She's given up trying to call him, suspecting he has thrown away his cell phone — it would just be another way for the thugs to track him down, or the police for that matter. She sleeps, drugged, endlessly, aided by alcohol and the painkillers she takes to battle her constant headache.

After two weeks of steady snow, finally there's a break in the weather, and as is usual for this part of the world, it's a complete reversal. A storm on the west coast generates a chinook that swarms over the mountains and slams into Sweetgrass — the Snow Eater wind arrives overnight. The west wind rises and rises more, until it's a hurricane that scoops up the recent snow and sucks moisture straight from the ground, the trees, the streets. Weeks' worth of piled snow softens and turns to water, or evaporates entirely into the howling warm wind. Within hours, roofs are free of snow, eaves troughs are gushing like it's spring. Streets are thick with puddles, water pools at every corner where the gutters and storm sewers can't accommodate the onslaught of meltwater. The air, singing with wind, is unbelievably warm. People discard the heavy jackets they so hastily brought out of storage against the early onslaught of winter. They are happy about the warmth but annoyed about the sloppy mess.

Sometimes, the cure is worse than the disease.

West of town, a cowboy rides along his fences through the buffeting warm wind, looking for damaged or downed wire. His horse wades through the drifts, and his dog bounds ahead. Suddenly, the dog starts a frenzied barking, backing away from a spot in the ditch, circling in an odd way, and then whining and wagging its tail uncertainly. Then the cowboy's horse startles, ears pricked forward, all four feet dancing. The man looks around to see whether he can discern what's making his dog and horse so uneasy. He scans the featureless white landscape, and his gaze lands on something utterly unusual, which at first he mistakes for a rag of plastic.

In the ditch, protruding from the snow, is a human foot clad in a bright blue boot.

The community hall is jammed and too warm. It seems the whole town has come for Marta's memorial service. The kitchen is crowded with women making coffee, setting out cups and milk and sugar, arranging plates of cookies and squares. Lucie is among their number, taking her place amid the legion of women who simply show up and do what needs doing.

The hall fills and fills. The doors never seem to stop swinging open. By two p.m. it's full of people sitting on uncomfortable, stiff-backed stacking chairs, others standing along the walls. Lucie confines herself to the kitchen, washing dishes, making more coffee, not looking around or engaging with anyone.

At last the hall is quiet, and Marta's two sons step to the podium. Shay and Chase speak quietly and sincerely about Marta, while in the front row family members weep and hold hands. But in the brothers' speeches is the open end, the loose thread — what happened to Marta? Yes, they have a body, but they have no story. Tom's sons do not address that topic. Instead they simply speak of their reverence for their mother, their memories of a sweet, kind, gentle person. They cry.

Members of the community also speak, relating stories about Marta's kindness and her knowledge of plants and ecology, her fine baking and knitting, the little things they remember about her. The entire hall is populated by people wiping away tears, and passing boxes of tissues up and down the rows.

And who thought to bring a supply of Kleenex boxes?

Tom's daughter Corrine does not go to the stage to honour her mother. Instead she sits in the front row, clenched and angry, looking straight ahead with thunder in her eyes. Tom spends the entire service looking at his boots. His daughter leaves as soon as the ceremony is done. Soon after, Tom himself slips quietly out a side door.

What is Lucie to do? She is adrift. No Ray, no chef, no restaurant, no job. No Tom. It's mid-December, nearly two weeks since Marta's memorial service. Tom has not ventured back to the café, nor has he tried to contact Lucie, who suspects he's holed up in his house in a state of permanent drunkenness. Yet Ray asked her to take care of Tom by finding a new chef, and Lucie is determined to respect that request. She goes to the café, but there's nothing to do; she can see no direction forward. She paces around the empty kitchen, ranting to the silent room.

"Find a new chef, as if. Just like that, find a new chef. Wave your magic wand, Lucie. Pixie fucking dust. How the hell am I supposed to do that? Damn it, Ray. Or Danny, DJ. Whoever you are."

As she paces up and down along the hallway, she notices the phone's message indicator is flashing. She punches the password code, praying it's a message from Ray.

It isn't. Instead she hears a pleasant voice with a Scottish accent. Incredibly, the message says, "Hey, this is Neil, and I don't know whether this will work out, but I understand you may be looking for a chef. As it turns out, I am a chef looking for a job. I'm in Calgary, here's my number."

For what seems the first time in weeks, Lucie laughs out loud. She replays the message again and again before she thinks to retrieve a pen and scribble the man's number on a scrap of paper.

I guess if it happened to me, the accidental server, it can happen again. Neil, the accidental chef. Pixie dust it is.

She dials the number and speaks to the owner of the Scottish accent, Neil Christie. He tells her, "I was teaching in the college's culinary program, but I quit last September. I really want to get back into the kitchen — more creative. I love the challenge of running a restaurant. I had a pub in Calgary for years. And news travels fast. It's a small world as they say, or at least the local culinary community is pretty tight. It's no secret that The Sow's Ear is closed and I assumed—perhaps wrongly—that you're in need of a new chef."

"You are not wrong," Lucie says. "Listen, I'm not the owner, so I can't make any promises. But why don't you come out and take a look at the place, and we'll talk."

"How's tomorrow?"

Neil Christie proves to be tall, mostly bald, and crackling with energy. His large, raw-looking hands are covered with nicks and scars. "I've hands like clumps of bananas," he says sheepishly, "but I do have proper knife skills."

"So I see," she returns.

Banana hands on his hips, he surveys the kitchen, then browses through various cupboards, shelves, the coolers and freezers, asking what Lucie considers to be intelligent questions about the business. "You've got quite an inventory to go through," he says. "I wouldn't make any drastic changes to the menu, at least not right away. We'll clear out the backlog of meat and stock and such, then maybe switch up the program in the spring when new fresh stuff shows up in the markets."

She ignores his use of the word 'we.'

He continues looking around, asking Lucie about opening hours, revenue, what his pay might be, she responds as best she can but she's not listening closely. Finally he says, "What's so funny? If I may say, you look like the cat that swallowed the canary."

"Sorry, it's just ironic — I started working here in a similar situation, very much by accident. My car broke down here, and I needed money to get it fixed. I walked into The Sow's Ear just as the only server walked out in a fit of rage. Next thing I knew, I had a job. I've been here for a year and a half now. It's a great place, people here are friendly. The town, I mean. And the restaurant too."

Now it's Neil's turn to chuckle. "Well, not too friendly, I hope. We're counting on them needing legal advice from time to time. My wife is a lawyer and the local law practice is for sale, which is why I gave you a call in the first place. If she and I can both find work here, we'll relocate from the city."

"Wow, you've gotta love it when a plan comes together, eh? For both of you. But there's something you need to know. The guy who owns this place has had some trouble lately. His wife disappeared and was found, um... dead," — the very word makes Lucie shiver. "You may have seen it on the news." Neil nods, thick brows knitting in a frown. Lucie continues, "The owner has never been the easiest guy to talk to, but right now, well... I'll let him know you're interested. I can't imagine he'll say no, but I can't promise anything."

"I presume you'll continue running the front?"

Lucie looks away, gazes absently out the window. "Yes, for now. I can't make any promises about that either, but I expect to be here through the winter."

That evening, Lucie drives up the long hill to Tom's house. The sun is long gone. It's nearly winter solstice; daylight is short. There's been no more snow lately, though as Lucie well knows, anything can happen.

Words to live by.

She pounds on Tom's front door but doesn't expect to rouse him. She turns to watch the western sky, noting the gradation of colour from midnight blue and cobalt overhead, to pale greenish teal and pale yellow at the horizon, and it's only four o' clock. She's mulling what to tell Neil if, as she suspects, she doesn't speak to Tom tonight. She's getting ready to leave when the door opens behind her.

To her amazement, Tom is dressed in clean jeans and a fresh blue and red plaid shirt. He appears to have lost weight. The skin of his cheeks seems soft and loose. But it's his eyes that arrest her. Far from being bloodshot and watery as she anticipated, his gaze is clear and steady. He does not smile, but nods at her and steps back from the open door, which she interprets as his invitation for her to enter. The house is warm and smells, incredibly, of fresh baking. For a tiny moment she almost believes it's all been a terrible hoax and Marta is about to step to the door, a plate of cookies in her hands.

"Want coffee?"

"No, thanks Tom, it's too late in the day, coffee keeps me awake. Listen, I won't keep you. But I need to talk."

"Come in." It's a command, not a request. "Take your boots off, the floor is clean."

Indeed it is. Lucie kicks off her boots and follows Tom into the kitchen, which is also neat and orderly. "Tryin' to keep the place up," he says. He pulls out a chair for her and moves away to lean against the counter, folding his arms across his chest. Scowling.

She doesn't know what to say, so remains standing. Gets right to the point. "I think I've found a new chef for the café."

"That so?"

Lucie explains the situation and her impression of Neil. "He says he's got loads of experience. I'll ask him for references but I think he'll be OK. Assuming you want to keep the café going."

Tom nods. He is gazing steadily at her but she doesn't feel assessed, sized up, the way she normally does when Tom fixes her with his steely regard. Instead, tonight he seems thoughtful, like he's on the verge of saying something remarkable — which he does.

"Come for dinner Sunday."

"I don't need your sympathy. I'm not a charity case," she snaps.

"Yes you are. Dinner, yes or no?"

A pause. "Can I bring anything?"

"Appetite."

They glare at each other for a silent moment, until Lucie impatiently turns and walks to the front door, pushes her feet into her slightly damp boots. She opens the door and steps outside into the chilly air. A couple of stars have popped out overhead. Far away, a coyote yips. She is halfway toward her car when Tom calls, "Lucie."

She turns.

"Hire him."

She nods. It's only when she's driving away she realizes Tom has never before addressed her by name.

—>///<—

Lucie arrives at Tom's front door with a freshly baked apple pie and a bottle of wine in hand. Tom swings the door wide and, as before, wordlessly stands back to admit her. Typically, his first words are not exactly welcoming. "I'm grateful for the pie, but you can take that bottle back."

Surprised, she sets the wine beside the door to be collected when she leaves. He takes the pie from her, but doesn't offer to hang her coat. Instead he turns toward the kitchen, leaving her to follow when she's got her boots and coat off.

"I quit drinking," he says bluntly.

"Oh? Well, that's good. Not that I'm passing judgment or anything."

He regards her frankly, then offers the barest of smiles. "Course you are, and you're right. That night the police came to say they found her, I dumped every ounce and smashed every bottle. Made a mess but felt good to break that habit. Literally. Done with it."

"That's impressive, Tom. I'm happy to hear it."

He goes even quieter as he lifts the lid from the only pot on the stovetop. "Stew and fresh bread. Not fancy." He stirs the pot's contents with a wooden spoon, sets the lid aside.

"Smells fantastic." Their conversation lapses, but unlike the companionable silences with Amanda or Ray, Lucie is nervous and eager to fill the void. She starts chattering. "I hired the new chef, Neil. He starts this week. He'll be driving out from the city every day for a while until he and his wife move out here, so I guess we'll stick to our usual winter hours. He'll probably want to close over Christmas like we did last year. But nothing else will change for now. We'll serve the same kind of food, same financial arrangements—only, listen Tom, I'm going to have to hire a bookkeeper. Ray used to do the books, but Neil says he'd rather not do all the accounting, though of course he'll order the food and such... "

"And you?"

"I'm terrible at that kind of thing. You'd think somebody who has a commerce degree would have a head for numbers and math, but really I don't. I'd prefer to hire someone."

"No. What are *you* going to do?"

Ah, the question of the century. What, indeed, am I going to do?

She takes time deciding how to answer. She sighs, crosses her arms. "Thought I would stick around for a bit. That is, if you want me to keep running the front end." She doesn't mention Ray's request of her to remain in Sweetgrass, should he ever be able to return.

In fact, she's told no one about Ray's note, his declaration, or the turmoil it's generated in her.

'I love you,' Ray wrote.

"Do I love *you*?" she'd spoken into the dark, silent air of her empty room after re-reading his note for the umpteenth time the night her car keys turned up. "I guess so. Yes, I think so. But what stopped us from saying that to each other when we could? Were we just too scared by our nutty lives and the fact we couldn't plan anything? Or did you not trust me? Did I not trust you? Or did I not trust myself? After all these years and all my escapades, do I even understand what it means to *love* somebody? Hell if I know."

Lucie suddenly realizes Tom is looking her way expectantly. "Sorry, what? I was thinking about something else."

"Tea OK?"

"Tea's fine, thanks. Want me to make it?"

"You know where the kettle is." Tom ladles steaming, delicious-smelling stew into bowls, places slices of bread on a plate, and carries everything to the kitchen table where he pulls out a chair and sits. Lucie puts the kettle on to boil, finds the teapot and tea bags, readies them. Then she joins him.

"You'll stay the winter," he says. It's a statement, not a question.

Again she talks to fill the available space, aware she's saying too much. "Yes, I guess so. I don't have anyplace to go, nothing's calling me back to Vancouver, that's for sure. I'll help Neil get things running. He doesn't want to be hiring new staff right now, he needs to figure out his menus and how he's going to pick up where Ray left off. He says he might change things in the spring, but for now we'll keep doing what we've always done. People seem to like it. And you didn't answer my question." She stops for breath and takes a spoonful of stew. It's rich and tasty, the carrots and potatoes are not overcooked, the gravy is thick and spicy.

"Bookkeeper."

She nods, rising as the kettle whistles. She makes the tea and returns to the table with the pot and two mugs.

"Can we afford it?"

She nods again. "Yes, the cash flow was good before we closed, so I see no reason we can't pay someone to do the accounting. This stew is terrific, nice and peppery, and do I taste lime juice?"

He regards her as he butters a slide of bread. "Miss him?"

To her chagrin, Lucie's eyes instantly fill with tears, she looks away quickly. "Sure, of course, what do you think?"

"I called him a liar. I'm sorry. He's got his reasons, as you said."

His words completely undermine her. She rests her elbows on the table, she presses her fingers into her closed eyes in an effort to stop her tears but instead starts sobbing. She hears him pour tea. "Have some tea," he says gently. She nods, wraps her fingers around the mug, and sips carefully. He asks, "You believe his story?"

"*Yeah.*"

"Me, too. Eat some more, you're skinny, and you've lost weight since he left. Nobody to cook for you." She nods again and takes another bite of stew. Tom continues, "I can do that. Cook for you once, twice a week. You can tell me what's going on at the restaurant. I don't feel much like going out."

She's so astonished she nearly drops her spoon. "Sure, if you want. I'd like that, too. And Tom — what are you doing for Christmas?"

"Same as any other day."

"You are so right. My heart's not in it."

"I'll roast a chicken."

"You're on."

—⟶〉∭〈—

And so they begin twice-weekly dinners in Tom's kitchen. Sometimes he cooks, and sometimes she phones to say she's bringing leftovers from the café. His gruff manner and frequent silences still make her nervous, but she tries to relax, which becomes easier as he starts telling stories of ranch life, kids, chickens, storms, good horses, difficult horses.

But there's nothing easy about Christmas day. Tom roasts a chicken accompanied by mashed potatoes, even cranberry sauce and Brussels sprouts. Lucie contributes a salad and cupcakes for dessert. They make a valiant effort to cheer each other by enjoying the meal — which is delicious — but after only a couple of hours, Lucie is exhausted from trying to keep up a jolly pretence.

Tom seems to agree. "I'd say let's watch TV but there's only Christmas movies on."

"I know. It's sad how this season that's supposed to be so full of friends and family can make you feel so lonely. Did your boys call?"

"Shay invited me for dinner, but I said no — rather stay home."

They clear the table, wash and dry dishes, standing side by side in silence. "When was the last time you were even outdoors, Tom? Get your jacket, let's take a walk."

He does so without protest and presently they're strolling along the street, side by side but decidedly not touching, crunching over the snow that's fallen in the past week. The night is bracing but not terribly cold, and there's a half moon to light their way. They reach the end of the row of houses, where the street bends to the west and becomes an unlighted road that connects to the highway a mile away. They keep walking, passing fenced fields on either side and gradually approaching a grove of tall conifers that stand black against the moonlit sky.

"What's *that*?" Lucie asks suddenly, spotting a strange fluttering shape about halfway up on a tall, broad spruce near the road. Then she laughs out loud. "Look, somebody's put Christmas decorations all over that tree." They come to a stop beneath the tree, which is festooned with garlands and ornaments.

Tom bends stiffly to retrieve a fallen ball, finds a branch, and fastens the ornament tightly on a branch. "Funny," he says. "All the years we lived on this street, I've never walked out here. Never seen this, but I bet they do it every year, whoever they are — neighbours I guess. Maybe the kids even sing songs. I always liked Christmas music." He stands for a moment, then abruptly he turns toward home.

Lucie remains a moment longer, marvelling at the makeshift communal Christmas tree, and then jogs to catch up with him. When they get back to Tom's house, she squeezes his arm, which is encased in his scuffed sheepskin coat. "Going home now. Merry Christmas, Tom."

"And you, Lucie."

She drives back to the ranch. Amanda and Keith are at a friend's for dinner. The house is quiet except for the cats that come mewing and rubbing against her legs as she stands in the dim kitchen. She's wondering what to do next. She grabs a squat glass from the cabinet and pours a shot of rye. She sits by the window and raises the glass, noticing the glitter of Ray's ring on her finger. She's worn that ring every day since last Christmas. She's become accustomed to its presence. But tonight as she holds out her hand, she takes a good long look at the pale blue stone that twinkles in the moonlight.

Two Christmases without you. My sweet man, where are you tonight? How long until you can call me, send a letter, something so I know you're OK and that you'll actually come back for me? Are you even OK? Are you safe or scared, have they hurt you? Ugh, I can't even think about this.

She sips.

And can you tell me, please, what the hell am I supposed to do with Tom? It was so easy to hate him, but now it's hard not to like him. I've utterly misjudged him, though he made that easy enough. I can't cut him too much slack. He's been an ass, and I do believe he's more responsible than anyone for what happened to Marta. Then again, he's not alone. We all had a part, we all let her down. It's not

*as black and white as I might have thought once. And now — Tom
is so lost. As lost as you, Ray.*

"Maybe lobster. And now I flounder."

With Christmas behind her, Lucie dedicates herself to helping
Neil to resurrect the café and recapture its energy, reputation,
and customers. She even does a couple of radio interviews, lined
up courtesy of Tash, to promote the café's re-opening. She doesn't
mention the local tragedy, nor Tom or Marta by name, certainly
not Ray. Neil and his wife Linda buy a house in Sweetgrass. Lucie
helps them get moved and settled, and she throws a welcome party
at the café, inviting everyone she can think of.

Despite the brutal early cold and snow in October and November
and December, it's turning out to be what everyone calls a typical
foothills winter: some snow, some cold, some chinook warmth that
blasts over the mountains and melts everything. The hiking group
schedules ski or snowshoe trips, only to be stymied by continually
changing conditions. More often than not, they hike instead of ski,
and Lucie buys crampons for her boots — strap-on spikes that help
her grip the ice and frozen ground.

She works, she bakes, and occasionally she caters a party. She
rides Quincy in the arena. She hikes or snowshoes with the group.
She hires a bookkeeper for the café, and she helps Neil design
weekly menus. He is not the curious, passionate cook Ray was, but
still he's a trained and competent chef. Business picks up.

One afternoon she phones Tom and says, "Hey, come to Amanda's
for dinner tonight. Keith has a horse problem and I think you could
help, but don't tell him it was my idea." She has an ulterior motive:
Tom has not budged from his house for weeks. He never comes
to the café, and to her knowledge he never even walks up the
street and back. Lucie does his banking and collects his mail. She's
tired of being his social buffer. And Keith does, in fact, have a

recalcitrant horse to deal with.

When Amanda arrives home from work, Lucie is prepping the meal and says, "Tom's joining us for dinner." She now knows better than to be direct about what she wants from the encounter between Tom and Keith. Over pork chops and grilled vegetables, they talk together about weather, the price of hay and cattle, a bit of local news. Tom and Keith are, predictably, less voluble than Amanda and Lucie. Finally, the talk turns to horses. Lucie makes tea, and the men move into the living room to sit before the fire while Lucie and Amanda clear the table and wash dishes. When they've finished, they go into the living room to find the men are nowhere to be seen, although the fire crackles and pops.

"I guess they're in the barn," Amanda says.

Lucie grins.

And so begins Tom's gradual re-emergence into town life, courtesy of Keith's difficult horse. Over the next few weeks, the two men work together, trading ideas and wisdom on training the animal. Then one day, Tom appears at the café, and Lucie almost hugs him. "C'mon in, I'm so happy to see you. What would you like?"

"Pie and coffee. Same as ever."

Ha. Maybe I've got my cowboy back.

February. The weather is remarkably mild — little snow, not even much cold. The fields are drab and desiccated, the wind ceaseless. It nips, frets, and frays Lucie's nerves. Her sleep is broken by annoyingly long spaces of lonely wakefulness, hours at a time. She tries listening to radio, she tries deep breathing and yoga, but nothing dispels her anxiety. When she does sleep, she springs awake at the slightest sound. Mornings find her bleary-eyed, impatient, and unrefreshed. Her lack of sleep is starting to show in her baking. She suspends bread making for the time being, concentrating instead on simple cakes and cookies. It's all she can manage.

How the time drags, as if Lucie is hauling a boulder through deep water. She is bored and fretful, restless and lost. She's forgotten how to smile. She's in constant search of diversion, anything to settle her mind for an hour or two. Riding, like baking, is beyond her. She knows the therapeutic value of both, but cannot rouse herself sufficiently to catch a horse or knead dough. She's wallowing in despair. She knows it, but can't seem to stop herself. Bitterness is her faithful friend and companion. She tastes blood in her mouth from continually clenching her teeth.

Seated in the ranch house living room one afternoon with nothing to do, she flips through the local weekly newspaper. Car and truck ads, heroics of the local sports teams, the high school drama club's winter production. Local politics. She turns the page.

Cries out loud. There's a picture of Ray.

It's the same strange photo that appeared on television before Christmas. The headline reads, 'Local man no longer subject of police search.' The terse article, just three paragraphs, tells her the police don't consider Ray to be 'a person of interest in the disappearance and death of Marta Williston of Sweetgrass.' She flings the pages to the floor, then dances and stomps on the paper until it's wrinkled and mashed.

"Damn you, Donny! Damn damn damn all of you! You've stopped looking for him! You *must* know something! *Somebody knows something and nobody's telling me a single fucking thing*!"

She leaves the mess on the floor, grabs her coat, and storms from the house, her mind full of lightning, her body electric with fury. She barrels down the ranch road, heedless of the curious horses that follow her along their side of the fence. She walks and walks along the township road until her knees cry and her ears sting from the cold. It's dusk and she barely knows where she is when finally she stops to look around to catch her breath and stare up at the colourless, featureless sky. Feeling defeated and utterly empty, she trudges home.

Luckily, she returns in time to tidy up the storm she left on the living room floor before anyone else arrives to see the evidence of her rage. She tears out the article, wondering again where the police got that photo of Ray. It must be old; he looks so young but stern and unsmiling, perhaps his bizarre story had already started to unfold when someone took that picture of him. Nothing in the photo's background is discernable, just a blur of shapes, perhaps it was taken outdoors. Maybe at his farm. She folds the scrap of newsprint and tucks it into her back pocket. Straightens the rest of the damaged paper and leaves it on the coffee table as though nothing had happened, as if there's no fresh gash in the universe through which her heart is bleeding.

She phones the police station.

"RCMP. Constable Duggan speaking."

"Hi Matt, it's Lucie from the café. Can I talk to Donny please?"

"He's not available, Lucie. Can I help?"

"No, I need Donny. When will he be back?"

The constable pauses, and then says, "About a month. He's away on training. So — you sure I can't help?"

She grits her teeth. "Um... no, it's OK... Wait, yes maybe you can... Matt, is there any news about Ray? I mean, I just read a newspaper story...?"

"I can't say anything more than what was in the paper."

"But... do you know where he is? Ray, I mean."

"No."

She tales a ragged breath. "OK, well... thanks."

One late February morning, Lucie and Amanda are in the ranch house kitchen, tensely gulping coffee before each heads out to work. Silently they watch the horizon above the eastern hillside.

It's glimmering, ever lighter with each passing minute, but gauzy clouds veil the sky.

"I recall having this conversation with you last year, about the days getting longer," Amanda says softly. "It still lifts my mood when we get more daylight. Don't you think?" As she speaks, the sun pops above the hillcrest and rises visibly, if slowly. Daylight floods the ranch's tiny enclosed valley.

I have to admit, you're right. I do feel better. A little. Sometimes. And I know you're treading carefully around me because I've been a bear with a sore butt lately. Ah, once again, look where I live. Amazing landscape. Amazing friends.

Lucie responds, "Yes, I do. And look at that, rainbows on either side of the sun. Gorgeous."

"Mmm, maybe. Those are called sundogs. In theory, they foretell a big change in the weather. If it's been great, which it has, local wisdom says we have a storm coming."

"Really? How accurate is that? I mean, is it true?"

"Kinda, maybe. I don't pay attention. It's as accurate as the other famous piece of local lore, which says ninety days after a dense fog there will be snow."

"Come on."

"I know, it sounds silly. The thing is, whenever there's a spring snowstorm in April or May, somebody's bound to say, 'I knew this would happen because three months ago we had fog.' And everybody goes, 'Oh, yeah, of course, you're right,' but nobody really remembers when the last fog was, even though fog is rare here, so you'd think it would stick in people's minds. In my humble opinion, bad memory feeds the local so-called wisdom about the connection between fog and snow. Maybe about sundogs, too."

Sure enough, though, the next morning arrives with angry skies and the radio announcing a heavy snowfall warning. But it's a short-lived event, a pasting of wet snow and ice that makes driving, even walking, treacherous for a day or two. Then the moisture-sucking warm wind returns, and the snow disappears. Rocking horse weather. Back and forth.

Lucie's frame of mind continues to be as volatile as the weather, bouncing from dour to angry to desperate to, occasionally, hopeful. She takes deliberate steps to distance herself from The Sow's Ear. Neil, banana hands and all, is very capably running the kitchen, and he's brought in a couple of young trainees he knew from his teaching days. Lucie has found and trained no fewer than five new servers and created a roster for them, so her presence at the café is increasingly unnecessary. She goes in early to bake, she takes shifts serving tables — after all, she still needs an income. But increasingly, she escapes back to the ranch.

She knows she is hiding, but she has good reason. She's recently noticed a disturbing problem: gossip. People seem to be talking about her. She's trying to avoid the sidelong glances and whispers at the café. It's puzzling and disappointing to realize such talk is swirling around town, perhaps still linking Ray to Marta's disappearance and death, even after the police statement exonerating him — although it was such a tiny article, buried deep in the local paper, who has seen it? And who believes it? Some don't, it seems.

Gossip. It's no different from Vancouver. The secrets about Brad and Elaine, opinions and smirks on every hand, inescapable. And here in Sweetgrass, despite Ray's constant cautious behaviour, everyone in town seems to know Lucie and Ray were a couple. And perhaps she was not as cautious as she should have been. Now, people openly stare at her when she's at the bank, at the post office, on the street. Occasionally, when she brings food to a table at the café, conversation suddenly ceases and customers won't meet her eyes.

It's been increasingly difficult to maintain her friendly banter and professional demeanour at work. She'd like to smash plates, throw hot coffee, spit, yell. Scream, 'You have no idea! You don't know the first thing about him!' but that would only add fuel to the gossip fires.

Instead, she finally returns to the refuge she's come to trust:

horses. She catches Quincy and works the mare in the arena, often under Keith's guidance when he's there training another horse. Occasionally, Tom is present too. Like Keith, Tom proves to be a patient teacher, offering tips and ideas on everything from how to hold the reins to controlling the speed and cadence of the mare's trot and canter, to understanding horse psychology. To her surprise, Tom's suggestions are gentle and kind, spoken softly. For Lucie, exploring non-verbal communication with a horse continues to be fascinating and absorbing, exactly the right diversion from the constant ticking anxiety of her clockwork brain. The right antidote to spiteful talk. These two men know her history and Ray's, yet they don't judge her. She's safe with them.

I never would have expected this from you, Tom. I thought you would yell at me. Or just stare at me like I'm the stupidest person alive, and how could Keith ever trust me with a horse? But you're actually patient, you explain, you make it about the horse and how I should respond, not the other way around. Damn you, Tom. You keep making me like you more all the time.

As ever, being on horseback and concentrating on riding skills calms her whirling thoughts. Town talk falls away, she forgets about it, at least until she hangs up her saddle, brushes Quincy's mane, and turns the mare back out to pasture.

But there's been something else, far worse than gossip. Phone calls.

The first call came in January on an unusually cold, dark, snowbound day. Lucie was at the café, serving tables. In her back pocket, her cell phone buzzed, and — ever hopeful it was a call from Ray — she scurried to the kitchen to retrieve the message. But it was a voice she didn't recognize, and a message she didn't want. "We're watching you. We know who you are. And we're waiting for him to come back. Just like you." Lucie yanked the phone away from her ear and instantly deleted the message.

Since then, it's happened maybe a dozen times. She's taking care now to note the incoming phone numbers, but usually the caller's identity is blocked, and even when she can see the phone number, it's never the same one twice. More than the increasing town gossip, more than her own desperate state of mind, these calls are deeply unsettling. She's agitated and finds herself looking over her shoulder all the time — at work, walking down a street. Neil notices her nervousness and asks what's wrong. She only says she's not sleeping well. But when Tom notices, she can't keep the truth from him.

Lucie and Tom are fixing dinner together at Tom's house. Lucie has filled him in on café business. She tries to remain detached and professional, but as usual when she's with Tom, his long silences provoke her to nervously talk talk talk. At length he says, "What the hell is spooking you, girl?"

Lucie stops chopping and looks at him, wiping onion-generated tears from the corners of her eyes. "Tom, you see right through me. So... I've been getting creepy phone calls, I think from the drug guys who are looking for Ray. But maybe not, maybe it's just some locals having their fun at my expense. Though that doesn't make sense, now I think about it, because nobody knows his story except a handful of people. And who has my cell number?"

He raises a bushy eyebrow. "Like what?"

"The phone calls? They say they're watching me, know where I work, where I live. Sometimes I don't believe it but sometimes I do. The druggie guys clearly have their methods, because they found Ray, smashed his car, and sent a crazy spooky guy to his apartment. Oh, Tom. I can't even imagine what might have happened if that guy had found Ray instead of me. Then again, I *can* imagine. That's what keeps me awake at night. And thinking about where Ray is now."

"Told Donny?"

"About the phone calls? No. For one thing, Donny's away and I don't want to talk to the other Mounties here. To say what? That I'm getting crank calls? Complain to the cops, no way. Come on, I'm tougher than that."

"That's not the point."

She resumes slicing onions. "And what *would* be the point?"

He places a gentle hand on her arm to halt her work, the same way he would rub the neck of a nervous horse to calm the animal and assert his presence, his authority. She knows. She's seen him do it.

"You don't have to be tough with me." She's astonished by his observation, but he continues before she can protest. "The point is, and you know it, the police need all the help they can get."

"Tom, telling the cops might make it worse. If the goons know I'm running to the police, they could terrorize Ray's family the same way they might be threatening me. And if they *do* know where I live… And what about Ray? Do they have him, are they threatening him by saying they'll hurt me?"

"Nope, I don't buy it. You're not doing Ray any favours. Tell the Mounties. Then get a new phone number."

She looks up in surprise.

"I wasn't born yesterday," he says. "I don't know much, but I know you can change your cell number like changing your underwear."

For the first time in weeks, Lucie smiles.

But, Tom, if I get a new phone number I lose Ray entirely. He has no way to find me, to call me. I'll be lost. So lost.

No snow for weeks. The fields are the tawny gold of pale ale, the soil is dry and undernourished. Highway traffic kicks up dust like it's the middle of dry July. Everyone's on edge about the lack of moisture and the threat of grass fires, bush fires, poor soil conditions for the upcoming spring seeding. The highway maintenance crews have had an easy time this winter, likewise the farm wives and husbands who support their ranch habit with city jobs. Their daily commute to Calgary has been a breeze. But everyone's worried. The county imposes a fire ban.

Despite Tom's advice, Lucie has not informed the police about the insidious phone calls. But after one especially graphic message, she relented and obtained a new cell phone number. She can't help it. Ray will just have to find another way to contact her.

I'm so afraid you'll think I've dumped you, that I've lost hope, cut you off. That's not true. But I cannot keep getting these crazy phone messages. I don't know what to do, except protect myself, and trust that you'll call Amanda or even Donny to find me. Find me, please. Ray. Danny. DJ. Whoever you are. Find me.

Lucie calls Judith. "The saga continues," she begins lightly.

"And?"

"Um, so... it's about the phone calls. I get these messages saying the thugs are watching me, waiting for Ray to come back. I feel like fish bait."

"Have you told the police?"

Lucie explains her reasons for not telling the police. "But I do have a new cell number. And, Jude? There's more. Besides this terrorizing, there's stupid gossip in town. I used to be the impervious one, I could blow off gossip. Now I'm second-guessing myself. I don't know what to do."

"Oh, Sweet Pea. Come here, come back to Vancouver. It might not be your permanent home, in fact Vancouver probably isn't home for you at all any more. But it might be a good place to hide for however long it takes."

March roars into town on a wave of wind and dangerous, galloping grass fires, creating a stir and much nervous conjecture among the café's patrons, who talk about weather and dry soil, about fire volunteers, about how much water is in the town reservoir and where else fire fighters could find water if they had to. The local talk now washes over Lucie, unnoticed. She tries to maintain her enthusiasm for the café, for her life in Sweetgrass, but each day seems longer and bleaker than the one before. She feels alien.

She's once again a tourist in town.

Pull me, push me. I'm here, I'm not. I'm part of this town, trying to make a home here. Then again, I'm a stranger. It's not even two full years yet. I might have made some connections, but really I'm an outsider and maybe I always will be. Is this home? Or is this just where I live?

One sunny, breezy day after the lunch rush, Donny of all people comes into the café. He's by himself and the room is quiet. Neil is in the kitchen and Lucie happens to be serving tables alone. She takes Donny's order without so much as a 'Welcome back,' ferries his plate to the table, and then goes into the hallway to pace. She is determined to speak to him, and finally, after much trepidation, she strides to his table, pulls out a chair and sits. He looks up with surprise.

She leans forward and speaks in a low, imperative tone. Gets right to the point. "Look, Donny, I have to know what's going on. I am so worried. This is making me crazy. Is there any news, anything at all you can tell me? Where is Ray, do you know? *Please.*" She doesn't mention the newspaper announcement or the threatening phone calls.

Donny leans back in his chair but keeps her gaze. Like the frigid December day when he took her in for questioning, his eyes are guarded, but she senses honesty and compassion, perhaps by the tilt of his head, or maybe in the set of his shoulders. He looks at her for several moments—so long in fact she's afraid he won't say anything. But he rewards her. He nods curtly and says, "He's safe, Lucie. That's all I can tell you."

"Is he in jail?"

"No. And he's not under suspicion any more. We put out a news release, the local papers and TV picked that up. He's not part of our investigation, he's been cleared. I'm not able to tell you anything else. Lucie, everything will turn out in due course, but it will take time. You have to trust me. He's OK, that's all I can say."

Well, that's a start. It's a slim thread, but it's all I've got.

She stands abruptly, scraping her chair backward. "Well, thanks. I really appreciate it." She turns away before he can see her crumbling face, her tears.

Her rage.

Lucie drives north from Sweetgrass and turns west onto a secondary road that winds between close hills. Aspen groves give way to dense stands of tall spruce, black against the buckskin-brown fields. Eventually she finds the unmarked gate, the blue mailbox, the gravel road that leads to Sweet Water Woman's house. She guides Agememnon along the rutted drive and stops when she can't make any further headway. Lucie strides boldly up the trailer's steps, wipes mud from her boots, and knocks loudly on the door.

No response.

Lucie nearly loses her resolve, but recalls Daisy's advice from the mushroom-picking day last June — so many months ago, a generation ago. She stands at the door, takes a deep breath, then pushes the door open and steps into the long, open room she remembers from her previous visit. She heels off her boots and walks into the kitchen, where Sweet Water Woman stands at the stove stirring a pot full of water and bones.

"Hiya," says the Native woman without looking up.

Christ, girlfriend, I could be a serial killer or a tax collector or some other equally odious person you don't want in your house.

"Hello," Lucie says in a low voice, drawing another deep breath. "That smells so good. Soup stock, yes?"

Sweet Water Women nods and continues her work, straining bone chunks and shards of boiled meat from the liquid. She jerks her head to indicate that Lucie should take a seat at the long table, which Lucie does. After several minutes, when she's finally ready to step away from the stove, Sweet Water Woman sits across from Lucie and says bluntly, "Your man's gone."

Without so much as a smile or nod, Lucie covers her face, hiding. She mumbles, "Yes, he's gone and I know why. It's a long, terrible story. I believe him, but I can't tell anyone the real reason, and even though the police have cleared him, I think people still believe he's responsible for what happened to Marta, but he had nothing to do with it..." She folds down until her forehead rests on the table, spreading her arms wide. She has never felt so free to let go of her load, to simply lay her trouble on this broad, worn surface.

"Go away."

Lucie jerks upright in alarm and looks at the woman across the table, who meets her with a gaze both challenging and empathetic. Sweet Water Woman says, "Maybe you think I'll get out my wampum beads and sage leaves, wave my peace pipe, give you wisdom? Tell you where he is?"

Lucie frowns. "I have way more respect for you than that."

"Why did you come here?"

Those words might once have sparked Lucie's temper, but instead she takes a deep breath and ponders her reply. On the stove, the soup stock bubbles and hisses.

Lucie takes another breath, holds Sweet Water Woman's gaze. "Because I think maybe you can help me calm down, think straight, and it's got nothing to do with sage leaves or whatever." She pauses and starts again. "Of all the women I know, I think you could give me some direction. Not because we know each other — in fact, exactly because we don't. I've only been here once, and you said I could come back because I don't talk too much, but I was intimidated that day. Normally I talk all the time. I analyze and blather. I'm doing it right now. I'm not a good listener. I don't sit still and listen to my own heart. I don't know what's in there right now, except confusion and disappointment and worry. But you have a stillness, a... *patience* I'll never have. I don't know how to do that.

"Here's what I do know. I've met people who have taught me about horses, the land, the birds and bush, the sky. You, but not only you, others, too. And I've been out walking, alone. I've been to the mountains on horseback. I've walked by the river on a November day that felt like June. I'm starting, only starting, to see and listen. And I've met good people, good, solid, got-your-back people.

"But I've got trouble now, and I don't know what to do. The two people I really want to talk to are gone. Ray is on the run. And Marta..." She pauses again. *When you're going through hell, keep going.* "Marta is gone too. I never really knew her. A lot of the time when we were together, we were quiet. I miss that. I should have spent more time with her. Much more.

"So — there's terrible talk around town. I don't know who to trust. I don't know if the town is on my side, on his side, on nobody's side. I'm in a maze. I don't know what to do. I thought you could help." Drained, Lucie sits back.

Sweet Water Woman gazes across the table as if she's looking across centuries, as if Lucie's concerns are tiny, insubstantial, inconsequential.

Lucie tries to match that penetrating look. She may not be a Native elder, but Lucie knows her own terrible history and what she's learned from it, and that informs her fierce gaze. The two women lock eyes for what seems many minutes to Lucie, but is only a few profound, intense seconds.

"Go away."

Stung again by this blunt remark, Lucie fumbles in her pocket and withdraws her car keys. "I'm sorry." She shakes her head. "I'm so sorry to come here whining..."

Sweet Water Woman leans forward with a resonant chuckle and warmth in her eyes. Says, "Shut up, girl. I don't mean *right now.* You're right, you don't listen. Look at me."

Again they look at each other, intense and electric. But Lucie sees kindness too.

You're looking at me like I'm some silly girl, but I think you are challenging me. I need to step up. If I say the right thing, maybe you'll help me. Maybe this trip was not the wrong idea.

Sweet Water Woman says, "It's simple. If Sweetgrass is not safe for you, then *go away* to some place you feel safe. For a short time, long time, it's up to you. I don't know you, but here's what I see: I think you're bigger than talk, but you have to make a choice about how you deal with it. Run or not, either way there will be talk, maybe for a long time. You're part of the local folklore now, and some people will always look at you sideways.

"You choose. But if you run, understand what you're running from. Is it the talk? Your man? Something else? Maybe you need to go away to find the stillness you want. I think so. Breathe different air, hear different birds, see the same moon — because we all see the same moon, remember that. Figure it out. You'll know when it's time to come back. And I think you'll come back. You've set roots here. Anybody who talks about birds and air and horses like you do, has roots here. You can't help it. This place has grabbed you."

Lucie's look is quizzical. Sweet Water Woman continues, "I think you love this place. I think this is home for you. That's what I saw in your eyes on our mushroom day. You looked around, quiet, you learned. You fit here. You might not know it, but I see it. Your man is gone. I don't know him, but I believe what I hear about him from people I trust. He is a good person. Some of the town believes him, some of the town is full of shit. It's always that way." She smiles, a broad quiet smile that crinkles the corners of her eyes.

Sweet Water Woman sits back in her chair to regard the whole room, and the woods beyond the windows. "I have a graduate degree in psychology, and I'm a practicing counsellor, mostly for addiction but other issues too," she says. "I know stress when I see it, and I'm seeing it in you. So, my advice to you is: take a break. Go visit your mama, your friends, whoever you go to for help. But don't forget to come home. That's what I see in you. This is home. This place has your heart. Go away. Heal. Come home."

Sky overcast, the same pale, silver-grey of the river's water-washed stones, or of the old scarred cutlery at The Sow's Ear that needs to be replaced. The air is so cold it feels hard, like bashing through a wall. She labours up the muddy, slippery hillside behind the ranch house, intent on challenging her physical self: her lungs, her legs. Her shoulders are tight and hunched up to her ears, and her lower back complains. There's a high-pitched whine at the back of her head. Her teeth are clamped, her jaw hurts.

She thrusts her way up the hill with sharp steps that jab for traction into the caked earth and dead grass. She curls her hands into the sleeves of her fleece jacket, having forgotten gloves or mitts. As she toils to ascend the slope, Lucie feels exposed, like a stone outcrop on the hill, an obstacle, a blockage, something to overcome. Her ears ache from the cold wind, and her cheeks feel flayed and raw.

Lucie is fuelled by rage, disappointment, her need to make a decision. Puffing, she achieves the crest and turns to face west into the full press of the breeze. In this iron-hard, cloud-covered morning, the mountains are smoky blue and sharp, like the razor-edged flints Native people once fashioned to cut meat, to scrape bone.

She faces the insistent west wind and strips off her clothes to stand naked against the bullying river of air.

Lucie braces her legs apart and spreads her arms wide. Wind in her hair. Throws her head back, looking up. It makes her dizzy. She sits, arms still raised to the sky. The last time she was up here, she laid back on the grass, holding Ray's hand, watching stars appear. That made her dizzy too.

What the hell am I doing? This limbo is even worse than when I left Vancouver. I feel friendless, I feel like nobody is willing to help me.

She drops her arms. Feels the smooth rush of air on her skin like a lover's caress.

And I know that's not true. But still, I can't live like this. I expect Sweet Water Woman is right, I need to go away, to disappear like Ray has disappeared. He asked me to wait, and I have never been more committed to anyone. But but but. But I am alone and he is nowhere. *And who's going to look after me, if not me, myself?*

Is that what I came to Sweetgrass to learn?

On the cold windy ridge, Lucie stands, naked. Lifts her head to the wind, and howls. Howls. Howls more.

Cries.

Screams.

Rages into the wind until her throat is raw and her mouth is dry and her voice is exhausted.

She hugs herself for warmth, grabs her clothes and quickly dresses, then makes her way back down the slope in the gathering dark, mindful of each step. Just like last time. Only today, she's alone.

She stops, listens. Coyotes sing to the west.

They can't hear me, the wind is blowing their voices to me instead.

She cries loud and long into the dusk, into the early stars, into the flying wind, into her own heart.

—⟩⫸⟨—

"Jude? Honey, it's time I came to see you."

"Yes! When?"

"Ah... how's next weekend?"

A burst of indulgent laughter. "Nope, no good. But the weekend after is wide open. How long?"

"Not sure. But I might be moving in for a bit."

"Oh, Sweet Pea, of course. Are you OK?"

"No. I need a break from the local action."

"Then come home, or what passes for home right now. For as long as it takes."

"Don't get me wrong, this is just a visit, maybe extended but not permanent. I'm not moving back to Vancouver."

At least, I don't think so.

—⟩⫸⟨—

Lucie calls Tom, but typically he doesn't pick up the phone. She leaves a message. "Tom, hi, it's Lucie, and I'm so sorry to be saying this by voicemail instead of in person, although I think you might already know or at least suspect — I'm, *oh*, I don't know how to say this... I'm frustrated and... exhausted... I'm sorry, but listen, my friend, I'm going to Vancouver. Tomorrow. Maybe for a while. Amanda knows how to find me, if you even want to. Oh, Tom. I'm so sorry. I'm leaving. Goodbye." She disconnects before her voice breaks.

Poor Tom. The women in his life leave him, one way or another. And Ray? I think he's running from guys who want to hurt him, but maybe he's also taking this opportunity to run from the woman in his life. And now I'm running from him.

BIGGER THAN DOUBT

Amanda drives Lucie to Calgary's airport over roads thick with wet, sloppy slush. Exhausted and forlorn, Lucie heaves open the truck's door, slides out, and retrieves two suitcases from the back. In the chilly, damp air, loud with circulating traffic, the two friends embrace and Amanda asks solemnly, "Are you coming back?"

Lucie wraps her arms around herself, turns to regard the busy, bright airport, and then looks back at Amanda. "You've got my car, girlfriend, I'd say that's a good indication I'm not leaving Sweetgrass for good. I might be in Vancouver for two days, two months, two years. I doubt it will be that long, but who knows? I'm staying with Jude for a while until I figure out what to do next.

"But, Amanda, my sweet friend, Bag o' Dirt," Lucie places her hands on Amanda's shoulders, holding her friend at arm's length and locking her gaze, "thank you, always and ever, for *taking care of me*. You've been kind to me since the first day I met you. You are a true friend. *I love you*. I've never said that to a girlfriend before, I reserved it for men who didn't even deserve it. Now I know better."

Lucie hugs Amanda with the most energetic, fierce, and honest embrace she's ever bestowed on a friend, even Judith. She and Amanda turn away to hide tears from each other.

Lucie's flight arrives in Vancouver later than scheduled. At the luggage carousel, she slings her heavy bags onto a cart, which she trundles out to find Judith in the waiting area. Surveying the pile,

Judith says skeptically, "Buddy, this is way too much luggage for a weekend."

Lucie encircles Judith in another long, warm hug. "You were warned."

"OK, I get that you're moving in. But you'll have to share me."

Lucie grins and punches Judith's arm. "You've been holding out! There's someone new in your life, and you're telling me *now*?"

"Don't get too excited," Judith says over her shoulder as she leads Lucie toward the exit. "I have a dog."

Arriving at Judith's house, they are greeted by a whirling tornado of black, tan, and white fur. The tornado sports a fluffy tail that whips and thumps, and amber eyes that gaze at Judith with absolute devotion. "This is Barney," Judith says. "He's a rescue dog, he's got some issues. In particular, don't hold your hand over his head. Pat his sides or back instead, and if he rolls over, you can give him a good tummy rub. We're working on trust, and getting over some of his habits. He's a sweetie, though. I mean, Luce, look at those eyes."

We're working on trust. No kidding. We're all working on trust.

Judith and Lucie heft Lucie's considerable luggage inside Judith's house. Lucie installs her things in the spare room, and then Judith opens a bottle of wine. "Hope you're not too exhausted from your terrible one-hour flight," Judith winks, "because Gwen and her howling child are going to stop by. Gwen and Patrick have moved, did I tell you? Not enough room in their teensy downtown condo for baby, equipment, etcetera. And you know what they're like, they've bought every kid gadget on the market, including a crib, high chair, and stroller that could pass for an urban assault vehicle. So to accommodate their new life and acquisitions, they bought a very nice gigantic house in Coquitlam."

"Seriously? That's one hell of a commute."

"Patrick has started working from home; he only comes downtown as needed to meet his clients. And Gwen's still on maternity leave, though she says she can't wait to get back to work. She's a good mom but also career-focused. So she's got some life balance challenges coming up. And yeah, definitely a long drive once she goes back to work."

They clink glasses. At that moment the doorbell rings, launching Barney into tornado mode. Gwen carefully makes her way through the door, beset by whirling dog and friends, all overjoyed to see her. Trying to pat Barney and hug Lucie at the same time, Gwen's arms are too full with her purse, tote bags, and baby Cleo herself, strapped into an enormous padded car seat and screaming for all she's worth. While Judith calms the dog, Lucie extracts the infant from Gwen, who kicks off her sandals, sets various bags on the floor, and collapses into the nearest chair.

"Want a drink?" Judith asks.

"Do you mean a drink or a *drink*?"

"Whatever you want. We've cracked a bottle of Pinot Gris."

Gwen rolls her eyes. "Oh, how I would love just one glass of wine. Yes please, but make it short. For the record, I'm not nursing, my little darling rejected me so she's on formula. It's all about driving home sober."

Unaccustomed to handling infants, nonetheless Lucie has unsnapped the baby's harness and hoisted her, still crying full throttle, from the car seat. Lucie joggles and rocks and tickles to no positive response. Scarlet-faced Cleo continues to wail until Gwen retrieves a bottle from the tote bag, relieves Lucie of the child, and settles on the sofa to see whether she can coax the baby into comfort. After a few minutes, success. "Tell me again why I wanted kids?" Gwen says, gazing with rapture into her daughter's face.

"They say you're most nostalgic about the baby years," Lucie says.

"Yeah, but not til they've graduated from college and have gainful employment."

"You look wonderful, Mom."

Gwen beams. "Right back at ya, Luce. And your new short hair! That is an amazing cut, it really changes you. And you've got colour in your cheeks. Love and fresh air agree with you." Her fond gaze returns to her baby, now sucking the bottle contentedly. "Which brings me to my next question: how long are you here? Jude says you've had some troubles, and you've split from your guy. What's that about?"

Lucie takes a long sip of wine, meeting Judith's eyes over the rim of her glass. "It's a novel in the making, maybe a screenplay."

"Ha, I'll settle for the study notes version. I have a short attention span these days, I have baby brain." Gwen reaches for the glass Judith has set beside her, considers the small volume of wine. "Ugh, such is my life now. Two sips of wine a week, and they're both right here, right now. Bottoms up, girls! Welcome back, Luce."

I'm not driving anywhere tonight. Time for a refill already? How did that happen? Oh, let me guess. And how much do I tell you, Gwen? What do you already know? How much do I trust you, or anyone, with Ray's story? But my own story, and why I'm back in Vancouver, makes no sense without Ray's story.

Lowering her glass, Lucie says, "Not sure how long I'll be here. I'm headed back to Sweetgrass at some point, but I had to get away and do some thinking about this guy. But besides that, I've been working my ass of for eighteen months without a break, so this is an official vacation. Or an official escape. Maybe I'll need to find a job here for a while. I don't know. Right now, I'm just so happy to see you both, and your new additions, human and otherwise. I need some familiar faces around me, and some time to decompress. So here I am among my best friends, and *their* best friends," she says with a grin.

Tough girl rides again.

Gwen removes the bottle's nipple from the pink bow of her drowsing daughter's mouth. She grabs a cloth from the apparently bottomless tote bag and spreads the cloth over her shoulder, then shifts the baby up and pats the infant's back, pacing across the room. Barney lifts his head and thumps his tail on the floor, then settles again as Gwen, patting her baby, passes back and forth through shafts of light coming from the living room's tall, narrow windows that remind Lucie of the first time she stepped inside The Sow's Ear.

"And where are you staying?" Gwen asks.

"Here, for the moment," Lucie responds. "Until Barney can't stand me and throws me out."

Gwen stops pacing and faces Lucie, rocking Cleo in her arms. "I'm asking because — you'll think this is so 'Gwen and Patrick,' two people who can't make a decision — we now live in Coquitlam, at the extreme edge of the known universe. But we haven't sold our condo downtown. We decided to sublet it. Why? I dunno, it seemed like a good idea at the time. I have baby brain, did I say that? I don't remember what I did this morning, much less the thinking behind that decision. The point is, our condo is empty right now. We had a tenant but that didn't work out. That's a whole other story," Gwen casts a conspiratorial look at Judith. "But Lucie, if you're going to be here for a while, even a couple of months, you could live there. You could just pay for the utilities, and maybe help with condo fees if you're here long enough to get a job. Whatever. I'd be so grateful."

Once again, Lucie locks eyes with Judith, who tips her glass to her mouth and simply shrugs.

Lucie says, "Gwen, sweet friend, you come to my rescue yet again, as you've done a hundred times in a hundred ways before. Not that Jude is any slouch in the rescue department either. Listen, I'd be oh so happy to live in your condo, but I've got no clue how long I might be here. Could be three days of intense meditation and yoga, a body cleanse, get my poop in a group, and then I'll bolt back to Sweetgrass in less than a week. Or I might be here for weeks, or months. Or years. I doubt it, but I'm just sayin'. I don't know. *I don't know.*" Despite herself, tears sting Lucie's eyes. "Oh, girlfriends, I don't know what to say. I only know that, as usual, I am leaning on you for help."

Gwen says. "Patrick and I need to figure out what to do with the condo. Meanwhile, it would help us to have somebody living there, even for a short time. That would give us a deadline for making a decision about whether to sell it. If you want, we can get your furniture out of storage so you've got your own stuff around you. But the place is already furnished..."

Lucie shakes her head. "Nope, there is no way I'm ready to go through my storage locker. But Gwen, I can pay for that myself now, let me at least do that. You've been so great, footing my storage bill all this time. And, did I say 'yes' to the condo?" Lucie looks again at Judith, who is grinning widely. "Um, let me repeat. *Yes.*"

Gwen and Judith exchange triumphant looks. Lucie notices but doesn't comment until Gwen has repacked her numerous bags, snapped her sleeping child into the car seat, and departed. Lucie refills both wine glasses and says, "OK, what just happened?"

Judith places her glass on the coffee table with a deliberate thunk. "Two things. It's true that Gwen needs somebody in her condo, if only to make the place look occupied. They have a liability—an empty flat that costs money—and you can help. Plus," Judith sighs, "Barney is not my only recent acquisition."

Lucie bows her head. "Jude, you are the best. You never say 'no' to me even when it interferes with your life. You have always, always been my safety net. You're what my mother should have been. And I've always taken such advantage of you. So, I want to hear what's up with you.

"But first, let me just say this: I think I've done some growing up in Sweetgrass. Not deliberate, more like osmosis. I see now that I know how to *take*, but I don't know how to *give*. I know I'm needy and distrustful, I'm judgmental and harsh. I'd also like to think I recognize when my friends need me in return, though I'm actually not very good at that — but I'm learning.

"Thanks to you, I found Sweetgrass, where I've made a life for myself on my own terms. And, to my amazement, that simple non-city life is fine with me. I *love* Sweetgrass.

"But the man I want is on the run, it's been *months*, I have no way of knowing... Oh, I just don't know anymore. *I don't know.* And that's why I'm here."

Grinning, Judith says, "Luce, maybe you should get a dog." She pours out the remains of the wine. "Don't get me wrong, we have lots to talk about. But you've just rolled over me like a rogue wave."

Lucie continues, "Yeah, sorry. I don't expect you to solve my problems. I love that you are a listener. Lucky you, Jude, you've been doing that for years. OK, that's more than enough out of my mouth, it's your turn. Clearly, I'm only staying in your spare room for a few days because something is up. Tell me what you're not telling me."

Uncharacteristically, Judith starts pacing. " I've met someone who is, um... Luce, she reminds me of you. She is smart and funny, she is vulnerable and needy, but I think I can give what she needs. And she is so... sexy, in a way that is warm and welcoming, a way I've never known. I'm wary of her need but, oh Sweet Pea, she is so... *good*."

Lucie grins her trademark wide, illuminating smile. "Oh Jude! She sounds like Ray. Warm and funny, someone who makes you feel great about yourself and makes you laugh. And sex is great, nobody needs to apologize for that. In the end, Jude, it's about laughing, don't you think that's the best thing?"

Judith empties her wine glass. "No. Maybe. Ah, maybe companionship, affection, a sense of belonging, maybe that could the best thing. A sense of ha-ha? It's good, a big thing for sure, but not the best thing. Then again, I love to laugh. Oh Hon, what makes two people click like jigsaw pieces? Who knows?"

"So, do I get to meet this woman? And meanwhile, you and Gwen had my move into her condo cooked up before I got here," Lucie accuses.

"Yep," Judith says. "Got a problem with that?"

"Oh no. Never. You two are my guardian angels. You, and Amanda, I miss her already. So, come on, who is this new person in your life, apart from Barney? When do I get to meet her? Details, girlfriend! Jude, I'm so happy for you."

—⟩⫞⟨—

Lucie meets Mona the next evening. Mona is half Italian, half Lebanese, with huge dark eyes and olive skin, corkscrew brunette hair, and a mercurial sense of humour. Lucie likes her immensely.

Mona's schedule is somewhat haphazard, so some evenings the three women have dinner together or meet for a movie or drinks. "Just like old times," Lucie muses to Judith. Other days, when Mona is working late or out of town, Lucie has Judith to herself. They walk Judith's dog and talk talk talk.

"I'd forgotten how lovely spring is here, if I ever really knew that in the first place," Lucie says one evening as they meander through Judith's quiet neighbourhood, surrounded by kids playing, dogs barking, and gardens in full, riotous bloom. "Funny how you have to go away to appreciate the finer points of where you came from. I guess if Marta has a legacy, that's it: she taught me about simple enjoyment of your surroundings. Look around, pay attention. I hope I don't lose touch with that presence of mind."

But there's a reason for Vancouver's lushness: rain, and lots of it. Sometimes it pours, sometimes it sprinkles, other times it's foggy, misty, or just plain humid. She'd forgotten about this aspect of coastal life, something she was never acutely aware of before but now occupies her to the point of annoyance. Lucie's clothes, sheets and towels are constantly damp. She's chilled all the time in a damp, bone-deep way that's different from being cold in Sweetgrass. And here in Vancouver, the sky is frequently overcast. She longs for the bluebird skies of Alberta, even the dry hills and fields that are more brown than green.

Another thing she's unaccustomed to: city noise. Traffic, air brakes, garbage trucks. Sirens especially. It's appalling how often a police cruiser or ambulance screeches by. In Sweetgrass, sirens are unusual and cause for speculation if not downright alarm. Here, they yammer continually like a pack of coyotes.

Despite sharing with Judith her dilemma concerning Ray, despite Sweet Water Woman's advice, Lucie finds no quick resolution or solace in her escape to Vancouver. She is restless, sleeps poorly, and daily she tills the same earth she did in Sweetgrass. Lucie talks endlessly to Judith about how rootless and aimless she feels, repeating the same information Judith already knows, and then she apologizes. "I've got such a one-track mind right now, Jude. I'm sorry, you must be getting sick of hearing the same song over and over."

Whether or not she's getting impatient with Lucie's discourse, Judith listens patiently as Lucie mulls her reasons for leaving Sweetgrass over and over. Judith says reasonably. "He'll get in touch with you eventually. Amanda knows where you are, and he can track you down through her, right?"

"That's my story and I'm sticking to it."

"For how long?"

Lucie bites her lower lip. "I am totally, one hundred per cent in love with him. How long? As long as it takes. I can't even think of anyone else, taking up another relationship. Not now, maybe not ever."

After two weeks, Judith finally suggests to Lucie that it's time to take up residence in Gwen's condo.

"You're right. I've been the third wheel for way too long," Lucie agrees, placing her fingertips tenderly against Judith's lips to keep her from politely protesting. "I will be back for dinners and dog-walking at least once a week. But you and Mona need your life back. Meanwhile, I need to move on with moving on. I've talked your ear off about Ray and Sweetgrass, and I'm really no closer to making a decision. Enough talk, already. Let's get the keys from Gwen and get me moved."

Lucie lies on a pillowtop mattress, under satiny sheets and an airy duvet. It's two in the morning and she's wide awake, staring at the

ceiling in her new home, a swanky if pocket-sized condo in downtown Vancouver. The room's ivory walls are softly lit by reflected
light from the street twenty-seven storeys below. The window is
cracked open slightly, admitting moist air and the remarkably loud
swish of traffic on the rainy street. She is so far from Sweetgrass
and the nighttime voices of wind and owls.

*You need a job. You can't just spend time spinning your wheels
and wondering when Ray will turn up. Amanda will let you know
if he calls. When he calls. And meanwhile, beach walking, I can do
that again now. Surf. I love surf. I never knew how much I missed it.*

"Surf, yeah I've missed that. But tonight — I miss coyotes."

Finding work in Vancouver proves to be laughably easy. With her
experience at The Sow's Ear, and backed by glowing references
from Neil, Lucie gets a job in a busy hotel café only a few blocks
from her new condo. Regular shifts, regular pay. What a difference
from her desperate search so many months ago. A lifetime ago.

She's been working for some weeks now. Spring has drifted into
summer — April, May, now June. No news from Ray, direct or
otherwise. Lucie has phoned and emailed Amanda constantly to
catch up on life at the ranch, the town. She's been reluctant to ask
whether there's been any sign of Ray, but Amanda never fails to
say, "No word yet, Lucie. Hang on, I know he'll call."

Lucie's Vancouver life has settled into a routine comprising
three elements: work, sleep, and seeing Judith and Mona. She's
ventured to Coquitlam to visit Gwen, Patrick, and baby, but she
hasn't looked up anyone else from her old crowd of acquaintances.
At the restaurant where she works, she's polite and efficient, but
doesn't befriend other staff. She's taken out a library membership
and signed up for Netflix. She lives a hermit life and that's fine.

On her days off, despite the persistent rain, she walks and walks
She strolls along West 41st Street, along Robson, through False

Creek and Granville Island, along the waterfront, the Seawall — places that used to lift her spirit with their bright shops and cafés, wheeling gulls, and cheery little passenger ferries chugging back and forth. Now that she has an income again, she's not afraid to browse racks of funky clothes, or buy a coffee and pastry and then sit by a rain-splashed window to watch the endless traffic. But nothing cheers her. Her shoes soak up the wet, her jeans wick moisture. She doesn't carry an umbrella and sometimes doesn't bother to pull up her jacket's hood. Instead, she allows the rain to soak her hair and trickle down her neck. It seems like penance, though for what she's not sure. She's done no wrong except to vacate Sweetgrass. To abandon Ray and any chance for him to contact her directly.

As one week leaks into the next, Lucie begins to lose hope. "Guess I'm not good at waiting for something I don't even know may happen, if ever. I need a sign," she says to Judith.

"Patience, Hon. That's all you can do."

"Got any pixie dust you could spare me?"

One warm June day, when the streets are shining after last night's rain, Lucie is in the hotel's coffee shop kitchen, sipping tea as she takes a break from serving tables. It's late morning and the café is quiet but for a few lazybones such as the couple at a corner table, quietly holding hands and smiling sleepily at each other. Brenda, one of the servers, taps Lucie's shoulder and whispers, "Some cowboy out there wants to see you. Asked for you by name."

Lucie looks through the window of the kitchen's swinging door and glimpses a familiar profile, hunched shoulders in a sheepskin jacket. Something in her face seems to startle Brenda, who says, "Do you know that guy, is anything wrong? Want me to call security?"

Lucie smiles. "No it's fine, I know him. I might talk to him a while though, can you cover my section? There's only a couple of tables right now. Keep the tips."

Brenda nods.

It can't be anyone but Tom. Typically, he hasn't removed his worn jacket, although the room is warm. But his hat rests on the table at his left hand. He is crouched over his coffee, staring into the mug with such intensity he could be watching a movie in its depths.

She pulls out the chair opposite and faces him, this proud, powerful man hunched over the table. He doesn't immediately acknowledge her. Instead he grasps the cup handle in his blunt fingers, his hand shaking. She watches the cup's perilous journey. He drinks, and then wipes coffee from his lips with the back of his free hand. The cup rattles when he replaces it on the table.

At last he raises his gaze with what seems a huge effort; he almost has to arch his back to bring his eyes up to meet hers. But then he gathers himself, and before she can say so much as 'Good morning,' he growls, "They found him."

"*Ray?*"

He stares at her uncomprehendingly, as though she's just spoken to him in Martian — or Ukrainian — then shakes his head slowly. "No no no. Huh, you don't know what happened to Ray? Donny never told you?"

"Donny said nothing, about everything."

"Hmm." He raises the cup again, more steadily this time. Drinks and places the cup down carefully. Meets her gaze. "The Mounties traced Ray's cell phone to his sister in Saskatoon. She backed up the story you told them, about the bad loan, the drug guys. Then when me and my kids did that TV thing, it was all over the news. Ray was in some bar in Prince George. Saw himself on TV, went straight to the nearest police station and turned himself in. He told them everything, named names in return for identity protection. So the Mounties busted a big drug and car theft ring thanks to Ray. Guns too. It was a big deal, maybe you saw it on the news, but maybe you didn't make the connection. Why would you? They gave him a new name and set him up someplace, I don't know where.

Donny does."

Romantically involved... and yet another false name, which I don't know. How can I find you? I can't. You have to find me. And you haven't done that. It's six months and you haven't done that.

Her jaw is clamped, she's grinding her teeth. She seethes. "So all this happened when? Before Christmas? Ray has been living somewhere *since then* and *nobody told me*? Not you, not Donny? Not *Ray*? I don't believe this." Her fists are clenched in her lap. She considers raging away from the table. She considers screaming.

"Hold your horses," Tom says quietly. "I thought you knew. I assumed Donny told you, so I never mentioned it."

"I saw that newspaper article months ago. That's the only way I knew they'd stopped looking for him. One day Donny was in the café and I asked him straight out, but he just said Ray was safe and I shouldn't trouble my pretty little head about it. Agh, I could spit nails right now."

Tom regards her calmly. "Yeah, maybe it's wrong of Donny not to tell you. Then again, maybe he thought you'd try to call Ray and that's not a good idea yet, still dangerous for you and for him. Maybe they've told Ray to sit tight for a while — six months, a year. These things take a while to blow over."

She sits back and looks straight at him, considering what to say next, deciding she has nothing left to lose. "The thing is, Tom... oh, I haven't told this to anyone." She pauses, willing herself to continue. "When Ray mailed my car keys back he sent a note too. Said he loves me, asked me to stay in Sweetgrass, so he would know where to find me."

"So you ran away to Vancouver. Not real smart if you ask me."

"He *promised* to come back for me, and I waited for *months*, but he didn't come back, did he? No call, no nothing. What am I supposed to think? And then the gossip, and the awful phone messages. I was scared. Yeah, I ran and I changed my cell number. Like new underwear, as I think you've said. So now I'm treading water in Vancouver, waiting for something to happen." She has picked up a fork and is rapping it on the table. Ting ting ting.

"He probably can't right now," Tom says evenly, like he's calming a jumpy horse. "And is that mutual?"

Lucie ignores his question, suddenly remembering Tom's opening remark. She swallows and sits back, her fury dissolving. "Oh Tom, I'm sorry. You didn't come here to listen to me rant about Ray. You said they found the guy who, who... crap, I can't even say it."

"That kid, Jason."

"*What*? That druggie kid? Drunk or stoned all the time? How do they know it was him?"

"He did it again."

"*Killed somebody*?"

"Kidnapped a girl in Calgary. Drove her out of the city, who knows what he had in mind? But he was high on something and she happened to have a mickey of rum on her. She talked him into drinking it all and when he passed out, she ran to the nearest farmhouse and they called the cops. Found him snoring in the van. They noticed blood on the doorframe and the seat, ran some tests or whatever they do."

He falters for a moment, and then continues, "They charged him with manslaughter. Best they can do because he swears he was drunk and doesn't remember, and there was likely no intent to harm Marta. He just wanted money. Thing is, when they found her, they found the cash in her pocket, the café money you gave her, two thousand dollars. If she'd just handed it over to him, she'd still be..."

Lucie reaches across the table to grasp his hand. She cannot think what to say. She sits back. "I'm so sorry."

"Plus it was him that smashed up Ray's car."

"*What*? Why the hell would he do that?"

"He was pissed off because Ray underpaid him for some job or other."

Lucie pauses as she sorts through this new information. She speaks aloud, but softly. "Yeah, Ray hired that kid to paint the restaurant, but he did a crappy job. So he smashed up Ray's car? That's crazy. But... there was that ugly guy in Ray's apartment... that was *after*... after Ray took off, because he thought... So that kid actually did Ray a favour by busting up the car and scaring him into leaving town. Otherwise the thugs would have found him. Ray got away just in time. Ohmygod, Tom. What a story. What a strange coincidence."

"It's good they got the kid. I thought you'd want to know."

"Of course, thank you. But Tom — you drove from Sweetgrass to Vancouver to tell me this?"

He regards her for a long moment. Once again, he seems to be appraising her, sizing her up, the look that infuriates her.

I am still not stupid, and I am still not a bale of hay.

"Keith sold horses to a guy in Hope. I trailered them out. So I was sort of in the neighbourhood."

Ah, lovely Hope. Been there.

Abruptly, he stands and reaches into his pocket. She thinks he's going to hand her something but he only places ten dollars on the table and grabs his hat.

She can't let him go, not after a twenty-minute conversation. "Tom, do you want, um, I could bring you a sandwich or something?"

"Done what I wanted. Headin' home," he replies, pulling his hat low over his brow like he's expecting bad weather. Shoves hands into pockets and looks up but doesn't meet her eyes; he gazes instead into some middle distance over her shoulder. Says, "Come back."

"What?"

"Come back to Sweetgrass. I need you at the café. People miss you. And Ray needs to know where to find you when he's ready."

She rolls her eyes.

"You didn't answer me. He loves you. That mutual?"

A pause, an exasperated sigh. "Yeah, I guess."

"Not exactly a ringing endorsement."

Another pause. "OK, OK, *yes*. I'm crazy about him. There, satisfied?"

"Then come back to Sweetgrass. Believe in him. He'll call you when he can."

What business is it of yours? Ach, didn't you say that to me one day on a sidewalk? We're in each others' pockets, you and me. We see through each others' crazy masks. Cowboy Tom. Tough girl Lucie.

Tom steps away from the table and walks to the door, bent forward as usual, like he's walking into a strong wind. Lucie follows his progress but makes no attempt to stay him.

With his hand on the door, he turns and looks at her. "Well?"

"*What*? I'll *think* about it, OK?"

That remark causes Tom to do something she's never witnessed before.

He laughs.

"You're busted, Lucie. You left your car in Sweetgrass. And your saddle." He turns to fling the door wide open.

Margaret's Waltz

I'm not the kind to sit and pine for places far away
Every town I travel to has its charms and its delights
But something about the moon tonight sends a longing to my soul
To be at a dance with the one I love on a warm prairie night

So please forgive me but tonight my thoughts are far away
To the place my memory will go if I give it half a chance
I smell the sage upon the air and I'm walking arm in arm
With the one I love toward the sound of an old-time country dance

Chorus:
And I can hear that Margaret's Waltz, the fiddle plays so sweet
And I can feel the spring of the hardwood floor beneath my feet
I close my eyes and I see the lights of town twinkling at night
They say that home is where your heart is — I guess they're right

– Connie Kaldor

THANKS TO THE FOLLOWING

First, disclaimers: The characters in this novel are entirely fictional, created from my imagination. Any resemblance to persons living or dead is coincidental.

Likewise my portrayal of the Canadian BSE crisis — the impact on ranch families described in this novel is my fictional interpretation of events, although the crisis itself was all too real. In May 2003, bovine spongiform encephalopathy (BSE, also known as mad cow disease) was discovered in Alberta, and the United States immediately closed its borders to Canadian beef. Some forty countries followed that ban. Although the U.S. and Mexico partially lifted their bans in August 2003, the damage was done. Statistics Canada reported that farm incomes fell to the lowest level in three years, and federal and provincial governments announced a number of aid packages, which continued for several years. In April 2004, the U.S. again halted imports of Canadian beef products. By the end of 2004, Canadian beef producers had lost some $5 billion in sales and income. The U.S. ban was fully lifted in July 2006. Other sanctions were ongoing.

My imagination (and probably too many movies and TV shows) was also the source of the police investigation described in this book. Any mistakes or misrepresentations regarding the RCMP and their investigative process are mine alone. My descriptions are a work of fiction.

And now the fun part: acknowledgements!

To the many people who generously gave their time, energy, expertise, love, support, and encouragement — thank you. I've tried to be thorough, but I'm sure to have forgotten someone. If you don't see your name here, I'm sorry for the omission — and you know I couldn't have done this without you.

KDW. Thanks to youse. You're all that and a ham sandwich... My life, my love, my best friend. Plus, no slouch in the kitchen, and a dab hand behind a camera lens (that's his photo of me on the back cover). Lucky me.

This novel was the basis of my master's-level diploma through Humber College's Creative Writing by Correspondence program. My mentor and editor was Joan Barfoot, to whom I give thanks and appreciation for her insight and guidance. She made this a better book. And, dear reader, you should read her books. Google her and get busy.

Sue Ridewood and Patrice Haan, fine friends and insightful readers, gave me expert commentary on early drafts.

Gervais Goodman, friend and photographer extraordinaire, provided the front cover photo. It was sooooo hard to choose from his library of terrific images. The Alberta foothills where we live is a photographer's dream for exceptional light and colour, wildlife and birds, horses and hay bales, seasonal changes. It's awesome, and Gervais' work captures it with reverence and passion.

Thanks to the tremendous, supportive crew at FriesenPress: Tammara, Bret, Galia, Sarah, Dahlia, Oriana, and my exceptionally insightful editor Rhonda. I hope you're all as proud of this book as I am.

Thanks to John Gilchrist for information about Route 40 Soup Company.

Many friends helped Ken and me establish home and community in Turner Valley and Black Diamond; living here reignited my life and inspired this novel. Thanks to: Sharlene Brown and James Lozinsky; Betty Foran; Carol Gauzer and Andy O'Laney; Karen Gimbel; Darlene and Mal Kirkland; Sue and Murray Knowler; Mady Kopstein; James Lee; Pat and Doug Lothrop; Janice McDougall and Gervais Goodman; Margot McMaster and Doug Munro; Diane Osberg; Suzanne Searle and John 'Hoogie' Hoogstraten; Evonne and Robert Smulders; Joyce Teskey; Jane and Dick Toews; Linda and John Walsh; Dixie and Tony Webb; Denise Withnell and David Wilkie. Etc. You know who you are.

Thanks to friends and family for support, encouragement, and, "Come on, you can do this.": April-Dawn Best and Larry Dziedzic; Colleen Brown; Korina Fandrick; Garry Fry and Karen Huggins; Kim Kartushyn; Diane Kossman; Jaybird LeBlanc; Kelly, Gwen, Olivia and Julia Palmer; Scott, Nancy, Kelsey, and Sarah Palmer; Marcia Pilgeram and Ken Keeler; Kathy Richardier; the late Richard Staker; Sue Staker and Peter Yaholkovsky; Sharon Lynn Williams; Adrienne Wong and Nathan Medd; Chandra Wong and Kirk Safford; Karin Wong and Mathieu Paré. And so many others, a swarm of precious bees. Thanks thanks thanks. You make honey in my life.

The songwriters who generously gave permission to use their lyrics are:

* Epigraph: *Hold Your Ground* - James Keelaphan, used by permission © ℗ James Keelaghan 1993 (" Hell, yes!" he said. Thank you James.)

* Chapter 1: *Insensitive* - Anne Loree / Frankly Shirley Music / Universal Music Publishing, used by permission

* Chapter 2: *Love What a Road* - James Keelaghan, used by permission © ℗ James Keelaghan 1998

* Chapter 3: *Hold Your Ground* - James Keelaphan, used by permission © ℗ James Keelaghan 1993

* Chapter 4: *Cowboy Boogie* - David Wilkie & Stewart MacDougall, ©1990 Ghost Writers in Disguise & Trouble Clef Music Ltd. (admin. by Bumstead Productions Inc.), used by permission

* Chapter 5: *Good King Wenceslas* - public domain

* Chapter 6: *Blow On Chilly Wind* - Jesse Winchester, used by permission, jessewinchester.com (Thank you, Cindy.)

* Chapter 7: *God Rest Ye Merry, Gentlemen* - public domain

* Chapter 8: *Does Your Mother Know?* - Gordon Lightfoot, words and music by Gordon Lightfoot ©1968 WB Music Corp., all rights reserved, used by permission Alfred Publishing LLC

* Chapters 9 and 10: *Wood River* - Connie Kaldor, used by permission, www.conniekaldor.com (" Go right ahead!" she said. Thank you, Connie.)

* Closing song: *Margaret's Waltz* - Connie Kaldor, used by permission, www.conniekaldor.com

ABOUT THE SOW'S EAR CAFÉ

The building that inspired this novel is the Wray-McRae building, a historic structure in the town of Turner Valley, Alberta.

The building was originally situated in Longview, Alberta, where it housed a laundry; the building's age is unknown. When the laundry business closed, two separate structures were bolted together and moved to Millarville, Alberta in the early 1940s. It was then sold to the Municipal District of Turner Valley and moved to Turner Valley, Alberta in 1944. In 1954, Percy Wray bought the building to house his insurance business. On his retirement in 1974, he sold the building and business to Mary McRae.

The building remained an insurance office until 1985, when it was sold and converted to a teashop and café. Several restaurant businesses have occupied the space since then, including the renowned Route 40 Soup Company, which Calgary food writer and restaurant reviewer John Gilchrist named as Calgary's top new restaurant in 2006 (although the café was clearly *not* in Calgary). As of this writing in 2017, the Wray-McRae building is still home to a restaurant.

Source: Culture and Tourism Alberta. www.culturetourism.alberta.ca/heritage-and-museums/resources/historical-walking-and-driving-tours/docs/Tour-Turner-Valley.pdf

Printed in Canada